SHE IS VENGEANCE

THE DAUGHTER OF DARKNESS

P. S. WHYTOCK

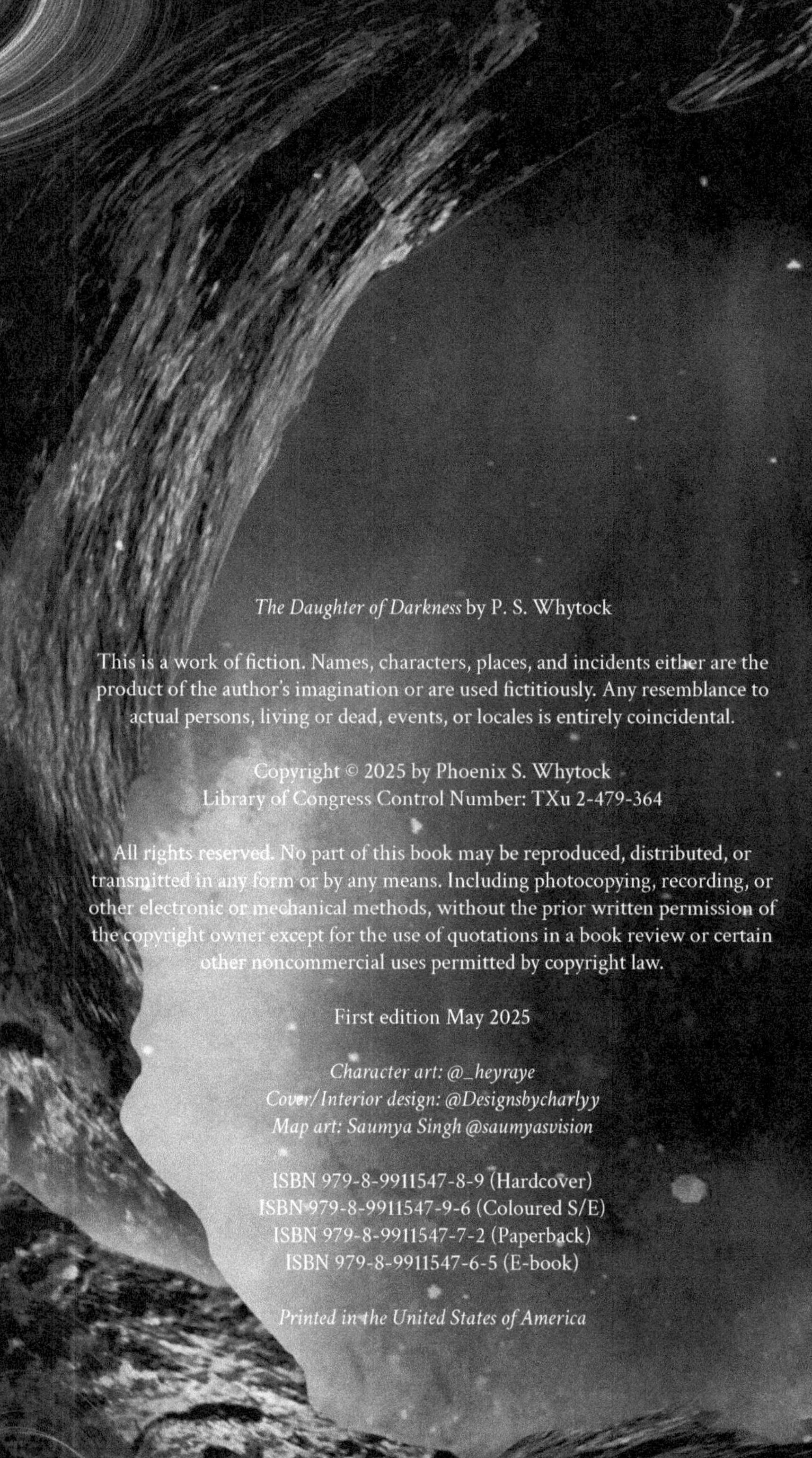

To myself.
You did the damn thing.
Fuck yeah

ABORG

NA
MOU

THE FOREST
LOST SOUL

DAUÐINN
MOUNTAINS

KI
VAL

THE BLACK
FOREST

ZARREN CITY

NS
EVENGILE
THE BLACK FOREST
ELDUR
NTAIN
ALLÚIN
THÓRS
EHAMM

PRONUNCIATION

PLACES:

Carpathian: *Car-pay-th-ian*
Origin: The mountain range spanning across Central and Eastern Europe.

Sighișoara: *See-ghee-SHWAH-rah*
Origin: A city in Romania

Tambiln: *Tam-b-lynn*

Tor'oc: *Tor-auk*

Dauðinn: *Doi-th-inn*
Meaning: Death
Origin: Old Norse

Dyagin: *Die-a-gin*
Álfheimr: *Alf-eh-mer*
Meaning: Land of the Elves
Origin: Old Norse

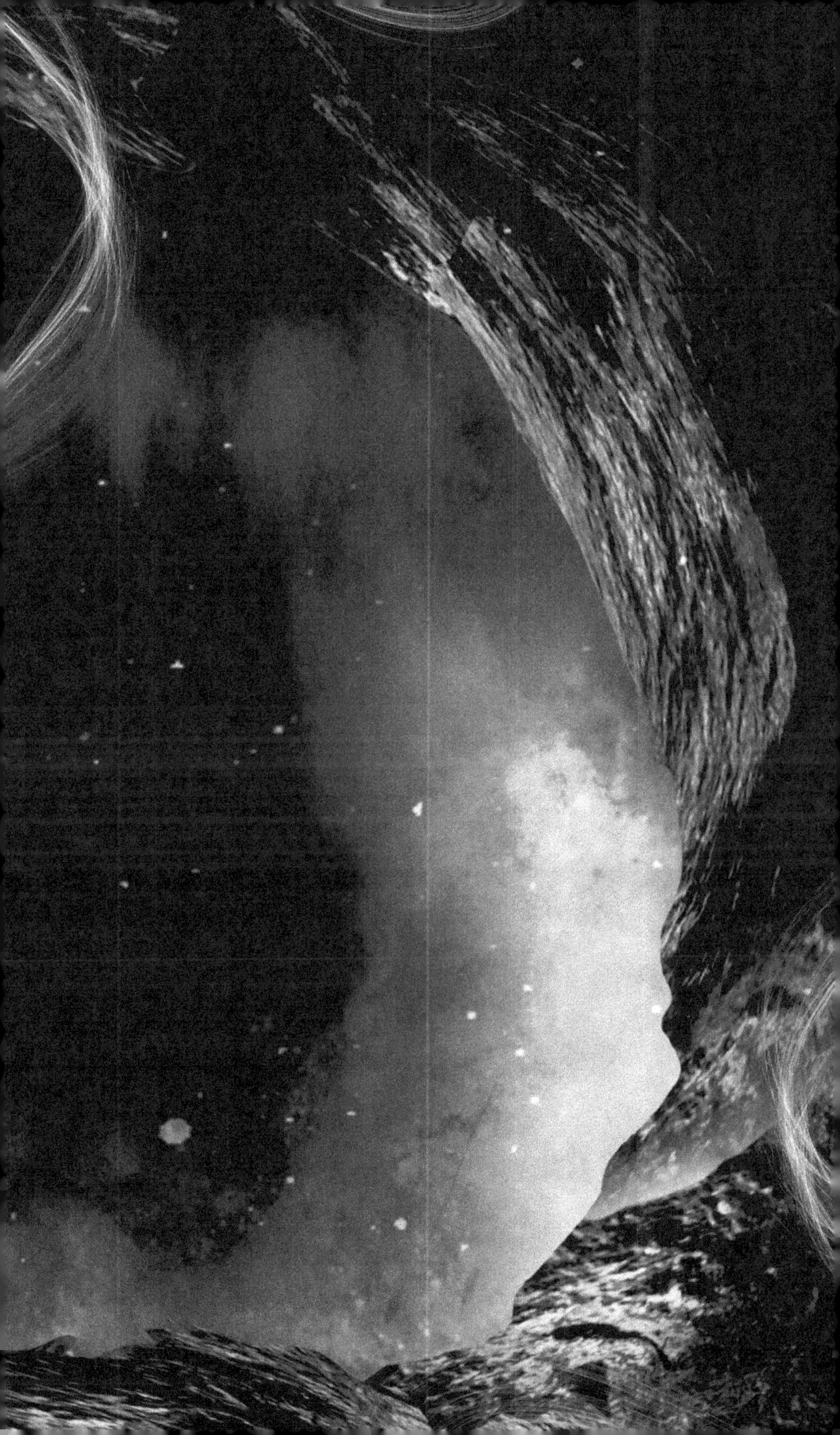

CHAPTER 1

It was one of those rare moments when Sarah wished she was anywhere but on a hunt. She found herself in the heart of Rome, trapped behind the walls of the decaying Roman Coliseum. The rain came pouring down like an angry horde as she waited, her clothes clinging to her body, crouched behind one of the ancient archways that led down into the many corridors of the lower structure.

She had been requested by Mario Capozzi, Rome's Chief of Police, after he texted her on a burner number she had given him, asking for her assistance. She was both shocked and unsurprised. Capozzi had saved her ass by chance once upon a time when she was cornered by an Orc high on a new street drug. Since then, she owed him—and she had known the day would come to pay up.

According to Fae historical texts, humans had been changed by magic when the wall separating their worlds fell, merging them. Over time, however, humans had become skittish around certain creatures—and the ones terrorising their city were among them. Hunters were no better. They were not a group the police were particularly fond of, let alone willing to ask for help. Still, she found herself in the middle of a covert hunt for the Chief himself, drenched and cold.

His message explained that a race of *Vilons* has been terrorising their city—and more importantly, their home—for the past month, with minimal impact from their police force. Vilons were a mixed race between humans and Gargoyles. They had large leather wings protruding from their backs, twisting horns, and, while mostly human in form, sharp claws and a deadly tail that could cut a man in half with a single flick.

Vilons were cousins to the *Drago*—half man, half dragon. The Drago came from the old world, where Fae and Gods ruled the earth and sky, where magic consumed their very essence. Though the Drago no longer roamed freely, hidden from human eyes for nearly a century.

The grit and sand from the ground made little sound under her feet as she waited silently, listening for her target to arrive. It was rare for Rome to experience a storm of this calibre, but Sarah thanked the heavens as her scent was washed away, letting her move with ease and without detection. Everything was pitch black except for the occasional flash of lightning in the sky. Years of consistent training kicked in, and her other senses took over as she crouched against the crumbling rock.

They're close, she thought as she shifted on one foot to peer around the stone wall. She could smell them. The strong scent of decay and rot from their breath hung in the air. And then she heard it. The sound of claws on stone and rocks breaking off from the coliseum wall. Sarah closed her eyes momentarily, taking a deep breath and exhaling silently. Her senses heightened in the rain, and she knew she would have to rely on her hearing and sense of smell. Her vision obscure in the darkness.

Standing slowly, she waited for them to move. Hearing their

claws scrape against stone as they took off into the sky, she set into motion. Moving with the shadows that lingered around the edges of archways, their dark spaces growing as the storm raged on.

Sarah could hear them cry out into the night, a sound she knew well enough to know meant they had caught something. Keeping her ears alert, she moved forward, blind to what was before her. The earth shifted under her as she moved to her right, grabbing one of the lower walls and swinging herself up. Loose gravel on top of the wall rolled under her feet, and she lost her balance.

Her body hit the muddy earth with a thud, dirt streaking across her face as a small groan left her lips. She held her breath, her eyes flickering in the darkness. Thunder roared, and lightning lit up the sky, letting Sarah see the Vilons as they tore through their victim. Sarah counted three bodies, quickly taking note of her surroundings.

Sitting up, she wiped the mud from her cheek with the back of her hand and pushed herself off the ground. *It's not as bad as it could be,* she thought silently.

Noting her mistake, she went left instead of right in hopes of coming up behind them. That plan was soon forgotten. Standing in the middle of her path, back turned, was one of the large creatures. She halted in her tracks, breath hitching as her body froze.

Her moment of surprise was short-lived as she retraced her steps and hid. Fingers itching at the thought of a fight, her hand slid down her leg, grabbing hold of one of the blades she kept concealed in her boots.

Sarah could feel the tension rising as she waited, and waited… and waited. And there it was. The roll of thunder boomed across the sky, lightning giving her sight. Sarah sprang into action, sprinting around the wall towards the offending creature. Sand and gravel flew behind her as she leapt into the air and hit the side of the wall with her foot, using it as leverage. Her back arched as she flew, the blade glinting in the storm.

The Vilon turned upon hearing her advances, a snarl twisting on its sharp-angled face as it caught sight of Sarah launching herself towards it. Opening its mouth, a wild screech erupted from deep in its belly.

"Shit!" Sarah exclaimed, twisting her body just in time as its tail sliced through the air, just inches away from where her stomach had been. She hit the ground, rolling out of the fall with ease. Crouching, she watched her opponent just as he watched her. Her lessons wafted through her mind briefly.

"Never make the first move. Wait, watch, and listen. Watch your opponent, wait for that small movement, and listen for when they will attack. Once they do, counter it and then strike!"

The Vilon shifted its stance, its grey-blue skin rippling with ridges of muscle, and Sarah tightened her grip on the blade.

"Why are you here?"

Surprise flickered across Sarah's face as it spoke to her. Its voice was low and rasping, a slight hiss following its words.

Her eyes narrowed as she replied, "I don't answer to beasts."

It bared its teeth at her insult, long canines flashing dangerously, a growl of warning whispering out. "Why are you here?!"

She gritted her teeth in annoyance. "I was asked to be here."

"Why?" it snarled.

Raising her eyebrows, she retorted, "Why do you want to know?"

"I asked a question!"

She clenched her jaw, annoyance creeping in as the rain beat down on her. "So did I! If you won't answer my question, then answer me this: Why are *you* here? Why this city?" *Why am I even talking to it?* she berated herself silently.

An emotion crossed over its sharp face that Sarah could not place.

"We came here because there was no food left in the western caves of our home! What was left was nothing but a few rabbits! That isn't enough to quench our hunger!"

"Why come here then?" she yelled above another bout of thunder. "Why not go to another cave or another mountain? Why come here?"

It shook its head, defiance on its face. "Things are happening, Halfling. Things you may not realise yourself. Armies are rising. Where, I do not know. They take over the land within weeks— days, even. Taking the food that we live by, the animals we hunt."

The beast swiped the air in anger, eyes darkening in rage. "That is why we come here! Here, there is food! Even if it is human, we must survive."

"Once people realise what is happening, the authorities will take drastic measures. They will kill you. Staying here is worse than starving."

"We have nowhere else to go."

"Expand your horizons," she answered dryly.

"It is not that simple! I do not wish to fight you, but my clan is starving—"

A wild screech came from behind her. Sarah whipped around, knife still in hand, she came face to face with one of the Vilons. Diving to the side, Sarah ducked as its tail whipped out from behind its back, slicing the air, not missing her entirely.

"*Son of a-!*" She ducked again, coming up behind the beast. Her arm stung, and blood trailed down her skin. "I thought you didn't want a fight?!" she screamed.

The beast turned and came at her again, bringing down its claws in swift, angular motions that promised to turn her skin into ribbons. She brought her knife up, blocking the assault for only a moment. "Call… him… *OFF!*" She grabbed the other knife out of her boot and attacked the Vilon's open stomach as it lunged, teeth bared, claws extended towards her. With quick movements, the blade sunk into its belly. The sound of the metal connecting with skin and muscle filled the void.

Screams of pain soon echoed in the silence as the beast grabbed at the empty air. Its body bowed forward, stumbling back. It pulled the knife out and threw it aside. With a cry of outrage, it lunged.

Sarah stepped to the side in a fluid motion and embedded the other knife into its chest cavity. She felt bones break; her blade met resistance, and she pushed past it.

Stopping, it turned, making one final attempt to attack. Failing, it dropped to the ground with an earth-shuddering crash.

Sarah stared at the dead creature at her feet with vacant eyes, ignoring the pity she felt. Reaching underneath the body, she pulled the blade out and wiped it against the front of her pants. She did the same with the other. With both weapons in hand, she turned back to the other, who was watching her with casual interest.

She felt fury build in her core. "Why didn't you call him off?! Or better, why didn't you join him?!"

"I wanted to observe," he replied easily. The stony disposition changed to one of curiosity.

Sarah blinked the rain from her eyes as it fell harder, her brown hair plastered to her face. "Observe what? You wanted to see what?! Would you have one of your own killed just for curiosity?!"

"One who advances without orders is not to be trusted. Letting you kill him is a far less painful death than if I had my way." He flicked cold eyes to his dead kin, disinterest in their black depths. "Now, do you want us to leave?"

She raised an eyebrow, pursing her lips into a firm line. "You could leave, or I could do what I was asked to do—and kill you."

"While death is something we do not cower at, I will make a bargain with you."

She laughed dryly. This was almost comical. "A bargain? With a Vilon?"

He tilted his head as he watched her. "We will leave only if you grant us space to roam. Land is hard to find, and food is scarce. Give us space to live freely, and we will live in peace. On my honour, I give you my word."

Her tongue flicked against her bottom lip in thought, her mind reeling with the creature's words. She took a deep breath, trying to calm the opposing thoughts that waged war inside her head. Every bit of her training screamed to slaughter the beast, but something in her gut whispered to let it live.

"You will leave and never return," she said, biting the words out. The hand around her blades twitched against the idea of letting them go. The Vilon tilted its head in agreement. "You will leave and never return to this city or any other city. Agreed?"

"Agreed. Anything else?"

She bit her lip, hesitating. This was a horrible idea. "Yes. There is a place where you and your clan may reside. You must promise never to touch any humans, only animals."

"I agree to these terms. Where is this place you speak of?"

Her insides screamed at her to stop, and she felt a fire ignite her bones as she uttered her following words, "Sighisoara… Romania." Her grip on her blades tightened as she spoke, regret already welling up. *Stupid girl.* "This is my home. For over ten years, people have been disappearing from their beds. I need help." She let out a short laugh, her body vibrating with unleashed emotions. She had just asked it for help. *What* was she doing? "Do not let me regret this."

The Vilon nodded his head softly in understanding. His stony expression wavering. "I am sorry for the loss of your people. You have my word we will not touch the humans and will do what we can in regard to any outer lying threat. They will meet a swift end if they near your people. But we will not set one wing into your village."

Surprise resonated in Sarah as she stepped back. "Thank you, Vilon."

"My name is Fiason."

"Thank you, Fiason."

Fiason nodded, respect underlying his expression. "Pleasure, Halfling." With that, he turned his back to her, opening his wings, ready to take flight.

"Wait!"

Turning back to Sarah, he looked at her with questioning eyes.

"Why do you call me halfling?"

Fiason tilted his head in thought. "Interesting."

"What?" Sarah asked through gritted teeth. She could feel the cold seeping into her bones, her annoyance settling beside it.

"You have much to uncover of yourself and this world."

With those final words, Fiason opened his wings, and with one great leap, he was sky-bound. Disappearing from sight, Sarah was left pondering his words.

A moment later, she could hear the rest of the Vilon's take flight. The beating of their wings was heavy against the damp air. Tucking her blades back into her boots, she moved her wet hair out of her face and looked at the dead creature, shaking her head as she walked away. She left the body for the police to collect, just as the chief promised they would.

A sigh of relief escaped Sarah's lips when she stripped out of her black jeans and tank top. Peeling her undergarments away from her body. Sweat, rain, and mud caused the material to cling to her like a second skin. She'd already removed her boots and placed them by the door to dry. Her twin blades were on the desk, twinkling innocently in the dim lighting.

The Grey Willow Hotel was old, ancient even, and cramped. The walls were grey and sparse of any décor, and the furniture had lost its colour long ago. Still, it was warm, and there was hot running water, so she wasn't complaining... much, eyeing a cockroach that scurried into a tiny hole in the wall.

Leaving her clothes on the floor in a sopping pile, she stepped over them and walked towards the connecting bathroom, kicking the door closed with her foot as she turned the water on. Stepping under the hot spray, she closed her eyes while the water worked over her body.

Dirt fell at her feet as she scrubbed the complimentary bar of soap over tired limbs, lathering her skin until it was pink. The cut on her arm stung as she rinsed it carefully, blood pooling at her feet before being washed away. After a moment, she set the soap aside and leaned against the shower wall, letting out a long breath.

"Halfling," whispered the Vilon's voice.

Sighing, she reached over and turned the faucet off. Grabbing the thin towel on the wall, she wrapped it around her body and stepped out.

Water dripped from the ends of her hair, rolling down the crease of her back. Scrunching her hair with the towel, Sarah looked at her reflection in the mirror. Tired brown eyes stared back at her, mousy brown hair hanging around taut features as she hung her towel over the curtain rod.

Her naked body glowed under the fluorescent light, the scars across her skin glinting silver, her hands gripped the edge of the counter in a white-knuckle grip.

"You let him go," she muttered under her breath, eyes boring into her reflection. "You let them all go." *They don't all have to die,* her thoughts echoed back at her, and she took in a steady breath, ignoring her conscience.

"You have much to uncover."

Her jaw clenched, and she shoved the Vilon's words to the back of her mind. Ignoring the judgmental stare she was giving herself, she pushed off the counter and walked out of the bathroom.

Throwing on a pair of underwear from her bag, she moved her hair over her shoulder, grabbed her first-aid kit, and walked to the bed.

Her weight made the mattress moan as she sat, giving slightly under her weight. Opening the bottle of rubbing alcohol, she saturated a cotton ball, eyeing the gash on her arm. It was a clean cut, but the wound was dark red and angry.

Gritting her teeth, she cleaned the laceration, scrubbing the skin until it was raw and slathering antibiotic ointment over it. She grabbed a gauze roll and wrapped the wound, knotting the ends.

With a yawn, Sarah cleaned up her mess, throwing the used pieces of cotton away and putting everything else back into her bag.

Her new black burner phone lay unassuming in the open bag, having trashed her other one as soon as she had agreed to help Capozzi. She picked it up and clicked the lock button, opening the screen. The time projected from it, **0023,** rotates on an invisible force field. Her brow arched, and she quickly clicked the lock button again to watch the numbers disappear before she tossed it into the bag.

Florin, the head of her small hunter's guild, despised technology and only found it useful when it suited *him.* So, her phone was a secret and more of a paperweight than anything else. It was there for others to get a hold of her—for cases like these. If Florin found her with it, the consequences would be damning. They always were.

Not bothering with her dirty clothes, she stepped over them and around to the side of the bed, sliding into the welcoming warmth of the hotel sheets. She was asleep before her body fully settled into the lumpy mattress.

CHAPTER 2

Wrenching screams of pain and terror echoed through the mountains in a cacophony. The sound carried on the wind surrounding the dark figure that stood soundly on the rocky ledge, looking over the dark cover of trees that quilted the forest floor. He stayed with his back to the wind as it pushed at his cold body. Their cries pulsed through him like a drug, creating a small, menacing smile to twist on his pale lips. The look of death etched on his features.

The night was dark, a black cover over the small, rustic forest village of Tambiln.

Those who slept within the mounds made from wood and mud that night had not heard their intrusion. Even the dogs sleeping outside around the fire pit had not stirred. The intruders, like the wind, were silent. Like a deathly fog, they crept through the walls of the small dome huts, and with swift, cold hands, they killed.

Blood was everywhere as the creatures slaughtered the village. Tearing their fingers through their victim's flesh. They spared no one as they feasted on the wealth of blood that surrounded them, pooling at their feet, they set streams of rich cherry red flowing through the village. The smell was mouth-watering as it hung thickly in the cool air like a copper blanket. It was the smell of innocence, the smell of death.

With a single step, a figure fell from the ledge. Treetops, branches, and the needles of evergreens whipped past him. Solid earth rose to meet him, and the ground seemed to shudder as he landed quietly on the balls of his toes, even the shadows coiled in answer to his arrival.

Emerging from the cover of trees, he slipped from the darkness, watching as his newborns devoured their food. His unnaturally bright blue eyes surveyed the carnage before landing on a forgotten meal. The figure took long, graceful strides, his steps mute on the soft dirt. He looked down at the still-conscious man who lay on the soiled floor, his shadow cast over the human in the moonlight.

A gurgling came from the human's throat before a word was forced out. "*Why?*"

A smirk tilted the male's mouth, his dark brow rising in amusement. "Because..." He stooped low, taking a single drop of ruby blood and swiping it across his lower lip. His tongue snaked out, tasting it, "...we *crave* your innocence."

"You're *monsters*," the human spat out with a gasp, blood spurting from his lips.

"Oh, but we're not. We're so much more than monsters. We are *Gods*." The figure dragged a long, sharp nail across the human's cheek, watching his life drain slowly. "Humans are the real monsters."

The figure stood, turning his back on the dying human. The blues of his eyes glowed in the darkness as he watched his newborns feed.

"Reign," he said quietly.

A moment later, his second in command appeared by his side,

arms linked behind his back, face set.

"My Lord?" Reign asked, glancing at him before following as he walked through the village, watching the newborns.

They dragged the lifeless bodies into a large pile in the village centre. Limbs upon limbs and bodies upon bodies piled higher, their brown and copper skin now pale, glowing crimson in the light of the campfire.

They stopped in front of the growing pile of humans, and Reign observed him as he clasped his hands behind his back with ease once more.

"How many?"

Reign looked at the bodies as the headcount grew, his close-cropped auburn hair gleaming in the firelight. "A little over a hundred."

"Just enough."

"More than enough, Avian," he commented, dropping the formalities, his black eyes flickering with calm assertion. "They won't need to feed for quite some time. Most of them drained two or more humans tonight."

Avian was thoughtful for a moment, his head tilting like a predator assessing its prey. "And the other interested party?"

"They are working simultaneously to procure what you asked of them." Reign produced a letter from the pocket of his black button-down. "This arrived via raven earlier from them."

Avian opened it and scanned the letter quickly, a smile playing around his mouth. "Like pieces of a puzzle, everything is falling into place," he said, watching his newborns set fire to the bodies.

The flames rose with great wafts of smoke, the stench of burning flesh filling the ruined village. He tossed the letter into the flames. "Gather the newborns. We will return."

"Avian?"

He deigned him a glance. "We're expecting company."

Reign returned the look, watching as the flames played off his features in a dance. "As you wish," he said quietly, turning to watch the fire as it licked the sky.

Talan hid carefully in the shadows of the forest trees. His eyes glowed like embers in the dark, his jaw clenched, and a low growl escaped his throat. He watched as Deathwalkers slaughtered the village people, the smell of blood tingling his senses, teasing his animal side.

He watched as they tore into their flesh and drank deeply from their bodies. His blood boiled and steamed hotly with rage as they crept silently around the wolves surrounding the fire pit. In one swift movement, they lunged, gouging their fingers into his brothers' animal forms. They howled out in pain as the Deathwalkers let them go, and stepped back in disgust as his brothers shifted back into their human form. Their naked skin glowing against the firelight.

With snarls of outrage, his brothers attacked with everything they had left. Their fast movements caused their wounds to gush, and one by one, they fell.

Talan restrained himself as fire boiled within his bones. His hands dug into the bark of a black tree, nails becoming claws, leaving four gouges embedded into the wood. His body shook with rage as he looked at the carnage. He would have died with them had he not gone for a hunt. Guilt burned inside of him like acid, the rabbit he had eaten now churning in his stomach. Talan closed his eyes and turned away from the scene, running into the thicket of darkness.

The pain at the loss of his kin was deep, like a crack in his soul, his heart pounded in his chest as he ran. His pace didn't slow, it sped up, the feeling of his feet digging into the earth the only thing keeping him tethered to this life. His animal side took over as he ran, and he shifted from his human skin into a massive wolf. Silver and red fur shimmered under moonlight as it penetrated the forest canopy.

He could feel it. He could feel *them* as their life was slowly ripped away. He felt every pull on their pack bond, every tear as one more bled out or was drained by a Deathwalker. The string that tied them together was quickly becoming frayed. The hallow in Talan's chest marked every brother he lost as it grew, weighing like sharp stones.

The beating of paws on wet soil sounded mutely through the trees, mud flying behind him as the rain started to sprinkle down. Talan suddenly stopped, his breathing abnormal and loud in the untouched air. With exhaustion, his paws gave out from under him, and he fell to the ground. With a lone growl, he shifted. His naked limbs curled into themselves, his body wracked with loud sobs when the tears poured down his cheeks.

He didn't know how long he lay there, not moving. He let the emotions drain from him like a creek bed going dry until nothing was left except rocks. There was an empty space for every one of his brothers, whose voices he could once hear in his mind now just echo.

With slow, sure movements, Talan stood. Determination was embedded in his face, rage twisting his features. He was going to kill them all.

He shifted, the wolf ripping through the trees. Throwing his head back, he howled to the wind as the sky turned from black to red. The moon became the colour of blood as a hunter's moon took its spot.

No other thoughts creased through him, and with a snarl, he sprinted into the woods. Everything was a blur to his eyes except the ground that lay before him and the echo of his fallen brothers.

A high-pitched squeal pierced the air, and a scattering of giggles followed as a young girl rode on her father's back like a horse. Her small hands clapped happily as she told him to go faster.

"Any faster, little one, and you might fall off," her father said as he pulled her off his back and stood up.

She pouted, her pink bottom lip jutting out in obvious disappointment. "Papa! I don't want to stop! I won't fall off, promise." A stray wave of black hair fell in front of her eyes, and she blew it away with a puff of breath.

Her father just laughed and shook his head. His mass of black curly hair framed his handsome face in a long, dark curtain that hung to his shoulders. His bright green eyes danced as he looked down at her. Without another thought, he swooped down and threw her into the air, and she squealed in delight. He caught her as she descended and hugged her tightly, tickling her side.

She screeched and wiggled her way out. Dropping out of his grasp, she stumbled to the ground before quickly running as fast as her legs could carry her, her father laughing while he watched. She saw her mother and nearly tripped over her feet as she ran to her, hiding behind her jean-clad legs as she entered.

Blonde brows raised and hands on her hips, her mother stared at her father as she picked her up. "What are you two doing in here?" she asked, walking into the room with graceful strides. Both husband and daughter looked at one another and shrugged. "Uh-huh," she said, giving the two of them an amused look.

As her father was about to reply, the doorbell chimed thrice, and her mother set her down to answer it. Her mother's voice wafted through the house almost silently. Two other voices could be heard, and she saw her father look towards the door curiously as a slight panic could be detected in his wife's voice.

"Saskia, love, stay here," he said, looking at his daughter once before joining his wife.

Saskia watched her papa's retreating back, his footfalls heavy on the hard floor. Her young eyes were observant as she stared at where her parents had disappeared. A single knock vibrated against the windowpanes of the sliding patio doors. Saskia's head whipped around, she walked over to the sliding doors, opened them carefully and stepped out into the warm summer night air.

Her tiny feet touched the warm concrete, and the moonlight hit her white face. Vibrant, mossy green eyes peered around the yard as shadows shifted everywhere, curiously trying to find what caused the noise.

She took one step, then another, stepping onto the grass, the feeling cool on her feet. A shadow caught her eye as it moved, and she turned towards it as it shifted further away from the drifting darkness and into the moonlight. Her eyes landed on a tall male with long black hair and bright blue eyes. His stature was noble and proud as he stood with his chin held high, body clothed in a dark, all-black suit.

Saskia turned her head curiously at the male. "Who are you?"

The male smiled, his teeth shining in the darkness. "Who I am does not matter."

"Who are you?" Saskia asked again, her brows furrowing.

The stranger raised an eyebrow. "You're determined; that's a good trait. It'll be useful."

Saskia didn't sway, tilting her head as she stared at the male. "You don't belong here. This is my home."

Something flashed in the stranger's eyes, and he knelt. While trying to reason with the child, he never brought himself lower than her. "Then again, maybe it's an annoying trait. Saskia, you are, how to put it... a liability. But the power within you can be trained, and if you come with me, I can teach you how to harness that power."

"Why?" she asked, her facial expression only changing slightly.

"You're special," he repeated, his jaw twitching, the only sign of his irritation.

"Why?"

A low growl came from deep within his throat. "Because—" He stopped short as a crash and a yell was heard from inside. "Damned to hell, they're early," he muttered through clenched teeth, and he lunged for her.

Saskia screeched and darted out of the way.

The man gave a twisted smile as a cry broke from inside. "Go and run, little one. They will catch you for me."

When Saskia blinked, he was gone. She didn't care though where the strange male went; she heard another crash, and her attention was turned towards the house. She ran as fast as her young legs could, sprinting through the door. Her heart was beating profusely as a sudden worry overcame her small mind.

The living area was empty, and she stepped forward, slowing her pace, following the previous footsteps of her parents. The house was dark, and moonlight drifted in through the windows. Her footfalls were light and mute on the wood floors, and the three people who loitered in their hallway didn't hear as she approached. None of them were her parents.

Saskia licked her dry lips as she came to a stop. Her heart pounded in her ears, and her eyes locked on the hand she saw lying limply on the *floor. She took a small, deep breath and walked around the people who stood there.*

Her eyes widened as she saw the bodies of what used to be her parents. Her father's throat was slit, and her mother's head was cut clean off, blood pooling around them like red and black mirrors. Their bodies lay together on the floor, her mother's head having rolled off to the side.

Saskia felt her heart stop in her chest, and her breathing quickened as her body began to shake uncontrollably. Her mouth opened wide, and what came out wasn't a sob nor a cry but a blood-curdling scream.

The people there jolted in surprise as they turned to find her behind them. Her vision was blinded by tears as she threw her body to the ground, grabbing her father's hand, blood soaking her clothes.

Hands grabbed her, and she fought them. Saskia kicked and screamed, trying to fight her way out of the iron grip. Blood covered her arms and legs, streaking the side of her face as she threw all of her strength into getting them off of her.

"Stop squirming!" said a gruff voice in her ear.

"No!" Saskia screamed, hair whipping around her as she lashed out, nails digging into the hands that held her. "NO!"

"NO!"

Sarah jolted awake, beads of sweat dotting her forehead, heart racing in her chest as she tried to catch her breath.

Bed sheets twisted around her legs as she collapsed into her pillow, her breath coming out in small pants. Her eyes glazed over when reality sunk in. Licking her lips, she counted to ten, her finger tapping on her thigh.

Sarah swallowed thickly and sucked in a shallow breath, calming her racing heart. She could feel the blood pumping through her veins, her blood pressure rising and falling as she fought her emotions. She combed her fingers through her hair with shaky hands as she sat up. Pulling the covers back, Sarah stood beside the bed, feeling the wood beneath her feet.

Solid. The ground was solid beneath her.

The floor squeaked with her weight, closing her eyes for a brief second, seeing the faces of the girl's parents, their bodies bloodied and dead. She shook the nightmare from her head and strode towards the bathroom. The door squeaked on its hinges when she pushed it open, turning the faucet on and splashing cold water onto her face.

Sarah stared at her reflection as it stared back at her. Water dripped from her lashes, her expression curious. The nightmare befuddled her mind like an impossible puzzle she wanted to figure out. Pushing away from the counter, Sarah grabbed her towel and patted her face with it, sucking in a slow deep breath.

A knock came through, and Sarah hung the towel up, her feet squeaking across the floor. She cracked the door open just enough to see who it was. The owner of the dingy inn stared back at her through the crack in the door. "*Sì?*" she asked the old woman, who was looking at her with distaste. Sarah glanced down at herself and grimaced, realising she was still in her underwear and topless.

The old woman, who looked as faded and old as the inn itself, brought her eyes back to Sarah's. "Check out." Was all she said.

Sarah nodded and closed the door before the woman could say anymore. Walking over to her bag, she pulled out a small watch, biting her lip. A quarter past twelve stared back at her, and she cursed. Her flight back to Romania was in less than two hours.

She threw the watch back into her bag. Grabbing her clean clothes, she pulled them on quickly, taking little time to think about her appearance as she buttoned her faded jeans and straightened the black long-sleeve shirt. Sarah grabbed her dirty clothes and stuffed them into her bag, running her fingers through her hair in an attempt to brush it. She pulled out a pair of worn-out black trainers, sliding into them before she zipped up her duffle.

Her eyes did a quick scan around the room before she left.

She didn't bother to stop as she exited The Grey Willow, even when she tossed her room key on the front counter, and the innkeeper called after her in rapid Italian.

Spring was evident in the slight breeze that blew past Sarah, warming and chilling her simultaneously as she stepped onto the street. The city was a mix of both new-age technology and archaic architecture. Neon signs lit up the daylight along modern glass and chrome stores between ancient brick apartments and hole-in-the-wall shops. The heart of Rome was wide awake and in full swing for the day as people crowded the streets. Horns blared as a chrome solar powered car hovered behind an archaic vehicle from seventy years ago at a now green stoplight, the goblin in the rusted red Fiat flipping off the owner of the other vehicle behind him.

Raising her hand, she hailed a passing taxi, jumping back and glaring at the dark purple mohawk that flew past her on a hoverboard. A silver and black smart car with a neon yellow taxi strip along its side stopped in front of her. It turned red to show occupied as she climbed in, throwing her bag on the seat beside her. *"Colosseo, per favore."*

The square around the Colosseum was flooded with tourists of all species, massive electronic billboard displays for new Fae glamour serums, human anti-ageing potions, and the latest technology. At the same time, hologram-guided tours with their advanced AI systems took tightly packed groups through the crumbling structures. Despite the early season, the place was *crammed.* Families, groups, and individuals swarmed the ancient archways, cameras flashing at every crumbing rock they passed.

Sarah exited the taxi, holding onto the still-open passenger door, eyes scanning the crowds. Face set, she watched a family of fauns enjoying the sunshine. Her attention wandered past the people, gaze locking on a tall half human half Fae figure in the masses.

Dressed in a tailored dark blue three-piece suit with long chocolate brown hair neatly pulled back, Sarah instantly knew the lean half-breed. Mario Capozzi, Chief of Police.

Capozzi stood calmly amongst the families and tourists, offering them small, placating smiles as they passed. His dark eyes spoke to her silently when they finally met hers, and with a slight nod, he turned on his heels and disappeared into the crowd.

Sarah stood there silently for a moment, watching the spot that now stood empty. Her emotions were at odds as her conscience tried to rule her judgment. She had let all but one Vilon live. She had offered up the mountains around her *home.* She had let them *live.* Why? Was she forgetting how to act like a hunter? That question plagued her like a torrent storm that made her headache.

Gritting her jaw, she ducked back into the taxi, ushering the driver to the airport. The Colosseum passed Sarah in a decaying blur, and she looked away. No one knew she had accepted this hunt and would keep it that way. In and out, that's how she liked it. She was only gone overnight. No one would know.

Closing her eyes, Sarah sighed, leaning into her seat. Visions of blood flashed through her mind, and her eyes shot open, nostrils flaring as pain coursed through her head suddenly. A headache began to wrap around her skull with sharp nails, and she winced when the pressure increased. Images of her nightmare disappeared, and all she could think about was the pain. Her vision faltered, her heart rate sped up, and a small groan slipped past her lips.

Sweat dotted her brow, and Sarah fought the sudden torment. Her eyes glazed over, connecting with the driver's in the rearview mirror. His look of concern was evident, but she ignored him, forcing in a shuddering breath.

Slowly, the pain in her head lessened, and the muscles in her body relaxed. Sarah took in an unsteady breath, rubbing her temples. Sudden headaches weren't uncommon; she had them since she was a child, but lately, they'd been worsening.

Sarah leaned her head against the cool windowpane, reviling in the temperature against her hot skin. She just had to return home before everyone started to wonder about her absence.

CHAPTER 3

It was a rare day in Sighisoara, where the sun shone, and the sky was blue rather than its typical turbulent grey. Children ran through cobblestone streets without care, and women and men walked freely without worry. For a moment, there was peace within their old village.

Unlike the city, her quaint village was resolute in its heritage, with humans segregating themselves from any and all Fae. There was nothing new or modern about Sighisoara. Every building and home was made of crumbling brick, clay, and stone.

Sarah paid her driver and got out, eyeing the children who ran past her as the taxi pulled away. Hitching the bag on her shoulder, she trekked up to the manor. The sun beat down on her, and she tilted her face to the warmth, enjoying the sunshine.

The lightness in the air was short-lived as Sarah eyed storm clouds building in the distance, just beyond the mountain peaks. Shaking her head, she tried to embrace the little warmth left before their world became damp and cold.

She could see the manor up the hill, isolated from the town. Its grey stones glinting in the sun. For once, the brooding mansion didn't look foreboding and haunted like the old women in town claimed.

Sarah quickened her steps, walking the rocky path up the hill, tall grass swaying in the wind as it picked up. Thunder rumbled in the distance, and she eyed the dark clouds again, hands hovering over the iron handles of the manor doors. With a shake of her head, she pulled them open and slipped inside.

A small squeak echoed in the stone halls, and Sarah heard something drop. Following the sound, she found her double-sided katana lying discarded on the dark green runner over the stone floors. Kneeling, she picked it up, weighing it in her hands. The polished edges reflected the hall, the suits of armour lining the length of the walls, and she pursed her lips in amusement when she saw a head of messy blond curls peeping from behind one of them.

"You can come out now, Alec."

The curls rustled as he shook his head.

Sarah laughed under her breath, setting the weapon down. "I'm not mad. You can come out."

Alec peeked his head around the leg of the armour, his golden eyes staring at her, wide and guilty. "I only wanted to look at it, Sarah, promise."

"Come on out, I promise I'm not mad." Sarah held a hand to the boy, ushering him out with a small smile.

Watching her carefully, Alec took hesitant steps towards her, his dark blue shirt and jeans mused from hiding. His eyes darting between her and the blade at her feet.

Sarah saw blood drip, and her brows furrowed. "Let me see your hand."

Alec bowed his head in shame, showing her his palm. It wasn't a significant cut, but just deep enough to bleed.

Pursing her lips, she tilted his head to look up at her. "How did you get into my room?" He mumbled something under his breath, and Sarah urged him on. "Alec, you must be honest. What do I always say?"

His eyes widened, mouth pursing. "As humans, integrity is all we have."

"That's right. Now, how did you get into my room?"

"Naschta picked the lock. She wanted to know where you had gone."

"And you took my katana?"

He nodded slowly, his mouth trembling. "She said I would learn eventually and gave it to me." He shook his head, grabbing her hand with his bloodied one. "I only meant to look at it, Sarah! I wasn't going to hurt anyone! I promise you!"

Sarah sighed, ruffling his hair with a smile, ignoring the blood on her hand. "I know, I'm not angry at you. If you know something is wrong, you mustn't do it. Even if someone tells you, it's okay." Alec nodded, and Sarah set her bag down, pulling out her first-aid kit. "Do you understand, Alec?"

Alec nodded again, holding his hand out. "I understand, Sarah."

She pulled out gauze and applied pressure to the wound. "Good. Now, where is Naschta?" She wrapped his hand tightly, looking down the hall quietly as Alec shifted on his feet.

He looked down at his hand, touching the gauze as she put the first-aid kit away. "Is she in trouble now?"

Sarah hummed. "She did something bad, Alec. I have to find out why."

He nodded in understanding, his eyes darting down the hall. "She's in the weapons room."

Sarah ruffled his hair again and tucked in the small silver medallion necklace half draped out of his collar. Alec grinned up at her. "Alright, go find Haveaurd. Have him clean your wound properly." She stood, watching him run off, his small frame flying down the hall.

Haveaurd was Florin's brother. A giant man and a merciless hunter. Though he had a soft spot for Alec, a side none of them had the pleasure of knowing. It was a fatherly love.

Looking down at the now-dried blood on her hand, she pinched the bridge of her nose while picking up her katana. Slinging her bag over her shoulder, she stalked down the hall.

A wooden door, reinforced with wrought-iron bars, was tucked down a narrow hall that veered away from the main entry. Sarah wrenched the door open, ignoring it as it slammed against the stone walls. A secondary metal gate halted her path, and she shoved it out of her way, stalking into their armoury.

Gripping the weapon in her hand, Sarah stared at the head of russet curls before her. "Naschta!" Her voice was laced with anger as Naschta turned to look at her with lazy green eyes, disinterest clear in them.

Naschta fiddled absentmindedly with a dagger, twirling it between skilled fingers. "He just can't keep his mouth shut, can he?"

Sarah glared at the woman. Naschta was only two years older than her, but Sarah felt like centuries separated them. "At least he has something you seem to lack: honesty." Her nostrils flared as her irritation grew. "What were you looking for in my room?"

"Nothing of importance," she commented, shrugging.

"Don't lie, Naschta, you're better than that."

Naschta let out a dry laugh. "Is that so? Am I now? Says the liar. Where were you, *sis*?"

Her last word came out as a sneer, and Sarah restrained herself from flinching. They weren't related. None of them were. They had all been brought in by Florin, orphaned, and lost. While Sarah felt protective over Alec, she didn't share the same bond with Naschta. Since she was a child, Naschta never trusted her, and she made to show that every waking hour of their lives together.

Sarah tightened her grip on the katana. "I was in the mountains."

Naschta thoughtfully tapped the dagger in her hand, commenting, "Yeah, sure you were. I'm sure that's why I didn't see you on my hunt."

Sarah kept her face blank, staring at her supposed sister. "Maybe your tracking skills aren't quite as good as you thought, dear sister, or maybe I'm just better at evading you."

Rage flashed in her eyes, and Naschta let out a snarl before flicking her wrist in a blur of motion.

Metal glinted in the dim lighting, and with quick reflexes,

Sarah shifted her body to the right as the dagger flew past her head, between the metal bars, and embedded into the wood door behind her.

"Do not dare insult me!" Naschta screeched.

Sarah dropped her bag, gripping the blade in her hand. Her steps were quick as the tip of the katana flew and halted before it connected with the exposed flesh of Naschta's neck. Sarah gritted her teeth, forcing words past them, "I don't know what you were looking for, but to endanger Alec the way you did—"

"—Please!" she scoffed. "He's the same age as you were!"

"I was eight years old. He's only five!"

"Three years doesn't make much of a difference!"

"He got hurt because of you! How old were you when you went into the Carpathian Mountains?!"

"Don't bring me into this!"

"*Enough!*"

The deep voice invaded the armoury, and Sarah closed her eyes, jaw working, and forced herself to lower the katana. Pursing her lips, she turned on her heels to face Florin.

His expression was set in steel, his midnight eyes impossibly dark as they travelled between Sarah and Naschta, his dark, dirty blond hair shaved close to his head. He stood just under six feet tall but was stocky and solid. In contrast, Haveaurd towered over his brother, filling the doorway at almost seven feet tall. Alec poked his head out from behind Haveaurd's massive legs, guilt in his eyes.

Even though Florin had taken them in at a young age, trained and honed them into hunters, the man before them had no warmth or kindness for anyone. They were weapons in his arsenal, no more, no less. Though hope for parental love had been yearned for in her earlier years, Sarah knew better. Had been taught that love and kindness will get you killed; the ideal had been beaten into her, but that didn't stop her from wanting both secretly.

Alec made eye contact with Sarah. "Sarah, I didn't mean to." His voice was small, looking up at the two women.

Sarah gave a slight nod, replying in a clipped tone, "It's okay, Alec, you did well."

Her eyes stared straight ahead as Florin moved closer, hands clasped behind his broad back. She didn't dare show emotion in front of Florin. As a child, she would be beaten if she cried and would be forced to train until her hands bled if she showed fear.

"Emotions are weakness! Hunters are not weak! You will kill or be killed! Do you understand!?"

Florin gave a hard look to Naschta, whose mouth was set into a firm line, eyes staring straight ahead. They both knew the punishment for showing weakness.

"What," he asked quietly, "Is going on?"

Neither Sarah nor Naschta said anything.

Florin nodded his head, face glowering. "How did Alec get injured?"

Sarah restrained a growl from escaping when she realised Naschta wouldn't speak up. Clenching her teeth, she said, "It was my fault, Florin. I left my katana out, and he found it. I was careless—" She heard Alec yelp in surprise before the back of Florin's hand connected her cheek. The force caused her head to whip back, ears ringing. Her eyes glazed over from the blow. She was used to punishments, but Florin's strength still surprised her.

Taking a steadying breath, she straightened herself, keeping her face blank, ignoring the hot stinging of her cheek.

"I did not train you to be careless! If I find you've left your weapons unattended again, you will answer to me!"

Sarah jerked her head quickly. "Yes, Florin!"

Florin growled lowly, eyeing Naschta quickly before returning to Sarah. "Clean up and come find me in my study when you're done."

"Yes, Florin," Sarah said, keeping her eyes trained ahead as the brothers walked out of the armoury. Alec looked over his shoulder as Haveaurd took his hand. He gave Sarah one last apologetic look and followed the men.

Naschta let out a sound of triumph, slamming her shoulder into Sarah's as she stalked past her.

Sarah grabbed Naschta by her bicep, digging her nails into the skin beneath her shirt. She ignored her protest and pulled her in close, brown eyes darkening. "If you *ever* go in my room again, I will make sure it's the last thing you do," she said calmly under her breath.

Naschta yanked her arm free, glaring at Sarah before she swept out of the armoury. Sarah stood there alone for a second longer before she shook her head and bent to grab her bag on the floor. Touching the tender skin on her cheek with the soft press of her fingertips, she winced, pursing her lips defiantly against the pain.

Walking out, the armoury door slammed shut behind her, and she made her way through the maze of the manor. One day away made a difference, and she tried to ignore the feeling of the invisible shackles locking around her ankles.

Sarah dropped her bag on her bed, using her foot to shut the door. She looked around, eyeing the wooden desk in the corner. Naschta had been meticulous while searching her room. Everything was where it should be. Nothing was out of place as she walked around her room. She looked at the papers on her desk, thankful she had disposed of her burner phone when she had.

Next, she checked the wall of weapons beside her desk, placing the katana in the empty slot. Swords, crossbows, and guns sat primly in steel holds anchored into the stone wall. She did a quick head count, satisfied when she found them all in their rightful place.

Sarah dug out her short blades from her bag and put them in the drawer of her nightstand. She rotated the knob handle of her drawer, and the back of it sprung open. Tossing her new burner phone in there, she closed it, taking out a small push dagger in the process. She tucked it into her back waistband, closed the drawer, and walked over to the adjoining bathroom.

Her cheek was bright red, and a small cut had clotted around swollen, broken skin. She grabbed a bottle of rubbing alcohol beside her sink and a cotton ball. It was old work, muscle memory, as she cleaned the wound. She dropped the used cotton into the waste bin and let her head hang low, her eyes peering up at her reflection.

Sarah lived by her integrity, but right now, she was living in a lie. The secret of her hunt weighed on her shoulders, but she shook it off as she stood straight. Rolling her shoulders back, she gave her reflection a stern look.

"Stop it," she scolded. "You can't show emotion. You can't let him see you falter. You're better than that."

Her words were empty as she spoke them. Shaking her head, Sarah put a small butterfly stitch over the cut on her cheek before leaving the solitude of her room.

Like the rest of the rooms in the mansion, Florin's study was well-updated despite the archaic structure of grey stone, wrought iron, and arching ceilings. A brushed metal desk and sleek black leather chair sat in the middle of the room. Black bookshelves lined one wall, with books upon books on creature studies and world history—Florin's personal favourite; and a shining arsenal of guns lined the opposite.

One would never guess that hidden in a town filled with old traditions, even older residents, and a manor cloaked under the guise of ancient stone and thick timbers, was an arsenal of modern technology and training facilities.

Sarah eyed the weapons bracketed along the wall to her right as she entered the study. She faintly remembered a time when she questioned Florin about his collection of firearms.

"Even humans can be monsters," he had said.

Personally, she thinks he just enjoys the chaos and power behind each round. If there was one thing Florin liked, it was control, and Sarah suspected even the smallest gun in his arsenal gave him that rush.

She heard the click of his door and trained her eyes ahead, straightening her already perfect posture and locking her hands at the small of her back.

"Relax, Sarah, take a seat." Florin walked around his desk, gesturing to the black leather chair in front of him. The dimmed, inlaid LED lighting above cut over his face, making the sharp-angled planes of his features look less human and more monster—and for a second, Sarah watched the shadows shift and morph his face into the demon she suspected lay dormant under his skin.

But the moment passed, and he looked up at her with cold, dark eyes as he took his seat. His stare seemed to see right through her—assessing her. Tearing her apart until all her secrets and flaws were laid bare.

Forcing herself to remain neutral, Sarah took the seat offered, keeping her posture stiff despite his words to relax.

Relaxing around Florin was *never* an option.

His expression gave away nothing as he leaned back in his chair. He was studying her, looking for weaknesses. He wouldn't find one. Florin reached forward and opened one of the desk drawers, pulling out a small manila envelope and tossing it in front of her. "I have a hunt for you."

Sarah flicked her eyes to the envelope, but she didn't touch it, waiting for permission.

"Open it."

She picked it up, her fingers undoing the seal. A single piece of paper slid out onto the desk. A single word was written in the middle: *Dimmir.*

Florin leaned forward, looking at the paper briefly. "Dark Ones."

Her brows wanted to furrow, but she smothered the action before it gave away her tell of confusion. Dark Ones? The original Dark Fae from the old world?

When the wall fell, dividing their worlds, the Fae were the only ones who knew there had been a separation between humans and magic. Magic integrated itself into the humans when the veil fell, so they didn't even have a chance to remember a time when magic didn't exist. But the Fae remembered, they knew the truth. So, they wrote the history books, the very ones that lined the walls of Florin's bookshelves.

But Dark Ones, originally called *Dökkálfar*—or Dark Fae—had all but vanished once the veil was destroyed. Hunters today called them Dimmir—dark, death, *demon.* It was rare to come across a Dimmir.

Sarah set the envelope aside, looking at Florin. Her curiosity got the better of her, and she asked, "Are you sure they mean Dimmir and not Deathwalker?"

"All Deathwalkers are Dark Ones, Sarah," Florin said, picking up the paper without deigning her a glance. "The Dimmir are the original Dark Ones that stood on the side of power when the wall fell. Deathwalkers are simply newborns bred in this world. Lesser versions."

Sarah studied his face, seeing a faint smirk grace his mouth. Power. It was what Florin craved, and she would bet her life, not that it was worth much, that she knew what side he would have stood on if he lived before the veil had fallen.

"Then they grew in numbers after the wall fell? I thought Dimmir were in hiding due to the bounty hunters had on their heads." It had become a sport between hunters. Find a Dimmir, cut off its head, and you will go down in the history of hunters. Dimmir were not easy prey, though; not many hunters have lived to tell their victorious tales, usually succumbing to the wounds inflicted by the demons they sought to kill. She had only ever heard about a hunter killing a Dimmir through Florin, and it had been some time since she had heard it mentioned.

"Deathwalkers grew in numbers, but the Dimmir did not. Deathwalkers were created by the Dimmir, and they follow their creators closely but create their own law and order within their clans.

"The one you will be hunting controls what is left of the Dimmir. Word has it he's growing an army of newborn Deathwalkers, and they're eating their way across Europe." Florin's face turned to annoyance as if he thought of this Dimmir as a bug in his way rather than the enemy.

Sarah put her hands in her lap, looking down at the word scribbled across the paper. "Is there any more information?"

"Your target is named Avian. He and his newborns reside in the eastern ridge of the Carpathian Mountains."

"So close?"

Florin arched a brow, his lip curling as he looked at the name on the card. "It might explain the disappearances in the village."

It's been fourteen years since the attacks on their village started. What was once a city of thirty thousand remained a village for barely eight hundred. Deathwalkers crave blood. According to the history books, before the fall of the veil, they would feast on anything that had a pulse, anything to satisfy the demons that filled their bodies and controlled their bones. But the veil shattered, and they brought that hunger with them.

Humans called them vampires from their old superstitions, but hunters and Fae knew them for the beasts they really were. They were the creation of the Dimmir, the elves that turned from light and sought the land of shadows—and the power that came with it.

The attacks on the village were subtle at first, one happening every few months, but as time went on, their confidence grew, and the attacks came more frequently. They would steal people from their beds and those who walk alone at night, leaving only bloody remains and shreds of the person they used to be. But now, as the numbers dwindled and the attacks were slowing, the village remained in constant vigilance and fear.

Sarah didn't know who was behind the attacks, but from the state of the remains, it was easy to assume it was the newborns the Dimmir sire. Humans had the innate weakness of being mortal and without the strength of the Fae. Hence, the Dimmir let their creations take their time, and Sarah wanted to slaughter each and every one of them for it.

Noting the lack of care in his words as he mentioned the disappearances, Sarah ignored her annoyance and bit down on her tongue.

"Take out Avian, and you'll take out the rest of the Dimmir. What do they say, cut off the head of the snake, and the rest will fall?"

None of this made sense to her. At all. Her hunts were straightforward, usually a village being terrorised or a beast ransacking the surrounding areas, but this raised questions in her she didn't know how to ask. "Who's to say more won't take his spot?"

"I know they won't." Florin's expression turned steely, his gaze staring at her intently with a coldness Sarah had seen time and time again. "Only *you* can take out Avian."

That gave her pause, and she flittered her gaze between the card and Florin. "Why only me?"

His tone was abrupt as he snapped, "Are you saying you are unable to complete this hunt? Should I find a more *qualified* hunter?"

Sarah bowed her head instantly, regretting her question. "Forgive me, Sir. No, I can do it." Rejecting a hunt was a sign of weakness to Florin, and weakness was unforgivable. Weakness meant death, and Sarah had someone she needed to live for.

Florin breathed through his nose, easing the edge in his voice and relaxing into his seat. "Out of the entire Order of Hunters, you were selected for this. This hunt is no easy task. Can you do it?"

"Yes, sir." The Order was created when the hunters rose up in defiance against the demons and beasts of the old world. They refused to live a life in relation to the Fae and other magical creatures. Still, they only condemned the beasts that showed malice towards the peace they strived to maintain in their world. Sarah never truly understood their reasoning, but power is a fickle friend to those who taste it.

Nodding his head once, he tapped the card before sliding it off the metal desk. Sarah knew it would get incinerated the moment she left. "Rest tonight. You leave in the morning."

Her body tightened, and she stood from her chair. "Yes, sir."

"You may go now."

Hearing her dismissal, Sarah turned and left. Her head swarming with thoughts of the coming morning and what the fuck she was about to face.

CHAPTER 4

The rain hammered at her window, racing a path along the arching glass, the night sky lighting up with flashes of lightning in the distance. Sarah watched the storm from her desk, fiddling with a double-headed coin, thoughts elsewhere as she dwelled on the previous night.

"Things are happening, Halfling. Things you may not realise yourself. Armies are rising…"

The Vilon's words rang through her head, and she paused, watching the trees at the forest edge sway violently.

"Halfling?" she muttered quietly. "What did you mean?"

A soft knock interrupted her thoughts, she looked over at her door as it slowly opened on silent hinges. Alec poked his head into her room, and she smiled at him. He was in plain blue pyjamas, his mess of blonde curls flopping over his forehead as he rubbed his eyes sleepily.

"Shouldn't you be asleep?" she questioned, walking over to him.

He looked up at her, a frown on his small face. "I couldn't sleep."

Sarah heard the distant rumble of thunder and felt Alec grip her pyjama pants that matched his own. She knelt, bringing him close as she stood up, holding him. "You can't let Florin see you scared of a little storm."

He buried his head into her neck, muttering, "I don't, but with you, it's okay?"

Sarah walked over to her bed, putting him down gently.

"With me, it's okay," she agreed.

Alec grinned up at her. "I don't even cry in front of Florin!"

She laughed at his pride and ruffled his hair, nudging him to the middle of the bed. "Make some room. You can stay with me tonight."

He crawled to the middle of the bed, the silver necklace around his neck swinging in the air, before burying himself under the blankets.

Sarah crawled on top of the covers, laying her head in her hand. "I'm leaving tomorrow for a hunt."

His golden eyes widened. "No, you were gone last night! You just got back!"

"I know," she sighed, moving an unruly curl from his eyes. "I have to do this though. This hunt is vital to us; it involves the *Dimmir*." She knew he'd get excited hearing about them. He loved stories from the old world.

He sat up suddenly, his face hopeful. "A Dimmir?! That's so cool!"

Sarah laughed again, pushing him down gently. "Get back into bed, Little One."

"Will you tell me the story of the Dimmir?" he asked excitedly.

"Which one?"

"How they were created, how they came to our world."

Sarah nodded thoughtfully, peering at him. "If I tell you this story, will you go to sleep?"

Alec nodded his head vigorously, wiggling his body beneath the blankets.

"Very well," Sarah commented, getting comfortable on the bed. "It started with the veil. The world of man and magic was divided by an invisible wall that separated us. Two entirely different worlds within one. Once, the divide was almost non-existent, but as man began to doubt their belief in magic, it grew stronger. It protected the world of magic.

"There were those that wanted to corrupt the old world, to control the light in it. It wanted the world to fall into darkness. But a human girl who was a descendant of the first Fae created was taken across the veil by the Gods and the last living dragon, and she shattered the veil, making two worlds become one.

"Before the fall, there was one Fae; he belonged to a race called *Ljósálfar*—High Fae. His name was Ezra, and he was an elf of , the city of elves. While trying to protect the keeper, Ezra became infected by the darkness. He soon brought death and chaos to their lands. Many feared him, but some joined him because of the power he offered. They were called *Dökkálfar*—Dark Ones.

"Dark Ones were High Fae that fell into the shadows. They became corrupted and twisted versions of themselves, driven by their lust for flesh, death, and the control that came with it. The weak-willed became servants, puppets to Ezra. Then there were some who became walking nightmares that could wield the darkness into whatever weapon they desired. In the old world, Dark Ones feasted on anything that had a pulse, ravaging entire towns and villages. When the wall fell, they hid in the new world, feeding solely on animals until they grew scarce after a few years. Soon, the Dark Ones began to create newborns to help supply them with food. Those newborns who didn't become puppets to their creator became Deathwalkers. Deathwalkers would bring humans and Fae to their creator to feast on them. After too many killings, hunters rose up in order and placed a bounty on the Dimmir's heads and forced them to go into hiding."

Alec sat up, looking out the window as the rain slapped against the glass. "I read once that vampires can't go into the sunlight."

Sarah nodded her head slowly. "Those are just stories, Alec. Deathwalkers can walk among humans, day or night, as can

Dimmir. Their skin does not burn, garlic does not offend them, and they do not have teeth that can suck blood from your neck—most of the time. Their canines are meant for… tearing."

Alec gave a disappointed huff as he fell back against his pillow. "That's silly. How do they drink human blood then?"

"Alec… this isn't something you should know."

He made a sound of complaint, and Sarah sighed. "Okay, okay."

She ran a hand through her hair as she lay beside Alec, bringing him close to her. "They tear them apart, Alec. They don't just drain their blood. They eat their flesh until there's nothing left but bones. These are humans, Alec, you must remember that. They are just like us." Images of her past cases flashed in her mind, blood and limbs and… *pieces.* That's all that was left when she had gone to the home of a family torn apart by a Deathwalker. There was nothing left of them but piles of their pieces.

Looking at the boy, Sarah shook off the icy chill that went down her spine.

"Do High Fae eat humans too?"

She shook her head. "No. High Fae are elitist within social structures; they conformed easily enough to the new world but only for their own benefit. Some of them might be monsters morally, but they won't eat you."

Alec yawned, his eyes drooping. "Did others evolve?"

"All creatures evolve over time, even humans," she whispered, kissing the top of his head. "Especially when magic shapes them."

He grasped the front of her shirt, looking up at her with tired eyes. "You'll come back, right?"

Sarah paused before answering him. Death was something every hunter faced, and she never made promises she couldn't keep. "I'll do my best."

"Promise?"

"… Promise."

It was barely dawn, the midnight hours still masking the sky as Sarah slipped out of bed the following day, eyeing the sleeping child that curled deeper in the blankets. She smiled softly, leaning forward to kiss the top of his head.

She opened her closet and pulled out a pair of black jeans and boots, a black long-sleeve shirt, and her worn black leather jacket. Leaving the coat on the bed, she grabbed the rest of her clothes and padded softly to her bathroom, silently closing the door beside her as she turned on the shower.

The hot spray beat down on tired muscles, and she relaxed against the wall as steam rose around her. The wound on her arm was halfway healed when she removed the bandage. Sarah looked down, rubbing the pink skin gently. Since she was little, she always healed quickly. Florin said her body's first instinct was survival, and her ability to recover swiftly was an attribute to that, plus the bitter healing tonic he would force Sarah to drink when she was a child. He said it was a medicine to help her body's immunity. Sarah believed it was luck. The cut on her cheek had already nearly mended, the skin smooth and pink as she ran her hands over her face.

She was tired—mentally and emotionally.

Sarah turned her neck and let the hot water fall down her skin, soothing the aches in her muscles as stress coiled in her core. *The Dimmir,* her mind whispered from the depths of her subconscious, not letting her forget for even a second that this next mission could be her last. Letting her mind wander, she closed her eyes, imagining the layout of the Carpathian Mountain range. Their village lay at the base of a forest that spread for hundreds of miles in all directions. The Carpathian Mountains were just to their east, and locals might argue that the surrounding forest was a part of it.

Thunder cracked overhead, and she paused, listening for any signs that Alec might be awake. When she heard nothing, she turned the water off and grabbed her towel. She took little time drying off, wringing the water from her thick hair and throwing it into a wet ponytail high on her head.

She pulled on her jeans and tucked her shirt into the high waistband. She grabbed her boots, looking for the rolled-up socks she usually stashes in them before a hunt, nibbling on her bottom lip when she found them missing.

Opening the door softly, she peeked her head out, pursed her lips, and sighed.

Golden eyes glowed in the darkness, and Sarah walked over to the bed, patting the space beside her. "Why aren't you still asleep?"

"The thunder woke me up."

Sarah cursed silently, knowing it would have woken him. She patted his head, putting her boots on the floor. "I didn't want to wake you."

"You can't leave," he said softly.

Sarah walked over to her closet, grabbed a pair of socks, and walked back over to Alec, sitting while she pulled them on. "Why can't I?"

He shook his head firmly. "It's dangerous. I can't protect you if you're not here."

Sarah allowed her smile to widen as she kissed his temple. "You mean I can't protect you if I'm not here." His scowl made her laugh as she pulled her boots on. Standing up, she grabbed her jacket. The worn leather hugged her sides when she zipped it up.

Alec hopped off her bed and scurried into her closet. She stood there amused, watching as he dug around her things. A moment later, he returned with a belt in his hand.

"You can't forget this."

Sarah nodded, a serious look on her face. "You're right. What would I do if my pants fell off?"

Alec gave it to her, crawling back onto the bed.

Sarah looped the belt through and grabbed the push dagger on her nightstand, slipping it into the hidden slot. Next, she went to her daggers in the drawer and secured them inside her boots with a practiced ease, their pockets snug against her calf.

"Is that all?" Alec asked quietly, his head darting around the room before landing on her with wide eyes.

Pausing, Sarah looked at her wall of weapons. "No," she muttered. She walked over to her small armoury, eyeing the firearms quietly. She pulled her semi-automatic Glock G40 from its mount, weighing it in her hands. She never used firearms on her hunts, but something told her to bring it. Sarah grabbed the holster on her desk, slipping her jacket off quickly as she looped it around her shoulder, clipping the gun in.

She zipped up her jacket again, grabbed extra magazines from her desk drawer, and tossed them into her bag. She paused when she saw the cobalt-stripped 10mm rounds in the drawer. *Just in case*, said a small voice in her head. Tongue in cheek, she swapped out her standard rounds for the cobalt ones.

"Don't go..."

She let out a soft breath as she grabbed her bag, throwing it over her shoulder. Alec looked at her with large eyes, and Sarah knelt before him, touching his cheek gently. "You have to be strong, Alec. You have to protect me, remember?"

His chin trembled as he fought tears but jerked his head in acknowledgement. "I'll make sure Naschta doesn't come into your room again. I'll watch it day and night until you come back!"

Sarah gave him a crooked smile. "That's right. Be strong, Alec." Pressing a last kiss to his temple, she stood, adjusting her bag and walking to her door. She looked back, whispering, "I promise to try my hardest to return."

With her final words, Sarah walked out of her room. Quietly shutting the door behind her, Alec sat kneeling on her bed, his small face twisted with sadness, holding back his tears as he watched her leave.

The morning sky wasn't visible among the low ceiling of clouds. Fog rolled through the mountains like a dreary cloak, whispering untold secrets to the trees. Sarah faced off with the tree line, her village and manor behind her, the Carpathian Mountains looming ahead in the distance.

It would take the entire morning to trek through the forest before she reached the start of her journey. The crisp air and misty skies welcomed her like a friend as she hoisted her bag across her body and began her venture ahead.

CHAPTER 5

Sweat dotted Talan's brow, beads rolling down his temples as nightmares consumed his mind. Blood pooled in his memories, his brothers' slaughter replaying over and over again.

Ice water doused his nightmares, he was startled awake. Talan jolted upright, his naked body contracting against the frigid temperature. His breath fanned out in front of him, bumps rising along his skin as he glared at his sister Alani, who stood over him, her dark jean-clad legs standing by his shoulder. Moving his wet hair from his eyes, he shoved to his feet, letting out a low growl of annoyance.

"Was that necessary?" he gritted out through clenched teeth.

Alani gave him a trying look, one dark brow raised, wooden bucket in hand, as she shifted her stance, unfazed by his naked body. "You looked pathetic, Little Brother. I thought I would help you out."

Talan bent low and shook his head vigorously, spraying her with water. Alaini made a sound of annoyance and jumped out of the way, but not before she got splashed. His eyes caught the mud that coated his legs, and he paused. His nightmares were real, the blood he saw hadn't been a dream. His jaw worked tirelessly as his thoughts reeled back to the night before. Shoving his dark hair back, he straightened, looking at Alani with distant eyes.

Brows furrowing, she put the bucket down and crossed her arms over her chest, her dark green wool sweater making her blend in with their surroundings. "What's wrong, Talan?"

He had run all night and all day until he reached his clan. He hadn't stopped once, travelling the Carpathian Mountains in a single stretch until he collapsed from exhaustion inside the sanctuary of his clan's walls. Mud caked his skin, but he didn't care. He had made it to the wooden deck of his family's cabin before collapsing just outside the front door.

Talan glanced around their village, the ground muddy from the rain, forest walls surrounding them like a towering fortress. Log houses with thatched roofs were scattered throughout their village, there was a small school near the centre with a butcher and grocer mirroring it, the training area for the pups just outside of that. Guards patrolled their outer walls both in human skin and wolf.

Everything was peaceful and quiet, and he was about to destroy that. Talan closed his eyes, heaving a heavy sigh as that peace weighed on his heart. When his eyes were closed, all he could see was his brother's faces as they died, and he opened them, grinding his teeth.

"Talan?"

He looked at his sister, sadness and guilt riddling his expression.

Alani looked down at his legs, eyeing the mud, and then looking around the village. Her gaze was asserting as she wandered over the faces that passed them without care. Nothing was out of the ordinary, but something was missing. Talan saw the realisation slowly slip into her face when she couldn't find the males she searched for.

She turned back to him, uncertainty clear on her face. It was the same face their mother had when she was alive; their similarities were uncanny. Yellow hazel eyes, chestnut hair that framed high cheekbones, deep olive skin, and a narrow face.

"Where are the others, Talan?"

He looked at the ground, his shoulders dropping as his body turned to ice, rage slowly eating him. His fingers curled into fists, shaking to contain the fury coursing through his blood.

"Where. Are. They?" her words were bitten out as her gaze turned primal, the wolf in her wanting to come out.

Talan lifted his head to meet her stare, fire burning behind his eyes. "They're dead. All of them. They're dead."

Alani went preternaturally still. "What do you mean dead?"

He was shaking now, ice turning to fire in his veins. What could he say? All he saw was their faces, their blood, and heard their last cries that echoed down the bond before it went quiet. How could he put that into words? Instead, he rounded on his heels and stalked towards the door.

"Talan, answer me!"

He gritted his teeth, ignoring her as he shoved his way into his family's home. The wood door slammed against the wall, dry mud from his legs flaking to the wood planks as he stomped through the small house.

"Talan!"

He whirled around, his eyes burning as he looked at his sister. "What do you want me to say, Alani?! They're dead, and their killers are still out there!" His chest heaved with every breath, nostrils flaring, and he knew his eyes were glowing as the wolf in him snarled in return.

The short blue cotton drapes were strewn open along the two square windows on either side of the kitchen and dining area, but that was it. No lamps were lit, and the cabin was cold like the spring storm drenched them from the outside in. He needed to put clothes on, but he couldn't move, not when his sister pinned him in place with her words, demanding the brutal truth from him.

Alani took a deep, shaking breath, closing the front door behind her. Her fingers tapped the wood with anxious procession before she turned her eyes to her brother. "Who killed them?"

Talan's body began to shake, and he balled his hands into fists, nails digging into his palms. If he looked down, there would be little crescent wells of blood before his skin healed over.

"Talan?"

His nostrils flared, and his voice was rough as the words scraped against his throat. "Newborn Deathwalkers. They came in the night and slaughtered well over a hundred humans. They killed an *entire* village. Our brothers didn't stand a chance." Saying it out loud made his knees want to give out, but he caught himself, combing his fingers through his curly hair.

Alani's face paled at his words, and she stumbled back, her body falling against the door. "Does anyone else know?"

"No," he muttered, staring out the window, watching the children momentarily as they played outside despite the temptation of rain.

"How did you survive?" she whispered.

"I went out for a midnight hunt." Talan braced a hand on the back of one of the four simple oak chairs around the wood dining table. "If I had been there... If I hadn't..."

Alani took a single step but stopped, thinking better of it. "Do they know you survived?"

"No." He stared at the world beyond the window, frowning, his jaw flexing while he chewed on his emotions.

"Talan?"

Talan turned his attention back to Alani, amber eyes glowing from the wolf inside him that begged to be released to hunt down his brothers' killers.

"Are we in danger?"

He pursed his lips, his face falling as his mind reeled with images of blood. "Gather the elders and everyone else in the square. They have a right to know of their deaths." He didn't give her a chance to reply as he turned his back on her and walked into the cramped bathroom at the end of a narrow hall, slamming the door behind him.

The rain came shortly after, thunder rumbling across the grey sky like tormented giants. The village gathered in the square. Elders standing among the crowds of males and females, small children tangled in their mother's skirts as they shied away from the storm. Murmured whispers travelled through them as they tried to figure out what they were gathered for.

Talan watched the backs of his people from the porch of his home. The chilled mountain air held no notice of the warming season as his breath fanned out before him. Dark jeans and his black wool sweater kept the cold at bay as he stepped out from his cover. The rain pissed down on him, and the thick soles of his black boots sank into the mud, his steps squelching in the silence. His damp hair curled slightly as a chocolate brown strand fell over his brow.

As he neared, people parted and silence fell. While thunder roared overhead, shaking the trees, Talan stopped in the centre, his eyes panning on those around him.

"You've gathered us here, Talan. Speak your mind."

Talan's gaze focused on Torin, their village chief who stood in the rain dressed in dark denim and a black shearling coat, his long black hair braided back, amber eyes pierced his own in knowing. A shiver ran along his spine, but he ignored the ice that threatened to fill him. "A great tragedy has befallen our people."

Whispers rose again, and Torin held up a hand, the murmurs ceasing.

Water travelled the plains of Talan's high cheekbones and down the length of his nose as he turned his face to the storm. Closing his eyes, he took in a steadying breath before looking back at Torin. Water dripped from his fingertips and eyelashes as his mind reeled with what to say.

"Where's my son, Talan?"

The soft, decaying voice belonged to a female who had stood the test of time, giving in to her mortality after she had lost her mate. Wrinkles mapped out her skin, her hair white and braided down her back, and her yellow eyes grew tired and distant as she stared at Talan. Kallen had been her son, her only tether to this world, and he had died.

Talan closed his eyes, knowing he was about to serve her only bond remaining in this world. The sight of lifeless eyes staring at the forest edge where he had hidden tormented him behind closed lids. He snapped his eyes open and looked at the woman. "I'm sorry."

What was left of the life in the mother's eyes slowly dimmed, and she fell to her brittle knees, the long fabric of her patched blue dress pooling around her in the mud. Those around her rushed to her aid, but she ignored them. A deep wail rose, and she turned her head to the sky and let out a mournful cry. The rain beat down on her face, thunder echoed, and storm clouds twisted overhead in sorrow.

The village looked at Talan for answers, their faces pinched in shock, anger, and fear.

"Your sons, our brothers, and our kin were murdered by newborn Deathwalkers!" His voice echoed through the now eerily quiet village as he bit out his words. "They came in the night and killed over a hundred humans, and with them our brothers!"

Many more cries rose up from the families of those who had fallen.

"What does this mean, Torin?!" demanded one of the villagers, stepping forward. His long black hair hung in wet strands around his face.

Torin looked at his mate, who stood beside him, dressed similarly, a more petite, pretty female with pin-straight black hair to her waist. "We are not killers. We are not trained to defeat such an evil. We are peaceful people. This loss is great to our people, but this is not our war to fight."

Blinding fury enveloped Talan as he took a step closer to his chief. "You mean to say we won't do anything?! There is an uprising of Deathwalkers on the horizon, and you wish to do *nothing*?!" He swiped an angry hand through the air, roaring, "They *murdered* our kin! How can you stand by and do nothing?!"

Torin's mate stepped forward, her demeanour calm.

"Nolia—"

Nolia held up a hand to silence her mate, staring at Talan with careful ember eyes. "We cannot risk the lives of anymore of our people. We are not a clan of hunters. We would live as peaceful shifters. That was our promise when we came to this world."

"They were murdered, and you will do nothing?"

"We will protect those who still live." Her words were final, leaving no room for argument.

Talan looked at the faces that stared at him. Children gazed up at him with wide, frightened eyes, and he gritted his jaw, remorse lingering in his voice as he said, "So you have made your choice?"

Torin nodded. "Aye, Talan."

Whimpers from grieving families filled the silence, the rain continuing its onslaught.

"So be it," Talan spat, jerked his head once and turned on his heels. The crowd parted as he stalked from the village centre, dread knotting in the pit of his stomach.

"Talan!"

He ignored Alani as he stormed into the house, feet heavy on the wooden slates, mud tracking behind him.

"Talan, stop!"

Shoving the door open to his room, he grabbed a leather satchel from his small closet and threw it onto his bed, tossing items from around his room into it.

"Where are you going?"

Talan stopped, turning to face his sister, standing in the doorway. Her arms crossed over her chest, and her face hardened as she looked at him. He narrowed his eyes on his sister. "You can try and stop me, Alani, but it won't get you far."

She unfurled her arms, her features softening, and she sighed deeply. "Do you really think you can stop them? Hunt them down?"

"I don't know," he said lowly, sitting on the edge of his bed, the mattress groaning under his weight. "You weren't there…"

"What good will come of you chasing after a ghost trail? You know the town elders will want to relocate. When you return, we may not be here."

Talan drew a hand through his dark hair, wet curls tangling around his fingers. "Do you stand by their decision?"

Alani tilted her head, sitting beside him. "No, but I do understand it. These people, our people, they are cultivators and peacekeepers. Some have never felt the weight of a weapon in their hands. Trying to go against the Deathwalkers would be suicide—especially newborns!"

"Deathwalkers killed our parents, Alani. Can you really sit by and do nothing?"

"Are you doing this out of revenge? They wouldn't want this life for you."

Talan stood abruptly, looking at the image of their parents that sat primly on his bedside table in a small wood frame. His sister was a mirror image of their mother, but he was a combination of both of them. He had his father's strong jaw but his mother's high cheekbones; his father's build but his mother's leanness. He was split right down the middle between the two. Their calm expressions reflected at Talan as he remembered a time when peace was evident in their lives, and there was more laughter than tears. "You didn't see what I saw, Alani."

She squared off with her brother, looking up at Talan with a determined gaze. "Then tell me! Explain to me! Tell me what I can do to help!"

Flashes of that night flared in his vision, and he snarled, "There was so much blood, Alani! It was everywhere! It covered the ground like rainfall! They fought them while their blood still spilt from their bodies! I watched them die, all of them!" Talan grabbed his bag, looking inside at the contents. A growl of frustration slipped out, and he threw the bag against the wall. The items inside were scattered across the room as they crashed on the floor.

A knife slid towards him, and he bent to pick it up. Nostrils flaring, he stared down at the weapon in his hands. It was the first blade his father had given him. It was what he had learned to fight with.

"Talan…"

"Our parents wanted us to know our legacy," he said, interrupting her. "They believed every Shifter should know how to fight and defend their home. They did not shelter us from the truth, Alani. They knew one day we would have to face it."

His sister moved in front of the door, desperation in her tone. "Is today that day, though? You were barely a young male when father passed. You're not a warrior, Talan."

He grabbed the leather and wool coat from behind his closet door and shoved his wallet from the bedside table in the inside pocket. He lifted the hem of his jeans, shoved the knife into his boot sleeve, and looked at his sister. "I don't know if today is that day, but I am willing to find out for our brothers and for our parents." He gently moved Alani out of his way, kissed her temple softly, and gripped her shoulders as he gave her a tight smile. "I love you, sister, no matter what happens."

Alani followed Talan to the porch, wrapping her arms around her waist. "Talan!"

He stopped and turned to her.

Her familiar amber eyes were pale in the grey overcast. She held up a hand, a small smile on her lips. "Be safe, Brother."

He nodded once before turning his back on her. The forest loomed ahead, and he stalked for the outer treeline, embracing the dark woods as they engulfed him.

CHAPTER 6

Sarah looked up at the canopy of trees, eyes blinking against the rain. The forest was cast into shadows as the storm bawled overhead, her small fire snapping in protest at the water. Though the rain fell, the forest was calm. Silent. The wind was still, the air hanging around her like a thick blanket.

She poked at the flames, throwing on some extra kindling, stoking the fire until they caught. She watched as the embers sparked into the wet sky, floating into nothingness before they exhausted.

Memories of the early morning floated through her head. Alec, wide-eyed and afraid for her. Then there was Naschta. She had been waiting for her in the entry hall. She could still see the dark look in her eyes as she watched her from the door.

Sarah looked wary at Naschta when she saw her leaning against the double doors of the manor. "What do you want?"

Naschta cocked her head, peering at her with a small smile, though it didn't reach her eyes. Her gaze was cold and unwavering. "I just wanted to witness you walking to your death," she said in a snide voice.

Sarah paused her steps, staring at Naschta momentarily. "And when I return, then what?"

Pushing away from the door, Naschta took a step closer.

Sarah could feel her breath fan across her cheek and resisted stepping back. "What will you do when I return?"

Naschta leaned in close, her lips grazing against Sarah's ear. "You won't," she whispered.

Sarah's stomach churned with contained rage at the confidence in Naschta's words. Closing her eyes, she tried to wipe the memory from her mind. As the stillness increased and the rain lulled a hypnotic melody, Sarah felt her mind drift. She could see darkness surrounding her and figures standing around something. A shiver ran over her body as blood pooled at her feet. She could almost feel its warmth on her fingertips, its tacky wetness.

Hands grasped her, and her memories changed. Blue eyes stared at her in the darkness, and sweat dotted her forehead.

"Saskia."

Sudden pain stabbed through her skull, and her eyes shot open. A gasp left her lips, and her hands went to her head as the pain wrapped around her in a vice grip. The world around her faltered, her vision becoming hazy. Sarah could feel her heart beating in her chest, and the sound of her blood rushing in her ears overtook the noise of the forest. The pain intensified, it was all she could think about as her body doubled over. Sweat dotted her forehead, mingling with the rain as she fell to the ground, her cheek pressed into the cold, mossy earth.

Sarah's head pounded, and her breathing came in shallow pants, but as the pain slowly eased, her eyes rolled back into her head, and she fell into the void.

The smell of wet earth and evergreens filled the air as Sarah trekked through the cover of trees. She had awoken to a dry night sky, darkness all around her, and a pulsating headache that throbbed at her temples with every beat of her heart. Her hair was dry when she awoke, but her clothes were damp, and the freezing temperatures in the mountains threatened to ice her over. The fire was nothing but embers that she quickly restarted, huddling close to it, eyeing the shadows with a familiarity that dipped closer.

She wasn't afraid of the dark; she had been trained to become darkness itself. To use the shadows to her advantage. It was beat into her as a child. The scars that marred her body were evidence enough, they were tally marks of her mistakes. If Florin found her, he would mark her as a lesson. She quickly learned that to be hidden was her only refuge.

The floor was soft underfoot, and she pushed a low-hanging branch out of her way as she scanned the forest bed. She was never given information about her assignments except the location and who she was hunting. Florin told her once that it was for the safety of The Order. What he meant was in case she was tortured, she wouldn't have any information to give them.

The Order was particular about their cases. They shrouded them from outsiders and hoarded them from other hunters. Sarah never understood why The Order did what they did or how they did it. Still, Florin told her to never question them, and she never questioned Florin for the sake of the flesh on her back.

The mountainside was a steep vertical climb, the path soft and uneven as Sarah dug the toes of her boots into the ground, hiking the terrain with ease. Her muscles sighed at the welcomed exercise, stretching and tightening, propelling her up.

She had discarded her bag by the fire pit that early morning, stuffing it into a small burrow and covering it with dirt and leaves. She would collect it when she was finished or buy a new one. She didn't care either way. She had only brought it with her out of habit, but as she smothered the fire that morning, she found herself eyeing the trees and terrain around her. Her bag would only be in the way. So, she stashed her extra magazines into the pocket inside her jacket along with a lighter and left the rest behind. Her first aid kit and food rations she kept in the bag for emergencies were left with the rest. She would hunt off the land, and if she got injured, well, she would deal with that when it happened.

The morning passed slowly, the air damp and cold as Sarah climbed higher. Thick clouds rolled overhead, leaving trails of mist to linger through the trees. The smell hit her before she reached the crest. Death and decay lingered, coating the scent of pines and earth. Lips pursed, she let out a breath through her nose and trekked up the last mound before the ground evened out into a plateau.

The Carpathian Mountains crested and peaked, rolling from one pinnacle to another, vibrant green earth surrounding her. Among the walls of mountains and trees sat a village in the valley below. Low-hanging clouds shifted above them, concealing most of it from view.

Tambiln.

From a rocky ledge, Sarah stared down at the village, eyeing the distance between them. She knew this mountain range from memory, knew the villages and clans, knew the prey and predators that roamed. Tambiln was a human village occupied by the Romani of the old world that now dabbled in cheap fortune-telling and farmer's markets as a way to get by. They lived off the land, their habits from the old world still woven tightly into their way of life.

Dome huts shaped from mud and long wood shafts scattered the village, fires lit throughout, and carriages and wagons moved back and forth from the village centre.

The oily stench of rot still wafted up through the air, and Sarah bit back her revulsion. She was used to the smell of decay, the last fibres of a body holding on while nature slowly took what was left bit by bit. She had seen and inflicted enough death to know that the smells would linger long after the bodies were gone, but why was it coming from Tambiln?

Eyeing the sheer drop one last time, she turned on her heels.

The descent was faster than the climb up, but the rocks threatened to dislodge under her feet as she hiked down them. The sheer face of the mountain's edge lurked nearby, only feet away. Sarah ignored its taunting presence and zipped her jacket up to her chin as the wind broke across her face.

Tambiln was a mess of chaos and haggard faces when Sarah reached the bottom, entering the village with assessing eyes, a stony wall came up on her face as she took in the mess. The open-walled lean-tos, where Romani sold their trinkets and potions, were empty and destroyed. The roofs caved in as if someone had cleaved right through them, and the wooden work tables were in splinters; feathers, bones, and beads littered around what was left. Wagons were overturned, and some of the shacks had been completely shattered. Tarot cards were scattered like snow in the mud alongside animal hides and household debris.

Sarah sniffed the air, nose wrinkling at the heavy tang of copper. The ground squished underfoot, and she looked down. Mud threatened to engulf her feet, but that wasn't what made her jaw clench and her gut coil. A pool of muddy red sloshed over her boots, a stark reminder of what had happened in the village.

Blood.

It saturated the ground they stood on.

Pulling her feet free, she cut through what was left of the village. Fires roared throughout, trying and failing to warm the hallow cold that had come to settle on Tambiln.

Sarah noted a woman walking towards her. The woman's shoulders were hunched, her once all black hair, now littered with streaks of white, a sheet around her face as she stared at the ground.

Reaching out a hand, Sarah stopped the woman. "Excuse me—" Her words died on her tongue as empty black eyes stared at her.

The woman's eyes went wide, her face previously empty like the life had been drained from her, contorted in fear and panic. She shook her head quickly, her limbs trembling under Sarah's hand. Sputtered sounds came out, but the words did not follow.

"It's okay, Myda."

Sarah turned a sharp eye to the gruff male voice behind her, forcing herself to relax when she saw a man probably in his late sixties.

The woman—Myda—shook herself free of Sarah's grip, and Sarah dropped her hand, watching as Myda tucked her head down and disappeared like a mouse hiding from a cat. Sarah supposed she was the cat to the gypsy woman. Pursing her lips, she turned to the older man.

Assessing dark brown eyes worked over her, eyeing her from boot to head. She was a threat; these people had been slaughtered, and she knew that all outsiders from that point on would be the enemy. Relaxing her body, she breathed through her nose and let it out, softening her features. She wasn't their enemy, but they had a common one.

A firm mouth pressed into a thin line under a bushy salt and pepper beard, the paled olive skin from the winter season crinkling around his eyes as they narrowed slightly, and with a jerk of his head, he said, "Come."

Sarah followed the older Romani man through the village. The people of Tambiln were just as Myda had been as they passed Sarah and the man. Faces void, hollow, and grey. Fear lingering over their shoulders like a Reaper waiting to stake its claim.

At the edge of the village, lingering through the wall of forest trees, was a wagon with bright blue glass that hung from its rafters, shells and petrified woods mingling through the glass. Sarah eyed the soft shards as they clinked together like a little bell against the shells, the colour reflecting like bits of life that might offer the village and its denizens redemption.

The man opened the wagon door and ushered her in, eyeing the outside world with one hard look. He shut the door firmly behind him as soon as Sarah passed the threshold.

Sarah's fingers twitched towards the knife hidden in her belt, her gaze never leaving the man who scrubbed a hand over his well-worn face.

He peered at her through his fingers, dropping his hands to his side. He stood only a couple inches taller than her five foot ten inches, and though his age marked his face, he stood like one of the evergreens. Old, unfaltering, and strong.

Shifting her weight, Sarah turned her body as the man walked past her to the desk in the back of the wagon. Noting the small size of the inside, Sarah looked around the wagon, lit only by oil lamp. Shelves lined either side, scrolls and books encompassing them. Elaborate red and gold runners lay underfoot, a small wooden desk at the end of the wagon with a carved wood chair behind it.

"You may sit, Girl," he said, eyeing her, adding, "If you like."

Sarah noted the small stool across from him but shook her head. "I'll stand. I won't be long."

He nodded his head as if knowing she would say that. "Aye." Moving the books from his desk, he lay a hand on the wood and leaned back into the chair. "What brings you to Tambiln?"

She turned to face the bookshelf beside her, her fingers brushing the worn edges of three large scrolls piled in one corner. With a curious tilt, she gave the man a sidelong look. "What happened here?"

"What business is it of yours, Ms...?"

Sarah held the man's stare momentarily before saying, "Rawan."

It was only a partial lie and one that came easily. It was her middle name, and because there were no records of her full name, she felt compelled to use it on her hunts. Another form of protection from people willing to sell her out to destroy the hunters and what they—she—did.

"Last name?"

"What business is it of yours, Mr...?"

His words echoed back at him in the wagon, and his lips twitched as he stared at her. "Luca."

"Last name?"

His lips crested into a small smile. "I like you."

Her memory was the only record of her full name: Sarah Rawan Viche. Florin had let her look at her birth certificate once when she was younger, the only living document that had her information on it before he burned it in front of her. She had read the name and date over and over again in those few minutes before he took it, engraving it into her memory.

Sarah Rawan Viche was born on February tenth of the year twenty-one thousand eleven.

She was twenty-two years old, and that was all she knew of

herself. She didn't know her parents' names, and Florin, who had scratched them out, never deigned to give them, where they came from, or where she'd come from. They were dead, and knowing their names wouldn't rise them from their graves. The part of her that had yearned to know what happened had been beaten out of her. They were dead, most of her was dead with them, and nothing would change that.

"What happened here?" she asked again, stepping away from the bookshelf.

Luca pulled leaves of sage out from a drawer in his desk and piled them onto a silver tray. Lighting them with a match as if the name he would utter was cause enough to smudge the evil from the room. "Deathwalkers, they unleashed newborns into our home. There was a Dark One, I saw him in my visions."

"Dimmir?" Sarah questioned, inching closer and found herself taking a seat on the stool.

Luca's brown eyes darkened, nostrils flaring as he said lowly, *"Dökkálfar."*

The air in the room went stale at the name, and Sarah felt her blood chill.

"This one came from the old world. He stood like night—like death and night were one, and he came to deliver the Reaper's request. His newborns stole over a hundred souls."

"When?" Sarah asked sharply.

"Two nights ago."

She had been in Rome during the slaughter. Guilt roiled in her gut, and she took a steady breath, trying to disarm it. There was nothing she could have done, whether she was in Rome or not. She knew they would have died regardless, but still, the guilt came and settled. The small part of her that Florin could never beat out of her wept at the loss of innocent lives.

"They came in the dead of night. Feasting on their bodies, draining blood, and bathing in it." Luca's face blanched as he stared at a spot on the desk, his gaze distant and wide while he recounted the events. "These newborns did not kill just to quench their thirst; they *ripped* my people apart. They killed them for sport as much as they did hunger." Anger flared in those dark eyes as they met

Sarah's.

Sarah glanced around the wagon, her gaze narrowing at Luca.

"Why are you not dead," she asked lowly.

Luca tilted his head, understanding crossing his features. "Aye, I would be had I been here. So would the others that you have seen." He opened a drawer, the sound of wood-on-wood scraping in the silence. A plain black cell phone was laid out on the desk.

Sarah raised a brow at the phone that sat very out of place in the ancient wagon.

Luca pursed his mouth, eyeing the device. "I find this to be both a revolting and annoying contraption but also increasingly convenient."

Amusement flickered through Sarah, but she kept her features schooled. "What does a phone signify?"

"You must understand, Rawan, that I and my people came from the old world. Though my people were only a few, those numbers grew, and soon Tambiln was created to house the families that made a home within our caravan." Luca turned the phone on, and the screen lit up his face as he swiped it open. "Those who died did not come with us. They were bred into the new world, descendants of the old world. My people, those who were with me when the veil fell, still enjoy our traditions." He opened an app and scrolled through some of the files before opening one and turning the phone to face Sarah as a hologram popped up on the screen. "We took our wagons and goods and travelled to the markets in the outer-lying towns and villages. We have been selling our spices and remedies for the last week and doing readings."

Sarah leaned forward and looked down at the digital image floating above the phone. There was Luca, his arms crossed over his barrel chest, another man holding a beer in his hand, and two women holding a tray of spices and herbs. They looked happy— carefree. She looked at the time stamp and found it marked for three days ago.

They looked very human in the image, and Sarah had to blink back her surprise, pushing away the phone.

"How old are you?" she questioned, glancing up at the older man with a raised brow.

Luca let out a low chuckle. "We were gifted with long life when we crossed the veil; when it fell, that didn't change. Though a gift, it is also a curse I find sometimes. If only they had also made me a little younger," he said with a cheeky smile.

So, he was old—very old.

He grabbed the phone and looked at it momentarily before closing the image. The hologram vanished, and he tossed it back into the drawer without a care. "As I said, the device is both an annoyance and a convenience."

Sarah pulled the edges of her jacket down, straightening it as she stood. "Do you know where these newborns have gone?"

Luca stood from the desk, his face turning serious. "No, and I don't suggest you try and find out either, Girl."

She appreciated the concern, a small part of her warming to it, but disregarded it quickly. "Noted, Luca, but if you do know anything—"

"—Would you like to see it?"

Her brows lowered. "See what?"

The camp was quiet as Sarah and Luca walked through what was left of the huts. He led her to the centre of the village; a large bonfire winked in the misty air as it began to sprinkle; embers floated free while the timbers crackled. A wooden cart sat stationary beside it, one loan form laying across the planks; a woven red tapestry covered the body. Sarah eyed her surroundings when dust floated around her as she stepped towards the wagon.

A strangled wail pierced the loamy air, drawing her attention and her eyes darted to a woman on the other side of the fire who was staring at her feet in horror. Sarah was already looking down when Luca placed a hand on her shoulder. Black and grey ash caked into the ground, but small piles still mounded between the lumps of mud, splintered, charred bits of bone sprinkled in like macabre confetti.

"They burned the bodies," he murmured quietly.

Unease rolled through Sarah, and she stepped back, looking at the woman holding a hand to her mouth, tears streaming down her face.

"Come." Luca put a gentle hand on Sarah's arm and steered her from the woman's gaze.

She stepped around what was left of the ashes and followed Luca to the back of the cart. He glanced around them quickly before he pulled back the tapestry.

Sarah's jaw clenched as she looked down at the angular Fae face. It would have been handsome if not for the sharp plains of its bones and the hollow of its cheeks. The creature looked almost human, but Sarah knew better.

She reached for its mouth and exposed its teeth. Nothing was out of the ordinary; their canines were only slightly longer than most humans.

"Shifters sometimes camp within our village, patrolling and aiding us as allies against common enemies in the forest or just to seek refuge for the night between their hunts. One managed to take this newborn down before he was torn in half. We found his remains beside this ones."

Sarah nodded slowly, pulling back the tapestry further, eyeing the chunk pulled from the newborn's stomach. Everything had been ripped out from within. It was a lucky kill.

"What of the Shifter?"

"Burned and ashes scattered in the forest."

"Good." She didn't need to say more. The Shifter died honourably. Pulling back one of the closed eyes of the newborn, Sarah heard Luca's quick intake of breath and the curse he let out. Black as night and completely unseeing, the newborn stared up at the sky—the green mountains above reflected back.

"Sever the head and burn the body," she said coolly, replacing the tapestry.

Luca stared at her momentarily, glancing at the body and returning his gaze to her. "They went east; we didn't dare track them, but the blood trail followed them east. If it continues, I do not know."

The hair on Sarah's neck stood on end, and a chill crawled down her spine. Her gaze sharpened as she scanned the village slowly, noting the faces that came and went and the quiet that seemed to blanket them.

Something in her stirred, pulling her to the forest. Her eyes were scanning the treeline when Luca said something, but his words fell on deaf ears.

She pulled her eyes from the trees and looked at the older man. "Sever its head and burn the body," she repeated. "Take your people and rebuild."

"We will stay here; we won't flee like pups with our tails between our legs."

"That is your decision to bear, I hope the outcome is favourable." Her words cut through her as she turned on her heels. They might have marked their lives on Death's roster if they decided to stay, but that wasn't Sarah's burden to carry. She learned long ago that everyone makes their own choices despite death's welcoming embrace.

She left Luca standing there, staring holes into her head as she walked away. The treeline loomed overhead like a massive wall as she stalked toward it, stopping when something slipped under her foot. She picked up her boot and looked down at the mud.

There, staring back at her, were two tarot cards.

A chill went through her as she stared down at the seemingly innocent cards.

The Fool and Death.

CHAPTER 7

    Talan crouched below the bushes just beyond Tambiln, eyeing the village and its occupants. It was worse in the daylight than it had been at night. Ruins of what had been lay like grave markers for the forest to see. Images of blood and the echo of screams flashed through his memory, the sounds of limbs being torn from bodies ripping through him. Nausea coiled in his gut, and he closed his eyes briefly, opening them once it passed.

    He saw the bonfire that roared in the centre of the village and the grey and black ash scattered around it. Bodies on fire, limbs torn, and the pale faces of terror filled his vision. The stench of rot and burnt flesh filled his nostrils. With a low growl, he shook his head, clearing the images.

    Rain began to sprinkle down, the flames crackling against the wet sky, and he shifted his position, keeping low as he moved behind a thick tree. The village was sparse with people; he knew Tambiln to be full of life—vibrant and alive, but this was not what he saw. What was left of the people was barely more than a shell as they picked up the remains of their loved ones.

Talan spotted Luca, the village head, as he rounded around one of the last standing, *whole* huts. A woman trailing behind him. Her brown hair tied back into a high ponytail, and she was dressed in all black. Her body was thin and athletic, and he could make out the calm swagger of her gait as she followed behind Luca. She was aware of everything around her, Talan let his curiosity bubble up as he watched her.

Hunters were common in these parts. Lone rangers who lived in run-down establishments and slunk around at night. Hitmen for hire, as they were known to civilians. Talan had seen them often enough when he ventured into the outlying city as a teenager. Almost every dive bar he had graced willing to serve him at seventeen had a hunter lingering in the corner, a drink in hand, looking as worn and dark as a back alley at night. He had stayed away from them for the most part, the air of danger emanating from them making it easy for him to mind his own. But sometimes when his curiosity got the better of him, he would ask them questions. They usually scowled at him and told him to get lost.

Rarely had he seen a female hunter, though, and this one looked nothing like the ones he was familiar with.

He pushed closer, keeping his body hidden behind the massive trunk. He watched the woman as she looked down at her feet. He could make out a flicker of unease, and maybe disgust, flash across her face before becoming neutral again.

Luca whispered something to the woman, but Talan couldn't hear it. Instead, he eyed the cart Luca gestured to. His heart hammered in his chest, threatening to burst from his ribcage, as he stared at the lump that lay covered on the cart.

The woman pulled back the cover, and Talan felt his skin boil with rage as his blood ran hot, then ice cold; the wolf in him growled, and the sound escaped his lips. His eyes turned molten, and the beast inside of him clawed to shift, to tear out of its confinement of human flesh and limbs.

He could smell the rot of the newborn, and he knew it had killed his kin, along with the rest of its kind. A low warning rumbled through him, and he dug his hands into the tree's bark, willing the wolf inside him to stand down.

Shaking his head, his eyes fixated on Luca.

"One managed to take this newborn down."

Talan's blood froze. One of his brothers had killed a newborn. Then there's a chance he could still—

"Given back to the earth."

No. No, his brother was dead, along with the others. There were no survivors, and he was a fool to think otherwise—to hope.

"They went east."

Talan's head whipped to the east, searching for any sign of the Deathwalkers, but there were none. He knew there wouldn't be any, but a growl of irritation rolled through him regardless.

The woman was watching the village, assessing her surroundings. There was the faintest tug on his mind the longer he stared at her. Something that made him want to come a little closer.

She said something even his keen ears couldn't detect and spun on her heels.

Without hesitation, Talan moved. He darted from the tree and cut through the forest, the earth beneath his feet silent as he went. The trees seemed to shift around him, his eyes never leaving the village as he darted around low-hanging branches. The woman disappeared briefly before pausing at the forest's edge. Talan took that moment to disappear into the shroud of greenery and overgrowth that hung from a tree, pressing his body to the trunk. He willed the forest around him to envelope him entirely, opening his senses as the woman stepped into the trees, pausing.

Her eyes darted through the trees, and Talan's body tensed as she paused in his direction. After a moment, her eyes moved on, and she made quick work of the forest, heading east just as Luca had said.

He held his breath momentarily, watching her figure as it retreated. When she was almost out of sight, he sniffed the wind.

Humans had a distinct scent shared between them, like flowers that had begun to wilt, sweet but sour. He sniffed again but smelt nothing. The woman disappeared from view, and he cursed silently. If he couldn't track her by scent, he would have to follow her closer than desired, which he did not want to do.

Talan waited a few minutes before moving, treading into the dense forest on near-silent feet.

The woman was quiet, almost completely silent in the dense woods; the only thing alerting Talan to her movements was the occasional brush of her feet against the pine and the light scrape of her boot against bark as she stepped over an uplifted root.

He had nearly lost her once, cursing silently when she disappeared, causing him to tread closer. It had been an hour already, and he was beginning to feel impatient. He wanted to shift, to see if he could pick up her scent, but knew it would be for nothing. She was scentless, and his curiosity peaked as he followed the sway of her ponytail.

Talan didn't see the moss-covered root as he took a step and found himself tripping forward. He threw a hand to steady himself on the tree, and when he looked up, she was gone. The curse was audible this time, his eyes darting through the trees, searching.

Pushing away from the tree, Talan quickly stepped over the uplifted roots. The forest was empty except for him. She was gone.

"Shit," he muttered.

A soft gust of air was his only warning before a hand was tangled in his hair, jerking his head back sharply, a blade pressed to his exposed throat.

"*Shit*, would be correct," said a low voice.

Talan's body stiffened at the cool female voice that pressed against his ear. He swallowed, and the blade pressed into his skin, the sharp edge digging deeper. "Is this a kink of yours? Restraining men in the middle of nowhere, maybe inflicting a little pain? I hear some like that." The grip on his hair tightened as she pulled his head back further.

"Don't you know it's creepy to follow women in the forest?"

"I thought you were playing Red Riding Hood?" Talan said with a rough chuckle, the sound barely escaping with his head yanked back.

A low hum from the woman vibrated through his back, her voice cold and humourless when she drawled, "Let me guess? You're the big bad wolf?"

"Something like that," he commented with a crooked smile that became a wince when she jabbed the tip of the blade deeper.

Hands pushed him from behind, and Talan found himself tumbling forward. Whirling around, teeth bared, he faced the end of a very sharp blade pointed between his eyes.

Light brown eyes stared him down, their gaze cold and calculating as her lips pressed into a tight line. "Why are you following me?"

Sarah's body tensed as she stared at the man at the other end of her blade. His amber eyes flashed dangerously, hinting at the predator beneath his skin.

"*Why* are you following me?" she demanded again. Her shoulders constricted as she shifted, and she took a silent breath, relaxing into her stance.

The man just smirked, his eyes never leaving hers.

Red Riding Hood, her ass.

Tilting her head slightly, she took a step closer, her short blade steady as it remained fixed between his eyes.

"Tell me, is this how you treat all men or just me?" he drawled lowly, a dimple appearing on his cheek as his smile turned sharp. "I'm flattered you think I deserve this." He put a hand to his heart. "Truly."

Annoyance ticked in Sarah, and her wrist flicked quickly, the tip of the blade slicing his cheekbone.

Jerking back, the man hissed through his teeth, his eyes

narrowing into a glare. "That wasn't very nice, Princess."

"You'll live, Asshole," she retorted.

The laceration was small and shallow, blood dotting the surface of his cheek. She could see his skin already beginning to knit back together. Soon, there would only be a faint pink line.

"Not human," she muttered, her brows lowering as she quickly assessed him.

"But still an asshole?"

Her annoyance ticked again.

"Listen, Princess, I wasn't following you."

"Don't lie."

"On my honour as a man."

"You're not a man."

He raised a brow at that and looked down at himself. "Last time I checked, I was; losing it would be a shame." A wicked look mingled with amusement as he said, "It's one of my favourite parts."

She ignored him, refusing to follow his gaze to his *favourite part.* "You're a male, but you're not a man."

"Not human," he corrected.

"There's no difference."

He shrugged his shoulders. "Depends on who you ask."

The forest around them seemed to still as the sky opened up and rain began to fall; a small creek and the snap of a branch followed. She needed to keep moving.

Sarah lowered her blade but kept it ready in her grip. "Stop following me, or I will make it a very big problem for you and your favourite appendage."

He had the decency to look pained.

Stepping around him, she didn't bother to look back as she started walking away.

"Aren't you going to ask what I am?"

Her eyes rolled into her head when she heard him start following her.

"You're a shifter. You're old enough that you've probably reached maturity." She only then looked over her shoulder, shaking her head. "But only in the immortal sense."

"You wound me, Princess." He paused, his steps faltering only for a moment. "How could you tell?"

"I could practically smell the dog on you."

"Ouch."

Sarah stepped around a fern, stooping for a moment as she brushed it back. Dried black blood stuck to the leaves, and she swiped a finger through it, bringing it to her nose. Copper and rot mingled together.

"I might not be a hound, but I could be useful."

Her annoyance ticked again, and she let out a deep sigh through her nose, standing to look at the man—*male.*

"And afterwards, I'll give you belly rubs and tell you that you're a good boy," she said dryly, altering her course as she walked away.

"How did you know that's my favourite?" he asked with mock surprise.

Sarah felt her fingers twitch around the blade still in her hand. "I don't need your assistance, Shifter."

"I have a—"

Sarah whirled around, the short blade glinting in the light before it was pressed against the column of his throat. There were only inches separating them, and Sarah could feel the hot breath of the male rush out of him as it brushed her cheek; tilting her head to look up at him.

"I don't care what your name is, *Shifter.* Stop. Following. Me," she bit out through clenched teeth, her heart hammering in her chest. She needed to go; the rain threatened to wash away her only link to the Dimmir, and time wasn't on her side.

The male looked down at her and raised a brow. "We need to work on your people skills."

Her nostrils flared with irritation, but it was the only sign that her mood was darkening.

"Listen," he said lowly, the humour slipping, "I understand you don't need my help, but I *can* help. I can make your life a hell of a lot easier."

Sarah stared at the male, hoping her gaze would burn holes into his head. "I doubt that."

He dared to lift a hand and raised a brow when she twitched the blade closer. Tapping his nose, he said easily, "Wolfy senses."

"Shifter—"

"—Talan."

Sarah ground her teeth together. "I don't have time for games, and you're playing a very dangerous one right now."

Talan shrugged, ignoring the pain from the blade as it scrapped over his skin. "Aren't dogs good at games?"

Her eyes held his ember gaze before sweeping over the thick black lashes dripping with rain and the high plains of his cheekbones framed by a firm jaw and mouth. Something clicked in Sarah, and she took a step back. "You were watching me in Tamblin," she said, more of a statement, and then a slow realisation dawned, her blade slowly lowering. "They were your brothers."

"*Are* my brothers," he corrected, shifting his feet when the knife dropped from his throat, a shadow flickering across his face. "Death does not change that."

She nodded her head slowly. "It's why you're following me."

Talan's chin tilted up, the muscle in his jaw twitching.

"What did you think was going to happen?" she said with a short laugh. "I wouldn't notice you? That I would lead you right to the Dimmir and their Deathwalkers—"

"—No, I—"

"—And you would—somehow—"

"*Stop*—"

"—Kill them all?" Sarah finished with a scoff. Rolling her eyes, she slid the knife back into her boot.

Talan's nostrils flared with leashed rage, and Sarah's brow ticked when she noticed the almost feral stare.

"Is the puppy wounded?" she asked drily.

Something in Talan snapped, and he lunged for her. His teeth bared, the wolf in him letting out a tearing snarl. Sarah spun, the ends of her ponytail whipping across her cheek. She grabbed his outstretched hand, twisting it back as her foot lashed out to the soft spot behind his knees.

He fell with a roar of defiance, twisting in her grasp and bringing her with him. Hips turning, he grabbed her with quick reflexes, flipping them both and slamming her into the earth, pinning her between his legs.

Sarah bit back her yell, the edge of a rock jamming into her ribs. "Asshole," she spat, her head jerking up and connecting with his nose.

Talan reared back his nose crunching, blood spurting.

With a quick thrust of her knee, she connected with his favourite appendage, and Talan howled, his body bowing in pain, hands going to his crotch. Wrapping her legs around his waist, her right hand grabbed the opposite lapel of his leather jacket, and she snapped her hips in a quick arc.

Talan grunted as his head slammed into the ground, his eyes pinched closed in pain, teeth bared.

Sarah stared down at the male, head cocked, sizing him up with calm assertion. "I expected more from a shifter," she stated, brushing the dirt from her clothes as she stood.

His only response was a low grunt.

"If you can't even beat a human in a fight, how did you expect to take out a clan of newborns?" She stepped away from him, crossing her arms and eyeing him.

Talan finally opened his eyes, biting back his groan, his balls aching as he sat up. He hadn't planned to fight her, but something about the woman irked him, and the wolf in him wanted nothing more than to rip the smug look off her face. Though when he looked up at her, it wasn't smugness he found, but disbelief and pity.

The leash on his primal side slipped at the sight of her pity, and he ground his teeth together. "Save your sympathies for someone else."

Sarah didn't say anything, watching him stand. She knew what he was feeling. She knew it all too well. Something in her tore open as the rain fell around them, and she sighed. "You won't survive, and you'll only be endangering the rest of your clan."

He picked a pine needle from his hair, dropped it, and glared down at her as he wiped the blood from his nose. "The safety of my people is none of your concern."

"You're right, it's not," she agreed, stepping around him. Ignoring the glower of his stare.

"So that's it?" he said in disbelief, turning as she walked away. "I can't help?"

"You would be dead before you could." She turned slightly to look at him, a small frown etching her mouth. "Go home, Talan."

Talan raised his brows when she used his name, ignoring the sudden lurch of the wolf inside. "They'll be gone by the time I get there."

"Then find them, but go home." She looked at the forest behind him when a twig snapped, her shoulders tensing and relaxing when a small hare skirted from the underbrush. Her hands twitched to her push dagger. "This isn't your fight."

Talan scoffed, laughing bitterly. "The night they killed my parents, it became my fight, and everyone else's that has lost loved ones at the hands of Deathwalkers."

Blood. So much blood flashed through her head. Images of the unknown little girl covered in her parent's blood, her curdling scream that followed. Sarah's nostrils flared. Her fingers were quick, the push blade slipping into her hand, and with a snap of her wrist, the knife glinted in the dim light before sinking into the hare.

Talan flinched, shifting his body, but it was too late. He hadn't seen the blade until the hare was pinned to the ground.

The hare jerked, its body spearing back a couple of inches at impact before stilling. Sarah stalked over to the animal, slipping her blade from its head and stabbing it into the dirt, not caring that it might dull the edge; she would sharpen it later. The blade came back stainless, and she slipped it into her belt. She said a quick prayer of thanks to the animal's spirit and grabbed the hare by the hind legs.

Sarah spared Talan a glance, stepping around him, his eyes like pools of fire and gold that watched her every move. She jerked her head to the forest behind him with a tight smile. "Go home."

Talan didn't say anything and just watched her walk away.

CHAPTER 8

Night fell quickly in the forest, the trees looming overhead. The crackle of fire snapped through the dense foliage, shadows playing off the underbrush and the long fronds of ferns that cloistered around her.

Blood dripped down the flat stone in front of her, trickling through the crevices of the log she straddled. Her short blade glimmered in the flicker of firelight, working through the pelt of the hare she was skinning.

The hair on her neck was standing on end and had been since she had made a fire and set up camp. Ignoring it with every bit of self-restraint she had.

She removed the brown pelt, the hare no more than muscle and tendon now, and threw it into the fire. The flames crackled, eating up the skin.

The tingling at her neck had her letting out a soft sigh, annoyance ticking the muscle in her jaw, and she flexed her fingers. She cleaned the edges of her blade using moss, slipping it into her boot. The forest spoke around her, the whisper of wind etching through the treetops, mist rolling across the ground like a bleak blanket of shadows and secrets. She ignored every instinct she had that was yelling at her to find, fight, and kill.

Rolling her head, loosening the tension in her neck, she grabbed the makeshift wooden spit she whittled and skewered the hare down the middle.

Standing, she kicked the stone to the ground, out of her way, and sat on the log again, facing the fire. Holding the spit over the flames, she watched the crackle of embers fizzle in the damp air.

"You can come out now," she said lowly.

The forest was quiet.

Sarah rolled her eyes, then looked to her left, glowering at the inky darkness just beyond her camp. The silence was palpable as she waited, her finger tapping the spit.

"If you make me come get you, we will have problems."

The snap of a twig and the swift rustling of foliage had Sarah raising her brows as Talan stepped from the shadows. His mouth pressed into a thin line. He stared at her, taking a deep breath through his nose.

Sarah turned her attention to the hare, turning it slowly. "How long were you going to just sit there?"

Talan crossed his arms, leaning his shoulder against a tree. "Until you put that knife away."

Snorting, she deigned a glance at him. "As if that would help?"

"No," he said shortly, walking over to a buried stone beside the fire and dropping his haunches to it. "Though it's more welcoming to know you don't have a weapon to gut me with."

Sarah's lips curled into a dark smile, pointing the spit at Talan, oils from the hare dripping to the ground. "I could gut you with this if you prefer?"

Talan winced, moving away from the wooden spike, eyeing the animal still skewered to it. "No, thank you."

"Then don't tempt me," she replied coolly.

Lips quirking, he rubbed a hand over his jaw to hide his smile lest she take it as a personal invitation to ram the spit down his throat.

"Didn't I tell you to go home?"

He shifted, watching her above the flames. The firelight cast a gold glow across her high cheekbones. "Yeah, well, I'm not really good at listening."

She looked up at him. "Clearly."

"Don't act like you're not happy I'm here."

Sarah sighed. "You're going to die, and it's not going to be on me."

"And if I live, what then?"

"Well, then it'll be a damn miracle."

Talan barked out a laugh. "You have such a sunny disposition." With a warning look, Sarah moved the spit towards him, and he held up his hands in surrender. "You're going in the right direction, at least," he said after a moment.

Sarah glanced at the forest, turning the hare over the flames.

"You never told me your name."

The spit paused in her hands, and something stirred inside her, tugging at the back of her mind. Her name. She looked at Talan, his eyes glowing in the firelight, and that tug in the back of her mind stirred again. "Rawan," she said, watching him.

Talan rolled his eyes. "That's a damn lie."

"Is it?" she challenged, raising a brow.

"What's your real name," he asked, bracing his forearms on his knees.

"Who says it isn't?" His answering cocky smile made her want to punch him.

Tilting his head, his nostrils flared slightly as he sniffed the air. "I can't smell you, but I smell the lie. It hangs in the air like something sour."

Interesting, she thought. "You can't smell me?" she questioned.

He held up a wagging finger. "Name first."

Irritation flashed through her, and she bit down on it. Sucking on her teeth, she turned the hare as one side began to turn black.

"What's—"

"—Sarah," she said, cutting him off. "Rawan is my middle name." If the puppy decided to turn on her, she would gut him before he could breathe her name to anyone else.

Talan nodded slowly.

Sarah removed the spit from the fire. "So, you can't smell me?" she asked, tearing a leg off the hare and tossing it to him.

Snatching the leg from the air, Talan nodded his thanks.

"I thought you had some magical wolfy sense?" she asked, smirking while she chewed on a piece of meat. It was bland and a little tough, but it would suffice.

His hand paused, lowering the leg as his gaze darkened, lips tilting in a sly grin. "I could come over there and see if I'm wrong?"

Her eyes narrowed, and said with a challenge in her voice, "Do it, and I'll stab you."

"Promises, promises."

Leaning the spit over the log, she unzipped her jacket, shrugging out of it. "I can feel you watching me," she drawled lowly, adjusting the holster around her ribcage.

Talan shifted, brushing his fingers clean on his pants.

Sarah peered at him from the corner of her eye, noticing his stare. She knew what he was looking at and refrained from pulling her jacket back on. "Are you going to ask or not?" she snapped.

He rubbed the back of his neck sheepishly at being caught again. "I figured I would respect your boundaries?"

Sarah snorted. "Yeah, okay, that's bullshit."

He held his hands up in defence. "I was trying to turn over a new leaf, Princess."

"Call me princess again—I dare you."

He smirked, opening his mouth, and Sarah slid the blade from her boot, cocking her head, waiting.

Talan rolled his eyes. "Fine."

Slipping the blade back into its holster, she brought a hand up to where her neck and shoulder met. Sarah traced the puckered edges of the scar that curled from under her top. She knew it was stark against her pale skin, like a deformed silver tattoo.

"How did you get it?" he finally asked.

"How I got most of my scars," she replied, licking her lips.

There was silence, and she flicked a glance at him. He was frowning, brows furrowed.

"I want to know, but… but if you don't want to…"

Sarah snorted softly, glancing at the fire, her mind wandering to the day she got that scar. She wasn't ashamed of them, but it was no one's business.

"Hunters are an anomaly to me. Forget I asked," Talan said, poking at the fire with a stick he found on the ground.

She watched him briefly and said, "When we're trained, we're not rewarded when we succeed. When we fail in that training— if we're caught—we're punished. Some punishments are left as reminders."

He paused, setting the stick into the flames to give her his attention. When she said nothing, he slowly asked, "How old were you?"

"Thirteen." She picked at the moss growing through the crevices of the log, staring at the ground. These weren't secrets; they were simply facts. Facts of a hunter's life, so she added, "Whips to punish, cables to restrain, knives to torture." The firelight caught the thin silver scars that wrapped around her wrists, barely visible, and she rubbed the pad of her thumb over it.

Disgust lined Talan's voice, "I didn't realise hunters… you were only a child."

"Train them young, and they're yours forever," she said bitterly.

"Why didn't you leave?"

That bitterness grew into contempt, her smile turning cold. "Why would I?" She slipped her jacket back on, covering the scar. "My parents were murdered in cold blood by Deathwalkers just like your pack. He saved me, and I couldn't ignore that debt. I owe him my life, regardless of the scars I've earned from it. That is the price I must pay."

Rage kindled in Talan's gut, spreading like fire down his limbs, and the wolf in him growled.

Sarah's eyes snapped to Talan's, seeing the black rage under his golden stare. Silence hung between them, and she jerked her head to the earthy patch beside the fire. "Get some sleep. We have a long day tomorrow."

"Sarah," he said lowly.

The tug on her subconscious made her still when he said her name. Something on the tip of her tongue made her want to tug back, but she couldn't because she didn't know what she was tugging at. Instead, she ignored it, saying, "I'll keep watch."

His dark gaze was enough to make Sarah soften hers. "Sleep," she said, slipping off the log to the ground and leaning against it.

Talan watched her with guarded eyes as she got comfortable, wrapping her arms around her waist. He knew the conversation was over, but it took everything in him to keep the wolf leashed as he lay out beside the fire. Folding his arm under his head, he trained his eyes on the flames.

The night was blessedly dry despite the sliver of mist that rolled across the ground like a creeping spider. Sarah paid it no mind, watching Talan as he slept. His chocolate brown hair was unruly, falling across his brow in a curled mess. Tawny olive skin glowing under the flames he was sprawled out beside, dark stubble shadowing his jaw, framing the ridges of his high cheekbones and straight nose.

Sarah pulled her gaze away from him, ignoring the tug on her mind as it pulled again. The flames licked the darkness, embers wafting into the air, and she glanced at her wrists, dark memories flooding her mind.

"What is the punishment for failure?"

Hot, wet red blood rolled down her forearms, and Sarah fixated on the ruby beads that trekked a path across her skin. Nails bit into her palms until the skin broke, and her shaking was controlled.

"Death," she bit out through cracked lips. Dirt and sweat caked into her pores, her braided hair hanging in limp strands around her face. She knelt on the wet concrete floors of the underground training arena, her black shirt torn and hanging around her aching knees, in only a black sports bra from the waist up. Even that was held by a thread. Her wrists

were bound in a garrotte wire and restrained in front of her face by a cable attached to the wall.

Florin positioned her so the cable remained taut, her arms aching, the wire cutting into flesh no matter how still she tried to stay. She sat there, kneeling, legs slightly spread to brace herself, booted feet crossed at the ankles, back arched forward. On display like a bloody canvas, Sarah could feel every muscle in her body screaming. Begging for it to stop, but she bit down on the pain and made her muscles stop their trembling. She refused to show Florin an ounce of weakness.

"And what did you do?" he asked quietly, his voice the calm before the storm, echoing in the chamber. He knelt before Sarah, his eyes cold and void of human sympathy. There wasn't any room for emotions, not in the arena. Florin adjusted the whip in his hand, his fingers rolling the slick tip between them, red glistening on his skin. Her blood.

Her eyes flickered to the training arena. It was a massive concrete jungle beneath the manor. Weapons lined the far wall to the right with various blades, guns, and wooden staffs. A training ring in the left corner with its massive grey mat, and in the centre of the room was a black maze of solid adamant. The labyrinth was shrouded in darkness, filled with traps and secret crevices. It taught them to become the darkness. Florin would hunt them, and they would have to hide. To become nothing more than smoke in the air, and if he caught them...

"What did you do?" he asked again, his voice turning brittle.

Sarah gritted her teeth. "I failed." She had. She had failed. He had caught her. He had come from nowhere and everywhere all at once, and she hadn't had a chance to slink into the shadows before he had a knife at her throat in one hand and another at her ribs in the other. She could still feel the pull at her neck, blood trickling from where he had punctured her skin.

"And do you think you deserve to live?"

"No," she said, her gaze still fixated on the blood dripping from her wrists. Her body tensed, waiting.

Florin stood, leaning over her, his mouth brushing her ear, whispering, "Correct." He straightened, the tail of the whip dragging across the cold floor, her blood trailing behind it. "But you will. You will learn, even if I have to beat it into you."

Her nails bit into her palms further, refusing to tremble despite the *fear that went through her; her mouth became flat, and her nostrils flared with the breath she forced herself to take. He had whipped her already—ten lashes for the ten minutes it took for her to fail. She was meticulous. She had learned to become shadows and ash and smoke. To become nothing but the world around her—but he found her. She hadn't sensed his presence, and she knew she had fucked up. She didn't know how, but she had, and now she was paying for it.*

"How many more lashes do you think you deserve?" Florin asked, his finger dragging across an angry, welted strip of flesh where her sports bra had ripped open.

The muscle in her lip twitched as pain rocked down her spine, and she barely contained the low whimper. "As many as it takes for me to learn that failure is-isn't an option," she gritted out, stumbling on the last bit as he dug his nail into a section of her back that she knew wept bright red.

Florin hummed, contemplating her answer. She could feel his eyes on her back, raking down her spine, following the trail of blood that soaked into the waistband of her black training leggings.

"Ten lashes. Count them."

She had barely taken in a readying breath before fire cleaved through her. Back arching, her muscles clamped down, and her fists shook with sweaty palms. A sliver of a pained moan whispered from her lips, and she bit her tongue to contain it, tasting copper, tears burning her eyes. "O-one," she bit out through a trembling jaw.

The second struck down the middle of her back, right along her spine, and stars flashed across her vision as her skin threatened to tear in half. "Two."

And so, it continued. The bite of the whip was like a white-hot fire that left rising red welts over her back like latticework, her sports bra hanging off her shoulders, her back almost fully exposed, but still, she counted, even as her whimpers of pain slipped through, mingling with the crack of the whip that echoed in the arena.

Her body shook despite her best efforts to constrain it. Blood dripped down her ribs, soaking through her leggings and painting the steely grey concrete. That rod of lightning bolted through her bones as the whip licked over her back, and she panted against the pain. Chest heaving with every shallow breath she took, saliva dribbling from her lips as her head hung between her arms, shoulders straining as the wire bit into her wrists.

"Ten," she said, her voice barely above a whisper.

"I didn't hear you," he seethed, his footfalls jolting in the pained silence that followed.

"Ten!" she spit out, her eyes narrowing on the splattering of her blood before her.

Florin sniffed, and she could almost see him wipe the blood on his face that she knew freckled his skin. The cable holding her wobbled, her legs having widened their stance. She was almost parallel to the ground.

Pain—that white-hot, ice and fire pain—lanced through her like a knife, and she felt time stop, and a scream tore from her lips as her skin split open. Flesh, muscle, and fat tearing as the whip wrapped around the curve where her shoulder and neck met and ripped it wide open. Darkness dotted her vision, and her knees slipped in her blood, giving out. Her body, still held up by the garrotte wire and cable, jerked violently.

Seconds ticked by into what seemed like an eternity. Sarah could hear his near-silent breath even over the roaring in her ears.

That breath brushed over her broken skin, causing her to shiver as a wave of pain rolled through her muscles.

"Say. It," Florin said darkly.

Her lips didn't want to move, her throat constricting with every pull to make her voice work, but she made them work. They would work. "El..." The words caught, and she choked on them, but she forced breath into her lungs and made the word come out. "El...even."

"What?"

She flinched at the sound of his voice, the harsh growl like a talon splitting into the numbing silence that was beginning to envelop her. "Eleven."

The wire was released, her wrists slipped free, and she crumpled to the ground without a sound. Blissful cold seeped into her bloodied, sweat-covered body, her clammy brow pressed against the ground, uncaring that blood streaked across her cheeks.

Florin's footsteps were barely audible as he walked away. The hiss of the whip on the ground disappeared, and the door to the arena opened and closed with a deafening click.

Only when she was alone did Sarah let out a broken sob, her thin body shaking until it was uncontrollable, and she was too weak to rise or even curl in on herself. So, she lay there on her stomach, the red concrete a *vision of Florin's abstract work of art.*

Sarah's mouth pressed into a thin line, her thumb absentmindedly rubbing over one of the scars when the memory faded. The fire cracked, and her eyes fixated on the ruby-red twigs glowing beneath the flames. She swallowed the lead weight in her throat. Nine years later, she could still feel the sting of the whip, could still feel it tear through her skin. She closed her eyes briefly, and when she opened them, she found Talan watching her as if he could feel the phantom pain that was etched permanently into her bones.

His golden eyes were unreadable as he watched her but said nothing. The fire spoke for the both of them as it cackled into the night.

CHAPTER 9

Dank, black stone walls encompassed the dungeon hall of Dyagin Castle, wooden doors laying in a neat row as Avian stopped in front of an empty cell.

A whining yowl cut through the stale air, and he cut a cold look to the small wolf pup held in Reign's vice grip by a tuft of hair at the nape of its neck.

The pup thrashed violently, stilling when Avian's blue eyes became a shimmering pit of wrath, blinking up at the Dark One. With a loud yelp, its body was tossed into the cell, slamming against the back wall. The door slammed shut as the pup leapt for two males dressed in all black, teeth bared in a twisting snarl, crashing against solid wood.

A thud rocked against the wood, but Reign and Avian simply

stared through the iron bars that caged a small cut out in the door. The pup backed up until its hindquarters were pressed to the back wall, teeth bared, simmering amber eyes glowing in the darkness.

Holding up a small silver necklace, Avian looked at it hanging in the air, bored, and tucked it into the pocket of his fitted black slacks. "Now that is dealt with," he said coolly. "Let's see how the feedings are coming along."

Reign nodded once, eyeing the pup, who stared back at him with wide eyes, hackles standing on end.

"Reign."

Avian's voice was cold, commanding. Reign blinked once, turned from the pup, and followed Avian out of the dungeon.

CHAPTER 10

Fire and ash coated the night sky, embers glowing like fading stars while Tambiln burned around him. Talan's chest rose and fell rapidly, eyes wild, turning as screams surrounded him in every direction.

He stepped forward, stopping when his foot sunk into something wet. Talan's face blanched when he looked down. An ocean of blood filled the village.

"Brother!"

Talan reared to his left, and a sea of bodies floated among the rising blood waters. "Jai!" he yelled, wading through the floods, pushing limbs and unseeing faces out of his way.

"Talan!"

He saw Jai among the ruins, his amber eyes glowing in the crimson tide and black skies, clinging to the side of a hut, black hair sticking to his *terror-filled face. Talan yelled for his brother and friend, throwing bodies aside, snarling when his feet sunk into the mud and the earth gripped him there.*

"No!" he screamed. "Jai!" He watched as the mud hut gave out, crumpling. Jai howled, shifting, his midnight fur stained red.

A piercing howl cut the night, and pain cleaved a path through Talan's soul as Jai was pulled under. Panic filled him, and he yanked violently at his feet, but the mud held fast. The waters were rising, the ocean of blood at his chest, and he screamed into the night.

"Talan!"

The water was to his chin, and he craned his head up, eyes glued to the black sky. His breathing was rapid and shallow. He could feel death raking its watery breath down his back.

"Talan!"

The water covered his head—

"Talan!"

Talan jolted, body going ridged. Breath heaving from his lungs in gasping breaths, he snarled, grabbing the hands that shook him and flipping them to the ground.

Sarah let out a harsh breath as she was slammed into the dirt. Talan pinned her legs between his, eyes wild and glowing. His teeth bared, more animal than male, canines elongated and threatening to rip her neck open.

She stared up at him, barely a breath between them. "Talan," she said quietly. Talan jolted, but he didn't move. He stared down at her, and she knew he didn't see her.

Claws dug into her shoulders, she contained the wince and glared up at the male. "Talan," she said again, firmly.

His chest heaved with every breath.

The bite at her shoulders stung again, and she glowered, snapping her head up. Talan roared, and those claws released her. "Wake up!" she snapped, flipping him off her.

He crashed into the ground with a howl, teeth still bared, eyes feral as Sarah straddled him. "Talan! Wake up!" she commanded. When he didn't respond, her fist lashed out like an asp, connecting with his cheek. "Wake up!"

His head snapped back, and Sarah exhaled sharply when she

felt his body relax under her. Blinking, those gold eyes quieted to amber and fixated on her, seeing her annoyed expression.

Talan's eyes travelled down her body where she sat on him, and his brows raised. "I knew you were kinky," he said roughly, his voice raw.

Sarah's annoyance simmered, and she shoved off him.

Talan sat up, watching her sit on the log. He looked down at the claws that grew from his fingers.

"You were having a nightmare," she said softly, watching him.

He blinked, staring at the forest. Dawn was beginning to fill the woods in a blue glow, the quiet morning hush laying over them like a blanket. His throat felt like sandpaper, and he licked his lips quickly, standing. He took a deep breath through his nose, relaxing the tension in his shoulders. There had been so much blood, and seeing Jai's face, his pack brother, made nausea coil in his gut. It wasn't real, but it felt real. There was nothing he could do, and there was *so much blood*.

Sarah kicked dirt over the still-smouldering fire pit, and what remained of the hare was tossed in with the ash and embers.

"Was I screaming?"

Sarah only had to look at him, and he knew the answer: yes.

She watched his claws retract, straightening her jacket, feeling her skin pull, and she knew blood stained her shirt underneath. His cheek was red and swollen, the skin broken from her punch, but it was already beginning to heal.

"Thank you," he said gruffly.

Tilting her head, she let her eyes rake down his body and back up to his weary stare. "I couldn't have you telling the whole forest our location," she said shortly.

Talan's lips twitched.

"Come on," she said with a nod of her head.

He watched her ponytail sway with every step she took, her shoulders back with that confident swagger he noticed in Tambiln. His eyes travelled down her waist to the jeans hugging the curve of her ass. When she paused, he snapped his eyes back up. Running a hand over his face, he breathed through his nose, straightening himself, and brushed the dirt and pine needles from his jeans.

The dawn light caught on her jacket, and he saw eight perfect punctures in her shoulders, four on each side. He knew if she turned around, he would see two more, one on either side. "What happen to—"

Sarah cut him a glare over her shoulder, her brown eyes shadowed with irritation, and he snapped his mouth shut.

"You owe me a new jacket."

Despite the ageing hours of the day, the sun somewhere overhead, the world was only a fraction warmer. Talan found himself zipping his coat up to his chin the farther they walked, stuffing his hands into his pockets.

He caught himself as Sarah stopped suddenly, eyeing her.

She scanned the never-ending growth, kneeling beside a half-destroyed footprint stamped into the dirt. Her fingers brushed over the dark grains, hoof prints marking half of it. Letting out a rough sigh through her nose, she stood.

"Well?"

She rubbed a hand over her eyes, turning to look at Talan only when she was sure she had a leash on her tongue. Too much time had been wasted, he was only slowing her down. "They're careful, very careful," she said, if not a little bitterly.

He sniffed, turning his face to the mist that crawled through the treetops. There wasn't any wind; the air was almost stale, and he could smell the lingering scent of rot that stained the forest with an oily cast.

"Not careful enough," he said, jerking his head just to the left of where they were walking.

Sarah followed his direction, looking over her shoulder. Nothing but forest. She looked back at him, raising a brow. Whatever he could smell was lost on her.

He widened his stance, staring back at her. "Would you like to sniff the ground yourself, Princess?"

Sucking on her teeth, she turned on her heels, following his directions. "I guess your *wolfy senses* are good for something," she muttered.

"What was that?" he quipped, turning an ear to her. "Was that a compliment?"

Her brows dropped in annoyance, and she ignored him.

Talan chuckled lowly, stepping over a rock as they changed direction. He watched her back, glancing at the punctures in her jacket. Jai's face flashed in his mind, and his stomach turned leaden. Blood, the screams of his brother's being torn apart, death. Talan hissed under his breath, raking a hand through his hair while visions of his nightmare and reality flashed across his mind.

Sarah tilted her head, listening. She could hear Talan's change in breathing and could practically feel his pulse become a staccato behind his ribs. Yielding a glance to her right, she watched him quietly, her face blank while his was a storm of emotions.

Talan's rich olive skin had paled, his mouth pressed into a firm line, gaze distant. She knew that look, had experienced it herself. Regret. Guilt. It had eaten at her until she couldn't remember who she was before. She had become guilt and breathed in regret daily.

"There was a village deep within the Transylvania Alps," she said casually, walking around a large tree. "That I, and another hunter, were dispatched to by The Order." Naschta's name lingered on the tip of her tongue, and she bit down on the temptation to just say it. Maybe the forest would hear and take matters into its own hands. She stifled the smirk from that thought and continued, not daring to look at Talan. "They claimed that one of their own had been cursed and returned as a Draugr. So we went, and we saw."

"And did they?"

"Yes."

The wind was bitter—even under the summer sky, stinging Sarah's cheeks as they keeled on the crater's peak surrounding the tiny village nestled in its core. The shards of rock cut into her palms when she shifted on the uneven surface, slate stones sliding underfoot.

Naschta surveyed the area, palming one of the daggers strapped across her chest in a black leather bandolier. Fitted across her chest, the bandolier hooked onto the holster strapped around her left thigh that sheathed a bowie knife, its carbon fibre handle shadowed against her black jeans.

"What do you want to bet that they're all dead?" she said mildly.

Sarah's jaw tightened, sliding a calculating look in Naschta's direction. Her curly russet hair was pulled back in a bun atop her head, her green eyes were cold as she stared down at the village of Tor'oc.

"Always so optimistic, Naschta," she replied sarcastically, adjusting the neck of her shirt. They were dressed identically: black long-sleeved shirts with high necks, black fitted jeans, and black flat-footed boots. Work as a unit, act as a unit, dress as a unit. Just like the good little puppets they were.

"I like to see the best in every situation," she sneered.

Rolling her eyes, Sarah quickly checked her own bowie knife strapped down her right thigh and the shorthand knives tucked into her boots. Eyeing Naschta one more time, she sucked in a quiet breath, and they slowly advanced on the silent village.

The path down was treacherous, the slate ground shifting and threatening to give way at any moment. Rock siding provided enough cover from prying eyes but not enough from Mother Nature as Sarah tucked the loose strands of hair behind her ear, the wind tempting to pull her braid free.

Halfway down the crater, the wind ceased, and Sarah said a silent prayer of thanks. Her head thrummed with the insistent onslaught.

Tor'oc was quiet—too quiet when they entered it, jumping the last few feet off the steep pitch as it ended abruptly into a drop. The white thatched cottages mapped the village, dirt roads trodden into winding streets, and the peak of the crater walls surrounding them was like an imposing fortress, breaking off into a long cavern where light glimmered at the other side.

"Why didn't we just use the front door," Naschta drawled, eyeing the long narrow valley, tucked between mountain sides.

"I don't know, why don't you go back up and try that way? Maybe the Draugr will give you a head start?" Sarah snipped dryly.

Naschta only rolled her eyes, inching her way around the stone siding of a cottage.

Death lingered in the air, not in the way of decay and blood, but as if you could feel the haunting tips of the Reaper's claws down your spine. The chill of ice and something more, something that lacked life. It was the middle of summer, but it might as well have been the end of winter.

Rolling her head, Sarah breathed through her nose, releasing it slowly, her muscles relaxing. She followed Naschta around the cottage, the dirt muting their steps.

Tor'oc appeared abandoned. There was no one around.

Naschta's brows raised, looking around the deserted village. "Maybe they are dead," she mused, loudly enough for Sarah to growl a warning. Naschta smirked, tossing it over her shoulder.

They trekked into the desolated village, noting the druid runes painted on their simple plank doors in blood. The villagers had been warding themselves.

Sarah tested a door, watching it swing open with ease. Passing through the threshold, she noted the sparse kitchen. A sturdy wood table sat in the centre, two long benches framing either side. Worn black pots hung on the brick walls, and a loaf of bread lay forgotten, half-eaten, on the slate counter, mold growing in patches over it.

Wood planks squeaked under her boots, creeping through the empty remnants of the home. She paused in the doorway of a tiny room. Two straw beds on wooden slate frames pushed against opposite walls, a narrow glassless window latched shut with a single wood shutter. Rough grey wool blankets lay dishevelled across the beds with matching grey wool pillows. But that wasn't what Sarah was staring at.

She crossed the room and knelt, cradling the stitched doll on the floor beside one of the beds in her hands.

This was a child's room.

The doll was only as big as her hand, if not a little smaller, and made of light grey wool. Pale yarn mimicked blonde hair, its black stitched smile, and eyes stared up at her, with a dark blue dress made from a scrap of fabric.

She didn't know why, but she pocketed the doll. Slipping it beside her blades tucked into her boots, feeling the press of it against her calf.

"Could you imagine?" Naschta commented, her voice dripping with disdain.

Sarah glanced at her, watching her flick dust from her sleeve. Disgust curled Naschta's lip as she looked at the children's room.

Standing, Sarah shoved past her counterpart, ignoring her even when she growled in warning when Sarah's shoulder rammed into her own.

The bitter air made even Naschta shiver as she ambled out of the cottage, commenting on it. Sarah didn't respond, rounding the side of the cottage and following the dirt street that wound through the core of Tor'oc.

"Guess we know where the blood came from," Naschta said lowly.

Sarah stopped, looking to her left, to the pen housing multiple sheep, their grey wool glinting in the sunlight. Blood coated their fronts, their throats slit. Her fingers twitched by her blade, eyeing the felled animal before walking on.

A large barn loomed ahead, weathered and sun-bleached. Boarded-up square windows cut low into the sides. A shack sat across from it, almost identical, yet much, much smaller. Those blood runes painted on both, across their doors.

"Check the barn," Sarah said, jerking her chin towards the small side door next to the large hinge barn doors.

Naschta strolled over to the barn as if she were doing nothing more than taking a walk in the park, and Sarah bit back the words she wanted to snap at her—to take the hunt more seriously. But she didn't. Walking to the shack instead.

The shack was commonplace. Small, packed tight with handmade farming equipment, those square windows boarded up with thick planks. The villagers had taken the time to make sure nothing could get in—to anything.

She turned to the barn to find Naschta leaning against it, the door open. She flicked a bored glance at Sarah.

"It's empty," she said monotone. "Wherever they went, it was far away from here."

Scrubbing a hand over her face, Sarah groaned, but the sound was swallowed by a snarling growl.

The growl ripped through the stale air, high-pitched like a wild animal.

Awareness crawled down her spine, and Sarah slipped the blades from her boots. Flipping them skilfully, she widened her stance, eyeing their surroundings.

Naschta followed suit, sliding out one of the longer daggers from her bandolier and pushing off the barn siding.

The smell followed next.

Putrid and overwhelming, Sarah and Naschta crinkled their noses in *disgust, the heavy scent of decay wafting in.*

Wood creaked, and Sarah snapped her eyes to the barn roof. Heart hammering, her gaze met the pale whites of the Draugr's eyes that stared down at them.

"Shit." And then she was moving, throwing herself to the ground and rolling out of the fall. The Draugr leapt from the roof right for her.

The once very human man crashed into the dirt, twisting with a snarl, digging its feet into the ground, watching them with a feral gaze. His skin, now greenish and weathered, was sunken in, clinging to every muscle and tendon in his body. What was left of his black hair was only strings swaying against the side of his caved-in skull. A simple cream shirt and black pants in tatters, laying limply over his skeletal limbs.

Sarah could see his ribs carving through his skin, and she tightened her grip on her blades, dropping her hips into her stance.

The Draugr sniffed suddenly, his white cast eyes searching. He sniffed again like a hound, and his decaying face stretched into what Sarah could only take as a smile. His lipless mouth revealed broken yellow and brown teeth.

"While this is all highly entertaining..."

Naschta's words registered in Sarah as she spun quickly, the Draugr leaping towards them with hunger in his eyes. Her blade glinted in the light before cutting through the Draugr's back. Steel met rotting flesh, and the skin flayed from his bones.

Reeling, the Draugr sliced a hand through the air, knocking Sarah to the ground with a heavy blow.

Stars flashed in her eyes, the Draugr's strength tenfold compared to her own. She flipped to her feet, watching him stalk towards her.

Wood creaked, and its attention turned, sniffing the air once more.

Naschta moved then, her dagger's hurtling through the air. They lodged nearly in sync, burying into his chest.

That animal sound ripped through it, tearing the daggers free and dropping them to the ground. Its attention turned to the barn, rearing for the open door.

Sarah sprinted after it, ignoring the faint latch of the door clicking shut behind them. Darkness enveloped her, and then the hot copper tang of blood filled her mouth as it splayed across her face.

Screams. Soul-wrenching screams rose like a choir. Men, women, even the terrified shrieks of children—she heard them all. Could feel their bodies shove into her with blind panic. Sarah closed her eyes, stepping from the mass of bodies that suddenly pressed into her.

She could smell the decay, but there were too many, too many bodies. She couldn't navigate the barn without being caught in the slaughter. Her back pressed into the wall, her fingers searching for the boarded windows.

Her ears rang with their shrieks, hearing limbs being torn and the gurgle of blood as they choked. She heard them die, one after the other. Taking in a steadying breath despite her heart threatening to rip from her ribs, she slipped one of her blades back into her boot.

The screams began to dim as the Draugr cleaved a trail of blood.

Where was Naschta?

Sarah refused to let the desperation she felt brimming peak. Fingers curling around a windowsill. She latched onto it, sliding her hand up until she felt the lip of a wooden plank. Teeth bared, Sarah pushed with every ounce of strength she had.

The wood moaned but stayed.

Decay and copper were heavy, nearly burning her eyes. Biting back the yell of frustration, Sarah raised her fist, snapping it into the wood over and over again until her skin split at the knuckles and blood coated her hand. Over and over and over—

Light burst through the darkness, and the board fell away.

It was enough.

Sarah whipped around, the screams turning to silence, but she didn't let herself think of that. Scanning the beams above her, she took a step and another, ignoring the squish of flesh underfoot.

The hair on her neck stood on end, and she whirled as the Draugr leapt from the shadowed alcove.

Slamming into her, her breath rocketed from her lungs, and they barrelled to the ground. Her blade flew from her grip, forearm bracing against the snapping jaws above her face.

The Draugr was covered in blood, his skin red and glossy in the single beam of light.

Sarah gritted her teeth, grunting as pain lanced her arm where the Draugr gripped. Rancid breath cut across her face, and she brought her other hand up, smashing it against the concave skull.

Howling, the Draugr shook its head, and it was all Sarah needed.

Slipping her second blade free, she rammed it between its ribs. The scream that pierced the air was enough to make her ears ring. Flipping him off her, she rolled to her feet, spotting her second blade and leapt for it as the Draugr leapt for her.

They met with a collision of limbs, fingers tightening around the carbon fibre handle as she landed over it. Hands grabbed her braid, nearly tearing her head from her shoulders, and she was airborne.

Her body slammed into the wall on the other side of the barn, spine whining and threatening to break. Hissing, Sarah stood, watching the creature through lowered brows.

That same twisted smile lifted its face, scenting her blood.

Sarah could only spit the copper from her mouth, her own crooked smile turning her lips in response. "Come and get me."

Sprinting through the blood and bodies, Sarah shoved the steel between her teeth and shoved off the ground, flying forward. As she flipped through the air, her body arched past the Draugr before it knew what was happening. Wrenching the blade from her mouth, she slid it home.

Landing on her feet in a low crouch, Sarah watched it stumble, making to turn, blade still nestled where his skull met his spine.

The Draugr dropped with a solid thud.

She stood, walking over to it carefully and twisting the blade for good measure until it severed its head from its shoulders.

The large barn door opened then, and Sarah snapped her eyes to the green ones that peered inside.

Something similar to the Draugr's rage filled Sarah, and her hands shook with the effort not to unleash it all on Naschta as she peaked her head in, lips curling at the sight.

Light filled the barn, and Sarah had to reel in the sudden urge to lose her stomach contents, empty as it may be.

Blood. There was so much blood. It coated the rafters, sliding down the walls like paint, right to the mounds of bodies and flesh that lay on top of one another.

Half-seeing gazes, reaching fingers.

The entire village of Tor'oc lay in decimation.

Sarah blinked. It was the only thing she could do. Her gaze slipped from one face to another until it stopped.

A head of pale blonde hair, nearly concealed in blood, glimmered faintly from under a woman, almost as if the woman had thrown herself atop the body it belonged to, with only a prayer that it would save her.

Naschta stepped into the barn, making a sound of revolt. "Well, that was entertaining," she said coolly, turning her attention to Sarah.

That same inferno of rage boiled beneath her skin, and Sarah stalked towards her with ice in her eyes. Before Naschta could move, Sarah's hand lashed out, gripping her neck until the air sputtered from her lips.

"You knew," she growled, her face inches from Naschta. "YOU KNEW!" she bellowed, her voice carrying through the crater.

Naschta's lips moved, her throat constricting. She brought a foot up, and Sarah quickly blocked her before it could catch her knee.

"I don't fucking think so," she seethed, fingers biting into the soft skin at her throat, pressing her body flush against Naschta's so she couldn't move. White hot, blinding rage. That's all she felt when she slammed her counterpart against the barn wall, blood raining down from the rafters.

"You fucking knew," Sarah said again, watching her turn blue.

Naschta refused to struggle, her green eyes turning to shards of ice, blood dripping down her temples from overhead, the vein in her forehead popping.

She could snap her neck and call it an accident. She could do so many things and blame it on the Draugr. Sarah wanted to do them all, but a soft, gentle voice in her head brushed against the rage she was boiling in, telling her to walk away.

With a final slam, Sarah released her grip, watching Naschta pull in a sucking breath.

Stepping away, she watched her with a heaving chest, nostrils flaring with leashed emotions.

Blood flecked across Naschta's olive cheek, and she wiped her thumb over it, tongue flicking out to lick away the dribble of blood. "Delicious," she whispered. Assessing eyes turned to Sarah, and she tilted her head. "It was an accident. I couldn't get the door open."

The lie was hollow, and Naschta knew it, but her small, knowing smile was enough to let Sarah know she didn't care.

"You knew," Sarah bit out, stalking away.

"It was too dark. I couldn't see anything."

Sarah closed her eyes, forcing a breath through her nose as that rage began to churn again.

The head of blonde glimmered softly like a beacon in the nightmare.

Grabbing the woman by the shoulders, she rolled her off, ignoring the silent scream still etched into her face, throat ripped out.

Sarah fell to her knees, blood pooling around her, sopping into her pants.

Pale blue eyes stared, half-lidded, into oblivion. Soft cream skin, now ashen, lips slightly parted. Blood stained her neck and chest, her stomach ripped apart. A dark blue dress lay in tatters around her petite frame, hands grasping her intestines as if that would keep them in. A trail of tears cut across her cheeks where they had fallen.

Hands shaking, Sarah pulled the doll from her boot, brushing a bloodied hand over it. Schooling her features, she closed her eyes to whisper a prayer for the departed.

"They're only human. They would have died, regardless."

Naschta's words cut like a knife, and Sarah snarled.

"We're human, Naschta," she spat out.

Naschta rolled her eyes, walking out of the barn.

Sarah didn't take her eyes off the child, reaching out to lay the doll on her chest, numbness creeping into her limbs as she sat there, kneeling before the dead.

Blinking back the clouding emotions in her eyes and the dark memories, Sarah sucked in a steadying breath, seeing Talan watch her from her peripheral.

"What happened after?" he asked softly.

That pale blonde hair and unseeing blue eyes still haunting her memory were enough to make Sarah want to stab something—or someone. Instead, she gritted her teeth, saying, "Kill the monster, save the village." She scoffed under her breath. "Tor'oc is a graveyard now, nothing more."

Talan shook his head, ducking under a low-hanging branch. "It sounds like the Draugr wasn't your only enemy."

"It would appear so," she muttered.

"Why do you think she did it?"

Sarah's laugh was as bitter as the air. "I can't prove that she did it." She paused, chewing on the inside of her cheek, before adding, "But I should have known. I should have checked."

"You can't blame yourself for their—"

"—I can," she cut in sharply. "And I have. Someone had to take responsibility for it, and it would have been me anyway."

Talan's eyes darkened, narrowing. "What do you mean?"

But he knew, even as she shifted her jacket, her face impassive. "They marked you?" he asked lowly.

A whisper of a smile shadowed her face, and Sarah looked at Talan then. "Like I said, some punishments are left as reminders."

And they were. Each of her scars is a tally of her faults—of her failures.

Talan growled, eyes turning molten, his hands balled into fists at his side. The mere idea of anyone laying a hand on her, on any woman, made him want to tear—

"Who's Jai?"

Her words were like a splash of cold water over his growing anger, and he sobered.

"He was my brother—they all were, but Jai and I were the closest. He was the closest thing to a brother I could have."

Sarah nodded in understanding; it was how she felt about Alec. She would destroy anyone who dared to lay a finger on him.

"Was he there that night?"

"They all were."

Talan let himself smile faintly, memories glazing over his eyes. "Jai and I were up still. The others had shifted and camped around the fire for the night. He was giving me a hard time because I told him he couldn't court my sister, Alani." Talan shook his head, a genuine smile tilting up his mouth. "A little while after, I got hungry, so I told Jai I would be back. I left... I had left him and the others. By the time I heard their screams and made it to the treeline..." The words halted in his throat as if he couldn't make himself say them.

Taking in a steadying breath, he said, "I watched them die. It took everything in me to not sprint into that chaos and be ripped apart with them."

"And what good would that have done?"

Talan's snarl ripped through her words.

"You don't understand, Sarah," he bit out. "*Bonds*, Shifters have bonds. They tie us to our packs; the bonds we form in a pack are ones that, when broken, we feel forever. That emptiness. It never goes away; it only fades until its more manageable."

Sarah blinked past the sharp tug on her mind when he said her name.

"Well," Sarah said, contemplating her next words, "You're not alone. So, take that for whatever it might offer."

# CHAPTER 11

It took an hour for his anger to simmer down. Talan knew it wasn't directed at her, but even so, he glared at the back of Sarah's head.

Her ponytail shifted as her feet walked nimbly over the uneven terrain. Her voice drawled through the darkening forest, "I can feel you staring at me."

The farther along they trekked, the darker it became. The world dimmed as the overhang of trees grew dense, and the light fought to penetrate its tangled brambles. Moss hung from tree limbs, whispering in the sticky air, as an unseen storm approached overhead.

Talan's brows lowered in annoyance, and he snapped back, "If I had something else to stare at other than your ass, I would, but unfortunately, my options are limited." He had meant *head*, not *ass*, but that's what had come out, and that's what he found himself staring at now, and it only made his annoyance grow.

Sarah paused, looking at him over her shoulder. Her face was neutral even as her gaze stripped him bare from head to toe, and a smirk edged her lips.

The wolf in him simmered beneath his skin at that, and he gritted his jaw.

"Would it be more appetising if it was covered in fur?" she quipped in a snide voice.

Despite his irritation, he found himself stalking towards her, his own smile roughish. "I don't know. Is that an option?"

Sarah shrugged one shoulder, spinning on her heels.

He watched the sway of her ass this time instead of the swing of her ponytail.

"I'm sure there's a man out here—somewhere—with a perfectly hairy ass, just *begging* for you, Talan."

Talan's eyes snapped to her head then, her coolly voiced words making him blanch with the thought of a very hairy bare ass wiggling at him.

"That is *foul*, Sarah." Talan gagged, the sheer idea making him want to upchuck everything.

Sarah's low chuckle was his only answer, but Talan found his annoyance ebbing and his own chuckle surprising him as it echoed back.

The tug in the back of her mind had been continuous the longer she was around Talan, and Sarah found a headache pulsating around her temples because of it. The pull had been faint at first, a nuisance. But the longer he spoke, the more he said her name, and the longer she was around him, the more it hurt.

"We can stop to take a break if you want?"

Her gaze cut to Talan, and he raised his hands in defence. She knew she looked like shit. Could feel the bead of sweat trail down her temple, and if she looked in a mirror, her reflection would be pale and ashen.

Licking her lips as a wave of pain sliced through her skull, she pushed on, shaking her head.

"Sarah," he rumbled lowly.

That tug on her mind pulled, and she stumbled, catching herself, hands on her knees as the pain increased.

"Stop," she gritted out, panting softly, the pain stealing the breath from her lungs this time.

Talan went to speak again, and she held up a firm hand. He snapped his mouth shut.

"Don't say my name… just…" she paused, taking a slow breath, working through the stabbing build of pressure, and then another. "Just be quiet for one moment," she said finally.

Talan watched her with those amber eyes, his brows pinched, mouth pulling into a frown. Sarah looked away from his concern, swallowing the knot in her throat.

Minutes passed, the humid air doing nothing to cool her skin. The pain began to ease, slipping its claws from her skull, and finally, she could breathe freely.

Straightening, Sarah smoothed clammy hands across her hair, tightening her ponytail. Sniffing, she looked at Talan. He seemed to blend in with the forest around him, making him appear at ease, but she knew he was anything but.

His body was ridged, watching her with fixated concern. She knew he could scent her pain, or maybe he couldn't?

She was scentless, apparently.

Sarah made a mental note to ask him about that again.

Rolling her shoulders, she eased the tension in her neck and back, breathing through her nose slowly. The remnants of the headache were scarce, but they left her feeling drained like every other time she had them. She would take a lashing over these headaches. A whip she could push past, being branded, she could endure. But the migraines? They were suffocating. They seeped energy from her like a succubus, and it took everything in her not to sit down and sleep.

She knew Talan was fighting not to speak, and she peeked a

glance at the Shifter. Her lips quirked at his face, sullen and hard. Sarah chewed on her bottom lip carefully, noting his eyes that slipped to her mouth when she did so. She quickly released it and shook her head in assurance.

"I'm okay." But her voice was rough. Clearing it, she tried again, "I'm okay. I get headaches frequently." As if that candour would ease the tension in his shoulders.

Talan took a step towards her.

Sarah found herself taking a step back involuntarily.

His hands balled into fists, and Sarah couldn't keep her heart from stuttering along her ribcage. With how tired she was, it would be an equal match if he wanted to fight.

Fingers flexing, Talan worked his fingers from their fists, almost like he was trying to expel energy. "Sorry," he murmured.

"Are you okay?" she asked, monitoring his movements.

His laugh was low and rough, and he raked his fingers through his hair, tousling the chocolate strands.

"I should be asking you that," he said with a press of his lips.

Those amber eyes seemed to glow, but Talan shook his head, and Sarah knew he was fighting the animal inside of him. Whatever primal part of himself that was telling him to shift.

Forcing in a breath, Talan let an easy smile slip into place, and walked up to her. Bending his head so they were at eye level.

"Did the big bad wolf scare you, Princess?"

Annoyance was bittersweet, and she let every ounce of it show.

"The only thing *big* about you is your ego." She let her eyes wander down his body to the front of his jeans. "Which leads me to believe you have a very *small*—"

Talan's warning growl was low and cut through her words, his eyes darkening. Though the twinkle of amusement was still there, softening the edge.

"Only one way to find out," he said with a chuckle.

Sarah rolled her eyes, turning around to stalk away.

"Don't be like that, Sarah!"

She flipped him off over her shoulder, and she could all but see the rakish grin on his face, hearing him huff out a laugh, following her through the darkening forest.

The forest thinned the deeper they traversed eastward; the air grew stale, and Talan commented on the smell.

Sarah could smell the tang in the air he talked about. The wind was still, every noise seemingly amplified, right down to the crunch of dirt that turned rocky.

Looking back, they stared at the looming forest that thinned before them and the slate rock rising above them with jagged edges. The sky was an angry dark grey horde, rolling clouds threatening to unleash a downpour.

Talan nodded in thought. "Back into the creepy forest, or follow the path that is probably the entrance to Dante's inferno? So many options," he mused dryly.

Sarah shook her head, raising a brow at him. "I told you that you wouldn't survive."

His cheeky smile responded in turn. "You would care if I died."

"You're going to be made into puppy-chow."

He barked a laugh, his canines lengthening just enough to cause her to give him a pointed look.

A wicked look lit up his eyes, and he leaned forward, only an inch separating their faces. Those elongated canines on display with his crooked grin. "If I survive, what do I get as a reward?"

His warm breath fanned her cheek, heat wafting off his body. And it took all of Sarah's self-restraint not to take a step back. But it wasn't from caution, fear, or even a desire to punch him—although the thought crossed her mind at one point during their travels. Her strange pull to him was there again, becoming a nuisance.

"Not me stabbing you for fun," she answered, hiding her smile.

She was growing a soft spot for the mutt.

He touched his heart, that minuscule space still separating them.

"You wound me, Princess," he said lowly, those amber eyes holding her own. "I thought I would get a treat if I was a good boy."

Talan winced suddenly; raising his brows, he glanced at the push blade currently pressed against his dick.

Sarah's face was full of mirth, tilting her head as she whispered, "Down boy."

Chuckling, Talan stepped back, that increasingly familiar light igniting his stare.

"You win."

Sarah slipped the blade back into its slot, hiding her smirk, and turned to the rocky dirt path winding around the mountainside.

Because that's what it was.

A mountainside.

The road was big enough for a small car but nothing more. Broken boulders and shards of rock and slate littered the seam where the mountain and road met.

Dante's Inferno indeed, Sarah thought to herself, snorting silently.

The Carpathian forest framed their other side, the scattered evergreens standing in observation as they made the ever-declining descent around the mountain bend.

Talan was right, though she wouldn't admit that to him. The forest and mountain both exuded an ominous air. Something dark had stained the earth here. She could feel it the longer they walked the road and the further they wound away from the forest, closer to the mountain's centre.

Silence slipped between them, and Sarah's guard went up when they rounded a bend in the mountain. The forest slipped away from view, and the road cut through a narrow gorge.

Nothing lived within these mountains. Their world turned to shades of grey and black, the mountainsides like sheets of obsidian.

Gravel crunching, Sarah contained her wince with every echoing step.

It was too loud and too silent all at once.

"Kinda makes you feel like you're in a graveyard," Talan murmured. His eyes scanned the sloping sheets of rock with a careful gaze.

Their steps slowed until they stopped altogether, just barely within the mouth of the gorge.

Talan scanned the towering peaks, frowning. "I feel like this is a fucked-up version of tag and hide-and-seek."

Without looking at him, she nudged his arm. "Tag, you're It," she muttered.

The air shifted, and Sarah's breath halted in her throat, her ears tracking every whisper of sound, but there was none. Everything was deathly quiet. The hair on her neck pricked, and her fingers itched for her blades.

"Do you feel—"

Sarah held up a hand, and Talan hushed, his voice seeming to fill the silence. Her neck pricked again, and her instincts took over.

They were in a graveyard.

And they had just walked into their own with nowhere to go but right into it.

Sarah let out a slow, steady breath and quietly slipped her blades free, keeping her eyes focused on the gorge.

Talan shifted his stance, slipping his own knife from his boot. Sarah quirked a brow at it quickly before returning her focus to the path ahead.

Her heartbeat was loud in her ears, her breathing too harsh in the dead silence. Her hands shifted the weight of the blades, trying to disperse the sudden adrenalin dump. Limbs itching to move, to do *something.*

Jerking her head to signal Talan, she stepped into the gorge.

A rock the size of her fist skidded across the ground, bouncing off a larger stone and rolling past her feet.

Ice went through her veins, and Sarah's head whipped around to glare at Talan, who mouthed *sorry.*

The echo the rock produced filled the mountain range, and it took all of a second for Sarah to whisper, "Run."

Dread wound around her limbs, encasing her body with no escape route but straight through a never-ending gorge and killing whatever watched them.

For once, she was the prey, and she refused to yield to it.

They flew through the obsidian mountains, Talan keeping stride with her, his eyes molten, and when he glanced at her, he flashed her a crooked smile, showing those elongated canines despite his olive skin paling in fear.

He had the nerve to smile at her. *Smile.*

She would kill him if they made it out of this pass alive.

A roar shook the gorge, the ground rattling around them. Something moved from the corner of her eye, and Sarah cursed, grabbing Talan from the back of his jacket collar. Yanking him back as shards of mountainside broke loose and shattered at their feet.

"Get down!" Sarah yelled.

Talan ducked as rocks the size of their heads rained down in a hailstorm, and they tore through the pass, a thundering roar following in their wake. Arms covering their heads, their bones rattling as the ground shook.

The ground cracked with a sudden impact, the rocks ceasing their fire, and Sarah and Talan whipped around.

Chest heaving, Sarah's eyes widened. Slowly dragging her gaze from the tan wire-fur skin boots past the strong muscular legs covered in straight, coarse black hair, the brown bear skin loin cloth secured around its waist the size of a tree trunk. A belly that hung just over the lip of the loincloth, that same tan wire-fur banded across its forearms with strips of leather crossing around it.

A bead of sweat ran down her neck, and Sarah steadied her stance, staggering her feet. Tightening her hold on her blades as her eyes stared up at the ugly slack-mouth face that towered nearly fifteen feet above them. Unnaturally blue piggy eyes watched them with hunger, its wild, long black hair standing on end like a lion's mane.

"That is one ugly bastard," Talan muttered.

"That, Talan," Sarah whispered from the corner of her mouth, "Is a Gogmagog."

The Gogmagog's face twisted into a horrible gaping snarl, spreading its beefy arms wide with a crashing roar that shook their insides. Its hands smashed against the mountainside.

Sarah eyed the cudgel held in its right hand; gnarly spikes stabbed around its bulbous head, threatening a painful death.

"Run," she whispered when the spikes lodged into the mountain and the beast's attention fixated on it.

Talan shook his head, face set. "Not a chance."

"Dammit, Talan," she snapped, the sound of her voice drowning in the cracking of rock.

The spikes came free, and the Gogmagog swung the cudgel

through the air; its brown and yellow square-tooth smile gleamed across its sagging face, and it advanced. Each step thundering underfoot.

"Move!" she screamed, leaping out of the way.

The massive cudgel split between them with a shattering crash as they leapt away.

Sarah rolled out of her fall, adjusting her blades and whipped around when the cudgel dragged across the ground, tearing a chunk from the road, and arched towards her.

Heart hammering in her chest, she launched herself at the beast, her feet digging into the side of the mountain for leverage. Back arching with one blade held above her head, she threw it like a javelin while her body twisted through the air. The steel glinted dangerously, slipping past the cascading limbs and lodging into its stocky shoulder.

Sarah's feet caught her before her body tumbled across the ground, using her arm to anchor her fall. She looked up at the creature, palming the other weapon.

The Gogmagog twitched when the blade sunk into flesh and muscle, those piggy eyes looking down at the protruding carbon fibre handle.

Its belly shook, and Sarah stared transfixed as what sounded like a garbled laugh erupted from its mouth before turning its attention back to Sarah and, with a bellowing cry, charged for her.

Eyes glued on its imposing form, her body lurched forward, the blade held tightly in her grip, and she threw herself to the ground. Her knees barked at the impact as she slid on them, turning through the opening between its thundering legs. The blade whipped out, slicing through muscle and tendon.

Crying out, the Gogmagog spun, its hand lashing out with quick precision, and Sarah saw stars. Her body flinging across the ground and bounding into the rock siding, her battered face reflected off the glass-like mountain. Blood streamed down her temples, cuts marring her cheeks.

A deep growl ripped through the air, and Sarah saw a massive wolf leap towards the Gogmagog, its silver and red fur reflected in the rock. Ignoring the throbbing in her bones, she pushed to her feet and watched the wolf sink its teeth and claws into its neck.

Bright red blood gushed from the deep gouges that trekked across its chest and shoulders, staining the silver fur crimson along its hind quarters. The wolf's jaws locked onto the side of its throat, and the Gogmagog roared in defiance.

With one hand, the beast grabbed the wolf and ripped him free, blood splaying through the air, and tossed him aside. The wolf yelped but got to its feet. Blood coated its maw, its ears pressed flat against its skull, nose crinkled in a silent snarl.

Sarah watched the wolf circle the Gogmagog, eyeing him with a hunger that promised death.

Arching the cudgel high above its head, the Gogmagog's sagging face twisted as it bared its teeth at the wolf.

The wolf lunged again, teeth bared, and bright golden eyes flamed brightly. Its teeth sunk into the exposed jugular, and a sickening tearing rang through the pass, followed by a sudden *crack*.

Sarah's mouth dropped open, impressed, watching the wolf tear the throat of the Gogmagog clean out, blood gushing like a river. The cudgel dropped from its slackened hands, and the spikes sunk into its skull. Those unnaturally blue eyes widened in surprise, blood trickling between its protruding brows.

Kicking off from its chest, the wolf landed on all fours, trotting proudly out of the way as the Gogmagog dropped to its knees.

The mountain rattled when it fell, its body heaving backwards with a lurching crunch as the spikes skewered through its skull and eyes.

Sarah grimaced at the sound before glowering at the wolf that watched her with those golden eyes.

"Talan?" she asked.

Silence, and then the wolf tilted its head with a whine of confirmation.

She looked at the shredded clothes on the rocky road and then at the knife sitting on a flat rock head like he had set it aside before he shifted.

"That was really stupid of you," she bit out.

Talan walked over to her, his maw and front stained red. He

was massive, standing nearly to her shoulder. His fur was silver with red and copper strands throughout it. Red tips on his fluffy ears and the tip of his bushy tail.

If he hadn't been covered in blood, Sarah would almost think he was pretty.

Nudging her shoulder gently with his nose, he looked at her, tongue lolling out with a huff.

It was the closest thing to a laugh Sarah could assume, and she raised her eyebrow when he sat on his haunches.

Pursing her lips, she sighed, relenting. "Thank you, though."

Shaking her head, Sarah stalked to the blade lodged into the Gogmagog's shoulder. Climbing on top of the barrel chest, she walked up its body to its shoulder and braced her feet on either side of the blade, pulling it out.

A shadow flickered overhead, and her head snapped up. Massive, feathered wings blocked out the light, silent as the wind.

"Talan! Overhead!"

A piercing screech threatened to blow her eardrums, the harpy nosediving straight for Talan, her razor-edge talons stretched in front of her, her half-human torso naked, long hair pitch black flying behind her.

The half-woman half-bird's wings flapped suddenly, catching the fall and sinking its taloned feet into Talan's fur.

Talan snarled, thrashing violently in the harpy's grip.

The talons tightened and the massive harpy easily lifted him from the ground.

Sarah sprinted for them, leaping from the Gogmagog, she threw the blade in her hand before she hit the ground. It pierced through the bottom of its left wing, clattering to the ground on the other side. It screeched in pain, but didn't halt its ascension.

Talan fought against the harpy, whipping his body violently, but it was all for nought. The creature had a firm hold on his shoulders, and all Sarah could do was watch as his blood dripped to the ground.

Anger welled up in her, until it came out as a low yell of frustration.

"You have got to be kidding me?!" She dragged a hand over her hair, trying to take in a calming breath through her nose. "I swear to the Gods if I need to rescue—"

A male roar of defiance and a bleating screech cut her off.

She let out a heavy breath, gritting her teeth. "*Fine.*"

Stomping over to her blade on the ground, she stabbed it into her boot sleeve and grabbed Talan's small hunting knife, tucking it through her belt.

"I told him," she muttered harshly.

Rounding on the road that led deeper into the mountain, she stalked past the Gogmagog's body, her face shadowed with irritation.

"I fucking told him."

CHAPTER 12

The harpy's talons suddenly extracted themselves, and Talan hurtled forward. Black stone walls cracked under the weight of his body.

Shaking his head, he spun, baring his teeth in a low growl.

The harpy glared at him with black eyes, showing a row of pointed teeth as she smiled at him, her talons clicking endlessly against the stone, tucking her black wings tight to her pale body.

Talan lunged for the bird woman, and she screeched, flapping off the gaping mouth of the mountain behind her. His paws dug into the ground, halting just at the lip of the entrance. The harpy flew out of reach and out of sight.

He huffed with annoyance, walking back into the stone mouth. His gold eyes flickered over his surroundings.

Black rock encased the cave above and below him. Shadows lingered near the back, enclosing the space, but his heightened sight saw the jagged wall beyond them and the open, narrow doorway.

Trotting through the small cave, dirt and tiny chips of rock rolling under his paws, he paused at the narrow passageway. Eyeing the carved stone steps that led into a yawning abyss of shadows. He sniffed delicately, his nose wrinkled at the faint sour tang of rot, and his ears flattened against his skull.

The air was stale in the stairwell; he could smell the Deathwalker's lingering scent. His growl reverberated through his belly softly before he silently crept down the stairs.

His broad body brushed against the sides of the stairwell that wound in a spiralling maze into the heart of the mountain. Even with his vision heightened in wolf form, he couldn't pierce the darkness, so he continued, using his sense of smell to guide him. Around and around and around until the mouth of the darkness opened and dim yellow light filtered in.

Talan blinked past the sudden light, eyes adjusting.

A scent he couldn't recognise sifted through the air, and he turned, snarling as a hand shot out, latching around his throat. His voice cut off with a choke.

"What do we have here?" asked a cool voice.

Talan's eyes raged with hatred as he looked up at the face that came into view.

Close-cropped auburn hair and brown eyes so dark they were nearly black stared down at him with smug curiosity. Hollow cheeks and angled features mapped a princely face; Talan would put money on it that he was an elf of the High Fae.

Talan's teeth snapped at the arm restraining him, his one canine catching on the sleeve, he yelped as the fingers tightened around his neck with impossible strength.

The male eyed the tear in the sleeve of his black button-down dress shirt. Letting out a deep breath, he gave Talan an annoyed look.

"Bad dog," he chastised with a disapproving tsk.

Talan growled despite the restraint on his neck, baring his teeth.

"I have a place for bad dogs just like you."

With a snap of his fingers, Talan was bound from tail to head in invisible bindings, hovering in the air. He lashed against them, and they only dug into his fur, searing the skin beneath. With a puff of breath through his nose, his eyes narrowed at the rocky hallway.

The *tap tap tap* of the male's shiny black dress shoes echoed through the hall, and the light from the embedded fixtures reflected off of them. Talan glanced at the small round lights set into the stone, turning on when they sensed motion.

Rounding the corner, solid wood doors lined the length of the hall on one side. Small iron cages sitting eye level cut through the wood.

They were cells.

Talan growled and lashed out again, fighting the bindings. The restraints branded his skin, and he snarled when he could feel the hot trickle of blood.

"Now, now," the male drawled calmly with a sigh.

A wooden cell door opened on well-oiled hinges, and they stopped before it. With a flick of the male's wrist, Talan's body flew into the cell, slamming into the rock wall, and a soft whine of pain slipped out. He still couldn't move, the bindings eating into his skin. Instead, he looked up at the male, his gold eyes glowing in the darkness.

The male flicked a piece of lint off his black trousers, lifting his brows when he looked at Talan, his gaze flickering to a shadowed corner before returning to him.

"Be good, and we *might* feed you."

Talan growled in response, and the cell door slammed shut, his bindings vanishing.

The burning of his flesh hissed in relief and his body sagged. A sliver of pain ran along his limbs and he shivered against it. Shaking his head, he huffed out a breath, forcing himself to stand.

The cell was dark except for the cube of light that filtered in through the iron bars. Talan stood on his hind legs, peering into the empty hall. He pressed into the door with a shove, testing it, but it didn't budge. The door was made of solid oak and almost as strong as the rock sidings surrounding it. He could feel the magic pulsing through the wood like an invisible shield, reinforcing it.

Dropping to all fours, he shook his head, wracking his brain. He had been so distracted he didn't notice the faint smell of pine and something sweet. It was a familiar scent, the one the children had in his pack before they matured at five years old and took their forms, the smell of earth and honey.

Talan rounded on the cell, annoyance and trepidation rolling down his back to his tail, his eyes pinned to the darkness in front of him.

There, huddled in the far corner of shadows, was a small lump.

Reaching out with a mental hand, he searched the shadows, brushing against a wall of pure undiluted fear. The pain and fear shot through him, and he quickly retracted from it like he had been shocked. Tail twitching, he sniffed once, then twice, stepping into the shadows until he stood before the tiny huddled mass.

He didn't dare touch the small child who sat curled in around themselves. Their thin arms around equally thin legs, a mass of hair concealing a face that was tucked into their knees.

Whining softly to get their attention, Talan pawed the ground.

The child's head snapped up, and they let out what would have been a scream had they not clamped down on it at the last minute. With his head up, Talan was able to see that it was a boy with his body pressed into the wall behind him. His chest heaved with every breath, amber eyes the size of saucers glowing faintly in the darkness.

Talan whined again, nudging one of the boy's knees with his nose.

The boy trembled, but his mouth pressed into a firm line, staring Talan down.

Laughing to himself, Talan admired his courage and took a step back. Grabbing the leash of his magic, he tugged on it once, and his bones cracked. The fibres of his muscle knitted back together piece by piece until he was once again human looking, or as human looking as he could be.

"I won't hurt you," he said softly, rolling his shoulders at the sudden change in his body.

The boy's trembling lessened, and he relaxed but just barely.

Kneeling, Talan gave him a soft smile and repeated himself. "I won't hurt you."

He just watched Talan with those wide amber eyes, his mouth still pressed flat in a stubborn line.

Nodding, Talan stood, jerking his head over his shoulder. "I'll sit over there."

The ground was hard under his bare ass, and Talan had half a mind to shift back. He grimaced as the stale air skimmed across his balls, and he adjusted his seat. With a deep breath, he leaned his head back, ignoring the stretch of seared flesh that wrapped around his ass, torso, chest, and back in a corkscrew. His blood already scabbing over the wounds.

Sarah was going to maim him if the occupants of this mountain didn't beat her to it. He groaned, running a hand through his hair and scrubbing it over his face.

Eyeing the door, he weighed whether he could force his way through. The wolf in him answered with a challenging *yes,* but his male side reasoned with a *no.* Rolling his eyes, Talan tapped his thumb against his thigh. Sarah's exasperated look of annoyance flashed in his mind, and he smirked. There was one thing he was finding he loved more and more: getting under the hunter's skin. He would love to put that look back on her face and maybe a couple other ones. She was attractive in a very human way. However, her features were plain by comparison to the Fae, her brown eyes light and full of different emotions she was shit at hiding. Her brown hair, while in a ponytail, was long, and her legs went on for days.

Talan shifted; a crooked smile tilted his lips as he thought of those long legs—

A quiet sniffle pierced his thoughts, and he glanced at the shadows.

Shuffling and the scratch of dirt on the rock were the only indicators before the boy was quietly padding out of the shadows, as naked as Talan was.

Sitting up, Talan watched the boy calmly, not daring to make any moves.

"You're... you're just like me?" he asked quietly, uncertainty wobbling beneath his words.

Talan nodded once. "Aye."

The boy shuffled his feet, his hands clasped tightly before him. "What are we?" he questioned. His voice was barely above a whisper, his eyes watching Talan like a prey that had been caught.

Propping his right leg up and sliding the other leg under it, he leaned his arm against his knee, watching the boy with understanding.

"We're shifters," he explained.

"I'm human," the boy argued.

Talan tilted his head. "From what I can smell, you're a shifter."

"I'm human!" he screamed this time defiantly, tears gathering in his eyes.

Lifting his brows, Talan leaned back, not saying anything and watched the boy with interest.

He didn't know what he was.

The boy's chest heaved with unshed tears, and he sniffed again, his bottom lip trembling.

"What's your name?"

Startled, the boy looked up at Talan with pale amber eyes. His mop of messy blond curls framed his chubby face and set off his olive skin with a glow that even the darkness couldn't contain. It was the glow the pups in his clan would get when they came into their wolf form.

Licking his cracked lips, the boy reshuffled his feet, glancing quickly at the door and then back to Talan.

"I'm Talan," he offered with what he hoped was a comforting smile. If he couldn't figure out how to comfort the same woman who was going to kill him once she found a way up here—if she decided he was worth that—then at the very least he could comfort a child.

The boy took in a deep breath, his face settling into that same stubbornness Talan had previously seen.

Apparently, he couldn't comfort a child either.

"Alright," Talan said with a shrug of his shoulders. "You don't have to tell me."

The cell door swung open silently, the trickle of light Talan's only warning, and he leapt for it.

He hit solid air, his bones groaning and threatening to break under the force.

A soft disapproving tsk followed when he collapsed on the ground, hand to his head to silence the ringing, and the same *tap tap tap* of those shiny black dress shoes as they entered the cell.

The Fae male knelt before him, the thin wall of air barely separating them. "Didn't I tell you to be good?" he asked softly, a halo of light igniting his auburn hair.

Talan bared his teeth, growling under his breath as he looked up at the male crouched before him.

With a snap of his fingers, a sickly pale male walked in with a tray, blond hair slicked back, his cheekbones too high, cheeks too shallow, dressed in black jeans and a black long-sleeve shirt that hung from his bones.

But the auburn male didn't give him a look, and Talan, his nostrils flaring as he scented the air, realised the blond male was human. His stomach roiled despite being empty.

Those assessing dark eyes watched Talan with interest even as he said to the man without looking, "Set it down and leave."

Talan subtly sniffed the air again. Nothing. He was scentless. Narrowing his eyes, Talan watched the male as the blond one disappeared.

"Don't make this harder for yourself, Shifter."

Huffing a laugh, Talan smirked. "Or what? You'll feed me to your pets?"

Something glinted in the male's eyes. "Don't tempt me."

He loosened the leash of his magic, letting his canines lengthen, and the brights of his eyes glow with a challenge. "I would like to see you try."

Dark eyes flickered with amusement, and the male stood, straightening the cuffs of his black dress shirt.

Talan noted the lack of tear in his sleeve.

"Perhaps we will," the male answered coolly. His eye slid to the corner where Talan knew the boy was huddled.

And then he was gone, the cell door clicking softly behind him.

The wall of air vanished when the door closed, and Talan's annoyance rumbled through him in answer.

Shuffling from the shadows, the boy stared at Talan with wide eyes, sniffling softly.

Eyeing the tray with the chunk of bread and two black metal cups, Talan jerked his head to the food. "Eat."

The boy grabbed the bread without a sound, tearing a chunk from it and inhaling it like it was his last meal. Talan grimaced; it could be their last meal.

"Slow down," he commanded.

Standing, he dared to put a hand on the boy's shoulder, ensuring he slowed down. Grabbing one of the cups, he sniffed it.

The boy grabbed the other cup and drank from it.

Talan opened his mouth to say something but snapped it shut. The boy had been here for who knows how long, so he took a sip.

Water.

"It's safe," the boy whispered, eyeing the door and shoving another piece of bread into his mouth.

Talan set his cup down, crossing his arms over his chest. "And you know this, how?"

Staring up at him with those pale amber eyes, brushing a blond curl away from his eyes, the boy said, "Because we're trained."

Talan rejected the piece of bread the boy held out to him. "You need it." Taking his seat back up against the wall, wincing at the scrape of rock on his branded flesh. Whatever magic the Fae male or this prison had embedded into it had made his healing process turn to molasses. "What do you mean trained?"

Washing the last of the bread down with water, his small belly already rounding in the slightest from eating too quickly, he turned to Talan. The cup clattered to the tray as he dropped it.

"We were told never to speak of it," he stated lowly, looking at his feet.

"Who will know?"

His eyes shot up, mouth pressed into that firm line. "They always know."

Talan inclined his head. "I promise it'll be our secret."

The boy shifted on his feet, his fingers twisting around themselves. He was scared, and Talan wanted to take that fear and shred it apart. Offering him a soft smile, he relaxed his shoulders and gave him an encouraging look.

"I haven't been trained, not yet like the others."

"Who?"

The boy fiddled nervously with his hands, eyeing the door.

"I have to get back," he said, brows furrowing.

"To where?" Talan asked.

His eyes became glassy and round, and the boy's bottom lip wobbled suddenly.

Talan's heart clenched at the sight of those tears, and he made a pained face, rubbing the back of his neck. He didn't know how to comfort the child, even if he wanted to. It was neither the time nor the place.

"I made a promise to my sister."

Footsteps scuffed the ground, and the boy tensed, whipping around to stare at the door.

Talan stood, pressing himself into the shadows, and quietly approached the iron bars. The hall was dim, nearly concealed in darkness, but a door clicked shut from somewhere and more shuffling, a motion detection light flickering to life. The same blond man and his sickly thin body passed their door without a glance.

He held his breath until he was gone, his body vibrating with unshed energy. When he was out of sight, Talan eyed the solid wood door, debating again whether he could break through it. He wanted to. He possibly could, too, but where would he go? Where would *they* go? He eyed the boy. He couldn't leave him.

Letting out a harsh sigh through his nose, he leaned against the cool rock. They would sooner die trying to find their way out of the mountain if he did get them out than if they waited.

And he refused to die because Gods forbid his snarky hunter found out. The smug look he knew she would have was enough for him to grit his teeth in defiance.

So, he did. He waited. Eyes bouncing between the boy, who shuffled back to the shadowed corner, and to the dim passageway. He waited.

CHAPTER 13

A bead of sweat dripped down her temple, leaving a salty trail across the dried blood that matted her hairline. A huff of annoyance left her lips as she stared up at the obsidian mountainside. Reflecting like a large shard of glass, its ridges and crevices threatening to slice her open if she fell across them.

Tapping a finger against her thigh, her neck craned back to look up at the camouflaged cave mouth. She weighed her options:

1: Let him rot. It would serve him right.

2: Climb up the mountainside and risk being sliced into ribbons.

3: Scope the surrounding area for another way in.

So far, she didn't like any of them.

If she left him, she wouldn't forgive herself, and she had a funny feeling he would haunt her for the rest of her days with that excessively annoying mouth of his. And if she climbed, there was a high risk the mountain would shatter at the touch of her blade. The last option would take too much time, and that was the one thing she didn't have.

Her finger continued its tapping, her thoughts reeling with cause and effect.

"Fine," she bit out with a harsh breath after a moment.

Slipping her blades out, her hands thrumming with energy right down to her bones, she twirled the blades, trying to expel the adrenalin. Taking a deep breath through her nose, she held it for a three count, releasing it through her mouth. She did it twice more before rolling her shoulders back and stalking up to the glassy rock.

A gleaming lip reflected the grey sky above her, and she ran a finger over it. A clean cut right through the pad of her callused finger, not deep enough to bleed but deep enough to warn her.

Taking in a breath, she stabbed her blade into the rock, testing its hold. The rock cracked with protest as steel sunk into it, but it held.

Saying a prayer to whoever was listening, she stabbed the second one higher and began her climb up. Her feet fought for even the slightest foothold as she climbed hand over hand. The higher she climbed, the worse the wind became, whipping at her back, her hair stinging across her cheek.

It was slow work, and she tried to drown out the warning bells in her head at every crack of rock and steel. If she was going to be caught, she would be damned if it were on the side of a glass mountain.

The small mouth of the mountain loomed closer, she ignored the strain of her muscles and the ache in her shoulders as she pulled herself up time and time again. Beads of sweat rolled down her back, and she could feel the cling of her damp shirt on her skin. Her nose was numb, her cheeks ruddy from the bitter wind that slapped her face, and her head ringing from the onslaught.

But still, she climbed. Higher and higher.

With the cave mouth within sight, she hefted herself up, eyeing the distance. Swinging her other blade back, her heart dropped into her stomach as the world shifted suddenly, and the blade she leaned on gave out.

Black rock shattered beneath her, and the world tilted. Her blade slipped free, and suddenly, she was falling. Sarah slammed against the mountain, stars flashing across her vision as her head smashed into it. Her blade that came free dropped from her hand, and she swung the other wildly, her arm stabbing at nothing.

Chest heaving, her mind racing, she swung again, and sparks flew as steel cut a path through stone, and then everything was quiet.

With trembling hands, Sarah wrenched her eyes open, chest heaving with every shaky breath she took. Licking her lips quickly, she glanced down. Her grave gaping open, waiting for her. Her blade lay on the ground, and she forced herself to look away, forcing her lungs to take in a deep breath.

She was hanging halfway between the cave mouth and the ground, and she could feel blood trickling down her cheek. Her shoulder started to scream at her as she dangled there, and she twisted her body to face the mountain again.

Feet fighting for purchase, she eyed the rock around her, spotting a hold just beyond her blade. Pulling herself up slowly, she reached for the hold and sighed with relief when she felt the solid weight beneath her fingertips.

Hand over blade, she made slow, steady work back up the mountain. Ignoring the beckoning death below her.

Her limbs were on fire when she finally reached the entrance, eyeing the ledge with wariness. She was out of footholds, and at least five feet were still separating her from solid ground.

She closed her eyes briefly and tried to quiet the excessive thoughts rattling her brain.

If you miss this, then you deserve to die.

Her subconscious's snarky comments didn't help anything, and she growled under her breath.

Looking at her blade, she slowly lowered her weight fully onto it. It held, but she could hear the creak of stone. Swinging her legs together in front of her, she rocked them back and forth until her body was a pendulum, and the wind propelled her forward with each push. The lip teetered as she tilted, and the rock around her blade cracked loudly. But she kept her eyes trained on it, snapping her legs forward, hips following. She let go as the blade shifted in the rock, and her body arched through the air. Hands outstretched towards the cave.

Her bones jarred as she slammed into the rock, fingers fighting for purchase, nails digging into the hard surface as she slid back.

"*No, no, no!*" she chanted, her hands grabbing at anything.

There was nothing to grab, and her body swayed in the air, slipping back and back until her fingers anchored into the grooves of the ledge. She stopped, hanging in the air by her fingertips.

Using every ounce of strength left, her muscles screaming for her to just let go, her fingers threatening to tear from their sockets, Sarah hauled herself up.

The ground was blessedly solid beneath her as she fell forward. A low moan left her lips, and her cheek smashed against the rocky surface, eyes closed, taking in calming breaths one after the other.

Dimmir, Deathwalkers, and harpies be damned. She didn't care.

Sarah lay there until her heart calmed in her chest, and her limbs didn't threaten to tear from her body. Standing up slowly, her shoulders aching but intact as she rotated one arm and then the other, she wiped the back of her hand across her cheekbones. Blood smeared across her skin, but she ignored the red stain on her hand.

The shadows seemed to shift and slither in the far region of the cave. The walls and floor were just a cutout from the mountain, big enough for the harpy to enter and exit at will and at least ten feet tall.

Glancing at her other blade that hung limply from the mountain, the wind causing it to sway slightly, Sarah knew it would be joining the other shortly. Her hand went to the small knife hooked into her belt and then to the gun still strapped into its holster.

She wouldn't use the gun, not yet, anyway. There was too much that could go wrong with a gun, and they were near useless with the Fae despite a killing round to their heart or between their eyes working just fine. They were too fast, and Sarah, while she hated to admit it, was too slow to get an accurate shot.

The little hunting knife would have to do.

With a crack of her neck, she pursed her lips and walked into the shadows.

Sarah found herself blindly stepping into a spiralling staircase that wound through the pit of the mountain. Her hand slid across the narrow passage walls that scraped against her callouses, her feet taking the shallow steps slowly.

The air was stale, her breathing obnoxiously loud in the hollow abyss around her, ears straining for any sound past her whispered steps and the brush of her hand on the stone. But there was nothing, only darkness. So down she went, around and around.

Light glimmered around a bend, and her steps halted, listening. Silence.

Hand dropping to her side, Sarah made the last turn, blinking past the dim light. She paused on the threshold, moulding herself into the shadows as she surveyed the area.

Floor-to-ceiling black stone encased the antechamber, though it didn't glimmer like glass. It was rough and worn down like years of use and wear had shaped it. Dim yellow lights were set into the ceiling, she raised a brow at the contrast of modern electricity and natural landscape.

Sarah stepped from the shadows, frowning when she felt its absence. Missing the comforting weight of her blades.

The antechamber morphed into a long dark passageway, and Sarah's finger tapped her thigh, walking into the hall.

Lights turned on overhead, two at a time, dimming seconds later when she passed them.

Motion censored. Interesting. Helpful, but also not.

The lights turned on with every section she passed under, noting the thick doors that lined the wall with their square cutout caged in iron. Sarah peeked into one of them, noting the darkness. If she had any money to bet, she would guess they were cells.

Homey.

Her neck pricked in awareness. The creeping sensation that

she was being watched made her stop. She didn't move; the light overhead went out, and she was encased in shadows.

Scanning the darkness was a futile attempt, the silence numbing. The absence of sound made Sarah step under the next set of lights. These lights were only slightly brighter than the ones in the antechamber but bright enough to fill the black void around her.

Awareness still ran its claws down her spine, but if she stayed where she was, there was a good chance she wouldn't get out.

"Those who hide, die. Those who fight... die less."

Florin's words rang from somewhere in her subconscious, and she had to stop herself from rolling her eyes. *Die Less* was right. They would all die, regardless. So, she kept moving.

She glanced at the ceiling above her, checking for cameras with every set of lights she stood under.

The hair on her neck stood on end, and she gritted her jaw in annoyance, glaring at the cell doors.

"Which one are you in," she murmured, moving her eyes along the doors to her left.

Her steps were quiet, sliding her body along the wall, pressed into the minuscule shadows that did nothing to conceal her. Door after door, her brown eyes flickered over them, straining to see what lay beyond the iron bars. But there was nothing. She couldn't see a damn thing, but she could feel someone, *something*.

Trenching further into the passageway, the feeling intensified, and she slipped the small hunting knife free. Her body thrummed with energy, and she paused at a door, just out of sight, as her skin itched in anticipation.

She eyed the door with a shake of her head. She couldn't do anything, but she also couldn't *not* do anything. Sarah adjusted her grip on the blade, staring at the door barely visible beyond her circle of dim light, its polished grey hinges reflecting the light.

Her finger tapped the blade, staring at those hinges, narrowing her eyes at the lingering shadows before the light overhead clicked off.

Something shuffled beyond the door.

Without thinking, Sarah flicked out her wrist, and the light turned on as she slipped into the shadows just beyond its yellow ring, the space between light sets, and followed it to the wall, to those hinges. Holding her breath as she pressed into the wall once again, she had to get past the door. That was it.

Another shuffle.

The light turned off.

Fucking motion censored.

Crouching, half kneeling, she began the slow walk forward. Pressing her shoulder into the wall on her left, looking up briefly when the light didn't turn on.

Gold flashed from the iron bars, and Sarah paused.

Two gold eyes peered from beyond, just above her head. They scanned the darkness, and she could see them narrow.

A hand shot out from the iron bars and grabbed for her, for anything, and she shot forward. Her head yanked back as that hand grabbed the swinging end of her ponytail.

Sarah snarled in answering, lashing out with the knife. The light flickered while the thing grabbing her howled in answer and retracted its hand.

Blood droplets sprinkled the ground, and she looked at the iron bars with a dark stare.

"Didn't anyone tell you that grabbing people isn't polite?" she snapped.

A pause, and then: "Sarah?"

Sarah jerked back at her name, scanning the door and the space beyond the bars.

Those gold eyes slipped from the shadows and widened, Talan's face appearing.

"Holy shit," he breathed.

It took her only a second to process the handsome face staring back at her before her hand snapped through the space between bars and latched onto a fistful of hair. Yanking Talan against the door.

"You *fucking* asshole," she seethed, glaring at him as he slammed into the wood.

Talan's surprise turned into that annoying smirk, and Sarah wanted to throttle him. He huffed out a laugh, the bars the only thing separating them, his breath fanning her cheek.

She wrinkled her nose. "You have dog breath."

His smirk only deepened, the dimple on his cheek peeking through the scruff on his face. "Woof," he said dryly.

"I told you," she replied, her fingers tightening on his hair, ignoring the softness against her skin.

"I knew you would come get me."

Her nostrils flared with rage, eyes flashing dangerously. "Don't you dare think for one moment I didn't contemplate leaving your ass."

Talan pressed himself into the bars, eyes roving her face quickly before sliding back to her angry stare. "You would miss me too much to leave me, Princess."

"I'm going to cut off your favourite appendage," she stated darkly.

"And what are you going to do with it?" he asked lowly, waggling his eyebrows.

"Dog!"

"Princess."

They stared at each other briefly, and Sarah's mouth pressed tight before she growled and let him go. Talan laughed softly, watching her with that annoying smirk still on his face, and she wanted to rip it off.

A mouthless Talan filled her mind, and she stifled her dark laugh.

"Sarah?"

It wasn't Talan this time.

A soft child's voice filled the space between shadows, and Sarah's heart stilled. Eyes snapping to the far corner shrouded in darkness.

"Sarah?"

That voice had every hair on her body standing on end, and she stared, unblinking, into the shadows. She could feel Talan's gaze on her, but she ignored him.

A small body and wide amber eyes pierced the shadows as they stepped into the dim light beam from behind her.

Her blood froze, and every part of her control snapped as pure, unadulterated rage took its place.

Shaking, she gripped the bars with white knuckles, whispering,

"Alec."

Talan raised a brow, looking between them. "I take it you know each other?" he asked Alec.

Alec turned pride-filled eyes to Talan. "That's my sister."

CHAPTER 14

Talan whistled lowly, but Sarah ignored him. Her focus was on the mop of blond curls and soft amber eyes that began to fill with tears.

"Alec," she breathed.

Alec's bottom lip quivered, and Sarah shook the door that separated them. The door held firm, and her growl of anger filled the air.

"I'm so sorry," he whispered in a small voice.

Sarah's chest cracked open at those words, and her knees threatened to give out. Eyes snapping to Talan, she bit out, "Open. The. Door."

Talan shook his head, eyes darting between the two. "I can't."

"Open it!" she snarled, her voice echoing down the hall.

His amber eyes turned molten at the command, and he stepped up to the bars. "I. Can't."

Her grip tightened on the iron as she shook it with every ounce of her strength, but the wood held without so much as a groan or creak. Laying her palm on the door, she looked at Alec with wide eyes, fear coating her mouth like poison.

"What happened?" she asked lowly.

His mop of curls shifted when he shook his head, biting his lip. "I don't know."

"It's okay, Alec. I'm not mad," she said with a soft smile despite the black cloud building behind her eyes. Florin. She was going to *murder* Florin.

"But I failed!" His voice cracked as tears fell down his dirty cheeks.

It took every fibre of her training not to ram her body against the door until it splintered. Taking in a strangled breath through her nose, she closed her eyes for a moment. Calming the war inside her that screamed at her to destroy anyone who laid a finger on him and the other side that told her to focus on the hunt.

Her finger tapped an iron bar, staring at the ground as she processed her next move. After a moment, she looked at Alec, softening her face. "You didn't fail—"

"But—" He snapped his mouth shut when she gave him a pointed look.

"You didn't fail," she said again. "Did you fight?" He nodded his head quickly. "Then you did exactly as you should have. And I am *so* proud of you. I'll get you out of here, okay?"

Alec's amber eyes glowed with pride, puffing his chest out at her praise. "Can we take my friend?"

Sarah's brows raised, sliding a look to Talan. Her lips twitched in amusement. "Sure."

Talan stepped up to the door again, and Sarah's resolve almost wavered when she saw his reassuring look.

"Talan," she ground out through the strain in her throat. "Protect him, he's all..." The words burned like bile, and she shoved it down. "He's all I have," she forced out. Sarah glanced quickly at Alec, and her knees wobbled again from fear before that raw, burning anger took its place. "I don't care how you do it, but *protect him.*"

Lips pressed tight, Talan lifted a hand and wrapped it around hers that still engulfed the iron bars. His voice dipped an octave as he said, "I will protect him with my life, Sarah."

The thread in her subconscious tugged when he said her name, but this time, it was almost comforting, familiar... grounding.

His thumb brushed the back of her hand, and his words settled over her with a promise. "I will take care of him. Now go."

As she stared into his bright eyes, something burned in her chest, she jerked her head in response. Chest heaving with every breath, her hand slipped from his warmth.

"Sarah?"

She looked back at him.

"Burn this fucking place to the ground."

Burn what? It was all fucking stone.

Sarah shook her head, eyeing the rocky passageway. If she was going to bring the mountain down, she was going to need a shitload of C4, and that wasn't something she had on hand.

The hall curved away from the cells, and every step led her further into the mountain's core, the motion sensor lights flicking on with every pass under them, only to turn off seconds later.

She didn't care anymore.

Let them know she was here.

Let them come.

Palming the small hunting knife, she inched around a bend in the path, peeking her head around it. Empty. She frowned. It was all empty.

Stone steps branched from the passage, carving down into the ground. Sarah hesitated, assessing the shadows that shifted and moved with a life of their own. Her fingers tightened on the blade, and she descended into the darkness.

Sliding her fingertips along the rocky wall, her steps silent and slow, she walked the straight steps one after the other. Seemingly going on forever.

Her patience was wearing thin, eyes scanning the darkness in front of her with no avail. Alec's wide, teary eyes filled her head, fuelling her growing irritation until the grip on her leash slipped, and she had to scramble for it before her anger reared its bloody head.

A near-silent growl rumbled in her chest, and she pushed on.

Down and down and down she went, step after step, until bright light spilt into the darkness. Bright and white, it filled the stairwell so suddenly that Sarah stumbled back, blinking.

Regaining her footing, she squinted into the light, stepped to the ledge where shadow and light met, and looked beyond the stairwell.

The same rocky walls and floors were carved out from the mountain; to her left was a silver metal railing with three rows of steel cables linking the poles along the ledge, and to her right, two black leather, overstuffed chairs, a round silver table between them.

Sarah stepped into the light, eyeing the otherwise empty space. Another step had her standing inside the modern lounge. Another step and a turn of her head had her blood draining from her face.

A sea of bodies lay stretched before her, hundreds restrained on clinical metal tables by steel cuffs attached to the tables. Row after row, hooked up to blood transfusions, dressed in simple white drawstring pants and matching white short-sleeved shirts.

Her heart seemed to stop cold in her chest, and she stumbled forward, gripping the railing. The icy metal bit into her palms, and she tightened her hold, keeping herself upright.

The mountain before her had been carved into a massive dome, with white clinical lights overhead, and it seemed to go on forever, disappearing under a stone lip until the bodies were concealed from view.

She turned to the lounge above the chamber, and her stomach dipped. It wasn't a lounge. It was a viewing room.

Bile rose in her throat again, and she clamped her teeth together.

Nostrils flaring, she forced in a deep breath through her nose, scanning the room. Eyes landing on a floating metal staircase.

Taking the steps two at a time, she met the landing and walked into the first row. Her steps were silent and slow as she walked the length of sedated bodies, stopping at one with ebony skin and softly arching ears.

Heart hammering, her fingers itched to reach out and touch the male before her. Instead, she touched the bag of blood that hung from a suspended cable and hook on the ceiling. A bold **H** was stamped on the clear bag as its contents dripped through the IV in their arm.

She curled her hands into fists at her side and walked on.

Pale like snow and dark as night, they lay strewn, males and females from all races. All Fae.

Tangled knots of dread wound tighter and tighter in her stomach, coiling around her shaking limbs the further she walked. The lip of the mountain loomed like a mouth, and the light dimmed as she passed under it. Bodies and bodies lay motionless on those clinical tables, and her heartbeat became lead in her chest when she saw the row of cages.

All were empty except the three closest. Sarah's blood turned to ice as wide, sunken eyes stared at her through iron bars.

Iron cages sat in a row, lining the length of the mountain beneath the lip. At least twelve feet wide and eight feet tall. They sat like prison cells, and within were its prisoners, starved and hollow shells of themselves.

She took a shaking breath and walked over to the first iron cage, counting the faces and finding seven. Young and middle-aged, they stood like living skeletons. Their bones threatened to tear their skin with sharp, jagged edges. Their clothes hung like torn rags around their frames.

Human.

They were all *human*.

Sarah's hands shook at her side, and it took everything in her to control it as one of the prisoners came forward.

A towering middle-aged man with salt and pepper hair that hung in limp strands around his sunken cheeks stepped from the group. His brown eyes were dull and too large for his macabre appearance. He lifted shaking hands, brittle fingers wrapping around the bars as he looked down at her.

"They'll kill you."

His voice was broken and guttural like he hadn't used it in some time, or if he had screamed until his voice broke—maybe both. Sarah contained her grimace.

"Who's they?" she asked, her voice barely above a whisper.

His eyes never strayed from hers, blinking slowly. "The ones who took us."

"Who took you?"

He shook his head, and Sarah could almost hear his bones creaking with each movement.

"They came in the night and took us from our beds. Many of us… now, only a few."

Sarah glanced at the row of empty cages before returning to the brittle man. "How many?"

"Hundreds, years, thousands."

Her brows pinched at his garbled words. "I don't understand."

"I have been here the longest," he stated quietly. "I have seen hundreds come and hundreds die." He paused; his gaze turned distance before sliding back to her with a vacant stare. "We will all die when they are done."

She glanced behind him at the hunched figures huddled together for warmth, following the bony ridges of a young female's spine exposed from a ripped nightgown. Unease roiled in her stomach, and she took a steadying, slow breath, looking back up at the man.

"Where did you all come from?"

He shook his head, those limp strands of hair barely moving. "Too many. Villages across the Eastern plains, too many."

Thousands. Hundreds. In the dead of night. For years. Her thoughts reeled, piecing his words together. Her village and its unsolved disappearances. Her bones cemented, riveting her in place as the realisation settled within her.

Horror morphed her face, and she covered a hand to her mouth to contain the gasp that threatened to spill out.

Steadying herself, she asked, "Are you all human?"

His arm lifted through the bars, pointing a single ridged finger to the sedated bodies. "Not the sleeping dead."

"Are they dead?" she questioned, eyeing the chest of the one closest to her. A female with blood-red hair and nearly translucent skin. Her chest didn't move, not enough for Sarah's human eyes to detect.

"No, and yes."

His cryptic words made her purse her lips and look back at him. He paid her no mind, lowering his hand and watching the female closely.

"Her soul feeds on my blood and the darkness within. Alive she may be, but dead she is."

Sarah stopped herself from rolling her eyes and raised a brow instead. "How insightful."

The man dragged his eyes to her in a way that made Sarah's skin crawl, and she shifted her stance with unease.

"Darkness eats the soul until only hollow bones are left." A low rasping sound followed his words, the likes of which Sarah could only assume was a laugh, and she couldn't stop the shudder that went down her spine.

His ribs heaved with a deep breath he took, the ridges peeking through the tears in his shirt, and something resembling clarity entered his eyes for only a moment. "He keeps us alive just enough, so we won't die when they drain us."

Sarah took a step closer, frowning.

A slow, methodical clap echoed in the chamber around them, and she whipped around as the man slunk back into the huddled group.

"Well done," said a deep, even voice from the shadows.

Sarah shifted her stance, raising the blade as she glared at the darkened alcoves of the cave. There were too many places the voice could be coming from, and she cursed herself silently.

You left yourself open, and now you're going to die because of your stupidity.

She gritted her teeth at her chastising subconscious. *Oh, shut up,* she snapped internally.

"You know," drawled that calm, even tone, "I'm quite surprised it took you so long to find my little *treasures*."

The voice came from everywhere all at once. The shadows crept and crawled towards Sarah like spindled fingers creeping along the ground in a fine black mist. She shifted on her feet, refusing to step back even as an inkling of fear dug its nails into her back.

"It's a delectable pantry, wouldn't you agree?" it asked. "Though sparse, I think it might be time to fill it?"

Her nostrils flared, her palms beginning to sweat as her tongue turned to ash. But she still held her ground. "Hiding in the shadows? How original," she drawled sardonically.

A low chuckle followed her words. "Now, now, why should I reveal myself to you, Hunter?"

Sarah stilled.

"Ah, yes, I know what you are," he stated humourlessly. "I know all things. I watched you climb your way into my mountain. I watched you fall, and I'll admit, I had hoped you wouldn't die." His tone was anything but reassuring with those words. Something dark underlined his tone, giving a frigid bite to his words that filled the already stale, cold space.

"Why?" she snapped.

The shadows whorled through the air as a male stepped from their inky depths. Dressed in a black tailored three-piece suit. The sleeves rolled a quarter of the way up his arms, the black vest hugging his slim frame and fitted with silver buttons embroidered with dark grey intricate patterns. His black slacks were tailored to fit his lean legs down to where glossy black dress shoes shone in the dim light.

Everything about him was darkness incarnate except his eyes. Where his hair was raven black and his skin pale, his eyes were a startling blue. His lips tilted into a cunning smile as he took one passing look at her.

"Why, you ask?" He tilted his head, assessing her like prey. "Because I have something you want, and you can get me something I need."

Alec.

Her jaw twitched with contained rage, and she wanted nothing more than to sever his head from his body, but she didn't. She waited.

"You know. I can see it on your face." He paused, sniffing the air, the quirk of his brow the only indication of surprise. "Interesting… I can't smell you. But I'm sure your fear smells *del-icious*."

A shiver went down her spine, and his answering chuckle made her stiffen her back.

"What do you want from me?" she ground out. There was no way in hell she would make it out of this cave in one piece, let alone alive while he was here. And something told her he had let her come as far as she had.

His assessing gaze lowered, and he smiled slightly. "Walk with me."

She didn't move.

"I don't bite," he paused, giving her a jilting smile. "Unless, of course, you want me to."

His back retreated into the shadows, and Sarah hesitated, her finger tapping excessively against the blade. With a parting glance at the humans behind her, she met the dull brown eyes of the man who had spoken to her. They stared at her, unblinking.

Swallowing, she followed the male into the shifting shadows.

CHAPTER 15

The shadows enveloped her like a cool blanket, wrapping around her limbs, face, and body. She waved a hand in front of her, and the darkness opened up. She was standing in a large, dark, eloquent room.

Polished stone floors reflected the arching ceiling above them. Obsidian pillars lined the hall, and steel torches hung in iron sconces along the path to the glass-like dais. A glimmering silver throne perched atop it.

The male walked ahead, and Sarah paused, her eyes trained on his exposed back.

He turned to her, his arms spread wide, his voice echoing. "Welcome to Dauðinn mountain. Here you stand in the Grand Hall, within the remains of Dyagin Castle."

The names were familiar, and the cold sweep of realisation overcame her.

He was her mission.

Avian.

He stood before her with a smirk, and she knew he saw her thoughts play out over her face.

Composing herself, she lifted her chin in defiance. "Dauðinn mountain was from the old world. This is now the Carpathian mountain range. This is not your old world," she bit out.

Avian huffed a laugh before striding to the silver throne. "Ah, humans and these new Fae. So innocent, so *stupid*," he muttered, dragging a hand along the arm of the throne, up the arching back as he walked around it.

His blue eyes pinned her in place, and Sarah barely dared to breathe.

"Hunter, human… human hunter. To think you can tame magic, to control it." He tsked softly. "Silly child."

Her rage flared, but she tightened her grip on it.

Avian's head ticked to the side, noting her slip of emotion. Amused, he sat on the throne, leaning into it with an air of arrogance.

"This was my father's throne," he commented, drawing languid circles on the armrest.

"How cute," she said ruefully.

He looked up at her through lowered dark brows, the shadows and light catching the sharp plains of his angled face. He was full Fae. There was no denying it. The unearthly handsome face that stared back at her with such unwavering coldness made Sarah tread carefully.

Sprawling comfortably on the throne, Avian watched her for a moment before speaking. "Everything evolves eventually. Time is the essence of change. It does not stand still, and it waits for no one. You know this world for its change, and I know this world for its core. I was born during the fall and raised through its ascent. The names may differ, but that does not change its nature, Hunter."

"What are you doing with those people?" she asked, forcing her tongue to work as it stuck to the roof of her mouth.

"Ah," he said with a short laugh. "They are to me what food is to you."

"Dimmir do not survive solely on blood," she stated.

He frowned at the name she used, straightening in his seat. "I am Dökkálfar," he bit out through clenched teeth, his face darkening. "Dark One. Fallen Elf to the High Fae. Your petty human terms for my kind will not be spoken in these halls," he seethed.

She let her smirk show just enough to let him see she enjoyed knowing she got under his skin. Avian bared his teeth in a silent warning. His blue eyes turned black momentarily before he calmed and leaned back into his throne.

"Do you know how Deathwalkers are made? How do Dark Ones differ?"

She gave him an unimpressed look. "Enlighten me."

"Dark Ones exchange blood from unadulterated lines. You drink from the creator, and they drink from you. An exchange of magic, of life, of sameness. But Deathwalkers, they are truly fascinating. Made from half-breeds, tainted bloodlines. I found that just a drop of my blood and I could control them like little puppets on strings. My essence flows through them, and with it, so does my ability to control their every move, every thought. The true powers of a Dökkálfar."

Sarah crossed her arms, giving him a bored stare. "I really see no difference."

"I am the first true Dökkálfar. I was not created. I was *born*." His crooked smile gleamed in the faltering firelight. "My father and mother were both Dökkálfar, true Dark Ones, and from them they conceived me. The last of the fallen High Fae and the firstborn of pure darkness."

She glanced at her nails with a sigh. "You're very dramatic."

Avian growled lowly. Standing, he stalked towards her. Sarah straightened, holding her ground as his pale hand latched onto her jaw in a vice grip, nails digging painfully into her flesh.

"As one born from darkness, who *is* darkness, I can control those I infect. I am both a salvation and a disease to all who meet me. And from the shadows, I will bring order to this new world."

She jerked her head from his grip, and she knew it was only

because he let her, but still, she met him with a hard stare, her mouth twisting in disgust. "And what about the humans you cage down there like animals," she spewed.

He waved a nonchalant hand at her, walking back to the throne. "A food source for my newborns, you saw. A drop of my blood, mixed with their human blood to keep them fed. I've commanded them into a sedated state."

She finally moved, forcing her steps to be casual as she walked towards the throne. "If they're sedated, then why have them restrained?"

"New pets must be leashed until they're trained. Wouldn't you agree?"

Nausea bubbled in her stomach, but she said coolly, "I wouldn't know, I don't like pets."

Avian leaned forward at her words, a cold smile cutting through his handsome face. "That's a lie," he whispered.

Sarah's brows shot up, crossing her arms. "Is it now?"

"I know all that happens within my mountains." He leaned back, snapping his fingers.

Her eyes widened slightly as someone appeared from a wooden door in the far-right corner of the Grand Hall. A man no older than she was, nothing more than skin and bones. Wearing black jeans and a long-sleeved black shirt. Feet bare on the stone floors, his dirty blond hair dishevelled but slicked back, skin gaunt over high cheekbones. He would have been handsome had it not been for the appearance of death that shadowed his eyes.

His feet slapped quietly against the ground in his wake, walking up the dais with a silver chalice in hand. He stood on Avian's left, holding it out.

Sliding a look to Sarah, his cold smile turned to the young man, taking the offered chalice.

Sarah saw the deadly points of his nails, painted black, as his hand shot out and grabbed the man by his shirt front. Dragging him forward so Avian could run his nose across his hollow cheek.

"The old world was truly depraved of such wondrous creatures," he murmured loud enough for her to hear.

His tongue flicked out and dragged a leisure trail over his jaw.

The young man didn't move, didn't even flinch. He stood there, bent at the waist, his eyes glossy as he stared at the wall ahead.

"While my blood may not possess them as it does the Fae, human minds are so easily broken. So easy to control." Avian's lips whispered over the young man's. "Such a good pet."

The young man twitched suddenly, and Sarah's eyes widened in horror as Avian's nail sliced across his neck, blood pouring from him into Avian's waiting chalice.

The thin body twitched again, eyes still glossy, mouth slightly agape. Avian sucked a drop of blood from the young man's bottom lip, sighing with contentment before he pushed him away when the blood stopped flowing.

His body crumpled on the dais; those eyes still open, unseeing.

Licking the rim of the chalice, Avian looked at Sarah as he drank deeply from his cup. Red staining his teeth when he smiled at her.

She felt like she would be sick.

"Blood may not be our only food source. But it's delectable, and I quite enjoy the taste of my pets."

"That can't be good for you," she forced herself to say casually.

He held out the chalice to her. "Want a sip?"

She blanched.

Avian laughed and sprawled on his throne. "Tell me, Hunter, what is your name?"

"And why should I give you that privilege?" she asked.

He took a sip, watching her. "Because you know my name."

She shifted her stance. "And you know this?"

"Why else would you be here? A hunter, hunting for its *prey.*"

His words whispered around her, and she whipped around as he vanished into shadows. His chalice of blood fell empty to the ground.

"Come out, you bastard," she seethed, holding her knife at the ready.

His laugh brushed against her ear, and she turned again, her heart pounding.

"A hunter who hunts a predator becomes prey," he whispered from the shadows.

She sliced through the air with a yell, and her body flew against one of the obsidian pillars. Her head slammed against the stone, and stars flashed across her eyes, her bones groaning under the banding pressure that pinned her against the pillar.

Head rolling to the side, she squeezed her eyes shut, trying to clear her vision. She could feel the hot trickle of blood going down the back of her neck, and she gritted her teeth, forcing herself to focus. Copper filled her mouth, and she spat out a wad of blood, licking the split in her bottom lip.

"I should have known you would fight dirty," she huffed, a crooked smile pulling at her split lip.

Avian appeared in front of her, dragging a finger through the blood that cut a path along her neck. He sucked it clean from his finger, his eyes darkening in the process. "An anomaly," he whispered, gazing at her blood with interest. "Interesting."

Head clearing, Sarah fought against the shadows that wrapped around her in a vice. "What do you want?!"

Doors groaned in the silence, and Sarah's attention snapped to the duelling wood doors that opened, standing nearly floor to ceiling.

Avian's gaze was riveted on Sarah, but she ignored him. Her limbs shook as Alec and Talan, naked as the day they were born, were brought in. He appeared unbound, but Talan's wrists were joined in front of him, his mouth pressed tight, and he looked like he wanted to say something. His eyes glowed, and she could see the anger that flamed brightly behind them.

Alec's eyes were filled with tears, snapping to hers. He tried to say something but couldn't. White hot rage boiled in her veins, and Sarah thrashed against her bindings.

A male strolled in casually behind them. His auburn hair cropped close to his head, and his dark brown eyes barely glanced at Sarah before turning a bored gaze to Avian.

"I told you it was a lie," Avian whispered against the shell of her ear. "You're surrounded by *dogs*."

Sarah's eyes bounced back and forth between Talan and Alec—dogs? Her eyes darted away, filing that thought, and looked at Avian and the other male. "Let. Them. Go," she bit out.

"Or what?" he taunted. "You'll kill me with this pathetic excuse for a knife?"

Her eyes flashed in warning. "I don't need a knife to kill you!" she spat.

"You'll need more than whatever…it is you have," he commented, turning his attention to the other male. "Let the boy talk."

"Alec don—!"

"—Sarah!" he cried, tears spilling down his ruddy cheeks.

"*Sar-ah*," Avian repeated quietly. "Such a beautiful name, *Sar-ah*." Disgust rolling over each syllable.

"Don't you hurt my sister!" roared Alec, lunging with his invisible bindings. His tiny body was yanked back by something unseen, and Sarah snarled when she heard his muffled whimper, his invisible gag going back over his mouth.

Her eyes blazed, willing holes to burn through the head of black glossy hair in front of her.

"Reign has a special gift of Fae magic," Avian explained, turning to the other male. "Controlling the very air around us. He can even control the oxygen within your body and suffocate you until there is nothing left. It's advantageous, wouldn't you agree?"

"You're a monster!" she said, spitting blood at his face.

Avian wagged a finger at her, tutting in disapproval. "Now, now, monsters go bump in the night, my dear Sarah. I promise you, I am much, much worse."

"This one is a fighter, stubborn," Reign said lowly, eyes fixated on Talan. "How I like them."

Talan glared at the male with disgust.

"Now, Reign, don't tease our guests," chastised Avian.

Reign answered with a jilting smile and casually walked over to a pillar, leaning against it with his hands in his pockets.

Sarah threw a withering glare at Avian as they walked towards Alec and Talan. "Don't you dare touch them!"

He paused, giving her a sidelong look over his shoulder. "And what will you give me in return for not hurting your precious dogs?"

Her nostrils flared, and her jaw threatened to snap with how hard she bit down. Forcing in air with a glance to Reign, she said, "You said you need something, something I can help with."

Avian walked over to Alec, bending at the waist to stare at him. "I will make you a bargain, Sarah Hunter of the Fae."

"I don't make bargains with Fae," she ground out.

He laughed softly, wrapping one of Alec's curls around his fingers. "Are you afraid?"

Sarah's lip twitched at the challenge. "What do you want." *Stupid, stupid, stupid.* She ignored her chastising thoughts.

Talan shook his head at her, his eyes wide in warning.

"Find my sister, and I will return this little one to you." He turned to look at her. "*Bring* my sister to me."

Talan's face turned to one of confusion, his eyes bouncing between them, brows furrowed.

Her bindings bit into her limbs, and she knew her skin was turning purple under the shadow bands. "Who is your sister?"

"Find the one called Saskia and bring her to me."

The name sent alarm bells ringing through her head, but Sarah rolled her eyes. "I'm going to need more than just a name," she said.

Avian strolled to her calmly, leaning forward until only a breath separated them. "Will you find my sister?"

"Why do you want her? I would run away from you too if I were her," she retorted bitterly.

His teeth bared in a snarl. "She was stolen from me!"

"Good!" she snapped back at him.

His hand lashed out, backhanding her across the face in a deafening blow. Her head jerked back and slammed against the pillar, head lolling in a daze.

"Without her," he seethed, "The prophecy cannot be fulfilled."

Blood dribbled from her split lip, her head throbbing with each heartbeat, but a manic laugh slipped out regardless. "So, without this bargain, you're fucked. Now *that's* interesting."

Avian's hand latched around her throat, squeezing until she sputtered for air. "The prophecy must be fulfilled. *Find my sister!*"

"Some prophecy if I haven't heard of it," she gasped. She was biding her time, scrambling to find a way out, but time was running out. And the last trickle of sand was slipping from her hourglass as the seconds passed.

Something shifted on Avian's face, and he released her, stepping back as Sarah sucked in a shuddering breath. "From shadows and mist and fire and ash," he said quietly, his voice echoing around them as he strolled over to Alec. "Walls will fall, and darkness will reign. As one is…" he grabbed Alec by a tuft of his hair, spinning around with black eyes, tears streaming down Alec's face, "The other shall be. From darkness and light, the world will rise."

"If you touch him…" she warned.

His eyes narrowed. "Find my sister."

Alec winced as Avian yanked his head back, dragging one razor-edged nail across his exposed neck. He was shaking from head to toe, and Sarah jerked her head.

"You do not hurt him! I give you your sister, and you give me Alec!"

A wicked smile split his face. "Deal."

Fire burned through her, and the skin on her arm seared. Sarah bit down on her broken lip, muffling her cry.

He cocked his head to the side. "Find the elves and the witch within, Sarah Hunter of Fae. Find the light, and within you will find the darkness. You have nine days. Mark them."

Sarah's eyes went wide as her bindings disappeared. Lunging for Alec with arms outstretched. "Alec!"

Avian snapped his fingers, and the world around them was engulfed in shadows.

His bedchamber was lowly lit by a fire in the hearth as Avian walked in, the yellow light flickering off the raw edges of stone around him. The red and black satin sheets of his massive bed glimmered in the light, the black four-post bed nearly swallowed in shadows.

Slipping his shoes off, he walked over the black plush rug strewn in front of his bed and undid his vest.

"What are we to do with them?"

Avian deigned Reign a glance as he dropped the vest to the bed, working on his shirt's buttons. His oldest friend, if he could say he had *friends*, and his right hand leaned casually against the wall beside the hearth, nearly shrouded in darkness.

"A bargain is a bargain, Reign," he commented, slipping out of his shirt.

His lean body flexed as the bitter air brushed against his abs, and he undid his black belt and the waist of his pants. He could feel Reign's stare, and he gave him a dark glance. "You don't agree?"

Reign shrugged. "What I think is minute." He paused, adding, "She understood our language."

He graced Reign with a sharp smile. "Yes, she did." His pants slipped down, and he stepped out of them, naked, and walked over to his friend, brushing his black hair over a pale shoulder as he went. "If she doesn't follow through with it, then she will die, and so will the pup." He paused before adding, "Go with them if you must. Keep an eye on my investment. Dear Sarah is keeping secrets. Her blood speaks lies; in fact, her blood doesn't speak at all, and I want to know why. I want to know why he didn't show up but sent his little pet instead."

Reign kept his features neutral, concealing his piqued interest at Avian's last statement.

Avian turned to the adjoining bathing chamber and strolled through the stone archway. He could feel Reign follow behind him.

Fire hung in torches on the walls, casting that same flickering glow in the bathing room. Water steamed within in the large stone basin in the middle of the chamber. Candles lit within the deep-set ledge against the wall that framed it. Two stone steps were carved from the ground to its perched dais, and Avian made his way up to them.

"Bring her."

Reign snapped his fingers, and a curvaceous human woman appeared from an antechamber naked.

Her long chestnut hair curled down her back, dusting the top of her supple ass. Full pouting lips lay slightly parted as grey eyes looked past Avian with a glossy stare. Large, full breasts sat prettily on her chest with rosy nipples that puckered in the air. Her waist dipped where her hips flared, and long, full legs met at the apex of her sex.

"Come," Avian said darkly, stepping into the steaming water and sitting on the ledge, facing Reign and the woman, the candlelight creating a halo at his back. His cock already hardening as he watched the woman saunter towards him.

There was something about blood and pain that turned him on, and today was no exception as he stared at the woman with hunger.

She stepped into the water, lowering herself onto the ledge within the basin before floating towards him. There were certain pets he kept for this special occasion, her supple body begging for him, and his mouth practically watered at the site of her. His legs parted for her to step between, the water coming to just below her breasts that floated for him to see.

He leaned forward, catching her chin between his thumb and forefinger. With eyes still on Reign, he whispered to the woman, "Let me see what that pretty mouth can do."

Without so much as a sound of protest and those glossy eyes still fixated on the point beyond Avian, the woman grabbed his cock and lowered her mouth to it. Tongue flicking against his tip.

He moaned lowly, rolling his head back as he hardened under her. Her tongue slipped down his shaft, teeth grazing against his balls, and his body jerked with pleasure. Turning his gaze to Reign, who leaned against the archway, watching him, expressionless.

Her mouth slipped over the tip, and Avian fisted a hand through her hair, thrusting into her hot mouth. She took it all without so much as a sound as he fucked her throat hard and fast.

Water sloshed over the side of the large basin, candles flickered, and Avian's groan of pleasure filled the chamber.

Reign walked out, and Avian's eyes trailed after him as he brought the woman's mouth down on his cock over and over again.

Pleasure coursed through him, and he roared his release, filling her mouth with his cum as he jerked into her with a final hard thrust. Yanking her off his semi-hard cock, hand still fisted in her hair, he brought her face level with his as he pulled her from the water.

"Such a good little pet," he purred, lust filling his eyes.

And with a quick motion, he slit her throat.

Blood gushed from her warm, supple body, filling the basin and staining it red. Avian dragged his tongue across her neck, his skin spraying with blood, and his eyes rolled to the back of his head as the flavour burst across his tongue. His cock hardening again at the taste.

He let her body go, watching it bob in the water, her blood pooling around her until the water was crimson.

Sinking into the hot bath, Avian leaned his head against the ledge, driblets of blood and water rolling across his skin as he combed a hand through his long hair.

The rich smell of copper and sweet death filled the air, and Avian closed his eyes as a dark smile gleamed in the candlelight.

CHAPTER 16

NINE DAYS LEFT...

"Wake up."

A boot to the ribs had Sarah groaning, her cheek pressed into coarse dirt. She was awake enough, or conscious at least, to know everything hurt—a lot. The back of her head throbbed, and she had to force her eyes open, fingers digging into soil and rock chips.

"Don't fucking touch her," snarled a voice behind her.

Sarah winced, head ringing, and she made to swallow the lump in her throat as her vision wavered. Blinking slowly, she focused on a mounded rock the size of her head directly in front of her face.

"Or what, Dog? You'll gnaw me to death?" the one that kicked her said mockingly.

A rumbled warning responded in answer. "I'll do a lot more than just that."

Talan.

"Promises, promises," the other said dismissively.

A warm hand brushed her head, and she held back a whine when it touched the bruised knot behind her hair. Her hand twitched in the dirt, ready to grab whoever was touching her, but a familiar earthy musk filled her nostrils, and she relaxed.

"Come on, Princess," Talan whispered softly.

It wasn't a request but a command.

Sarah didn't have it in her to nod, forcing herself to sit up. Her bones groaned, every muscle screaming. Her cheek and lip pulsated, and she knew they were swollen. Strands of brown hair fell around her face, and she lifted a hand to her hair, wincing when dried blood scraped under her touch.

"You look like shit," Talan teased.

Sarah glanced at him. "So do you," she muttered hoarsely, her tongue sticking to the roof of her mouth.

But he didn't. He wore black jeans, a dark grey long-sleeve henley, and black boots. His dark hair was dishevelled, his skin unmarked and just as golden brown as before, and his amber eyes stared at her with warmth and familiarity.

Sarah would never tell him this, but he looked good. Whereas, she felt like a train wreck and probably looked like one, too.

"As touching as this reunion is, time is of the essence." said a droll voice.

Sarah's head snapped behind her, and Talan grabbed her as she lunged for the auburn-haired male, Reign, who leaned against a tree.

"Down, Princess," Talan said roughly against her ear. Letting out a harsh breath when her elbow jammed into his solar plexus.

She fought in his hold, her body screaming at her to cease, but she ignored it. Thrashing like an animal, teeth bared and eyes flashing with burning rage.

Reign's answering smirk made her see red. "Cute."

Talan's arms banded around her, his voice deep as he commanded, "Sarah, stop!" Her foot met his shin, and he winced.

"Sarah, it's okay!"

"No!" She screamed, whirling on him suddenly. Yanking free of his hold. "It's not okay! Where the *fuck* am I, where is Alec, and why the *fuck* is *he* here?!" she yelled, jamming a finger in Reign's direction.

Talan gripped her shoulders, softening his hold when he saw her flinch. "He's here to keep an eye on us."

Her eyes narrowed. "And you know this how?"

"Because you've been passed out like the dead since I brought you here," Reign stated. "Because the pup woke up before you and reacted similarly."

Sarah's eyes bounced between Reign and Talan, narrowing once. Her mouth pressed into a scowl. "Where are we?" she snapped, stepping away from Talan, ignoring his frown as she leashed her anger.

Reign nodded his chin to a spot behind Sarah. "Brasov."

Following his gaze, she found the old city nestled within the mountain range, just down from the jutting forest ledge they were on. Its steeples and resplendent buildings painted a pretty picture of cream, gold, and russet red among green mountains.

"What are we doing here?" questioned Sarah, glaring at Reign.

He brushed some dirt off his black long-sleeve henley. He and Talan were dressed almost identically, except Talan's shirt was a different colour. "Catching a flight."

She crossed her arms. "To where?"

"Take a guess."

Glancing at Talan, whose jaw ticked with annoyance, she raised a brow. "Let me guess, we're a thropple now and going on our honeymoon?"

Reign rolled his eyes. "Funny."

Find the elves and the witch. You have nine days. Mark them.

Avian's smug voice filled her throbbing head, her memory returning, and the leash on her anger slipped.

"He was serious," she muttered in disbelief, eyes widening.

Reign's lips twitched with amusement, watching her as she ran a hand over her hair. "You'll find Avian is rarely anything but serious."

Talan's brows furrow. "What are you talking about?"

Laughing lowly, Reign slid a knowing look to Talan. "Interesting, isn't it? The Fae language has so many lovely qualities, especially the elven tongue."

Talan snapped at him in warning, "Don't speak in riddles, Dark One."

Reign gave him a crooked smile, something flashing over his face before it cleared, and he turned back to Sarah, who was staring at the city with distant eyes.

"I know where we're going," she said quietly.

"A-plus for the student," Reign said, walking up beside her. "Extra credit if you can guess why."

"The elves built an empire when the wall fell, disguised as an antiquities trade, but specialising in magical artefacts." Sarah paused, chewing on her lip and wincing when the scabbed split in her lip began to bleed again. "Frankfurt is a three-hour plane ride from here… when do we leave?"

"Tomorrow." Reign held up a hand when Sarah rounded on him. "You look like shit," he leaned forward, sniffing once and wrinkling his nose, "You smell like shit, too."

She glared up at him. "I have nine days. Nine. I can shower when I get there."

Reign gave her a calculating look, dragging his eyes from her face to her boots and back up. He quickly plucked a leaf from her hair before she could swat his hand away. "Would you rather walk around with two males while looking like you got into a fight with a tree and the tree won?"

She scowled but didn't say anything.

"One night won't delay anything. In fact, it might help. Gods know you might be less of a pain in my ass if you eat something." He said the last part mainly for himself, rolling his eyes at her answering glare. "Come on, I'll get us a room."

Sarah watched Reign amble away casually, walking around the rocky ledge and starting the descent into the city. Her stomach coiled with unease, flexing and fisting her hands repeatedly. Trying to regain some semblance of stability as her whole world tilted on its axis.

Talan reached out a hand to her, and she jerked her head in warning, pinning him with a stare that caused him to drop his arm back to his side.

Alec's teary gaze was all she could see, and her chest cracked open like someone had ripped out her heart. Pinching her eyes shut, she held back the tears that gathered and forced in a deep breath.

Commanding her legs to work, she followed Reign down the mountain.

The hotel Reign found was old and outdated but warm, and even though her body felt like lead, when he looked at her with that smug amusement as he watched her falter a step in front of the door to her room, she wanted to ram his head through the wall.

"I dare you," he all but purred, seeing her intent.

Glaring at his satisfied smile, she wrenched open the black door, the silver **10** sliding against it and hanging desperately to the nail as she slammed it shut.

She could hear his low laugh from the other side, and she rolled her eyes when she heard a door open and close beside hers. Stalking into the room, she heard the door opening again and Talan walking in behind her.

"I don't trust him," Talan said after a moment, watching her sit on one of the old springy mattresses.

There were two full beds with faded yellow floral comforters and two semi-flat cream pillows. The walls were covered in floor-to-ceiling cream wallpaper that had creeping floral vines and what was once bright purple flowers. The cream carpet was surprisingly spot-free, and navy drapes framed the lone window that overlooked the street from their first-floor room. A tiny, worn desk sat pushed into the corner with a single wood chair and a clock that read **15:00**. The day was nearly over, and the thought of losing a single day made her antsy.

"You don't say?" Sarah replied dryly, stroking the comforter's fabric, her thoughts drifting.

Talan scoffed, striding to the window and peeking through the gauzy white drapes that did nothing to conceal them from view of the outside world. He pulled one of the heavier navy ones closed when he made eye contact with a pedestrian, the light in the room banking to a dim.

"You should shower," he said quietly.

She looked up at him, noting the concern in his gaze. He held her eyes momentarily before jerking his head to the door.

"I'll give you some privacy."

Sarah watched him walk out, tracking his back until the wall blocked him from sight and the door to the room opened and closed. She let out a ragged breath, stood slowly, and rubbed a hand over the sore spot on her lower back.

The bathroom was tiny. The shallow tub, small counter, and toilet were yellowed with age, probably brand new fifty years ago if she had to guess, with once-white walls and three flickering, too-harsh white lights.

Turning on the hot water, she closed the purple floral shower curtain and faced the mirror, which covered nearly the whole wall above the sink.

She looked like absolute shit. No wonder the hotel attendant was staring at her with concern, eyeing Talan and Reign cautiously.

Her ponytail was nearly pulled free, strands of hair framing her face. The blood caking her hairline had turned brown, streaks of blood going down her neck where her head had been slammed into the pillar. A bright purple bruise puffed up her right cheek, minor cuts marred her brow and chin, and a purple cast to her split bottom lip.

Edging her jacket off, she shrugged it to the ground, unlatching her holster and setting it on the counter with the extra magazines. Her shirt was the worst of it, and her breathing was ragged by the time she got it off. Hands shaking, she had to grip the counter to steady herself.

Purple bruises marred her arms, chest, torso, and hips in perfect bands that wrapped around her. Bringing trembling fingers to the one that wrapped around her abs, she winced when pain bit through the tender skin. Turning, she eyed the trail of blood that went from her head down her spine, stopping between her shoulder blades, right over the scar that marked her there, looking at the bruise peaking above the waistband of her jeans.

She looked like shit, and she felt like shit. Reign's words mocked her, and Sarah shook her head with a low growl, the dark circles under her eyes practically neon in the too-bright lights.

The tattoo on her left forearm, just below her elbow, caught her eyes. She dragged a finger across it, watching it waver in the light. The brand the magic had chosen for her; a band of tiny flowers and their deadly thorns. Fae bargains, wrapped in sweet words, and deathly consequences if not fulfilled.

Sarah stared at the tattoo for a moment, her mind reeling, before slowly removing her boots and jeans. She slipped out of them, leaving them piled on the floor as she stepped under the scorching water.

Talan looked at the bathroom door and then at the bag in his hand. He was standing outside the door like an idiot—a helpless idiot.

Raising his fist, he hesitated, wavering when he couldn't hear anything on the other end. Letting out a sigh, he rapt on the door. Silence.

"Sarah?" he called.

Silence.

Knocking again, he waited a minute, and still, nothing.

"Sarah?"

Her bed was still made, no sight of her dirty clothes. She had been a mess when he left, covered in dried blood and smudged dirt from earlier. Her face was bruised and cut up, but she had looked fearless and angry… very, very angry.

He remembered the way she looked when she saw the boy— Alec. Seeing her tears and the distress made him want to tear apart the Dark One. If he hadn't been bound by Reign's bullshit magic, he would have ripped the mountain apart to get her and the boy out.

The wolf inside of him rumbled with promise.

Swallowing, he sucked in a quick breath to steady the wave of emotions and opened the bathroom door.

Talan froze.

Sarah's arms were braced on the counter, and she was staring at herself, unblinking. Clothes piled on the floor, and a damp towel hanging on the shower curtain bar. All the blood was scrubbed off, her pale skin bright pink, blending in with the purple bruises she was covered with. But that wasn't what made a pit of rage open within him, sharp talons tearing at his bones, demanding to shift, to *protect*.

It was the scars. They marked her back like latticework. The muscle in her back flexed under the clean silver lashes that shifted in the light. He could see the scar that wrapped over her shoulder, and his anger flared. But before he could say anything, his eyes fixated on the slightly pink scar raised against her skin, directly between her shoulder blades.

He didn't know how long he stared at it, but he flinched when Sarah spoke.

"It was my punishment," she said lowly, eyes drifting to his face in the mirror.

Talan's hands clenched at his side, barely breathing, still fixated on the raised scar that marred her pale flesh with puckered edges.

"It's a Druid rune. The one that was painted on the doors in Tor'oc. It was my punishment for their deaths." She turned to face him, naked and unfaltering, when his gaze raked over her quickly before snapping to her face. "He had me draw it out, and then he made a villager forge an iron in its likeness. And when darkness came, he had me strip to nothing and kneel on the manor's steps, overlooking my village."

Her voice had dropped to a whisper, and Talan held his breath as she stepped up to him, with brown eyes staring at him.

"I was made an example of. So that I am reminded, every time I see it, that I am responsible for my village, and I am responsible for the death of another." She didn't blink. She only cocked her head softly, staring up at his amber eyes that he knew were glowing brightly. "It means *death shall not enter,* but he forgets… I am Death."

Talan was shaking, barely noticing her warm hand on his cheek. "Breathe."

He growled at the command.

"Breathe," she said again softly.

The wolf in him rumbled with annoyance but obeyed, and he breathed as the beast within settled. He exhaled with a *whoosh,* running his free hand through his hair. "I'm going to kill him."

Her answering smirk was almost comforting as she walked past him, still naked. "Get in line."

He watched her saunter away with that same cocky stride he had come to know well. Eyeing the flex of muscle that corded her body from her shoulders down to her lean legs. His brows rose when he glanced at her ass. There was nothing soft about this woman. Every edge and angle had a muscle that had been shaped and honed from years of training, torture, and hunting.

That thought alone made him growl again, but even as anger rumbled in his chest, something else stirred as he forced himself to look away from her full breasts when she turned, but not before catching sight of the dusty rose nipples that hardened in the cool room.

He coughed, holding out the nearly forgotten bag in his hand. "I got you some clothes."

She laughed under her breath, strolling over and snatching it from him. "Oh, goodies for me? You shouldn't have," she teased.

Talan's shoulders relaxed, and he turned his back to her so she could rifle through it. "I don't know your size, so I had to guess."

She hummed in acknowledgement.

"I did knock, by the way, twice. If I had known you were in there, I would have waited."

The rustling of clothes paused. Talan could feel her staring at him, and he willed himself to fixate on the hotel door instead.

"I'm going to take a nap," she said after a long pause.

He nodded quickly. "I'm going to the bar next door. Find me when you're awake."

The bag rustled again, and she didn't answer, so he slipped out of the room, leaning his head against the closed door.

"Trouble in paradise?"

Talan narrowed his eyes at Reign, leaning against the door frame of his room. "That's none of your business."

He shrugged.

Pushing off the door, Talan made to walk past.

"Where you going?"

"To get a beer," he said reluctantly, the muscle in his jaw ticking.

Reign nodded, shutting his door. "Let me join you."

"Do I have a choice?"

The auburn male gave him a wolfish grin. "I wasn't asking."

CHAPTER 17

"Saskia... Sas-kia." A melodic voice sang from the darkness.

Sarah blinked, staring into the abyss. Waiting. There was that name.

"Sas-kia," sang that voice again.

Light burst across her eyes, and she flinched when two white wood panel doors opened abruptly.

"Aha! I found you!"

Sarah—no, Saskia squealed, crawling for the darkest corner of the closest she was hidden in. A hand grabbed for her ankle and yanked her out, and she laughed and kicked at the hand, rolling onto her back with a wide grin.

"Mamma!" she giggled, her mother tickling her sides until she screamed with laughter.

Wide, sky-blue eyes stared down at Sarah with so much love that her chest filled with a warmth she had never known, but it wasn't for her, it never was or would be. That love was for Saskia, the eyes she was looking through. Hair like dark sunlight fell in soft curls around a lovely pale face and rosebud mouth, the tips of her delicate ears arching through the folds of her hair.

"You can't hide from me, my little wildling!" her mother mused with a glowing smile, brushing her nose over Sarah's before kissing the tip of it quickly. "Come! Your father and brother just got home."

Sarah gasped, sitting upright. "Brother!" Laughing, she scrambled to her feet and ran from the room, her mother calling after her to slow down.

The world around her was a blur, like smeared paint, but still, she ran through the halls until a cozy kitchen appeared, where two males leaned casually against butcher-block counters.

"Brother!" she yelled excitedly, leaping at the tall, lean legs that were eye level with her face.

Laughing loudly, large hands grabbed her by the waist and tossed her in the air before bringing her in for a crushing hug. "How's my favourite sister?" her brother mused.

She leaned back to gaze at him, placing her hands on his chest. "I'm your only sister!" she giggled.

His flashing white smile was the only thing she could make out on his face. The rest was a blur, just like everything else around her.

"Ah yes, what would the world be like if more of these little monsters were running around?" he asked with a dramatic sigh.

Sarah giggled again. "Rawr!" she said, baring her teeth into a ferocious snarl, her hands making little claws at him.

He flicked the tip of her nose with a laugh. "That's the spirit."

"Ah, look at my little savage daughter," said her mother, gliding into the kitchen. She was the only one Sarah could see clearly. Her face was radiant and full of love.

"I'm a monster, Mamma!"

Her mother laughed. "Yes, my love. Very scary indeed!"

The world shifted, and Sarah felt like she was spinning uncontrollably until the world became dark, and she wasn't Saskia; she was only Sarah.

Naked, alone, and in the dark, covered in her scars and bruises.

The mother's voice filled the void around her, and pain lanced through her head with a jolting force that had Sarah screaming into the abyss.

"My savage daughter. My little Saskia."

Sarah woke with a start, her body covered in a thin sheen of sweat. The sheets were tangled around her limbs, and her fingers fisted into the comforter as the pain in her head throbbed uncontrollably.

Nausea bubbled in her throat, and she rushed for the bathroom, tripping over her feet before falling in front of the cool porcelain and heaving up bright yellow stomach acid. There was nothing in her to expel. She hadn't eaten anything in over twenty-four hours.

After her wrenching ceased, she laid a clammy cheek on the toilet seat, welcoming the cold against her overheated skin.

"Saskia."

The name whispered through her head again, and pain wracked her body, stealing the air from her lungs; the breath she sucked in was strangled as her bruised muscles contracted.

She pressed the heel of her palm into her temple, trying to soothe the deep ache that throbbed against her skull. After a few minutes and half a dozen deep breaths, her limbs stopped quaking, and she made herself stand. The world tipped, and she braced a hand on the counter.

"Easy," she muttered to herself, licking her dry lips.

She met the stare of her reflection, noting the bruise on her cheek and the faint purple ring around her neck she had missed before. The swelling had dissipated entirely, and she was thankful. The last thing she wanted to do was walk around with half a swollen face.

The bruise on her cheek was still purple and noticeable, covering the ridge of her cheekbone. Still, it wasn't the worst she'd ever looked, though certainly not the best, either. It had been a while since she had gotten her ass handed to her, and she had nearly forgotten the discomfort that came with its bruises.

Scratch that. She never forgot.

Slipping into the shower, Sarah quickly rinsed the sweat from her skin and stepped out. Towelling off and snatching her hair tie from the pile of her clothes, she banded it around her wrist and finger-combed her hair as she walked back to her bed and the clothes Talan had bought her.

Her lips twitched with amusement, and she raised her brows at the clothes: one black bra, dark-stonewashed skinny jeans, navy blue long-sleeve thermal, and a black canvas jacket with a plush knitted lining. Sarah plucked the pair of wool grey socks up, grinning now.

Chuckling to herself, she got dressed and grabbed the spare key from the tiny desk, quickly noting the time: **18:05**.

The door shut behind her, and she whistled lowly, ignoring the stare of a passing couple in the hall.

"You forgot the panties."

Talan choked on his beer, glancing at Sarah as she claimed the barstool beside him. She had snuck up behind him, and her whispered words sent a shudder of heat and surprise down his spine. He had been zoning out, staring at the stack of hard liquor behind the old bar, thinking of what had happened within the mountain and what he saw in that bathroom.

It was hard to think of anything else, actually. He had downed five beers in the two hours since he had been there, and Talan felt like his brain had been branded with its own mark.

Composing himself, he leaned his elbow on the bar top, giving her his undivided attention. "Did I now?"

She flagged down the bartender, nodding to the beer Talan nursed. "I'll have the same."

Talan looked at her clothes, and something in him nodded in approval.

"Your tongue is hanging, Puppy," she said with a wry smile.

He scowled. "Puppy?" he muttered under his breath. "I see everything fits," he said, gazing down at her. *Panties*, she had said. His eyes strayed to her lean legs, and suddenly, the world narrowed around him at the thought of her without panties, and he made himself look away. Shifting in his seat and ignoring the sudden tightness in his jeans.

"I didn't realise you paid such close attention to my body," she quipped, taking her beer from the bartender.

"It's kind of hard to miss when you walk away from me all the time," he retorted with an eye roll.

Sarah's answering smile as she sipped her beer made him pause before sipping his own beer.

She looked over her shoulder, assessing the bar behind them, and he knew she had spotted Reign lounging by himself in the far corner. "Guess we have a shadow."

He grunted, not bothering to look back at the male. "Yeah, apparently."

"Huh," she said, looking between Reign and himself. "Are you sharing a closet with our little bloodsucker?"

Talan frowned. "I ripped through my other clothes when I shifted."

Humming with a nod, she took a long swig of her beer, letting out a burp a second later.

Shaking his head, he said, "No wonder you have so many men flocking to you."

With a snide smile, Sarah leaned in close. "Well, I haven't been able to get rid of you—yet."

"I'd like to see you try, Princess."

She signalled to the bartender for a refill once she finished her pint.

"Hey-*y*," slurred a male voice from behind them.

Piss and stale beer assaulted Talan's senses as an inebriated man sidled up to Sarah's side. She rolled her eyes, not giving the man any time of day.

"What hap-happened to your cheek," the man questioned, swaying on his feet and using the bar-top as support. His grey eyes were glossy, and a red flush splayed over his cheeks. His bright blond hair hung in dishevelled curls around his round face.

Sarah sighed as Talan growled low in his chest, canines elongating. "Down boy," she muttered, sipping her beer.

"*Ooh*, you're… you have *magic*," he said, wiggling the fingers of his non-beer-holding hand. Turning his attention back to Sarah, his eyes narrowed as he peered at her closely. Hey, you're kind of cute."

"It's the alcohol," Sarah muttered, wrinkling her nose when his breath brushed across her.

The man frowned, thinking. "Yeah… prob… probably." His eyes glazed over, and he stumbled before catching himself on Sarah's arm.

She let out a sound of annoyance, shaking him off her.

Talan turned his full attention to the man, his eyes glowing.

Sarah noted Talan's eyes shift from warm amber to the intense glow that now consumed them. The man to her left was very close to becoming kibble.

Ignoring the rumbling warning from Talan, she cocked her head to one side, eyeing the man slowly. He was very human and very drunk. She didn't have the patience to deal with this, but all the same, she leaned against the counter with her head in her hand. Giving him an unimpressed look.

The man shifted under her stare, but his intoxicated state made him cocky enough to grab her arm. "Did… didhedothistoyou." His words jumbled together, and she had to gather all of her brain cells to pick it apart.

"No," she said stoically. He still hadn't let go of her arm.

The man tugged on her, trying to pull her off the stool. "You shouldcome home withme."

Her head was starting to throb again.

He tugged on her arm harder, trying to get her to follow. She opened her mouth to snap something at the man and tug her arm free, but before she could, Talan's warmth blanketed her back and filled her body as he stood, pressing himself against her.

"I fucking dare you," he rumbled darkly. The promise of pain lingered in his tone.

The man's eyes widened, nearly dropping his beer and scrambling to catch it.

Talan's hand gripped her shoulder, and she let herself lean into the touch. She watched the man with a dull stare as he stumbled back.

"Bitch," he muttered under his breath. That was the wrong thing to say.

Talan snarled then, flashing the deadly points of his canines.

"Well, if I'm a bitch, then what breed is your mother?" Sarah asked calmly, fiddling with her beer before sliding a pointed look at the man. She could feel the silent vibration of Talan's laugh against her back despite knowing he still glared at him.

Despite his intoxicated state, the man knew when to cut his losses, and shook his head, muttering under his breath that sounded a lot like, "Fucking magic dwellers. Was a plain ass chick anyways."

Sarah turned and touched Talan's bicep, trying to get his attention as he growled after the man. "Ignore him." She glanced at the counter, noting the splintered wood under his hand. "Let's go back to the hotel. Call it an early night. Watch trash TV."

It took Talan a moment to turn his gaze down to her, his eyes dimming to the soft amber she was becoming familiar with. He jerked his head, swigged back the last of his beer, and placed a hand at the base of her spine as he led them out of the growing crowd.

Reign leaned back in his chair from his shadowed corner, watching the human stumble away from Sarah and Talan. Getting lost in the gathering of humans and Fae that occupied the old bar. The creaky wood floors and brick walls gave the mostly tight quarters a cosy feel.

Finishing his whiskey, Reign watched Sarah and the shifter pay their tab and leave. He stood, stalking out of the bar, until his eyes landed on the back of the man. A slight smile twisted his lips, and he slipped into the shadowed alleyway that lay in wait between the stacks of cream and gold stores and hotels.

The man took a drink from his bottle, letting out a loud burp before wiping his nose on the back of his hand. Reign watched him with fixated fascination as he stumbled past the shadows. Quick as an asp, he snatched the man from the street.

"Fucking hell!" he exclaimed, dropping his beer. He sounded distressed, looking at the shattered bottle and lost liquid that left a wet stain on the concrete.

"Shh," murmured Reign, putting a finger to his mouth. "We don't want to cause a scene, do we?" he purred, his dark eyes turning nearly black in the shadows with a wicked smile cut across his face.

The man's face blanched, staring at the Fae male in front of him. "I-I-I'm sorry, Ididn'doanything!" he stuttered in a rush.

Reign tsked softly. His hand lashing out around his neck. The man's body slammed against the brick side of a shop, and he groaned with pain. "You touched something that doesn't belong to you."

The air around them grew bitter, like the Reaper's breath, and the man swallowed, trembling violently.

"I'm sorry," he said clearly, shaking his head wildly, sweat gathering on his brow.

Reign noted his jumping carotid that beat rapidly in his neck, and he licked his lips, showing his lengthening canines.

The tang of piss filled the stale air, and Reign's dark laugh followed as it dripped down the man's pant leg, mingling with his spilt beer.

"Don't be afraid," Reign whispered. "This will only hurt a lot."

"No! I'm—" His words cut off, eyes bulging from their sockets.

Reign tilted his head, lifting the man by his neck until he dangled in the air. "You're what? Sorry?" he asked softly. He hummed as the air around him shifted and moved under his command. "Have you ever wondered how much oxygen actually takes up space in the human body? It's interesting because the Fae can survive on much less than you silly humans," he mused as the man's face began to concave, gasping for air that didn't exist. Reign let him go, keeping him suspended above the ground, watching his body shrink slowly, painfully.

He stepped over the puddle of beer and piss, ignoring the choking babbles from the man as he peered into the street. It wasn't too busy. He turned back to the now nearly skeletal human in front of him.

"It's amazing how much space oxygen takes up in your body. But soon, your muscles and blood cells will shrivel up and be nothing more than dehydrated meat in its casing. Too bad you're not my taste."

The man's body twitched once, then twice, and his eyes shrivelled into nothing. His cheekbones were cut out, and his skin was grey and paper thin.

Releasing him, his body crumpled to the ground with a crack as brittle bones snapped under pressure.

Reign leaned forward, whispering into the shrivelled ear. "Next time, don't touch someone who doesn't want to be touched."

He slipped into the street when a crowd passed by and returned to his corner in the bar. Waving down the waitress to order another whiskey.

"You know what he said isn't true. He's an idiot. A drunk idiot," said Talan, slipping out of his shoes.

Sarah leaned back in her chair, her feet propped on the desk, sock-covered toes wiggling. The minute they entered the room, her boots and jacket were shrugged off, and the heat cranked up, making for a toasty environment. "Which part?"

He paused before putting his shoes by his bed. "All of it."

She nodded thoughtfully, fluttering a glance in his direction before turning it back to the wall. "What role do you think his sister plays?" Forehead scrunching, she replayed everything that happened.

"Maybe we should go back and ask him?" quipped Talan, sitting on the ledge of the desk.

She rolled her eyes, ignoring his sarcasm.

He shrugged. "What's the place called in America?" he asked, furrowing his brows in thought. "Alabama!" he said suddenly, leaning back and crossing his arms. "What if he's into that purest thing?"

Taking a deep breath, Sarah let it out through her nose, calming the desire to knock him off his perch.

Standing, hands held up in defence, he strolled towards the bathroom. "Maybe he dabbles in American reality TV. That's all I'm saying."

He kicked the door shut, and she could hear the water turn on. Shaking her head, she pinched the bridge of her nose. Nothing made sense anymore, she felt like she was losing control of the tether on her life.

Talan's off-key singing filled their room, and she huffed a laugh, eyeing the bathroom. With a sudden thought that made her reel with quiet laughter, she snuck over to the door with a coy smirk. She could hear his words get garbled, and she took the opportunity to open the door.

His singing drowned out any creak of the door, thankfully, the hotel kept their hinges well-oiled, and she slipped in silently. He was her prey, and her eyes lit up, seeing the silhouette of his body in the shower curtain.

She had to stifle her laughter, creeping closer. Without thinking, she reached forward and flushed the toilet.

A second later, Talan's yell filled the space, and before she could move, he jumped away from the scalding water, falling through the shower curtain.

Startled, she scrambled out of the way, laughing hysterically when he landed in a tangled heap at her feet.

Suds covered half of his chest, and he looked up at her, growling in warning.

Grinning, she leaned over him, saying sweetly. "Turnabout is fair play."

He lunged for her, and she darted out of reach with a laugh. Her eyes travelled down the rugged ridges of his sculpted body, where muscle cut a path directly to the apex of his waist. Sarah's laugh faded, and the air in her lungs shuddered out of her. He had been naked in the mountain, but she had been too busy to look or think about anything else.

Realising what she was staring at, she snapped her gaze back to his and found them glowing in awareness. This was a different predatory gaze, the kind that was filled with a heat that made her toes curl intrinsically. The pull between them she had noted tugging at her insides. She was acting irrationally around this male.

Giving him a slight smirk, she said, "I thought it would be bigger, being your favourite and all."

She tried to keep her breathing even as she sauntered out of the bathroom. The room suddenly stifling,

Talan's growl followed behind her, and she could hear him shoving off the curtain. Before she could make it to the side of her bed, his hand snaked around her waist, pulling her flush against his damp and very naked body. His other hand wrapped around her neck, fingers curling over her jaw.

"That wasn't very nice, Princess," he whispered.

Sarah's heart thundered in her chest, and her nipples hardened against her bra, the fabric abrasive against her suddenly flushed skin. Clenching her teeth together, she made to turn her head, but he kept her pinned in place. His muscles flexed against her with his own restraint.

Using his nose to brush her hair out of the way, he skimmed a path along her neck. His hot breath brushed over her skin, and she squeezed her legs together, trying to ignore the heat building in her core.

"Don't play games you won't win," she gritted.

His low chuckle reverberated through her back, and she pressed against it without realising until his arms tightened around her.

"I didn't think it was fair that you didn't get a proper look, Princess." His tongue flicked against the flesh behind her ear, and her body jerked in response. "I think you were curious. I think you wanted a little peek," he murmured, nudging them closer to the bed until the fronts of her knees bumped the edge.

Her breasts tightened at those words, and she tried to shake her head. At him, at herself, she didn't know. "You're so full of it," she retorted, a little breathless.

"Hmm," he hummed. "Am I, though? I can smell how wet you are."

He flipped her around to face him, his gold eyes darkening with need, nostrils flaring as he took in her body's betrayal. Talan's arm banded around her back, the other hand sliding into her loose hair, careful of her bruises and cuts. "Why did you come into the bathroom, Princess?"

Sarah made to answer, but she fixated on a bead of water that cut a path down his large chest, over his nipple, and she licked her lips, eyeing it.

Talan growled again, watching her tongue flick against her bottom lip.

His cock pressed against her belly, and Sarah swallowed the sudden flash of fire that engulfed her lips and threatened to consume her. Her breathing turned shallow as her eyes travelled up to his, and her knees nearly buckled at the heat she found in them, forced to press herself against his hard body for support.

His hand moved from her hair to cup her cheek, stroking the marked flesh gently. Bending his head, his lips dipped to her's—

A bang from outside jolted Sarah enough for her to step out of his hold, that cord between them dimming somewhat, licking her lips. Gathering herself, she gave him a look. "Go dry off. Otherwise, you'll smell like a wet dog. And I don't think I can sleep with that." But that was the furthest thing from the truth. He smelled edible. She could smell his intoxicating musk rolling off him, but she took another step back, crossing her arms.

Talan gave her his signature annoying crooked smile and took a step back, his cock still rock hard. She didn't dare look at it.

She didn't relax until the bathroom door clicked shut, and she let out the breath she was holding. Her core pulsated with need, and she had to squeeze her legs together, running a hand through her hair.

What the hell was happening to her?

"Fuck."

CHAPTER 18

Avian's shoes tapped on the stone floors, the sound reverberating in the hall. The lights flickered to life overhead one by one as he passed under them. One cell, another, another and another until he stopped.

A small whimper came from beyond the iron bars, and with a push of his magic, the wood door swung open.

The light from behind him pooled into the dark cell, falling on the small boy, Alec, who lay huddled on his side. Knees to his chest, his arms wrapped tight around them. Reign had given the boy a long-sleeved shirt to wear before his departure, and it swallowed his small limbs whole.

His sobs made Avian's brow twitch, the only indication of emotion on his otherwise cold face.

"Now, now," he cooed lowly, tilting his head in observation.

Alec's whole body jerked at his voice, and Avian watched his arms tighten around his knees, head buried between them and the neck of the massive shirt.

"Afraid, are we?"

The sobbing ceased, and Alec's body went still.

"Ah, the little pup doesn't like that?"

Tear-filled pale amber eyes glared up at Avian as Alec unfurled himself.

Avian's mouth tilted in a faint smile, eyes narrowing.

"I'm not afraid," Alec said, brows furrowing.

"I'm sure you're not." Avian frowned, stalking forward. His hand latched onto Alec's hair, and the boy's yell pierced the empty hall behind him. Thrashing in the air as Avian lifted him from the ground, his eyes turning black. "But I can change that."

Tears streamed down Alec's cheeks, eyes wide with fear. "My sis-sister will come for me!"

Avian's answering smile gleamed white in the shadows. "I know." His head tilted, and he brought his nose to the boy's hair, sniffing.

His grip on Alec vanished, and the boy fell to the ground with a yelp that turned into a whimper.

Sniffling, Alec tried to crawl away from the male, who placed his foot on the boy's back and halted him with a disapproving tut. Leaning forward, his hand lashed around the boy's chin, forcing him to turn and face him.

"Let us see what *he* is hiding," he hissed, nostrils flaring as he breathed in Alec's scent again.

The terror in Alec's eyes gave way to the emotions rolling within him despite the answering snarl he let out.

Black eyes staring into amber ones, Avian dragged a claw down Alec's face, watching the shadows transfer from him to the boy and whorl on his skin, and Alec's eyes rolled back.

Avian was sucked into Alec's memories, images wavering like murky pictures. Something bitter covered his tongue as he sifted through the frayed remnants of what was truth and what was a lie. That bitterness stood as a towering veil around a bundle of memories. Avian raised a cool brow, brushing aside the lies he had been sifting through.

Cracks in the veil shimmered and wavered in the fragments of the boy's mind, and it shattered easily under Avian's powers, falling away like shards of glass.

Blinding light tore through the boy's mind, and Avian had to shield his eyes as it cleared.

Walking into the protected memories, Avian's smile cut into a murderous grin. Familiar brown eyes and dark blonde hair wavered in the images around him as the person walked through a cave, blood pooling at Avian's feet and fading gold eyes staring up into a void.

"I see," Avian whispered darkly, glancing at the bundle that lay wailing, ruddy face blotchy and covered in snot as it screamed.

The person stooped to pick up the child.

Avian glanced at the male, who paid him no mind as he walked to the mouth of the cave and then to the mop of dirty blond curls and thrashing tiny limbs held in the male's vice grip. The male who looked nothing like the one writing to him, the one who gave him the boy to do as he pleased, but rather the one he had been searching for. Hidden in plain sight.

A soft chuckle emanated from Avian, and he released the hold on the boy's mind.

Blinking into the darkness, Avian let go of the boy's chin as he came back to reality, stepping away from the now unconscious child.

Avian's words echoed within the silence, "Eight days, *Sar-ah.* Eight days, and then the truth is set free."

The cell door slammed shut as he walked out, leaving the boy strewn on the stone floor, unkempt glee turning up his heinous stare.

CHAPTER 19

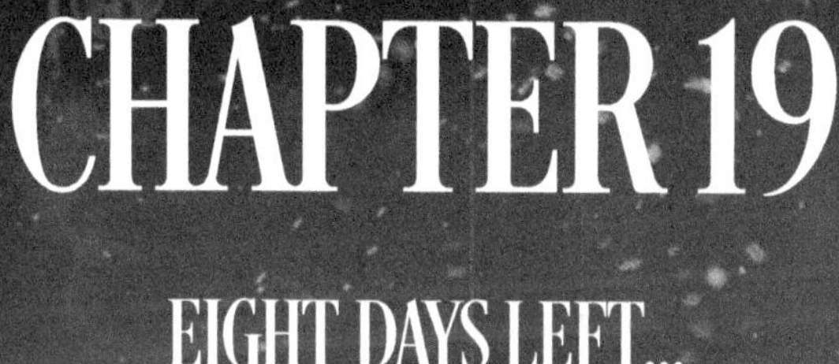

EIGHT DAYS LEFT...

Sarah reigned in her irritation as she glanced at the male on her right. His smug face stared straight ahead, watching the passengers board the plane.

"Was this necessary?" she drawled, fastening her seatbelt.

Reign blinked, sliding her a slow look. "Everything I do is necessary."

"I find that hard to believe," she said with a snort.

Sarah found the back of Talan's head peeking over his middle seat, two rows ahead of where they sat towards the back of the plane. A mother with her infant sat beside him in the aisle seat, and Sarah's lips quirked. Her mirth died when she caught Reign's equally amused expression.

"You planned this?" she drawled, giving the male a flat stare.

"Maybe," he said, clicking his seatbelt into place and fidgeting in his too-small aisle seat.

She snorted, watching him try to get comfortable. "Problem?"

He growled a low, frustrated warning meant only for her ears.

Sarah rolled her eyes. Fae males were the biggest prima-donnas she had met.

"Down, sweetheart," she said with honey and venom dripping from her voice. "Don't get your leash in a twist."

Reign's brows shot up. "Leash?"

"The one your master has you on. Do you also do tricks? Or is it only for him?" she asked, leaning on the armrest to her left and picking at her nails.

"Watch it, *sweetheart*, or you might find yourself on a leash."

That made Sarah laugh. "Get in line. I already have a ripcord around my neck."

There was silence, and Sarah stuffed her hands into her jacket pockets, feeling the comforting press of her gun against her ribs. She had refused to go without it, and more importantly, she had refused to go naked with the enemy into territory unknown to her. So, when she walked through the body scanner, it magically broke, courtesy of the male beside her.

The agent's frustration at their broken machine had her waved through, waiting for Reign and Talan while they were made to go to a different line with everyone else.

Talan had grumbled about having to be pat-searched, and Reign's smug smirk was enough to know he was responsible for it.

"So... do you call him master? The one holding your leash that is."

She glowered at him. "Do *you*?"

Reign huffed softly, watching people settle in their seats. His voice was low, so only she could hear. "Avian is an interesting character."

"Let me guess: he's not as bad once you get to know him?" she said snidely.

Something dark flashed in his eyes when he stared at Sarah, the depths of brown holding his secrets.

"No," he said quietly after a moment. "He is much worse."

Sarah held his gaze unblinking before Reign turned away.

"Then does that make you a monster or the monster's pet?"

"I may be a monster, but I am no one's pet."

She looked at the male beside her, really looked at him, and saw the strain at the corners of his eyes, the throb of a pulse in his temple, and the slight downturn of his mouth—all the things he concealed behind a cold smirk and narrowed gaze.

He had secrets, and she wanted to know what they were.

"Why did Avian send you with us?"

"Avian likes to protect his investments, and you just so happen to be on the hunt for his biggest one."

"His sister?"

Reign nodded.

"Why doesn't he just go get her himself?"

"Because he doesn't know where she is."

"Why?"

"Because she was kidnapped."

Those words made her pause, thinking of the little girl she saw in her dreams. The blood, her screams, and her parents torn apart at her feet. She could still feel the warm pool of their blood seeping between her toes. But it hadn't been *her*. It had been Saskia.

"What makes him think I can find her?" she asked after a moment.

Reign tilted his head, looking at her thoughtfully. "You're not the first hunter he's made to search for her."

"What happened to the others?"

He gave her a pointed look.

Dead.

Just like she'll be if she doesn't fulfil their deal. The Fae bargain would see to that.

"And he's sent you to babysit all of them?" she said snidely.

The captain came on over the intercom, and Sarah tuned him out when Reign said, "I volunteered."

"I feel so special," she spat with a roll of her eyes.

Reign shook his head. "He told me to come, but Avian wouldn't force me if I didn't want to."

Looking him up and down, she asked dryly, "Let me guess, he also doesn't force you in bed, but you tell him it's okay because you secretly love being a bottom and giving over control."

The plane jerked as it began moving.

Reign's smile could cut air, and he leaned in, saying softly, "You're testing my patience."

"It's my speciality."

His nose twitched, and he leaned back, laughing lowly to himself.

She pulled her hair from its ponytail with a huff, combing her fingers through it before settling into her seat.

Reign's body tensed beside her, and she could see him turn to stare at her from the corner of her eye. She glanced at him.

"What?" she snapped.

He leaned forward as she leaned away, but her armrest dug into the wounds on her back, and she winced.

Reign's face was only inches from hers, and he sniffed the air.

Her cheeks turned scarlet, annoyance bubbling beneath the surface again, and she had to gather every ounce of her control not to jab her fist into his nose.

"You better have a good reason for that," she hissed, her gaze throwing daggers at him.

His body was still ridged when he leaned away. His eyes were clouded in emotions he kept well concealed but now stormed his features.

"You're scentless," he all but whispered.

She rolled her eyes. That was it?

"So, I've been told," she said, turning away.

"Why?" he demanded.

She raised a brow, cocking her head at his sharp tone. He was toeing the line of her control.

"I don't know, why don't you ask him?" she said, jerking her head in Talan's direction.

Reign grabbed her shoulder, making her look at him. She slapped his hand away, earning them a look from the middle-aged man in the row across from them.

"Avian said your blood spoke lies…"

At the mention of Avian, Sarah's control snapped, plane be damned, and she reached for one of her knives… they weren't there. They were at the basin of the mountain, and she wanted to scream in frustration. The whole hunt had gone wrong, and it just kept spiralling out of control, out of her control, and she wanted to punch something.

Instead, she regained the leash on her temper and said, "Yeah? Want a taste?" Her tone held nothing but contempt.

His canines elongated, and he smiled, licking his tongue over their sharp tips. "Are you offering?"

Sarah jerked back in disgust, her lip curling. "Blood-sucking bastard." She didn't know their teeth could do that. That was new.

Reign barked out a laugh, his eyes lighting in amusement as he leaned back into his seat, his shoulders relaxing.

"Take a nap. Apparently, eight hours wasn't enough to make you less of a pain in my ass."

That was the issue, though, wasn't it? She hadn't slept at all, not with Talan snoring in the bed next to hers, not after what had happened between them, and certainly not with the thoughts of Alec on her mind. Her conscience bounced back and forth between the two males, and then the desire to kill the red-haired male in the room beside theirs and the restraint it took to keep from going over there and doing exactly that.

No. Sarah hadn't slept at all. She was exhausted. The Fae could withstand hours, days, and even weeks of sleep loss, but she could not. She was human, and she wanted to slip into a sleep-filled abyss and face everything with a clear head, but she couldn't, and so she had to refrain from broad daylight murder of the male beside her.

"I could give you a real pain in your ass if you like?" she snarked.

Reign's white teeth flashed at her. "If you can get a hit in, I won't talk the rest of the flight."

Sarah's hand shot out with a quick jab. A shot that anyone else would have taken to the nose, but Reign's Fae reflexes surpassed her own and caught her punch mid-strike.

She growled in anger.

"That's okay, one day… maybe."

She glared daggers at him and yanked her hand back. Sliding down into her seat and crossing her arms, she simmered silently.

The cabin's air conditioning turned on, and the rush of cool air made Sarah shiver despite her coat.

The air turned warm around her, wrapping around her like a blanket, and she stopped shivering. Her muscles relaxed with a tired sigh.

Gritting her teeth, she sighed, too tired now to fight. "Thank you," she said begrudgingly.

Sleep was edging around her mind, and she could feel the fog settle within her. That welcoming abyss.

Reign only chuckled softly, and she watched him pull the safety pamphlet out and begin reading it as she slipped into the darkness.

"Was that necessary?"

Talan's annoyance was clear as day on his face when they walked from the terminal.

"You had an open seat but stuffed me between a baby and an oversized man who smelled like piss and old potatoes."

"Someone had to buffer the baby from the piss," Reign commented coolly, stuffing one hand in his front pocket as he walked.

"Asshole," Talan seethed.

Sarah was still blinking the sleep from her eyes, feeling like she had slept for a year, sandwiched between the two males.

"I do have one," Reign replied dryly.

Talan made a sound of disgust, and Sarah arched a brow at the both of them. She wasn't awake enough for this. "Will you both shut up?"

Reign snorted under his breath while Talan growled at the male in response, but neither said anything.

The airport was stifling, making Sarah's skin itch, and she breathed deeply when they pressed through the doors to the pickup location. Despite the blaring taxi horns and the chaotic rush of Fae and humans looking for a ride, Sarah stilled her mind. Closing her eyes, she breathed through her nose, inhaling the spring air and fumes of the city around her.

Feeling more grounded than she had when landing, she opened her eyes, and found both males looking at her, waiting. She pursed her lips. "What?"

"You ready, Princess?"

Reign shot him a look from the corner of his eye. "She's not a princess."

Irritation flashed over Talan's face, and he turned a dark stare to Sarah. "I'm going to break his neck if you don't first."

Sarah sighed, rolling her eyes and shoving between them to hail a taxi. "Good fucking luck with that, Puppy."

Reign sniggered, and she looked over her shoulder at him, silencing him with a glare. "Same goes for you, Blood Sucker."

A white and black taxi pulled up, a blue light on the side mirror indicating it was auto-piloted. Sarah slipped into the seat behind the empty driver's side, hearing Talan mutter about having to sit in the middle again. His long legs were glued together and nearly folded in half in the tiny compact car.

The two males bickered like children, albeit quietly, or maybe she was tuning them out. Sarah couldn't tell the difference as she stared out the window, her finger tapping restlessly on her leg as emotions she couldn't decipher tunnelled in her gut.

An AI-generated female voice asked where they were going in German and then again in English.

"Álfheimr Towers," Sarah replied in German.

CHAPTER 20

Talan let out a low whistle. "That's impressive, even to me."

Frowning slightly, Sarah studied the gold twining pillars framing the circulating glass door. They were carved into large gleaming trees, their branches tangling together over the entrance and glass wall that allowed them to peek into the white marble foyer. Álfheimr Towers stood out in Frankfurt, the city of technological advancements, and modern silver and all-glass high rises co-mingling with Baroque and Gothic architecture.

Álfheimr Towers was gold, glass, and gleaming in the overhead spring sun that peaked through storm clouds, the smell of rain lingering in the air.

Sarah tilted her head, attempting to glimpse the top of the tower.

Cars honked relentlessly behind them, the city street bustling as pedestrians flowed from every direction, neon lights glimmering from storefronts. Tires screeched on the pavement, and drivers yelled at one another in German. Sarah blinked, pulled from her thoughts, and looked away from the top of the tower, turning a critical eye on the revolving door.

"You ready?" Talan murmured to her left.

"She doesn't really have a choice, *Puppy*," Reign intoned dryly.

Sarah held up a finger when Talan made to snap a reply. "One," she said to Talan, "Yes. And two," she turned a cutting smile to Reign, "Only *I* can call him Puppy. *You* can call him Talan."

Talan gave her a small, amused smile, his amber eyes roving over her face when she turned to look at him. He showed no sign of objection, and she looked at Reign, who stared at her curiously.

The Fae male was a closed book, and Sarah couldn't pinpoint the thoughts behind his dark brown eyes. He was pretty in the golden light that reflected off the tower, with his close-cropped dark red hair and princely Fae face. His casual yet confident stance alluded to the power hiding within him.

Reign only arched a brow at her.

Rolling her eyes, Sarah stalked towards the tower, hand outstretched to the slowly spinning glass.

The foyer was all white marble, from floor to towering ceiling, which travelled up and up and up in a hollow centre through the entire tower. Gold veins ran through it like little lifelines.

Sarah's brows shot to her hairline. She stared up at the hollow centre of the tower, barely seeing the glass top and sky beyond.

A security checkpoint to get beyond the white marble front desk stopped them, and Sarah sighed silently when an Orc male, filled her vision. All towering seven feet, bulky muscle, and dark green skin of him. Two small tusks protruded from his lower jaw and curled across his upper lip, black eyes looked between the three of them. He crossed his arms over his barrel chest, bare biceps larger than her head flexing.

"Can I just knock them all out?" Reign asked casually.

Sarah noted him eyeing the Orc from his black boots to the all-black security uniform he wore, a gold Álfheimr Towers crest on his left shoulder of a crossed sword and branch, and then the pretty blonde Fae female who stood from her desk watching them, waiting dressed in all black business attire, a similar gold crest on the left side of her blouse.

"Touch them, and I'll knock you out," she replied as equally casual.

"Do you have an appointment?" the Orc asked, his baritone voice echoing in the marble foyer.

Her finger started tapping softly on her thigh, deciding how to reply. She could see this going one of two ways:

1. She answers honestly; they get told to leave, and they leave quietly.

2. She answers honestly, tries to fight their way through, and sacrifices Talan and Reign as she runs for the shiny gold elevators just behind the Orc.

She was leaning more towards option two.

"I will kick your ass, Princess, if you try to run for it."

Sarah snorted, rolling her gaze to Talan. He was staring at her pointedly, studying her. "You've tried that already."

"Sarah," Talan warned.

Her mind nudged painfully when he said her name, but she pressed it down, ignoring it.

"Appointment?" rumbled the Orc at the same time. When they didn't answer, the Orc huffed in annoyance, pointing a large, green, beefy finger beyond them. "Leave. No appointment, no entrance."

Reign chuckled on her right, and Sarah closed her eyes, letting out a deep breath. "*Fine.*"

"Fantastic," Reign drawled darkly.

"What is he—"

The air pressed around them tightly, cutting off Talan's words. Reign stepped up to the Orc; even at his towering height, the male had to look up at the Orc.

Black eyes flashed with a warning, and a large green hand pressed against Reign's chest, pushing him back, but the male didn't budge.

A cutting smile carved his face, and Reign leaned against the hand. "You're an ugly son of a bitch."

The Orc roared in annoyance, lunging for Reign.

Moving faster than Sarah could comprehend, Reign stepped to the side, sending the Orc stumbling forward. The air pressed around them tighter, but a bitterness broke through it when Reign tilted his head, and Sarah shivered, watching the Orc pause, hand going to his chest.

The Fae female at the desk squeaked with surprise, eyes going wide, and Sarah watched her brown eyes roll back, before she collapsed just as the Orc did the same. The ground shook when his colossal frame hit the ground.

Sarah shook the creeping feeling off her limbs when the air pressing around them vanished. Eyeballing the Orc and the now empty space behind the desk, she rounded a glare on the auburn-haired male.

Reign shot her placating smile. "They're not dead. I merely stole the breath from their lungs… temporarily." Casually stepping over the legs of the Orc, he tucked a hand into his black jeans pocket and walked through the security checkpoint.

"Great," Talan muttered, "There's two of them."

Shaking her head, Sarah jerked her chin at Talan to follow, and she stalked behind Reign, her annoyance beginning to peak.

"I could kill them if you like?" Reign commented casually as they waited on the elevators.

"I say the same thing to myself about you," Sarah snipped with a tight smile.

The elevators dinged, and they filed in. Soft music played, out of touch with the Fae, the hunter, and the shifter who occupied the all-glass interior of the lift.

Sarah noted her reflection and winced internally. Her cheek was on the mend, her cracked lip healing, but there was a tiredness in her brown eyes—a weariness with an undercurrent of frustration within. Smoothing a hand over her high ponytail, her brown hair lacked life compared to the males she stood beside. Her cheekbones were a little too sharp for her round face, her mouth a little too firm, her chin a little too small, and her eyes a little too big. Everything about her was a little *too* much of one thing or another.

She wasn't plain, she wasn't pretty, she was just… a little too much, or not enough. The males framing her left and right were too pretty—too handsome, for their own good.

Reign and Talan nearly stood shoulder to shoulder in height, Reign an inch taller than him. The Fae male had the princely features of the Fae. Oval face framed by strong dark brows, high cheekbones, full firm mouth, and a narrow, strong jaw. His figure was lean, muscular, and entirely at ease, confidence rolling off him in waves almost arrogantly.

But where Reign was pretty like the Fae, Talan was rugged like the mountains.

Dark chocolate brown hair fell messy across his brows in thick waves. Sarah watched him comb a hand through it, musing the strands even more. Amber eyes caught her brown ones in the reflection, and they stared at each other silently. She knew those eyes turned golden when he wanted to shift or when his emotions rose to the surface; she had been subject to their change.

Breaking his gaze, she let her eyes wander over his face. He had a straight nose, black lashes framing his eyes, high cheekbones, a full teasing mouth, and a strong square jaw. Where Reign was lean, Talan was muscled. Large shoulders and biceps strained the grey henley he wore, fitted across a large chest and loose around his narrow waist. Her eyes travelled down and down to the black jeans. Memories of the imprint of his naked body pressed against her back made heat fill her stomach.

Her eyes snapped back to Talan's, finding them dark and questioning, like he was questioning himself rather than her.

"If you two are going to fuck, please wait until I leave."

Reign's dry tone made her eyes snap to his dark ones in the mirror.

Before she could reply, the elevators opened to the fiftieth floor.

Talan let out a low whistle. "Shit."

Shit was right. Sarah's mouth dropped just a little, taking in the massive white marble and gold foyer, the glass pyramid roof towering over them, acting like a prism as a rainbow wavered across the white floors.

White marble floors were webbed in the same streams of gold that flowed from four gold trees, one in each corner of the room like strong pillars. Their branches crowned the arching ceiling and stopped at the base of the glass. In the centre of the foyer was the gold crest of Álfheimr Towers.

Two large, duelling dark wood doors with gold handles opened, and a slim Fae female with copper hair and doe green eyes appeared. She wore a black pencil skirt and a black blouse with the emblem. Her black stilettos clicked softly on the marble, and she smiled at the three of them.

"Please follow me," the female said in a gentle voice.

The three of them didn't move.

Amusement flared in those large green eyes. "He's waiting for you in the conference room."

"Who?" Sarah asked, eyeing the female and the foyer.

"The King."

"After you, Princess," Talan muttered.

"Funny," Sarah snarked. But she followed first, eyeing the female cautiously as she turned on her heels and walked back to the door she had come through.

The three of them slipped into a long hall, several dark wood doors lining each side. The female held the one at the end on the right open.

Sarah stopped, eyeing the female before she went in.

Noting her hesitation, the female smiled kindly and waved an open hand to the door. "They're waiting for you," she said.

The conference room was more extensive than Sarah anticipated, brows shooting to her hairline. A long wall of floor-to-ceiling windows overlooked the city, white marble floors and walls, and a long circular dark wood desk sat in the middle, with black leather chairs around it. A large wingback leather chair sat at one end, and in it was the king of the Fae. But he wasn't alone as he studied a tablet in front of him, a hologram hovering above it. A stunning female with a mane of long, wild copper curls stood to his right, pointing to something on the tablet.

When they entered, two sets of eyes snapped up to them. One was dark blue like the ocean, and the other like living fire.

The female straightened, her eyes widening.

Sarah tilted her head, eyeing them. "If you expect us to bow, you're going to be shit out of luck."

CHAPTER 21

"Sit."

With a wave of his hand, three chairs pulled out, and Sarah flicked her gaze from them to the Fae king. His dark ocean-blue eyes watched her curiously, and she couldn't tell where that curiosity stemmed from.

"Are we sitting, or are we going?" Talan murmured.

Eyes bouncing between the male and the female Fae—no, that wasn't right. The female wasn't Fae, her ears lacking the delicate points that the Fae King had. Her gaze dropped to the chairs, hesitating. The tattoo around her forearm constricted, small thorns of her bargain digging into her flesh, making the decision for her.

Pulling out the chair in the middle, she sat, leaning back casually as Talan sat on her left and Reign on her right.

"What an interesting dynamic," the king commented. His eyes went to each of them, studying their faces. "A Fae, a human, and a shifter."

"It's like the start of a bad joke," muttered Talan.

The king ignored him, his eyes fixed on Sarah. She stared right back into the depthless blue. He was pretty, like Reign, but in the way the old Fae were pretty. Unearthly beauty, with blue-black hair, cropped short and coifed to the side, high angled cheekbones, a firm brow and a strong, narrow jaw. While relaxed and lean, his posture had an air of danger. His three-piece all-black ensemble straining against the muscle underlying, the cuffs of his black dress shirt rolled halfway up his forearms.

"Would you like to explain to me why you found it necessary to suffocate my security guard and receptionist, who are now being treated by my medical staff?" His words were casual, but there was warning beneath them.

Sarah cocked her head, not helping the tight smile on her face. "I believe it's called *making an entrance?*"

"Medical care was unnecessary. I only rendered them unconscious," Reign added unbothered, leaning back comfortably in his seat.

"Reign, what a pleasure, as always." From the king's tone, Sarah doubted it was a pleasure, and she slid the male to her right a questioning glare.

Reign tipped his chin at the king. "Savven, always a pleasure."

"I take it you two know each other?" Sarah drolled.

"Reign brings a human hunter, as I assume you are, to me for the last few years. How is your *master*? Has he found what he's lost yet?"

Reign's jaw tightened, the only indication of his dislike. "Not yet. But he's hopeful with this one. As am I."

"Hmm," the king, Savven, hummed, eyes sliding to Sarah. "Do you know why they bring the hunters to me?"

Reign's sigh was audible, and Sarah looked at him as he looked at her, something *almost* like hope glimmering behind his dark eyes.

"Why?" she asked, still looking at Reign, whose hope grew

noticeably. Weirded out by his reaction to the question, she looked at the king.

"Because Brean is a witch and can track lost things. So, he sends the hunters with Reign to her to try and find his lost thing so they may bring it back to him; in return, he stays far, far away from my city."

"And none have been able to find her? His lost sister."

"No, and I'm not partial to helping Avian anyway, but I do so for the sake of my city."

"Sarah…"

Sarah shifted in her seat, feeling Talan's gaze burning a hole in her head when he whispered her name. "And who's Brean?"

"I am."

Four sets of eyes turned to the pretty ginger standing beside the king. She was petite, with lovely features that looked both fearless and stubborn. Her fair skin was covered in a map of freckles, and a small nose and full mouth were offset by large amber eyes that looked like fire. Her mane of wild copper curls hung down her back, her slim figure dressed in a cream blouse with long gossamer sleeves cinched at her wrists, a dark brown fitted vest that hugged the curve of her breasts and narrow waist, and long wide-leg trousers that were accented with a small gold chain clipped to a brown belt with gold buckle.

"I am Brean." The witch took in a silent, steadying breath, the king placing a gentle hand on her forearm. Their eyes connected briefly, and Sarah watched the king's face soften at the witch.

Amber eyes locked on Sarah, sharp and unfaltering, and her gut coiled tightly with anticipation. She didn't know why, but there was something familiar about the witch. It felt like trying to remember a dream after waking. But now, as they stared at one another, her gut curled tighter and tighter.

"Hello, Sarah. I've been waiting for you."

A couple things happened at once when those words left the

witch's mouth. Talan rounded on Sarah, confusion marking his handsome face. Reign let out a deep breath, and pain split through her head like an axe.

Everything around her ceased to exist, her ears ringing as the pain lanced through her again, and she bowed forward. Fingers clenching into fists, Sarah willed herself to control the pain, to breathe through it, to own it so it didn't own her.

A gentle hand touched her back, and she jerked away from the touch, snarling at the intrusion through her pain.

"Sarah," said the intruder.

Her head *throbbed* uncontrollably at her name, sweat dotting her temples, and every muscle in her body clenched painfully.

"*Sa-rah.*"

Her name sounded like it had been whispered on the wind down a long tunnel, and she squeezed her eyes shut as her name resounded through her skull like a cudgel.

"Sar—"

"—Don't!" she managed to spit out.

Everything went quiet, and seconds ticked by endlessly until finally, the tension in her head slowly ebbed into nothingness, and she was left with the aftermath of its destruction. Her body trembled violently, her muscles turning to lead as the claws of pain retracted, sweat coating her hairline.

Gritting her jaw, Sarah forced air in through her nostrils, expanding her lungs. Again and again, until her fingers unfurled, half-moon crescents bitten into her palms.

"If anyone," she rasped, her vocal cords feeling like she had been screaming as the words grated against them, "says my name, I will *gut* them."

She could feel a hand hovering over her back like it was hesitant to touch her again. That was wise. She wouldn't recommend touching her right now.

"I see it's still in place," said Brean behind her.

Sarah turned to see the witch retract her hand to her side. She was watching her with those amber eyes. Pain, resignation, and… guilt lay in their fiery depths. "*What* is still in place?"

Everyone except her and the witch faded into the background

as they stared at one another. Sarah could see the words lingering on Brean's tongue; inner conflict raged in her face. Standing, she heard the males around her stand, too, but she ignored them. She faced off with the witch.

"What is still in place, Witch?" she repeated slowly, looking down at the female who stood a head shorter.

Notching her chin a fraction, Brean narrowed her eyes but didn't waver as she said, "The magic I placed around your mind fourteen years ago."

CHAPTER 22

"Did they really just kick us out?" Talan asked with a scoff, eyeing the conference room door.

Reign arched a look at him. "Feel like you're missing out on the fun?"

Talan pursed his mouth, walking down the hall. "I just don't like leaving her alone."

"I have a feeling she can take care of herself."

He shook his head, combing a hand through his hair. "It's not that. It's just… different. It *feels* wrong. I can't explain it." His stomach twisted with unease the further he walked away. It made the wolf in him tense, and he rolled his shoulders back, trying to offset the feeling.

"My secretary will show you to your rooms," the king said

casually, walking ahead and opening the large duelling doors into the foyer.

Reign and Talan both stopped.

"You *live* here too?" Talan asked, sceptical.

The king paused through the doorway, arching a brow at them before sweeping a look down their bodies and back up. "Is that a problem?"

Shaking their heads, Talan muttered a quick *no*.

Nodding once, the king turned on his heels. "You have nothing to worry about. Sarah is in good hands. I trust no one like I trust Brean."

"That's nice for you, but I don't." Talan walked through the doors, passing the king, who held his stare.

The king framed the doorway, his posture impeccable, his chin notched just a hair to allude to his title. "You can take my word as king. No harm will come to her."

Talan smirked crookedly at him, stuffing a hand into his front pocket. "Forgive me when I say you're not my king and don't know you. So, your title means nothing to me."

Reign tensed beside him, and Talan forced himself to remain calm even when the faintest smile tugged on the king's lips.

"Fair enough, Shifter."

Those three words made Talan relax and ease a tight smile over his face. Just then, the same female from before with her large green eyes and copper hair walked in, her heels clacking on the floor.

"If you'll follow me?" the secretary said brightly with a smile.

"Shifter."

Talan paused, Reign passing him and following behind the female. He raised his brows at the king, whose face gave nothing away, but his eyes looked at him as if he were searching for something or someone. "It's Talan."

The king didn't so much as blink, instead curiously asking, "Is it true that after the fall you can only change into a wolf?"

Talan faced the king fully now, head tilted and hands in his pockets. "I wasn't there for the fall, but yes, I can only shift into a wolf. Why?"

The king shrugged, and Talan thought the action looked odd from the stoic male.

"Just curious. I haven't met any shifters since the fall. My brother was a shifter but wasn't limited by form."

"The Fae bloodline tainted by us dogs? Interesting." Talan scoffed, disbelieving.

"Not in blood but chosen," the king said darkly at Talan's blatant disrespect.

Talan jerked his chin and stepped back. "Well, lucky him."

As Talan reached Reign, he heard the king softly murmuring, "He's dead." Talan turned around, but the king was gone.

The city below was a bustling, congested mess of smart cars and people. Sarah watched the pedestrians go about their lives as she stood in front of the wall of windows, blissfully unaware that someone was watching them from above. When she looked up, her reflection caught her, frowning. Her eyes drifted to a set of amber eyes over her shoulder and the face of the witch behind her.

Sarah turned, eyeing the female. "You have one minute to explain yourself."

Brean leaned on the ledge of the conference desk behind her, her face resigned. "Give me five."

Stepping away from the window, Sarah waved a hand towards the witch, telling her to continue as she stalked away from the glass wall. Bracing her forearms on the back of the high-back leather chair the king had been sitting in, she had a clear view of the door, the window, and the witch—who was currently standing in the beam of sunlight, watching the world outside with a frown on her pretty face, her hair looking like a wildfire.

"You have to understand that what I had to do was not easy and did not come without a price," Brean started, sweeping a hand through her hair before turning to Sarah. "I wasn't always a witch. I was born in Scotland a very long time ago; my family was murdered, and the magic pulled me across the veil to protect me. It made me into this" –she held up a hand, emerald sparks of magic igniting between her fingers— "from there, I was raised by the High Fae before my caretaker was also taken from me. Death is a fickle… I dare not call her a friend but a companion throughout my life. So, when I found a new family, and they were also taken from me, I took the chance to bring one of them back, so long as I did something in return for Death." Brean sucked in a deep breath, closing her eyes briefly as if she were seeing the events unfold in her mind.

"That was your first mistake, bargaining with Death," Sarah drolled.

Brean's eyes snapped open, flashing emerald, and the seat Sarah was leaning on jerked so violently it made her stumble back from the force. "It was not a mistake! I would do it over and over again for the time I've been gifted. You, of all people, should understand this!"

Power filled the room, and Sarah could feel the weight of the witch's magic pressing in on her, waiting.

"My family was murdered, but I didn't get another in their place," she snapped, gripping the back of the chair and shoving it back against the desk. But that was a lie, wasn't it? She had Alec. *He* was her family. The thought of him holed up in a cell right now made her see red and grit her jaw until her teeth groaned under the pressure.

"You do have someone," the witch murmured softly, the fire in her gaze lessening. "I can see it in your eyes."

Clearing thoughts of Alec from her mind, Sarah narrowed her eyes on the witch. She had to focus, for Alec's sake. "What deal did you strike with Death?"

"Life for life. They would bring me back, and in exchange, I would take care of something for them when it was presented to me. I exchanged myself for someone I love instead. A soul for a soul."

"Your life?"

Brean's shoulders sagged as if she had been bearing the weight of this secret for a very long time. "Yes."

"Who did you bring back?" Call her nosey, but Sarah had an

inkling she already knew who it was.

"That's none of your business," Brean remarked darkly.

Sarah arched a brow at her. "It was that king of yours, wasn't it?"

Brean's jaw flexed, and Sarah watched her leash her anger, but not before her eyes flashed like fire, promising to burn Sarah up if she spoke about the king again.

Suppressing her smirk, Sarah looked at her nails casually, still leaning against the king's seat. "You have two minutes left."

"She told me a child would be brought to me."

"*She?*"

"Death."

Sarah nodded thoughtfully. "I always knew Death was a vindictive bitch. All makes sense now."

Brean winced, glancing around the room as if Death heard her and was making sure she didn't pop up suddenly. "As I was saying," she muttered, rounding her attention back to Sarah. "She said there would be a child that would alter the course of history. Something about a prophecy, apparently." Brean rolled her eyes.

"And I was that child?"

"Yes and no. Many brought children to me to heal after the fall over the years, but you were the first child I was told to conceal entirely with magic."

Warning bells rang in Sarah's head, and she tilted her head. "How do you know I'm that same child?"

Brean's eyes swept over Sarah's face, studying her. "The air whispers secrets to me, and I feel my magic lingering all over you, like a film. But there's only one way to find out."

Ice went down her spine in trepidation, and Sarah pushed off the chair, backing up a step. "Times up." She didn't want to hear anymore. She wanted to go get Alec and return to the manor, bear her punishment for failing her mission and go about her life, or whatever would be left of it after Florin made his mark on her for her failures.

"Sarah."

She had started walking towards the door when the witch said her name and her head spiked with pain. "Do. Not. Speak. My. Name," she spit through gritted teeth, chest heaving as she controlled the wave of needle-like pressure across her skull.

"Have you ever wondered why you frequently get headaches? Why, every time you think of a certain name or event, pain comes with it." Brean walked around her to look her in the eye as Sarah tried to stand straighter. "That is because my magic was built into you to make you forget, to conceal you from the world. Your very identity lies within your name, so the magic makes you forget in hopes that the pain will be greater than the truth."

Amber eyes blazed earnestly, and Sarah cocked her head, staring down at the witch. "How do I know you're telling the truth?"

"You don't." Brean shrugged. "But what would I gain by lying to you when this marks the end for me?"

Her brows furrowed, and Sarah shot a questioning glance at the witch. Brean only shook her head in answer.

"So, what are you saying? You concealed my memories, why?"

"I concealed more than just your memories… and I don't know why it had to be done. You would be better asking that question to the one who brought you to me. I was only hired for my services," Brean said, taking a single step back as Sarah smoothed a hand down the front of her thermal, pulling on the hem of her jacket.

Sniffing, Sarah tightened her ponytail, glancing at the door briefly before returning to Brean. "Are you saying I'm not human?"

The witch opened her mouth when the door to the conference room opened, and the king stepped in.

Even Sarah had to admit the Fae King looked lethal and elegant in his slim black trousers, black dress shirt with rolled sleeves, and fitted black vest. Dark blue eyes swept over them, lingering on the witch, and Sarah wondered if something was going on between the two as they shared a look.

Sunlight filtered across his high cheekbones and angled jaw, highlighting the blue tone in his short, raven-black hair as he walked across the wall of windows. "Pardon the intrusion, but I need to have a word with my counterpart." He looked directly at Brean.

"Right," Sarah said slowly, stepping back. I'll be going then. Let me just go collect the bloodsucker and the puppy. Where did you put them?"

"I suppose they're comfortable in their rooms," remarked the king dryly. "Your room is also ready, my secretary will show you the way." As his words left his mouth, a soft knock came from the door, and the pretty redheaded Fae female appeared.

"Excuse me?" She was not planning on staying.

"The annual charity gala is tonight. You and your companions are welcome to attend. My secretary will bring appropriate attire to your rooms, as it is a black-tie event." The king finally looked at Sarah, his brow arching a hair. "Unless you would like to leave? But I assume there's still something you need from us. So, stay, drink, eat, dance… or don't. Be miserable if you wish, but as I stated, I need a word with Ms McKenzie." He waved a hand towards the door and his waiting secretary.

Sarah looked the king over from head to toe and back up. "Has anyone ever told you that you're insufferable?"

"Yes."

She smiled tightly at him. "Good. Just making sure."

Brean coughed into her hand, and at Sarah's glance, she quickly covered her smile.

Sarah gestured to the secretary as she walked out of the conference room, the door swinging closed with magic. "Lead the way."

CHAPTER 23

Talan stood outside Sarah's room, feeling antsy. He wanted to know what happened, but most of all, he just wanted to ensure she was okay. He groaned under his breath, combing his fingers through his tousled hair. He had been waiting in his room, listening for her arrival, and had heard her thank the secretary some time later. He waited ten minutes until he gave up and stalked across the hall to the door mirroring his.

The rooms were nice—unsurprisingly modern, with accents of dark wood, black marble instead of white, and gold veins running through the floor. A king-size bed pushed against a black marble wall with black silk sheets and matching black satin quilt; a sheet of windows overlooked the city, and a dark wood wardrobe took over more than half the wall across from his bed.

His small village and cabin paled in comparison, but he wouldn't give up his family home in the woods for a gilded high-rise, no matter how much they paid him. At the thought of his home, thoughts of his slain brothers infiltrated his mind, and a cold hand swept over him.

After everything they had been through in the last few days, he had nearly forgotten... no, he *had* forgotten why he was here for just a moment. But that was it, wasn't it? They die, and the world keeps moving; *he* keeps moving, their bodies turn to dust, and eventually, everyone forgets.

Guilt burrows in his chest, and his nostrils flare at the rush of emotion. He had forgotten them for a moment.

Before he could turn on his heels and stalk back into his room to hole up, Sarah's door swung open.

"Puppy," she commented, eyeing him. Sarah paused, eyes darting over his face before her lips pursed, and she stepped back, opening her door wider. "Come on, you look pathetic," she says.

He growled, wanting to snap at her comment, and he felt that if he did, she wouldn't bat an eyelash at him. She would weather his anger and guilt and not hold it against him because she knew—Sarah *knew* what he was feeling firsthand. He had seen the reminders on her body, the tally marks for every failure coating her like a second skin.

Her brown eyes were like melted milk chocolate, watching him openly with shuttered emotions. She wasn't candidly beautiful like some human women, though she wasn't ugly either. But it wasn't her physical appearance that made her pretty in his eyes. It was how her eyes looked to the sky when it rained, softening for just a moment, or the love and protectiveness when she looked at Alec. The dangerous smile and lethal glint in her eyes that graced her face when they first met. Or the soft, easy smile and laugh when they shared a beer; it was the first time he had seen her partially relax—if you could call it that. Her beauty wasn't born; it was created by her everyday little moments, and Talan wondered if she knew how stunning she truly was.

But instead of questioning her, he strolled into her room, whistling lowly. "They really outdid themselves with their gilded cage." Her room looked nearly identical to his, except everything was on opposite sides, the glimmering cityscape filling the long wall of windows.

"It's a bit much," she agreed, shutting the door.

Talan tracked her movements as she walked across the room. She shrugged out of her jacket and draped it over a small vanity built into the wardrobe, her eyes catching his in the mirror's reflection.

"What's wrong, Talan. You look like someone stole your favourite toy."

He let a wicked smile curl his lips as he said, "What if I said you're my favourite toy, Princess."

Sarah's reflection arched a brow at him. "I'd say bite me, but you might take it literally."

"I have a feeling you might enjoy it," he rumbled, chuckling lowly.

She rolled her eyes. "Whatever you say, Puppy."

Talan watched her slip out of her boots and pad over to the windows, watching the city. He could make out her faint reflection in the glass, seeing the conflict raging in those brown eyes. He couldn't help himself and walked up behind her, keeping a foot of space between them. This felt different compared to the hotel. They were both fully clothed and for some reason, *this* felt more intimate. He could feel his heart hammering behind his ribs. Stuffing his hands into his pockets to stop himself reaching for her, he just stood there, waiting.

"Tell me what's wrong," she murmured softly, head turning slightly so he could see her profile.

He shook his head, eyes trailing her exposed neck, stopping at the bruises marking her pale skin. "I'm okay, Princess. There's just a lot on my mind."

"There's a lot on everyone's mind." She turned around, the space between them narrowing.

His eyes swept over the bruises and the healing cuts. Something within him rumbled with a silent, deadly warning. He was going to *kill* the bastard for laying a hand on her. He was going to kill both of them—Avian *and* her master.

Sarah tilted her head, the movement pulling him from his thoughts. "If I can't protect Alec at this moment, then let me at least protect you."

Empathy instantly swept away his murderous thoughts, and he wanted to gather her into his arms and hold her. "Has anyone ever protected you?"

"No."

That one word made his body tense. His family protected him until they were taken. Then he took over that responsibility, but even so, he had his pack, his brothers… Sarah had no one.

"Let me," he said softly.

Their chests were nearly touching, her face turned up to him, and Talan had the briefest thought of how easy it would be to push her against the glass and kiss her. His heart nearly skittered to a stop, and he forced himself to breathe through the realisation that he *wanted* to kiss her. Sure, there was tension between them—a narrowing cord that tugged him to her. They bantered enough to make him want to say anything to provoke her and see the wicked glint in her eyes. But right now… right now, he wanted to pull her brown hair from its ponytail, comb his fingers through it, and kiss her until she couldn't sass him.

Talan watched her eyes drop to his mouth for a flicker of a moment before darting back to his gaze. He knew she could see it in his eyes, could see the desire, the heat causing his amber eyes to turn molten. He might not be able to scent her, but he could hear the hitch in her breath and see her eyes widen a fraction.

"Let me protect you," he murmured again, stepping an inch closer until their chests brushed with every breath.

Sarah's body tensed, and she arched her head back a hair to keep her gaze locked on his. But she didn't step back, and Talan took that as a win.

Her mouth ticked up into a shadow of a smile. "Aren't I usually the one saving you?"

"Maybe," he said, tilting his head. "But if you recall, I did save you from that monster in the gorge."

"And then I had to rescue you."

He chuckled at her dry tone. "Semantics." He dared to lift

a finger and brush it along her cheek, watching her closely. She didn't so much as flinch as he brushed the pad of his thumb over a bruise marking her left cheekbone. "Let someone take care of you for a change. Let me." He lowered his head a fraction, cupping the side of her face.

Sarah didn't move, but he could see her breath coming in faster as her breasts brushed his chest and her lips parted softly. He could see the flash of desire slip through her shuttered emotions, her body tensing, eyes flickering between his and his mouth as he lowered his head.

He knew she could feel it, too—the pull between them.

His lips were only a breath away when there was a loud knock at the door. He felt Sarah tense; the desire slipped away, and her emotions shuttered entirely. Talan dropped his hand and stepped back, giving her space despite everything in him commanding him to tell whoever was there to fuck off so they could resume.

But he didn't. Instead, he took a breath and walked over to Sarah's door, pulling it open with maybe a little bit too much aggression as the Fae female on the other side startled. She gave him a hesitant smile, and he frowned at her before noting the black garment bag in one hand and a clear bottle of purple liquid in the other.

"Your gown and a potion for your wounds, Miss," the female said quickly, holding the items for Sarah to see who was walking over in that familiar confident stride.

Talan shot her a look of regard, catching her guarded gaze for a second before he slipped around the female and disappeared into his room.

When the door was closed, he noted a similar black garment bag over his bed and scrubbed a hand over his face with a heavy sigh.

What the fuck was he doing?

Reign lay on his back on the oversized feather-top bed, arm

behind his head, staring up at the black marble ceiling, his eyes tracing the gold veins. He was still buzzing with the adrenaline that went through him when the witch said Sarah was concealed in magic. In that moment, he felt something so foreign to him that he had spent the last twenty minutes trying to identify it.

Hope.

That was the foreign emotion racing through him right now. Hope was a dangerous feeling, especially for someone in his position. He never thought there would come a day when he might have the opportunity to hope again. It was rarely found within the dark mountain, and it was not something Avian instilled.

At the thought of the Dark One, Reign's jaw clenched tightly. He had been by Avian's side for nearly fifteen years. A puppet to the puppet master.

Reign's lip curled back in a sneer. Little did Avian know, he had less of a puppet and more of a spy in his secluded castle.

Every time he had Reign capture a hunter snooping around the mountain, and even the few who made it within, Avian would make a bargain with them. Go to the Fae and seek the witch who finds the lost things, find his sister and bring her to him. Their days were numbered the minute they made the bargain. Reign had watched dozens of hunters fall to their deaths at his feet, not by his doing but by the magic that snuffed out the light in their eyes when the days finally ticked down to zero.

But with Sarah... Sarah had been different. Reign frowned, thinking of the moment within the castle. Avian had tasted her blood, and that's when Reign had first felt it. Small and hesitant, but it was there from that moment until now. Hope.

A knock at his door had him glancing at it. He flicked his fingers, and the door opened. The pretty female stood there holding a black garment bag.

"For you, Sir," she said, holding it up like an offering.

Reign didn't move from the bed, crossing his legs at the ankles, before he slid her a crooked smile, and a small gust of his magic snatched the bag from her hands and shut the door in her face. Letting the air go, the bag lay over the top of the vanity, and he directed his attention to the windows.

Hope. He frowned again. Hope is what destroys souls when your expectations get too high. But he dared to believe for a moment that maybe… just maybe, there was hope within the chaos. Because he was slipping into the darkness the longer he stayed with Avian, and he had to hold onto something.

And if Sarah was tied to his sister or could somehow find her, that hope would be his lifeline for the next eight days.

CHAPTER 24

Savven shut the door to his study as soon as Brean slipped within. Head bowing as his finger tapped the dark wood frame, he heaved a sigh before turning to the beautiful redhead who stood wide-eyed watching him.

"Brean McKenzie," he intoned lowly.

"Savven," she interrupted quickly.

He shook his head once, softly, and her full lips pursed. Fixing one of his rolled cuffs, he glanced at her, sauntering towards her. "Do you want to explain to me what I overheard?"

She huffed, rolling her eyes. "I knew you were listening."

Savven tapped the arch of one of his ears. "I can't really help myself, Witch."

"Careful, Prince," she murmured, arching her neck to look up at him as he stopped before her, towering over her petite frame.

Drawing up his left hand, he let his middle finger feather across her cheekbone and down the side of her face to the curve of her neck. "It's *King* now," he whispered.

Brean turned her chin and captured his wandering finger between her teeth as it made its way across her bottom lip, dragging her tongue across the marked skin before she released it and smirked up at him. "Careful, *King*, I still bite, crown or not."

A thrill shot through Savven, and a whisper of a smile parted his lips as he leaned down, his face hovering over hers. His eyes searched her face before dragging back to the vibrant amber ones that kindled hotly. "I do as well, Witch." His thumb brushed her bottom lip, his jaw flexing with restrained desire. "Now, Ms McKenzie, tell me your secrets."

Her breasts brushed his chest, their bodies nearly flush, and he sucked in a silent breath when she stepped away. His world turned cold without her close to him. His little firedrake.

Brean combed her fingers through her unruly copper curls, licking her lips before biting the bottom one, and he stopped himself from tugging it free.

"Talk to me," he urged gently.

Amber eyes met his, and the pain and sorrow in them nearly brought him to his knees. Grabbing a short back black leather chair from his study desk, he turned it towards her. Brean swallowed and nodded, slumping into the seat with a deep sigh.

"Tell me why I heard you say Tatius came to you," he said, casually using the God's name.

Scrubbing a hand over her face, Brean leaned forward, arms braced on her knees. "Because she did... after the final battle."

Savven's blood froze, and he went preternaturally still.

"You, me, and everyone else... we all died." Those last three words came out in a strangled whisper as if her body and brain couldn't bring herself to say it out loud. Brean blinked rapidly, clearing the tears that gathered. "She came to me and wanted to proposition my life in exchange for doing something for her. I told her I would only do that in exchange she brings someone else back."

"Brean... there's a balance—"

"—I know," she cut quickly, her tone sharp, jaw flexing when she stared up at him through furrowed brows.

"Then who…?" But he knew. He knew before the words even left his tongue.

"Me… for you."

Dread filled Savven hearing his confirmation, and he fell to his knees before her.

The tears finally fell from her eyes, her nostrils flaring with contained emotions.

His little firedrake, his witch, had… "No, you didn't. You couldn't have." Savven shook his head in denial, his hands cupping the backs of her knees through her trousers as he kneeled between her legs.

"It's only when the girl finally finds the truth will the God of Death come to collect my soul."

"Brean," he growled through clenched teeth. "Tell me you're lying—tell me you didn't give yourself for me." His chest was cracking open with every breath he took. The woman before him looked smaller than ever, but she still rolled her shoulders back, determination pursing her lips.

"I did, and I would do it again a thousand times over."

"Why?" he demanded, the tone of a king slipping through the word.

"Because they need their king!" she argued back. "Because I am only a witch, and you are a king of the land. They *need* you, Savven. They don't need me. But I needed you if I were going to survive this world. It was selfish. I brought you back because *I* needed you. *I* wanted you, even if it wasn't forever."

Savven leaned forward, cupping her face between his hands. "Don't," he whispered harshly. "Do not say that." He was shaking, whether from anger at the situation or fear at the idea of losing her, he couldn't tell. "*I* need you."

"But they don't," she whispered, her eyes downcast.

He forced her face to look at him, bending his head to catch her eyes. "Fuck them. Fuck all of them. *I need you.* I am King, and I am *telling* you that *I* need you."

Her amber eyes snapped to his.

"You're a king, Savven," she whispered. "I am only an orphan witch. Why?"

Fuck, because he… because he…

Savven's chest heaved as the words lingered at the tip of his tongue—his truth—the words he had felt in his heart for the last hundred years when they had awoken in a new world and built this empire together. But the look in her eyes told him she wouldn't believe him, not right now. So, instead, he leaned forward and kissed her brow gently, savouring the feel of her skin beneath his lips.

And in the tongue of his people, he bent his lips to her ear and whispered, "You are the heartbeat in my chest, the flow of my blood, and the hope of my every waking day. You are my darkest desires and the vision of every wicked intent. I am King, but only to you will I kneel."

When he pulled back, Brean stared at him with wide eyes and softly parted lips, her chest heaving.

"What did you say," she whispered.

"One day, I'll tell you," he promised, standing. Savven held out a hand to her.

Slipping her long fingers into his waiting palm, he pulled her to stand beside him.

"What about…"

"Let's not worry about Tatius," he said, stopping her worried words. "We have a gala to attend, and I can't wait to see you in your gown. The God of Death can wait." He would fight the insufferable God if needed, but for now, he ushered Brean towards the study door.

"You see me in one every year," she giggled softly, the tightness releasing from her shoulders.

Savven nodded. "And every year is better than the last."

Brean paused and turned to look up at him. He looked down at her with a raised brow in question.

Her hand pressed against his chest, trailing down until it tugged on the hem of his vest. "Thank you," she murmured.

Savven couldn't help himself and stroked a hand over her cheek. "Always," he promised.

CHAPTER 25

Sarah fidgeted where she stood in the doorway, eyeing the grand ballroom before her.

It had been six hours since Talan left her room, and in that time she had replayed what the witch had said to her. Turning every word over to make sure she hadn't missed anything.

"There's only one way to find out."

The witch's words were cryptic, and Sarah would be the last to admit it, but a slight brush of anxiety filled her chest. Eventually, she fell asleep and only woke up when a knock came on her door. Sarah found a slight Fae female with bright blonde hair and wide chocolate eyes standing in her doorway.

Her hair had been brushed, pulled, and prodded until it sat glossy and brown in a low, coiffed bun that pulled her hair away from her face. The female had done her makeup next, and Sarah could confidently say she felt like a doll. Never in her life had she worn this much makeup—not unless you consider blood splatters blush and long hours of sleepless hunts eyeshadow that smudged under her eyes in shades of purple.

The floor-length gown that had been selected was made of black silk that hugged her body. The open back plunged down her spine, and a single swath of silk stretched over her shoulder, across her open scarred back, to her opposite hip.

Sarah felt entirely exposed. She pulled at the fabric, feet shifting again in a pair of black strappy kitten heels. A doll, indeed. If Florin and Naschta saw her now, they would laugh at her. Her bargain with Avian—which was slowly beginning to cover her forearm as the days ticked down like it was an hourglass and the sand was running out—and every reminder of her failures was on display for every Fae and human eye in the ballroom who turned to watch her when the doors opened.

Nearly being forced out of her room by the blonde female and escorted to the ballroom had left Sarah with little choice. She scanned the room for Talan or even Reign. At this point, she wasn't picky and just needed a familiar face in a sea of the unknown.

Like their rooms, black marble with gold veins mapped the floor and walls, and high above glittered hundreds of floating candles that sparkled and created a dancing glow over the entire space. Along each wall, single-file, were gold pedestals with glass casings housing different artifacts. Some were made of stone and large, others so small Sarah couldn't see them. One, a long slab of rock, on the wall, anchored by steel pins and encased in a glass house over it.

Stiffening when a sneering male and his companion walked by her, looking her up and down slowly. His eyes lingered on her scars and then on the moving ink branding her left arm. The female scoffed, and the male pulled her along, but not before Sarah heard the female whisper, "*Whore.*"

Finger tapping against her thigh, Sarah counted to ten, willing herself not to walk up to the female and smack the smirk off her face. They figured the only reason she was there was because she had sold herself to one of the Fae, as noted by the bargain tattooed on her arm. And she had, hadn't she? But not for the reason they thought.

Fingers clenching, she let out a deep breath and let it go slowly before rounding on her obnoxiously thin black heels and stalking towards the stone slab.

Shoulders rolling uncomfortably, feeling the burning of eyes on her scars, drilling new holes into her back, Sarah pursed her lips and studied the stonework. It was old, chipped in places, a chunk the size of her fist missing in the middle and the paint faded, but the story was still clear: it was the birth and death of a world.

A corona of stars fell, and light bathed the world. Dragon fire was breathed into its core, and the old world was born. Sarah's eyes skimmed over the age-old timeline until her eyes tracked to the end, where a female with gold wings and blond hair hung suspended over a roughly sketched battlefield, light bathed behind her, and then the end of the mural was consumed in darkness.

"That is Hazen Solvaya."

Savven stepped up to her side, his trimmed blue-black hair styled in a way that was neatly combed on the sides but still messy on top. Sarah eyed him slowly, noting his all-black three-piece tux sans tie or bow, and the glass of amber liquid he held. Everything was tailored to his lean, fit body, and Sarah had never seen a Fae of the old world so comfortable in the modern world. He was stunning in the way all Fae tend to be, but there was an ease about him, something about how he held himself that made Sarah want to see how he fought.

"I think she was mentioned once in an old Fae history book I read," Sarah mused, returning her attention to the stonework.

"A travesty," Savven murmured. "She's the reason you're standing here today."

A human with Fae heritage who tore the divide and joined the two worlds into the one she knew today.

Sarah cocked her head, scanning the golden-winged woman. "What happened to her?"

"She died." Savven raised his whiskey glass and took a sip. "She refused the immortal cup and chose to remain human. She died of old age, followed by her husband, who was once the general of a great dragon army and who chose mortality to be with her. They have three children, who also have their own children now, and their lineage lives on to this day. They visit me every winter solstice."

"So, all's well that ends well," she muttered dryly, her eyes drifting down the wall to a long, thin, cracked-in-half stone slab anchored beside the timeline.

She could feel his gaze on the side of her face and raised a brow at his regard.

"You're an interesting one," he remarked thoughtfully, sipping his whiskey.

"So they tell me," she said, walking down the line of artefacts until she stood in front of the split stone. Something was etched into it, and she leaned forward, narrowing her eyes as she tried to decipher it. "All ends have a beginning..."

Savven hummed thoughtfully, following her. "Yes, it does say that."

She arched a brow at him.

"You can read this?" he inquired.

"I think anyone with a grammatical education can read it."

The Fae king nodded slowly, turning his full attention to her. "Do you know what this is?"

"I couldn't tell you."

"It's a piece of a Fae altar that stood beside the veil; this is all the remains of it after the fall. It was used in ancient traditions and ceremonies. I find it interesting that you can read it."

Sarah waved a hand out before her and half bowed to him. "I aim to entertain." Standing next to the king, she was starting to get antsy, and her finger began to tap against her thigh softly when she straightened. Her eyes darted at the faces around them and the eyes that peered their way. There were too many eyes, too many people watching them, watching *her*.

"Well," she sighed, "As fun as this has been. I'm going to walk away now."

His following words sent ice down her spine, and she stiffened as she turned away from him.

"The truth lies within your blood. No amount of magic can conceal that."

Her chest tightened, jaw flexing as her teeth clenched. Sucking in a silent deep breath through her nose, Sarah rolled her shoulders back and tilted her chin up a fraction. "I'm going to go find a drink," she muttered before walking into the gathering of bodies and whispered judgments.

Talan sipped on the flute of champagne in his hands, eyeing the crowd over the rim. His tux felt tailored to his body, and he wondered how they managed it, but he still hooked a finger under the stiff white collar, trying to loosen it. It was comfortable enough, but he himself was uncomfortable—with everything. He was surrounded by the elite, the High Fae of society and other creatures with enough money lining their pockets to earn positions of power within the archaic social structure.

He spotted nymphs, males and females draped in gossamer that scarcely covered their willowy bodies. A hulking orc pressed along a wall, dressed in black tux pants, his massive green chest bare and adorned in two gold hoops through his nipples. Talan winced at the thought of piercing his chest and the pain, taking another swig of his drink.

His eyes glazed over the faces, brows lifting when he saw a female shifter mingling with two Fae females, flutes of alcohol in their hands.

A waiter passed, and he put his empty glass on the tray they held as they went.

The air shifted around him, and he looked at Reign from the corner of his eye when the auburn-haired male stepped beside him, nursing a glass of what Talan assumed was vodka on the rocks based on the distinct smell of battery acid coming from the glass.

But that was all Talan could smell.

Frowning, he looked at Reign, eyeing him intently.

"You're not my type, Pup," the male commented casually, eyes tracking someone in the crowd.

Talan followed his gaze and saw the Fae king disappearing into the bodies.

Rolling his eyes, Talan shifted back to the male. "Why do you conceal yourself?"

The glass hovered over Reign's mouth before he took a slow sip, his dark brown eyes sliding to Talan.

"You use your magic to hide your scent. Why?" he questioned.

"Careful what you ask; you may not like the answer."

"Doubtful."

Reign's smile was wicked as he took another sip of his drink. "Tell me why you haven't tried to kill me yet?"

Talan's brows folded. "What?"

"You were there that night," Reign stated casually. "In Tambiln, with the other shifters."

Talan's blood froze, and his body went ridged at the mention of his slain brothers. The wolf in him growled deep, pulsating with checked rage. He couldn't scent the male, so he hadn't known. All he knew was the rotten stench of the black blood of a Deathwalker that he had followed from Tambiln.

"I just think it's interesting you haven't tried anything. What's made you turn into such a *good boy*." Reign's words oozed with sarcasm, and Talan gritted his jaw to repress the urge to punch him.

"You have no idea what you're talking about," he growled finally, glaring at the Fae and taking a step in his direction.

Reign cocked a brow at him. "Don't I? I was there that night. I watched them get slaughtered. I watched their blood saturate the ground—"

Talan lunged.

His body slammed into a wall of solid air, he grunted when pain splintered through his hand and he felt the bones in his knuckles crack.

Multiple pairs of eyes turned in their direction, and Reign clicked his tongue.

"Behave, puppy. Wouldn't want to draw attention to ourselves. Not until Sarah fulfils her side of the bargain and finds Avian's sister. You can *try* and kill me afterwards, but no promises."

Talan's blood was *boiling*. He could only see red and knew his eyes were molten as he tried to reign in the wolf. The bones in his hand were slowly mending, popping back into place as his fists trembled at his sides. Lips pulling back into a sneer, Talan spat, "I won't try to kill you. I *will*."

Satisfaction lit Reign's dark eyes, and the male leaned forward until his lips brushed Talan's ear, the scent of vodka on his breath. "Hold onto that anger. You're going to need it in the future." Leaning back, Reign eyed him up and down before taking a methodical sip of his drink. "Revenge is a game played between only the strongest competitors. Keep your wits about you here, and don't let anyone goad you into submission. I feel like things are finally about to get interesting."

He felt a soft pull of something familiar and looked to his right, watching Sarah stalk up to them with a scowl on her face. Talan narrowed his eyes on Reign for a second more before he looked down at Sarah. Her brows were furrowed, and a familiar scowl tugged her mouth down, but she looked beautiful.

They hadn't seen each other since their shared moment in her room. Now, seeing her in the backless black gown, confidence rolling off her in waves despite her scars being on display, brown eyes rimmed in black and flashing with her normal fire, Talan didn't think another female in the room could compare.

"Is the princess unsatisfied with tonight's event?" Talan drawled casually, some of his rage dissipating at Sarah's presence.

Sarah grabbed a glass of sparkling champagne from a passing tray and gave Talan a pointed stare over the rim. "If you know what's good for you, you won't goad me right now," she snarked before tossing the alcohol back.

Raising a brow, he held his hands in surrender, "Yes, ma'am."

The orchestra in the far corner of the hall started a waltz, and both Talan and Reign offered Sarah their hand.

Talan moved his hand in front of Reign's, but not before Sarah raised a brow at both of them.

Reign chuckled softly and retracted his invitation. "Next time. It would seem Talan has the first dance."

Rolling her eyes, she slipped her hand into Talan's. "There won't be a next time. This is the first and last dance I will be performing."

Shaking his head, Talan wrapped his fingers around hers and pulled her close.

"Be careful, Dog. Sounds like Sarah might have two left feet."

It was her turn to growl in annoyance, but he noted the way her shoulders tensed. Talan only pulled her closer to him, bowing his head so only she could hear him. He whispered, "Don't worry. I have two left feet as well. We make a perfect pair."

"Or a dangerous one," she replied, though her lips tilted in a hint of a smile, her shoulders easing as they began their waltz.

CHAPTER 26

Why was it always her name? Pain lanced through her head as soon as her name passed Reign's lips, making her whole body tense. The claws slowly retracted from her skull, and she was able to ease into the dance. Not that she can say that their dance was… easy—or graceful.

Both she and Talan had two left feet. Neither of them could dance gracefully to save their lives, much to her toes and his dismay.

He winced when she trod over his glossy black shoes with her toe again, the tops now thoroughly scuffed and her toes visibly red in the strappy heels.

But when she made to apologise, he only pulled her closer and shook his head, whispering a single word in her ear that made her shiver. "Don't."

His palm was warm and firm along the marked flesh of her back. His fingers splayed across her spine like her scars weren't there. Sarah could feel the warmth of his hand searing through her, making her back arch and chest press along his. The space between them was void. She could feel his heart race, pounding against hers.

Was he nervous?

Sarah glanced up at him through her lashes, and a blush rose to her cheeks when she found amber eyes glowing back at her with an intensity that made something bubble to life in her chest.

Was it her heart? Was it… beating faster? Her heart felt like it was jumping erratically as she stared up at him, even though she knew logically it wasn't.

Talan dipped his head, his arms tightening around her until she felt the air squeezed from her lungs.

"Sarah," he murmured softly.

But it wasn't soft enough, and pain split her skull in two.

The magic of their horrible dancing shattered into tiny, fragmented pieces, and Sarah shoved Talan off her, stumbling back, a hand pressed to her head.

"Sarah!" he said again, but alarm rang in his tone.

Why was it always her name?

The hem of her black gown caught under her kitten heels, and she tripped forward, spotting a hidden balcony in the chaos of her swimming vision. Desperation screamed through her, and Sarah stumbled towards it. A sea of eyes swayed through the pain as they stared at her, but she didn't care. She ignored Talan, especially as he called after her, and her name was like a death knell on his lip. Reign appeared on her heels until she shooed him away, his hand touching her shoulder and making her flinch.

Sweat coated her body in a thin sheen, her limbs shaking with sheer determination to keep her upright. Shoving people out of the way, their protests following her, Sarah grabbed the black marble handles of the French doors and forced them open.

Crisp air hit her face like a knife, and she sucked in a ragged breath, bracing a hand on the wall as she doubled over, her body wracked with tremors of pain.

"Sarah?"

She braced, but a wave of soothing warmth eased over her instead of pain, and her muscles relaxed.

Brean was staring at her when she looked over her shoulder. The witch's wide gold eyes filled with understanding and... *guilt?*

"What did you do?" Sarah asked, pulling in a deep breath as she straightened cautiously and turned to the witch. Brean was dressed in a beautiful navy-blue velvet column gown that hugged her body with a deep v-cut down her chest and long sleeves with diamond-crusted cuffs. Her ample cleavage was somewhat covered by a nude mesh fabric, and her long, wild hair was half pulled away from her face, untamed pieces framing her cheeks.

"I eased the magic binding you," Brean said, pursing her lips.

The warmth disappeared, and Sarah felt her limbs freeze all over again. "You did what?"

"The magic was designed to make you forget whenever you remembered something you weren't supposed to. But something special in you is fighting back, something powerful. Maybe magic of your own?" Brean's head ticked to the side curiously.

Sarah made to retort when the king appeared, and she raised a brow at them. "Please don't bring the party out here. Otherwise, tomorrow's news headline will be: **HUNTER PUSHES WHOLE GALA OFF BALCONY LEDGE.** It'll be very damaging to your reputation."

The king's head tilted, and a sly smile ghosted his lips. "We wouldn't want that, would we?"

Sarah noted his hand curling around Brean's waist protectively—possessively, she couldn't tell which. But she would assume both.

"You look ravishing," the king said softly to the witch, and a pretty blush stained her rosy face. "Let us return so I can claim your first dance."

She was intruding on their little moment, but that was no fault of hers. They followed her out onto the balcony, so she would be damned if she had to go back to the masses.

"Of course, your majesty," she murmured. Brean turned her shimmering black-rimmed eyes to Sarah. "Will you be okay? I can get the king's assistant to show you back to your room."

"I'm sure I can find my way back on my own," Sarah said tightly. "Your *people* await you." She couldn't help the bite in her tone; whether it was from the pain or the thought that everyone was attending a gala while her little brother was shivering in a prison somewhere, she didn't care.

The king's eyes flashed in warning, a frown tugging at his mouth. Sarah knew he was going to say something, but Brean laid a hand on his chest and offered her a small smile before turning to him and slowly pushing him back.

"Come, your majesty, let's return. They're about to start drawing winners from tonight's fundraiser."

Stern dark blue eyes flickered away from her and instantly softened when he glanced down at the witch. "How many times do I have to ask you to call me Savven?"

Their voices were low as they walked back into the gala, but not before Sarah heard Brean reply softly, "But the title of *king* fits you so well." And Sarah saw something pained but full of passion fill the king's gaze before they were swallowed by the bodies and the doors closed fully behind them.

Sarah walked to the curling black metal railing, designed to look like tree branches and leaves, and braced her hands on it. Stars blanketed the sky above her, and she sucked in a shuddering breath, the cold air making shivers run the length of her. Despite the city lights, they were high enough to see the glittering vastness, and Sarah walked backwards until her back hit the wall and slid softly to the ground. Staring up at the sky as she undid her hair, the pins scattering to the ground, and brown hair tumbled around her shoulders like a protective cloak.

Drawing her knees up as much as the gown allowed, Sarah wrapped her arms around herself as the duelling French doors opened, and Talan peered around the frame.

"Sar—"

The glare she shot him could curdle milk and instantly made Talan snap his mouth shut.

"Hey," he opted quietly.

She turned back to the stars, whispering, "Hey."

The doors clicked shut softly, the warm candlelight slipping out into the darkness through the windowpanes. Talan dropped beside her, his body brushing against hers, a whiskey glass held out.

He teasingly wiggled the glass and its amber content when she didn't take it. "I brought the good stuff and some better company."

A slight smile curled one side of her mouth when she smelled the whiskey. Shooting Talan a glance from the corner of her eye, she took the glass and sipped delicately. It was intense, a little fruity, followed by something spice. It was indeed the good stuff.

"Thanks," she said, taking another sip and looking back at the stars.

Talan shivered beside her, but he pulled off his tux coat all the same and draped it over her shoulders. "Sorry if my dancing made you run away. I know I'm horrible."

Sarah smiled to herself, smelling him in the fabric of the jacket and letting it fill her lungs as she leaned forward to adjust it before warmth hugged her arms.

"It's fucking cold out here."

Talan and Sarah looked to the French doors and found Reign there. He scowled at the icy wind, and instantly, a bubble of warmth filled the balcony.

"That's better," he intoned, smoothing a hand over his perfectly styled auburn hair, regarding them with a raised brow. His all-black tux made him look like a villain in an old Bond movie, whereas Talan looked like the James Bond character from a century ago—rugged and dashingly handsome.

Both were clearly up to no good, but either way, Sarah waved a hand to the space on her right. "Might as well make yourself comfortable."

"And what are you two doing out here?" Reign inquired dryly, sitting beside her but with space between them. "Plotting your escape?"

"Sitting with the dead." She tipped her glass back and drank half of the contents.

Reign's gaze flickered to the sky, a sadness lingering behind his gaze as he looked to the stars. "That's an old belief."

Talan frowned in confusion. "What is?"

Sarah offered him the whiskey. "That the sky is a graveyard of people from the past."

His fingers froze just before they curled around the glass, and Talan looked to the stars, taking the whiskey and tossing it back. "We're going to need the bottle."

Sarah watched Talan disappear back inside, leaving her and Reign alone.

Silence sat between them in their bubble of warmth, and Sarah glanced at the Fae male. Something about him put her at ease, and she frowned, not liking that.

"Do I entertain you?" he commented dryly.

Snorting, she turned away from the sky. "Not in the slightest. But I do find you peculiar."

Reign let out a short laugh. "I've never had a female tell me that before."

She adjusted Talan's jacket around her shoulders. "Holed up in a mountain with a psycho Fae lord, I imagine not."

"Careful how you speak about Avian," Reign warned, but it lacked any weight.

Sarah looked at him fully, frowning. "What do you actually want?"

A smirk lifted the male's lips, his eyes darkening. "What are you suggesting."

Tilting her head, Sarah leaned in close. "You don't fool me." She leaned away, observing him.

He frowned in response.

"You have been very accommodating to us when you could just let us stumble around and let time run out."

"I, for one, very much doubt you would do much *stumbling around* Sarah Hunter of Fae." It was Reign's turn to observe her, his eyes studying her face until she felt he would expose all her secrets. "Not that you need to know or care, but I have something to gain from this just as much as you do."

French doors opened and closed, and Talan plopped beside her with a nearly full bottle of Dalmore 64. "I snagged this from a waiter."

"Well, at least you didn't grab the cheap bottle," Reign mused wryly.

Sarah grabbed the bottle from Talan and held it up at eye level, inspecting it. "Plan on getting wasted, Puppy?"

Talan snorted and took the bottle back, popping the top off. "So, you can take advantage of my vulnerable self? You wish, Princess."

"As cute as this flirty banter you have going between you is," Reign stated unamused, reaching out a hand, "Please do try to keep it contained around me. I don't want to throw up such nice whiskey."

"We're not flirting," they said in unison.

Reign snorted. "Convincing."

Talan threw him a cutting glare and passed him the bottle.

They fell into silence. Leaning back against the wall, Sarah turned her face to the stars, watching them glimmer overhead, the city lights below seeming to mimic them.

"Do you think they're really up there?" Talan asked quietly, taking a swig from the bottle.

Sarah chewed on her words. Did she think her family was up there? The stars twinkled the longer she stared at them, seemingly glowing brighter. "I hope so," she said softly, almost to herself. *Hope* was something she rarely allowed herself to feel, but it trickled in like a stranger in that small moment.

The thought that her parents were up there as stars, constantly watching over her, comforted the cold, lonely parts of herself.

"Hope is a dangerous feeling," Reign murmured.

Sarah glanced at him as he drew a knee up and leaned his arm on it. "I know."

Reign caught her eye for a split second, and Sarah couldn't help but see something familiar in his gaze. Something she saw in her reflection from time to time—weariness.

He was tired.

She could see it in him despite his hard exterior.

In some sense, they were the same in that way. Every day was a new battle, a new mountain to climb, but they kept climbing no matter the scars they collected and the blood they lost along the way.

Sympathy bubbled in her for the briefest moment.

Flicking her gaze back to the stars, Sarah reached for the bottle.

"It's a graveyard full of nearly forgotten tombs." The whiskey burned going down, and she passed it to Reign.

"And yet, every night, we're forced to remember the loss," Talan said somewhat bitterly.

"I might like that opportunity when I meet my end." She moved the coat aside and looked at her tattooed forearm. The vines were twisting ever so slightly, digging into her flesh, reminding her that time was running out. "To be something beautiful after I die."

Talan's finger brushed against her thigh, and she glanced at him. The fire she found burning in his stare made her insides twist.

"You're already beautiful," he said so softly she barely made out the words.

Reign groaned in disgust. "Lord. *Please* keep it to yourself. I'd rather enjoy my whiskey without your sentimentality."

Talan didn't break her gaze, and Sarah frowned at her feelings curling hotly in her stomach.

Breath catching in her throat, Sarah forced herself to look away even as a hot flush crept up her neck. No one had ever looked at her like he did at that moment, and she didn't know what to do with that information.

She needed more alcohol.

Snatching the bottle from Reign as he was about to take a sip, she ignored his growl of protest and raised the liquor to the sky. "To the dead and those about to die, may we find beauty in our deaths." And she drank—deeply. Fire spilt down her throat, but she ignored it and drank until her head buzzed.

She drank to her upcoming demise. Because somewhere deep within her, she knew that she was going to die. And that realisation deserved a drink.

Talan chuckled and gently took the bottle from her when she was done. "Save some for me, Princess."

Sarah scoffed, her head falling back against the wall. Adjusting the coat around her, she let herself get lost in the sea of city lights and stars.

CHAPTER 27

Sarah stumbled, hand slapping against the wall to catch herself. A giggle, a fucking *giggle*, escaped her, and she moved her hand from the wall to her mouth.

Lord, the liquor was making her feel funny. She hadn't been drunk… ever. She wasn't nearly drunk enough to make her an idiot. Still, she was undoubtedly more forgiving and less restrained if Talan's arm around her waist was any indication.

The hall to their rooms was moving, or was that her? Sniffing, Sarah stood up straighter, leaning into the warm male aroma curling around her. He smelled good, really good.

"Thank you," Talan rumbled with low laughter.

She had said that out loud. Shit.

Sarah raised a brow, looking up at him. His amber eyes were

trained on her, a heat rising within their beautiful depths. "Don't let it go to your head, Puppy," she said with a scowl but doubted it was convincing as she leaned closer to him, inhaling.

Something about him made her defences want to melt completely, the smell of him more intoxicating than the alcohol. Her head was clearing by the seconds the longer they stood there, but she found her hand curling around his middle. Feeling the press of his ridged abdominal muscles flexing under her fingertips, a low, barely audible growl rumbled through him, and she felt the vibrations under her palm.

She smirked coyly.

"Behave, Princess," he warned, his voice wrapping around them in a soft warning.

He leaned his head down, their noses brushing, and Sarah's breath hitched.

They had sat outside on that balcony for an hour, drinking and not talking. Reign had left them to chase a blonde he saw from the French doors, and then it was just her and Talan, pressed against one another, a bottle of overpriced whiskey, and each other's quiet company.

Now, the darkness of the corridor and dimmed sconces created their shadowed privacy, which slowly pressed around them, and Sarah was too keenly aware of the lack of space separating their bodies.

Talan's arm tightened around her middle, pressing her closer to him. She knew that if she tilted her head just a breath, their lips would touch.

Her heart pounded in her ears, making her limbs thrum with a burning desire.

"Talan," she breathed, her skin tingling as he dipped his head, breath fanning across her neck, his jaw brushing hers as he skimmed his lips along her throat. Or was it an illusion, too faint to truly feel? But her skin burned with a trail of fire regardless, and she arched her neck.

"Sarah," he replied, pressing the sound into her flesh with a kiss that wasn't an illusion. Nipping the skin with his teeth.

Her gasp filled the hall, both with desire and pain, and Talan sighed deeply, lifting his head.

And then he stepped back.

The warmth disappeared, and Sarah was left standing there, her core aching and body humming with leashed desire.

What the fuck.

Her eyes opened, and she looked at him, frowning.

"I told you I would walk you to your room," he said softly, pressing a hand to her lower back.

She walked mutely, confused and sexually frustrated. This male tied her insides up, and she wasn't used to the lack of control.

Her door was not even ten paces down the hall from where they had stood frozen in their own world. But there it was, a stern reminder of where they were and what she was tasked to do. For a moment, she had forgotten Alec. No, not forgotten, but she put him aside for her own selfish desires.

Guilt made her frown, and she wrapped her arms around her middle, stopping in front of her door.

"You looked beautiful tonight," Talan said softly, turning to her. He leaned down and pressed a kiss to her cheek before reaching behind her and opening her door.

It swung open effortlessly without a sound.

He stepped back, fingers skimming her arm, staring down at her with reservation. But Sarah could see the lingering desire, the heat, but also the restraint flaring behind his glowing golden eyes. He was trying to be a gentleman, and Sarah couldn't stop her mouth from curling up.

"Goodnight, Princess."

"Goodnight, Puppy," she whispered, her fingers twitched against her forearms. She wanted to close the distance between them, but instead, she stepped back into the threshold of her room and gently closed the door.

The darkness and overwhelming silence greeted her when Sarah faced the room. Softly glowing city lights filtered through the large windows, spilling across the black silk comforter on the bed.

Kicking the kitten heels off, they landed by the foot of her bed as she walked to the extended wardrobe built into the far wall;

finding the zipper on the side of her dress, she shimmied out of it, leaving it in a pool of black silk on the ground.

Cool air brushed her exposed skin, her nipples hardening to peaks, and Sarah caught her reflection in the glass window.

Smokey makeup made her eyes seem darker than usual, and her brown hair tumbled around her shoulders. In the dark lighting, the mousy locks were rich like decadent chocolate. Her breasts were small but firm and full, and her gaze wandered down and down her muscled abdomen to the sheer lacey thong she wore.

Hands coming up, Sarah slowly skimmed her fingers along her skin, trailing them lightly across her breast, picturing Talan's hands instead of hers. Her breath caught in her throat, her core aching, and her fingers stilled their wandering.

Memories of his breath skimming her neck, his lips hovering above her skin like a tease, the feel of his body pressed along her back. Her eyes fluttered shut at the images, and her right hand slid down her stomach to the centre of heat between her thighs, finding the lace wet and waiting for not her fingers... but *his*.

Need, hot and spiralling, coursed through her until her body practically vibrated with it. It was going to consume her.

Sarah looked back at her door, and within two heartbeats, she threw on the long white cotton sleep shirt that was stacked on some other new clothes, courtesy of the female who had done her hair and makeup earlier in the day, and marched out of her room.

Talan's door was offset from hers, and she would gather it was also locked if she were to try it, which she nearly did as her hand hovered over the handle. Dropping her hand to her side, her finger tapped her thigh as she stood outside of it, alone in the dark hall, the sconce lights on the wall overhead barely casting light in her direction.

What was she doing? Sarah combed her fingers through her hair with a soft sigh. She was standing basically naked in a hallway where anyone could find her, and that thought alone shot a thrill through her, and she squeezed her thighs together with anticipation.

It was a soft knock, only one, but Talan's door opened seconds later. Sarah found herself staring up at amber eyes, trying to calm the sudden nerves clenching her stomach and making her heart race.

His collar was undone, the buttons open at his chest, and he looked like he had been combing his hands through his chocolate curls. He looked *edible*, and the nerves disappeared as she licked her lips and dragged her gaze back to his, staring up at him through her lashes.

She felt sexy, and a wave of feminine confidence rolled through her, something she couldn't say she felt often—or ever, and maybe it was the last legs of liquor in her blood, but she held onto it.

Talan opened his mouth to ask the question she saw on his face, but he paused. His eyes trailed down her body, nostrils flaring, and she knew he could smell her arousal.

"Sarah," he said roughly, jaw flexing and eyes turning molten.

"Don't," she replied, daring herself to take a step closer.

Their chests nearly touched, and she held his gaze, her nipples outlining her shirt, and she wanted his hands there, touching them. Her body practically begging for his touch, his mouth, his teeth.

He shook his head despite his eyes glowing with his need and hunger. "You're drunk."

"I'm not." She dared drag a finger along the exposed skin on his chest. His pectorals rippled, and he let out a strained growl. Sarah could hear the wolf in him rising to her silent invitation.

"You are," he argued lowly. "I'm not taking you to bed when you're drunk. I want to keep my favourite appendage."

Her eyes trailed down to where there was a noticeable hard bulge, and she licked her lips. "Let me taste it." The words were out before she could think about it.

Talan groaned softly. "Princess."

"Puppy," she purred.

She stepped closer until her nipples grazed his chest, and a breathy moan escaped her lips. Something about him made her want to pull her hair out, but... despite that, he had become something solid, something reliable, and steadfast in her chaotic, pain-ridden world. And for the first time in her life, she felt her burdens ease, just a bit, from her shoulders when she was around him.

Talan looked down at her with hooded eyes, but he still didn't move to touch her. "You're drunk," he tried again, but there was no weight to his words.

"No, I'm not." She pressed her palm to his chest and found his heart beating wildly. "I'm buzzed but not drunk. I'm sober enough to know what I want, and right now... I want *you.*"

"You don't mean that." But despite his words, there was hope in them. He wanted her just as much as she wanted him.

"Talan," she growled in feign annoyance, "I am basically naked in a public hall, practically begging you to fuck me. If you don't make me scream your name, I *will* cut off your favourite appendage out of spite."

A smirk curled his lips, and she had a second to register his words before he grabbed her.

"I like seeing you beg."

And then his mouth was on her. Hot and claiming, every inch of her body came alive at his touch. She felt like a livewire about to explode as his fingers slipped under the hem of her shirt, and she groaned at the contact, pressing herself flush against his body.

There was nothing and no one else at that moment. Her mind went blank for the first time in her life, and all she could think about was his tongue as it slipped past her parted lips and claimed her mouth like it was always his.

Hands grabbing her ass, he lifted her against him, her legs wrapping around his waist. His door slammed shut as he walked them to his bed.

Black satin sheets and a comforter identical to her own pillowed around her as Talan tossed her onto the bed. She bounced once and sat up on her elbows, arching a brow at him.

"Take it off," he growled, eyeing her shirt.

Sarah smirked and slid off the bed to stand before him. Her fingers tugged at the hem of her long shirt before slowly pulling it over her head. The shirt pooled on the floor, and she stood in only her panties, breast heaving and heavy, desperate for his touch.

"Fuck."

Rough calluses grazed the side of her breast and skimmed over one taut nipple. Sarah sucked in a breath, arching into his touch.

"Beautiful," he whispered.

Ducking his head, Talan kissed her shoulder, hands trailing down her sides. Fire enveloped where his mouth touched her, and she watched him through half-lidded eyes as he knelt before her.

"Talan…"

"Shh."

She couldn't respond as his mouth trailed kisses down her stomach to the hem of her panties, and he inhaled the smell of her arousal. She could feel his growl of approval straight to her core, and she sucked in a breath, his tongue trailing up her stomach, hands gripping her hips.

He paused at her breasts, taking a nipple between his teeth and sucking on the small bud until her eyes rolled back, and she gripped his shoulders for support.

"Talan, please," she gasped, her core aching painfully.

Tongue flicking over her nipple, he released it from his tormenting and straightened. "Get on the bed."

Chest heaving with desire, his dark tone made her nerves scatter with anticipation through her body. Eyes trained on him, she walked back until the bed bumped the back of her knees, and did as she was told.

"On your hands and knees."

Her lips curled at the new demand, and she tilted her head in defiance.

"Make me," she purred.

Talan's eyes flared gold at the challenge, and he undid the button of his tux pants, slowly undoing the buttons of his shirt. It gathered with hers on the floor.

She stared up at him, taking her time to gaze at his bare torso and the ridges of muscle cording it. "What's the big bad wolf going to do?" She smiled coyly. "Eat me?"

He leaned forward, grasping her chin between his thumb and forefinger. "I'm going to *devour* you, Princess." He leaned back, shifting his pants down until they hung loose on his hips. "Get on your hands and knees."

Sarah leaned forward, keeping her eyes locked on his, and dragged her tongue across the ridges of his stomach. A devious glint in her eyes when she felt him tighten under her mouth and suck in a sharp breath.

His hand wrapped around her throat, squeezing gently and making her look up at him. "Be a good girl, Sarah," he whispered, leaning in close.

Despite her name slipping out of his mouth, the pain didn't come. It was like whatever was happening between them was stronger, at least for the moment, than the magic that normally inflicted the torment on her mind.

The heat between her legs made her squeeze her thighs together at his words and scoot back, keeping her eyes on him all the while as she turned and did as he told.

"Good girl," he murmured, his fingers feathering over her ass.

Her stomach clenched, feeling his breath at the apex of her thighs. Jerking in surprise when his mouth pressed against the centre of her drenched panties, she gasped.

"Talan!"

His dark chuckle was her answer.

He pressed his mouth to her again, nipping at her inner thigh and dragging his tongue along the seam of her panties, teasing her until she moaned lowly and pressed into his face.

"Don't be a fucking tease," she panted, arms shaking when his tongue dipped into her centre and nipped at her through the fabric.

Talan's fingers dug into her hips and flipped her onto her back without warning, her squeak of surprise making him smirk.

He watched her with vibrant eyes, stepping back from the bed to remove his pants.

Sarah licked her lips. He wasn't wearing anything under them and was fully erect, a bead of precum dotting the thick tip that she wanted to lick off.

So, that's what she did.

Legs spread wide, she slipped to the edge of the bed and pulled him between her thighs.

His cock was large and heavy in her hand as she lowered her mouth to the tip, eyes on his, tongue licking off the precum with slow deliberation.

Talan's nostrils flared, lips parting, and his hand went to her loose hair. He fisted his fingers into the tresses as she sucked the head of his cock into her mouth, tongue curling around him, and he groaned low and guttural.

Sarah smirked in satisfaction.

Using her other hand to wrap around his base, she slowly worked her mouth over him, her other hand matching what she couldn't swallow. She dragged her teeth over the sensitive flesh, relishing in his low sound of approval, choking when he hit the back of her throat as he slowly fucked her mouth.

Spreading her legs further, panties rubbing against her sensitive clit, she let go of his base and brought her fingers to her aching core, rubbing herself through her panties as he fucked her face. Moaning when pleasure coursed through her, and her fingers sped up, pinching her clit and shoving the fabric aside when it got in the way.

Sarah let him guide her mouth while she used her free hand to grasp his balls, tugging on them softly, feeling them tighten.

Talan's growl ripped through him, and he pulled her off, snatching her wrist from between her thighs.

Sarah whimpered at the loss.

"I want to taste you, Princess."

With lust-hazed eyes, she stared up at him, nodding mutely. Slipping her panties off, Sarah spread her legs further, exposing herself to him while she played with her breast, pinching her nipple between her fingers as her other hand snaked to her drenched pussy.

"No," he said lowly.

She frowned, frustration welling up, watching him sprawl confidently on the bed. Hair beautifully dishevelled around his rugged face, he was the image of a God. Talan bent an arm back to lay behind his head, biceps flexing, thick muscled legs splayed slightly, one bent up.

"Come here."

"Talan—"

"—Come here, Sarah."

A part of her relished in the firm command in his tone, her mind turning off for a second. Crawling over to him, she straddled his waist, his cock pressing between her wet centre, and she rubbed herself over him. It would be so easy to slip him inside and to ride him until she came undone, but he held her firm when she started to edge him into her.

"Behave, Princess" he warned.

His hand went to her breasts, squeezing them gently and rolling her nipples between his fingers, tugging on them until she cried out.

She leaned forward, her lips trailing over his chest and neck to his mouth. He captured her mouth with his in a heated kiss, his hand going to the alcove of her neck and bringing her flush against him.

Moaning against his mouth as he rubbed against her heat, she tried to slip him into her, but his hand banded around one of her hips, holding her still with a rough chuckle.

Fire blazed within her, tunnelling down and down into an inferno that threatened to consume her, and she wiggled against him, trying to displace the sensation coiling in her core.

"I want to taste you," he muttered against her lips.

In a single breath that had a gasp flying from her lips, Talan flipped her around, her ass above his face, her juices drenching the inside of her thighs, and she could feel his breath grazing against her, and she quivered.

Fuck, she thought, licking her lips.

His cock dripped with precum before her, and Sarah couldn't help herself to the offering. Dipping her head to taste him on her tongue again. Moaning loudly when she felt his tongue drag from ass to clit, she bucked into his mouth, fingers fisting into the sheets to keep her upright.

She shook with every sweep of his tongue, tremors rolling down her spine to her toes, her core tightening when he inserted a single finger into her. She moaned around his shaft, his other hand gripping her ass. Her lips hollowed around the tip and released it with a flick of her tongue, kissing a trail down his cock, licking his balls and taking them one at a time into her mouth.

His groan was deep, and he grabbed her hips in both his hands and buried his face between her thighs. Teeth grazed her clit, and she saw stars when he gently pulled at it.

Dragging her hand along his base as she rimmed his head, licking his slit clean and savouring the salty taste of him in her mouth. She wanted nothing more than to make him cum, and swallow every drop.

"Fuck, Princess."

She could hear him mutter against her pussy, licking her clean until his tongue poked her entrance and her back arched, mouth gaping.

"Talan!" she gasped.

"What do you want, Princess?"

His fingers replaced his tongue, dipping inside of her and curling to hit the spot that made her buck into his hand.

"T-Talan!"

"Words, baby, tell me what you want."

"I need you."

"What do you want?"

"Fuck me! Now!" she growled in warning.

Her world tilted, and she was on her back, Talan above her, his knowing smirk making her want to punch him and fuck him all at once.

Spreading her legs, he threw one over his shoulder, his cock poised at her entrance. She braced her hand behind her on the bed's footboard, shaking as she watched him pause, hovering above her.

"Ta—" His name was cut off with a gasp as he shoved into her in one fluid movement.

He filled her up, her core stretching around his girth, and her free hand clawed at the sheets, back arching off the bed. Talan held her leg firm, using the one over his shoulder as leverage as he rocked into her slowly.

Every push felt like fire and wholeness, and his name fell from her lips in a whisper.

"I know, Princess," he said softly, rocking his hips faster.

She met his eyes and found them burning with unsaid promises and… safety. She was safe with him, even now when she was naked and spread before him for the taking.

Sarah's whimpers turned to moans with every quick thrust of his hips, and she felt her climax building with every push. Her brain had turned foggy, but she knew what she wanted.

Catching him off guard, she wrapped her legs around his waist and flipped them around, straddling his hips. His stunned expression almost made her laugh, and before he could complain, she slid him inside, hands braced on his chest as she rode his cock.

Her hips rolled, breasts bouncing, and Talan gripped them as she fucked him. Her movements became erratic, his other hand going between her legs to rub her clit, and her head fell back.

Riding him over and over again until she felt her release coming.

"Talan, I'm..." her words choked on a scream as his hands gripped her hips, snapping his hips up and fucking her hard and fast as she came all over him.

"Fuck, Princess, I'm going... shit..." he growled roughly, trying to move her off of him.

She smirked, leaning forward and gripping his shoulders, thighs locking around his hips as she rocked over him, whispering into his ear, "Fill me up."

His brows furrowed, his mouth parting when she squeezed around him. "Are... are you—fuck—are you sure?"

She squeezed around him again, her core sensitive and wet, every firm thrust of him making her see stars. But a secret part of her wanted him to come in her, a near-silent tug whispering for him to claim her, mark her as his inside and out.

Talan gripped her hips with a final hard thrust, and a guttural moan slipped past his lips, his release spilling into her.

She could feel it filling her, and a strange new desire shot through her, and she peppered kisses along his neck and cheek down to his chest as he calmed. His ragged breathing filled the silence.

When his grip on her hips loosened, Sarah slumped on his chest, letting out a harsh breath.

Talan rubbed soothing circles on her back, kissing the top of her head.

"Good girl," he muttered into her hair, kissing her temple.

Sarah's lips twitched. "Good boy."

His chuckle rumbled through her chest, and she snuggled against him, his cock still buried inside of her, and she didn't mind. She could feel sleep edge closer, her eyes drooping.

Thunder rumbled outside, rain pattering against the long wall of windows, distorting the neon lights of the city.

"Princess, I should get you cleaned up and find that assistant to get you a morning-after potion."

Sarah shook her head. "No," she mumbled into his pectoral. "Don't need one. Stay."

His chest vibrated, and she knew he was laughing softly. "What do you mean you don't need one? Don't tell me you want little pups running around? I wouldn't mind, but…"

"Florin made sure we could never have children," she muttered, sleep quickly approaching. "He gave us a medication as children that made us infertile."

Talan's fingers, which were lazily tracing up her spine, froze.

"It's okay," she said, trying to soothe him as her eyes closed, the rain outside lulling her like a song. "I'm okay."

Arms banded around her protectively, and she felt him pull the satin sheets over her. Talan kissed her head, and she drifted off to sleep.

CHAPTER 28

SEVEN DAYS LEFT...

The storm worsened into the dark morning hours, and Brean tossed restlessly in bed. Wild red curls fanned around her, a soft whimper tumbling from her as thunder split the sky like a hammer.

Her body tensed, fingers fisting into her comforter. She was unaware as her door opened silently, and Savven slipped in like the night, dressed in black joggers and a white crew neck.

If Brean could see him, she would have thought he looked more human than Fae, but his face would give it away every time. Far too beautiful to be mortal.

His short hair was in disarray like his fingers had worked through it aggressively.

Lightning spiderwebbed the sky outside before thunder followed, and he frowned, watching the witch toss in her bed. Her eyes scurried behind closed lids, and he knew she was reliving her family's deaths. The reason for her dislike of thunder and why he stood in her room now.

Every time there was a storm, Savven would wait up to see if it passed quickly, and if not, he would find himself outside Brean's door. Waiting to hear silence, but it never came. The air was always filled with her terrified whimpers, and it wrenched his soul every time.

He would slip inside her room and, just as he did now, crawl into bed with her and hold her.

Savven carefully scooped her close to him, brushing her curls away from her sweat-dotted brow, and wrapped his arms around her. Cradling her close to his chest, his head resting atop hers.

With a flick of his finger, the tangled green bedding righted itself and softly covered them both.

Thunder rolled violently, and Brean sobbed, shaking.

Savven frowned, pain making his heartache. Tightening his arms around her slight frame, he drew her closer to him, trying to smother the darkness in her mind.

She had lost her parents to hatred.

Her guardian to greed.

Her new family to darkness.

Herself… for him.

She had given all of herself to this life, and Savven wanted to give her something in return, but she wouldn't accept his heart, not with this bargain she made with Death. So, instead, he gave her this. Peace in the stormy darkness.

Brean slowly began to relax, and when the thunder rolled through the air again, she didn't move or make a sound. She was safe, and she softly began to snore against his chest, and he smiled to himself.

"Sleep, my little witch. I will fight the darkness for you," he whispered in the tongue of his people.

Savven laid his head atop hers and pulled her tighter as he closed his eyes, but he never slept. Waiting for the storm to pass so he could slip away, though until then, he would lay with her and fight the torments of the sky so his witch could sleep peacefully.

Talan watched Sarah sleep soundly, her lips slightly parted, breathing slow and even. His head was propped up by his hand as he lay on his side, elbow resting on his pillow.

She had fallen asleep so quickly that he found himself smiling, remembering her still seated on him, curled into his chest. He had to slowly remove himself before he cradled her close and sat up, laying her back into the pillows.

He had taken the time to get a warm rag and carefully clean her up and tuck her into the covers, his thoughts on what she had said about her master. His anger had nearly boiled over, and he had wanted to shift so he could hunt down the fucker who had done so much to such an innocent child. But he had held back the wolf in him and took a long, cold shower to cool the rage instead.

Sarah didn't stir when he had slipped into bed beside her, even when he pulled her close to him, and she cuddled against his chest. He was expecting her to wake up at any moment and punch him for being naked in bed with her, and a smirk lifted his lips at that thought.

His finger slowly moved a piece of hair from her cheek, and he frowned. He still couldn't scent her, not even the shampoo she had used or the perfume she had worn—if she had worn any, and a part of him highly doubted she had, but he had scented her arousal. His brows furrowed in thought. She and Reign were both scentless, but why?

Despite being unable to scent her, Talan found himself drawn to the hellion beside him since he saw her. Watching her in the ruined village surrounded by death, he had known, even as a near-silent part of him whispered it to him, that where she went, he would go too.

Talan stilled, thinking of Tambiln and then his brothers. He could still hear the screams that tore through his mind, feel the pain as they died, and then the silence that followed, the hollowness that filled him afterwards.

But the longer he stayed with Sarah, the less empty he felt.

Laying back, he hooked an arm behind his head, staring at the vaulted ceiling.

He had started this journey off as a plot for revenge, to track down the bastards who slaughtered his pack. He had left his village, his sister, and went into the forest to seek out Death. Talan hadn't cared if he lived or died then, but now… he glanced at Sarah. Now he cared a little too much if he lived or died, the weird pull between them growing stronger and stronger the more he stayed around the woman at his side.

When he faced Reign within the mountain, he realised then that his journey was never to avenge his brothers. They were gone. They had returned to the earth—spirit and all, and a part of him will always feel that pain. But when he saw Alec, terrified but willing to fight to the end, all his ideas of revenge melted away. His sole focus shifted to the boy in the cell, and the woman he knew was coming for him.

Maybe he should feel guilty for no longer seeking revenge, but Talan couldn't find it in himself.

He looked down at Sarah, the frown on his face softening.

Revenge was coming, but it wasn't by his hands.

Scooting down into the bed, Talan pulled the woman beside him close, kissed her temple, and closed his eyes.

CHAPTER 29

Fear clung to Alec as he huddled within his cell, knees hugged to his chest, old tears dried to his cheeks.

Tap, tap, tap.

The sound of footsteps filled the abyss around him, and he lifted his head and looked at the small square of light that had infiltrated the darkness.

Cold blue eyes gazed at him from the other side of the bars, and icy talons went down Alec's spine.

"Be strong until I return." His sister's words made him purse his lips in defiance, and despite his fear, he stood and faced the icy depths staring at him.

Baring his teeth in a snarl, something overwhelming consumed him, and his body felt too small and too confined. Fear, anger…

and courage spiked through him, and his snarl turned into a small savage growl as he was overtaken by his emotions, and his body turned from boy to wolf pup.

Digging his paws into the stone, Alec lowered his head and bared his teeth. The male smirked at him, and Alec lunged for his face.

Wood slammed against his body, and a soft chuckle filled the cell.

Footsteps followed as the male walked away, and Alec slowly stood, confusion, pain, and fear coursing through him.

Returning to his shadowed corner, he sniffed the ground before turning in a circle and curling into a small ball, head on his paws facing the door.

A soft whine left him as he thought of his sister and waited.

"Now, she breaks it now. Now, now, now—"

Brean's eyes flew open in the still dark morning hours. She could hear it, the air. It was whispering instantly in her ear.

"Now, now, she goes now."

Her heart stuttered in her chest. This was it. The final moments before the sand in the hourglass runs out.

"She breaks the bonds; she breaks the magic."

It was never meant to last forever. *She* was never meant to live forever, and now, time had run out.

"Now, now, go now."

Closing her eyes, she sighed and slipped from her bed.

Álfheimr Towers was silent.

Sarah slipped through the grand halls undetected, black marble and gold surrounding her as she entered the ballroom.

It was dark, the only light coming from the large windows on the far wall with hints of dawn on the horizon.

The gala had been swept away as if it had never happened. The artefacts were stowed, probably in a vault somewhere, but one remained, anchored to the wall.

The long stone slab, the *altar*, was still displayed on the wall behind its glass housing.

She had awoken to Talan snoring softly in her ear, his arms wrapped tightly around her. There was a comfort she had never felt before, lying in his arms. She wasn't a virgin, but she had never had sex with someone out of desire or actual attraction. It had always been to satisfy a hunt, to obtain information, or simply because she needed to alleviate her anger. But with Talan, it had been something entirely… different. It had been… nice. It had been something she wanted to do again.

Flashes of their shared night made heat crawl up her neck, and she dared to smile at the thought. She had been half tempted to slip beneath the sheets and wake him up, the urge to be with him again stronger now, insistent. Still, something anxious crawled through her body like a spider overpowering that desire.

So, she had found herself slipping out of his room to hers, showering and dressing quickly in her freshly washed jeans and dark blue thermal, thanks to the king's assistant. It had felt good to slip back into her regular clothes and boots, hair tied back into a high ponytail. She felt like herself again.

Now, staring up at the stone, that anxiety intensified. The words danced back at Sarah as she read them.

"All ends have a beginning."

Her skin itched, and she shifted on her feet restlessly.

The words were taunting, and her mind went to the ruined

village and the tarot cards she had stepped on.

The Fool and Death.

Her heart began to beat faster, pounding in her ears as the blood rushed through her head.

"All ends have a beginning."

The air turned thick, like the words were whispering to her over and over again, and Sarah could feel the magic in the air. It was *suffocating*.

She was suffocating.

Ever since she arrived at this Godsforsaken tower everything had begun to change, her world narrowing around her. She was going to break.

Her skin felt too tight, too confining. The creeping feeling over her flesh was too much, and she sucked in a ragged breath, something within pounding against her skull like it was trying to break free.

"Fuck," she gasped, rubbing a hand over her arms, nails clawing at the fabric of her shirt until it tore. It was too much. Her skin felt foreign, and the longer she stared at the words, the harder her heart began to beat, pounding like a drum behind her ribcage.

She was faintly aware of a door opening and closing behind her, and Sarah stumbled as she turned. The world around her was flickering like a candle. Images wavering back and forth, and her breathing turned ragged.

The pain was starting to wrack her limbs, fingers balled into fists at her sides, and her jaw clenched when she saw the witch.

Brean stood reverently, dressed in a black fitted blouse, black trousers and flats… she looked like Death in the pale light of dawn filtering through the windows. Her hair wild and untamed around her face.

Sarah focused on the vibrant amber eyes that gleamed through the haze of her vision. "What's… happening?" she gritted out, the words strangled, every one of her movements a struggle, a fight against herself. She felt like she was trudging through mud and slowly drowning in it.

The thick air seemed to pause when Brean opened her mouth. She knew in her very fibre that magic was laced into the singular word as it seemed to fill the ballroom, and the world around her shattered into fragments.

"Sarah."

She screamed as pain split her in two, and her very soul was torn down the middle. Darkness consumed her, but before the abyss swallowed her whole, she had one singular, gut-wrenching thought that pierced the pain.

The truth.

That wasn't her name.

CHAPTER 31

Fury blinded Talan as he stormed the hallways of Álfheimr Towers, the animal within him pulsating beneath his flesh like a rabid beast, demanding he shift and find her.

Sarah hadn't been there when he woke up, the spot still barely warm. He had lain there for a moment, thinking about their night together, and a smile formed on his mouth before a scream filled his ears that had him sprinting out of bed.

He barely managed to throw on his jeans before running barefoot and shirtless out of his room. Reign's door flew open when his did, and they shared a brief look before they were flying through the corridors.

Now, with the Fae on his heels, Talan stalked towards the king's office, following the scent of the male that led them to a dark wood door.

He tried the black handle, it was locked, so he banged his fist on the wood instead. The door groaned and rattled violently.

"OPEN THE DOOR!" he roared.

Reign was a dark force behind him; he could feel the male stewing in whatever emotions he was feeling, but Talan didn't care enough to look back at him. If he was worried about losing her because of his fucking dark lord, then he would be facing Talan's wrath as soon as he found her.

"OPEN THE DOOR!" he bellowed again, the wood cracking under his fist.

The door opened, and the fury of the Fae king greeted him. He wasn't dressed like the king Talan had seen the day before or just last evening. He was in dark jeans, a black button down, sleeves rolled, and collar undone, his black hair askew.

"Where the *fuck* is she?" Talan demanded through gritted teeth.

He had every mind to grip the king by his throat and shake him, demanding answers.

The king pursed his lips, blue eyes flicking between him and Reign and back to Talan. "Brean has her."

"If the witch hurts her, I'll kill her," Talan snarled.

Before Talan could blink, the king grabbed him by the throat and slammed him against the wall. Reign quickly stepped out of the way to avoid being smashed.

The king leaned in close, teeth bared and dark promise swirling in his gaze. "If you threaten, touch, or look wrong in that witch's direction, I will pull your head from your body and stake it to the front of my tower for all to see."

The silence was palpable in the hall, Talan's nose wrinkling as he fought to tame the beast controlling his emotions.

His. Sarah was *his.* His to protect. To care for. To *find.*

He didn't know where those innate feelings had come from, but they settled within him as if they had been there all along. Talan nodded, a quick jerk of his chin, silently vowing to kill them all if anything had happened to her.

Savven stepped back, smoothing a hand over his hair as he looked between Reign and Talan.

The shifter rolled his shoulders back and released the tension after being slammed against a marble wall, eyeing the thin crack spiderwebbing across it.

"Brean has your counterpart with her. I will take you to them, but only under the promise that you *refrain* from going to them, no matter what you see."

More silence followed before Talan relented and nodded, seeing Reign do the same. He just needed to see her, to make sure she was okay, that she was alive.

The scream he had heard made his blood run cold, and Talan never wanted to hear something like that again. So, he nodded again, pushed the animal within him down until the torrent of emotions became more manageable, and swept a hand out to the open hall. "After you, *Your Majesty.*"

Savven opened the door to the ballroom, and Talan and Reign slipped inside, the king following as the door clicked shut.

Soft beams of sunrise were filtering into the dark space, orbs of fire suspended in a circle in the middle of the grand room, and within its centre was the witch and...

"Sarah!" Talan gasped.

Sarah looked like she was sleeping but was hovering over the ground like a sacrifice to the Gods. Palms facing up, strange dark green symbols were marked on the underside of her wrists, her chest barely rising, ponytail hanging below her unmoving. The witch stood before her, dark green magic sparking her fingertips, hands raised slightly. She was chanting something under her breath, head tilted back.

"What the *fuck* is she doing?!" Talan hissed darkly at the king, who watched the females with fixed interest.

"Shut up, Puppy."

Reign's dark tone made Talan's attention snap to the male. Dark brown eyes were trained on Sarah, he didn't think Reign was breathing. He had gone preternaturally still.

Talan shifted his feet, looking between the king, the witch, Reign, and Sarah. What the fuck had they gotten themselves into?

There was a thickness to the air, and Talan could feel the magic weave itself around them through the fire, and then it stilled.

Everything became quiet. Even the fire didn't so much as flicker, and the witch's chanting ceased, her head falling back completely.

The magic was still there, like a film he could taste, smelling the bitter tang of it. Talan stilled, feeling the air shift, and the three of them waited with bated breath.

There was darkness all around her. It seeped out of her bones, through her blood, and into the shadows that curled around her limbs like the gentle caress of a long-lost friend. But within that darkness sparked the soft glowing purple light of magic, shimmering with flecks of gold. Sarah reached out a hand to touch it, and though she couldn't see anything within the darkness, she felt it curl around her fingers.

Where was she?

She looked away from the shadows and magic, straining to see into the void that surrounded her. Nothing was visible.

Sarah frowned, opening her mouth, but nothing came out. Hand to her throat, she tried again. Nothing.

A soft, glowing blue light made her blink rapidly as it appeared in the distance.

Leaving the shadows behind, Sarah walked towards the light, raising a hand to shield her eyes the closer she got.

When her eyes adjusted, she stopped, gaping at the light that turned into a shimmering blue veil that had no end. Towering into the darkness high above her and stretching into infinity on either side. It was a fortress. However, the closer she looked, Sarah saw small hairline cracks in the wall.

"Magic is strange," said a softly lilting voice.

Sarah's head turned, finding Brean standing to her right, gazing at the veil in question. She didn't ask why the witch was here; something about this place felt familiar to Sarah as if she had been here before with

Brean.

Dressed in all black, the witch seemed to merge with the shadows, her hair like a beacon of fire. Sarah tilted her head in question, looking up at the divide as Brean hovered a hand over the cracks and traced along it. They stretched across the veil unending.

Amber eyes turned to Sarah, and the two women stared at one another.

"Beyond this is your truth." Brean dropped her hand, facing Sarah. "We met once when you were a child, and I was forced to hide not only you but the others in your circle. Many like you were hidden by parents or guardians to fit in with human society when the fall first happened, but you were different and so were the circumstances. There was something strange about your magic; it was vicious against mine, protective of you, and your guardian was not... kind.

"Right now, we are in the farthest reaches of your mind, the parts that have been fighting against my magic since it was embedded within you. Not enough to alert you, but as you've aged, it has gotten stronger, and the closer to the truth you got, the more it tried to break the veil... which is why you began to feel pain every time someone said your name. Given the cracks in my magic, I'm sure it would have eventually succeeded."

Brean paused, thinking. "But that's not your name, is it?"

Sarah...

... that wasn't her name...

Something brushed her hand, and she looked down at the magic-imbedded darkness curling around her fingers, faintly seeing her hand disappear into their swirling masses.

This was her mind. This was her.

"Come," Brean said, stretching a hand to her.

Looking between the darkness, the veil, and the witch, she paused before softly walking over to Brean. Lifting a hand laced with curling streams of black and purple shadows, she placed it into the witch's.

Facing the fortress of magic that stretched across her mind, the two women stepped beyond the veil, and the world splintered into a million pieces as light bathed the darkness around her, and the truth was set free.

CHAPTER 32

Sarah was spiralling through flashes of memories, each one brief glimpses of the past until the world stilled, and she was taken back nearly fourteen years ago where warm wind brushed her cheeks, the sun was hot, and blood didn't bathe the world....

"Mamma!"

Tiny legs cut through tall green grass like the wind, long black hair, a banner behind her, and a bright blue sky above.

"Saskia?"

"Mamma, look!" Saskia outstretched a shadow shrouded hand towards her mother as she ran towards her. Pink lips parted with a gasp, heart hammering in her chest as she skidded to a halt in front of her mother. "Look what I can do!"

Saskia raised her hands, and clouds of dark purple and black flecked with gold floated in front of her face, twisting in the air. Her vibrant green eyes widened in fascination. She watched the magic twine up her arms and giggled, feeling it tickle her skin.

"Oh, my darling girl, what power you hold," her mother said in awe, kneeling before her and fussing with the hem of Saskia's dark green tunic that had twisted around her body, pulling a length of grass off her black leggings.

Her mother's bright blue eyes stared up at her as she gently grabbed Saskia's hands and lifted them to her face to observe the dancing power.

"Mamma, why is it two colours?" Saskia whispered as if it were a secret said between her and her mother.

She had always been able to control things, move items at her command, make flowers blossom and wilt. But she had never seen it come to life like it did now, and when her mother touched her, it disappeared. Saskia frowned when the purple and black shadows vanished.

Looking at her mother in question, her blonde hair gleamed like the sun, and Saskia couldn't help herself as she pulled on a strand, waiting for an answer.

Sighing, her mother sat in the tall grass, tugging on Saskia's hand to follow.

She sat, crossing her legs and playing with the grass, summoning the shadows again and watching a small stem of black and purple curl around her finger.

"Saskia..."

She looked up at her name.

"Once, a long time ago, someone hurt me, someone I cared for. He put a darkness in me that corrupted my magic—"

"—Is that why your eyes sometimes turn black?"

Her mother smiled sadly. "Yes. But I contain it and have learned to control the darkness."

Saskia tilted her head, thinking about the times she saw the shift in her mother's blue eyes. It wasn't often, but... "Does Papa have it, too?"

"No, my love. He does not," she said with a shake of her head. "You, my daughter, are a product of the dark and light. Which is why your magic is two colours. You are not one thing but many. You are more powerful than you realise, and one day, you will be able to harness it and change the world."

Saskia frowned, looking at the thin shadows curled around her index finger. "What if I don't want to change the world? I like my world as it is. You're in it, and papa and brother."

Her mother chuckled, fixing her sky-blue dress before pulling Saskia into her lap and cradling her. "Then you won't have to. Everything is a choice, love."

"Mamma, I'm not a baby!" she said, wiggling in her hold, but a smile lifted her cheeks.

"Oh, no. You are certainly not a baby," her mother confirmed, dipping her head close to kiss the tip of her nose. "You are my savage daughter, wild and carefree. Never let the world tame you, my Saskia."

The memory changed.

The faces of her mother and her younger self tilted and shifted until the world blurred and the sunshine disappeared. She was transported to another memory, this one warm, secluded, and felt like... home....

"Have you heard from him?"

"No."

"I'm worried about him. What if he's let them consume him? What if he comes for her—"

"—Levina—"

"—the prophecy—"

"—my heart!"

Her mother's frantic words quieted, and Saskia pressed closer to the crack in the door, listening to their conversation.

Her papa pulled her mother close as she wrapped her arms around her middle, tears spilling down her cheeks. Why was her mother crying?

"Avian is my son, Torin."

Her papa sighed, pressing his cheek to her mother's head. "I know, my heart, I know."

Hands grabbed her waist, and Saskia squealed as her brother picked her up and spun her before holding her in his arms. She wrapped her little legs around his waist, bracing her arms on his shoulders as she leaned back and smiled at him.

"Brother!"

"Hello, little hellion. Have you been good since I've been away?" he greeted with a broad white smile, his dark red sweater matching his hair.

Dark brown eyes twinkled with laughter, and Saskia grabbed him by his tan cheeks, drawing their foreheads together. "You were gone for so long," she said with exasperation, eyes going crossed as she stared at him.

Laughing, his chest rumbling with the sound, he gently bonked her head with his and squeezed her tight. "I missed you too, sister."

Saskia giggled, pressing out of his arms. "You're squishing me!"

"What is this?"

The doors opened, and her parents stood with amused expressions, arms crossed.

"Brother's back!" she squealed with delight.

"Welcome back, Reign," her mother said warmly.

"Son," her papa greeted, pulling him in for a hug. "How was the hunt?"

Reign shrugged, tucking a long dark loch of auburn hair behind his ear as he set Saskia down. "It was good. Caught two bucks in the eastern ridge. It'll last us the winter."

Her mother leaned over Saskia, pressing a kiss on her brother's cheek. "Thank you, darling."

Saskia tugged on Reign's dark jeans, staring up at him. "Brother," she whispered, crooking a finger at him.

Reign cocked a brow at her and bent down. "Hmm?"

"Can you show me?" she asked in a hushed tone, despite knowing her parents could hear her.

He snorted and looked up at her parents.

"Go on," her mother sighed.

Reign straightened, offering his hand to Saskia, who promptly took it, his large fingers curling around hers.

"You know, little hellion, I was your age when I learned how to skin my first buck."

"Really?!" she gasped.

Humming in acknowledgement, he led them to the garage. "Father taught me, as I will now teach you. The first lesson: after we've taken their lives, we give thanks to their spirits and to the Gods for providing the meat so we may be fed. Life is a circle, and everyone is prey to some sort of predator, Saskia, don't forget that."

She stared after her younger self and her... brother... *Reign*, as they disappeared. Her mother and father stood frozen in time. Both wearing jeans, her mother in a white long-sleeve and her father in a light brown cable knit. Sarah lifted a tentative hand to their faces. Hovering over her father's olive skin, the memory of his stubble-covered cheeks against her palm still imprinted on her skin, nearly feeling it now, but she knew it was only a memory.

His green eyes, olive skin, and black curly hair skewed on his head made him look untamed, like the forest and mountains.

Her eyes shifted to her mother, who, unlike her father, was like the sun and sea. Her honey blonde hair was silky and long down her back, loosely pulled away from her face where sky blue eyes were wide and full of light. Her petite frame was thin and delicate, and her father, who was tall and solid like a tree, stood a head above her. They made a beautiful couple.

She reached for her mother, but before she could, the memory warped, and her parents melted away into the image of a quaint, cosy bedroom. *Her* bedroom.

"Papa!" Saskia squealed, grinning ear to ear.

Her father tickled her mercilessly, and Saskia gasped for air, scrambling under her blankets to get away.

He chuckled, stopping, and brushed her long black hair away from her face as she flopped down into her pillow, giggling.

"Alright, little one, enough of that. Bedtime."

Saskia snuggled deeper into her patchwork quilt, her father tucking it around her body until she was cocooned. "Papa, look what I can do," she whispered, wriggling her hand free.

Without much thought, thin black and purple shadows twined around her tiny hand.

"Ah," her father said. "Your mother said you learned some magic the other day." He reached out and grazed the black shadows with the tip of his finger, and a slight frown tugged on his mouth, curling his finger away.

Saskia noticed and freed her other hand, tugging her father's finger back towards her. Slowly, a purple shadow reached out and touched the tip of his finger. The red skin where the dark shadows had touched slowly mended, and the redness faded.

Green eyes met identical ones, and her father smiled at her. "You are a true wonder, my Saskia."

"Mamma said I can change the world, but I like our world. I don't

want to change it."

He chuckled and leaned forward, brushing a kiss to her brow. "Change comes in time, slow and steady. We all must change and grow, just as the world does. It is the law of nature, Saskia."

"Will you, mamma, and brother be there with me?"

"Always," he whispered, his eyes shining down at her with promise.

Her father stood, but Saskia reached for his hand, curling little fingers around his pointer finger.

"Papa?"

"Hmm?"

"Who's Avian?"

Her father stilled and sighed deeply, tucking a black curl behind one of his softly pointed ears before sitting back beside her. "Avian is a Fae, like yourself. Very powerful, but... troubled. Your magic is similar to his, but he does not possess the same qualities you have."

Saskia raised her hand, tiny webbings of black and purple lacing her skin. "Like how I told it to heal you?"

"Exactly, little one."

"Maybe I can show him!" she said excitedly, eyes widening.

Her father laughed softly, the sound somewhat sad, and Saskia frowned, lowering her hand.

"I think that would be very sweet of you, and I bet he would love that. Maybe in the future, little one, when you're bigger. But for now, I think its best if your mother and I try and help him first."

"If you and mamma are helping him, then I know he'll be okay."

Leaning forward, her father hugged her close, the scent of the alpines curling around her. She hugged him back, squeaking when he squished her to his chest in one mighty bear hug before releasing her.

Tucking the covers back around her, she yawned as he flicked a finger to her light, and it dimmed to near blackness.

"I love you, Papa."

"I love you, my Saskia."

Her cheeks were wet, and she lifted shaking fingers to her face as the memory stilled. Her father had just left, and her younger self had closed her eyes. She stared down at the sun-kissed skin, youthful heart-shaped face, long lashes, and full, small pink mouth slightly parted as her younger self fell into her dreams.

My Saskia.

Not *Sarah.*

Saskia.

Saskia.

The name slipped into the hollow spots of her soul and stitched itself into her very fibre like a missing piece.

Saskia.

The memory shifted and changed, and the world was dark. It was nighttime, and bright, cold blue eyes stared down at her...

"...but the power within you can be trained, and if you come with me, I will be able to teach you how to harness the power within you."

"Why?" Saskia asked, her frown only deepening, brows furrowing. He made her tummy fill with butterflies, but not the good kind, and she shifted on her feet slightly.

"You're special," he repeated, his jaw twitching, the only sign of his irritation.

"Why?" she asked again. The hair on the back of her neck stood on end, and it felt like something was watching her.

Her heart rate picked up, and she dared to glance at her hand as something brushed her fingers. A shadow curled around her middle finger, but it wasn't hers, and she pursed her lips to keep from gasping. Saskia grabbed the strange shadow, her own shadows curling around her fingers protectively, and it skittered away at their touch.

A low growl came from deep within his throat. "Because—" The male's words stopped short as a crash and a yell was heard from inside.

Saskia gasped then, her head darting to the house.

"Damned to hell, they're early," he muttered through clenched teeth.

She barely had time to see him lunge for her.

Saskia screeched and darted out of the way.

The male gave a twisted smile as a cry was broken off from inside. "Go and run, little one. They will catch you for me."

When Saskia blinked, he was gone.

Another crash had her gasping and sprinting for the house. She ran as fast as her legs could carry her through the still open sliding doors. Her heart was going to beat out of her chest, a weird tang filling the air that had her wrinkling her nose.

The living area was empty, and she stepped forward, slowing her pace, following the previous footsteps of her parents. The house was dark, and moonlight drifted in through the windows. Her footfalls were light and mute on the wood floors, and the people who loitered in their entryway did not hear as she approached.

Saskia licked her dry lips, coming to a halt. Her heart pounded in her ears, and her eyes locked on the hand she saw lying limply on the floor. She took a small, deep breath and walked around the people who stood there.

Her eyes widened, and her blood turned to ice.

It was her parents... it was her parents.

The bodies of what used to be her parents.

Her father's throat was slit, and her mother's head was cut clean off, blood pooling around their bodies like red and black mirrors. Their bodies lay together on the floor; her mother's head had rolled off to the side, her blonde hair caked in black blood, and her mouth opened in a silent scream.

Saskia began to shake uncontrollably, her heart thundering behind her ribs, and her breathing quickened to short gasps. Her mouth opened wide, and what came out wasn't a sob nor a cry but a blood-curdling scream.

The people there jolted in surprise as they turned to find her behind them. Her vision was blinded by tears as she threw her body to the ground, grabbing her father's hand, blood soaking her clothes.

"PAPA!" she screamed, searching his once vibrant eyes for life, but all she found was a cloudy green haze that didn't look back at her, smile, laugh, or tell her it was okay... "PAPA!"

Saskia threw herself to her mother, one small hand pulling on the blackened blonde hair to bring her head to her body. Tears burned her skin, her vision watery as she tried to piece her mother back together. "Mamma..." But her voice was as broken as her mother was, and Saskia cracked from within, trying to put her mother's head back on her body. "Mamma... please," she sobbed under her breath, desperate. "Please..."

"Enough of this," drolled a male, almost as if he were bored.

Saskia ignored him, brushing her mother's hair from her face and kissing her cheeks as if she could kiss her injuries away, as if her kiss could heal her, as her mother had healed hundreds of her scrapped knees and injuries before. "Please, Mamma..." she whispered through her tears, her voice broken.

"Take her."

Hands grabbed her at the male's command, and she fought them. Saskia kicked and screamed, trying to fight her way out of the iron grip. The blood of her parents stained her arms and legs, streaking the side of her face as she fought them.

"Stop squirming!" said a snarky female voice in her ear.

Eyes flashing with rage, Saskia twisted her body and drew her nails across the female's face, limbs flailing wildly, trying to escape.

The female's green eyes widened with outrage, snarling, her teeth snapping in front of Saskia in warning. A russet curl slipped out of her bun as she fought to hold the little girl back.

"No!" Saskia screamed, hair whipping around her as she lashed out, nails digging into the hands that held her. "NO!" She grabbed the female's curl that had come free and ripped it out.

The female screamed, nearly dropping her.

"Stop fucking around. Get her to the car," the male said, stepping into view.

Shoulder-length dark blonde hair and dark brown eyes stared down at Saskia, and she bared her teeth at him.

"Savage little beast, aren't you?" he remarked cooly.

"Laud—"

The female's head whipped back as the back of his hand struck her hard and fast. Saskia froze, eyes going wide.

"What have I said about saying my name outside the manor?" he said coldly, brown eyes turning black.

Shifting, the female spit out blood and straightened, her hands tightening and bruising Saskia's skin.

"Apologies, Florin," she muttered, albeit bitterly.

Florin hummed dismissively. "Get her to the car. We're done here."

Saskia kicked and screamed, the female throwing her over her shoulder and keeping an iron grip across her back. Eyes trained on her parents' bodies, Saskia didn't take her eyes off of them until a car door was slammed in her face.

She lunged for the handle and snarled when it was locked, banging a shadow-covered hand against the glass. Magic flared in her veins, and she smashed her fist against the glass over and over and over again. It didn't give.

The black-haired male stepped from the shadows and pinned Florin to the side of the house. Saskia stilled, her fist against the glass. She watched the males with wide eyes.

Florin laughed while the blue-eyed male leaned in close and whispered something. Even from the window, Saskia could see his anger rolling off him.

In a flash, Florin removed the male and had him pinned in his place. Shadows pressed along both males, dark veins creeping along their forearms, but Saskia could see Florin outpowered the other—just enough, just for tonight. But something told her it wouldn't always be like that.

Shoving his body into the side of her home, she winced at the mark it left. Florin said something to the other male that had his mouth twisting into a snarl, his blue eyes turning to ice. Florin just laughed and walked towards the car.

Heart hammering in her chest, Saskia didn't take her gaze from the blue eyes that stayed trained on her through the glass. Even when the front doors opened and closed. Even when the car turned on, and they began to drive away.

Something caught her eye. In the shadows of the tree line, just off from her house, was a blur of red. She pressed an open palm to the glass, watching the flash of colour move in and out of the trees. Her breathing came in short pants, her heart racing.

The shadow burst from the treeline when the car picked up speed and pulled onto the road.

"Brother," she breathed, moving to the rear window, hope sparking within her.

Reign sprinted after the car, but they were too fast, even for his Fae speed.

He stumbled, hand outstretched, reaching for her with his eyes wide and face contorted with desperation. She reached back, but it was no use. They were too far—too fast.

The hope faded from her as quickly as it had come.

She pressed her blood-stained hand to the glass, her heart falling in her chest as she whispered, "Brother..."

The memory froze, putting a hand over the smaller one of her younger self, and though their skin never touched, light flared between them. She gasped as pain cleaved open her head and black and purple shadows exploded through the image, claiming her.

And finally… after fourteen years… Saskia awoke.

CHAPTER 33

Three things happened all at once:
1: The orbs of fire extinguished.
2: Brean collapsed.
3: Darkness exploded from Sarah and consumed the ballroom.
Talan sucked in a sharp breath as the world went black, arms going instinctively to shield his face.
Silence.
One heartbeat… two… three… slowly, he lowered his arms when nothing happened, a faint purple light illuminating from within the pitch.
Amber eyes glowing in the darkness, he tried to see through the swirling shadows that curled around the light. He looked to his left and couldn't see Reign, but he felt him move towards the glint of

purple, and a faint outline of his face came into view.

Slowly, the darkness began to melt away, retracting like something or someone was calling them back. Beams of sunrise filtered into the ballroom, bathing it in warm orange light, and the shadows disappeared entirely, but in its place...

Heart hammering, he looked at the woman who now lay on the ground, still as the dead.

It wasn't Sarah.

The king, who must have caught her before the darkness descended upon them, was on the floor, cradling the witch to his chest. One arm wrapped around her shoulders, the other cradling her head, but when he noted Talan, he followed his stare and frowned.

The witch stirred, and Savven looked down at her with a tender stare. She blinked twice, and Talan watched as she tried to stand, the king shaking his head. Brean smiled gently up at him, lifting a hand to cup his cheek, and the king sighed heavily. He stood with her in his arms and carefully set her down, waiting for her to find her footing.

Brean kissed Savven's palm when she was steady and faced the woman.

Talan approached when she stood alone, his breathing heavy in his chest, heart thudding behind his ribs.

She was dressed the same: dark blue thermal, jeans, and boots, but that was all of Sarah that remained. Before them wasn't a woman... but a female.

A delicate heart-shaped face, high cheekbones and full pink mouth were framed by sun-kissed tawny skin, delicately pointed ears, and long ebony hair strewn across and blending into the black marble floors. Her body was still lean and long, but his eyes narrowed on the curl of shadows, thin bands of black and purple that moved across her skin like a shield.

The silence was deafening, and Talan gritted his jaw, taking a single step towards her when the smell—the *scent*—hit him, and he fell to his knees.

His bones jarred at impact, but he didn't care, didn't pay attention as his world narrowed to just the female before him. The pull that had been there from the start tightened in his chest until he could barely think of anything else.

Her scent mixed with his, she smelled like the forest—like home. Like mountains in the winter, evergreens in the summer, and the earth in the spring just after rainfall.

The wolf within him stilled, in shock, and his world that had cleaved in two at the loss of his parents and his brothers mended at the single realisation of who the female before him was. What she had been all along.

His.

She was *his.*

His mate.

"Sarah," he breathed, barely audible.

Her name was like a calling, and the female's eyes flew open.

Eyes that were a beautiful, vibrant green like fresh moss turned to look at him. Power filled those depths, the shadows melting into her skin as she sat upright, long black curly hair falling down her back.

"Sar—"

Darkness fell across her face, silencing him. He had never seen anyone or anything so beautiful look so damning.

"Do *not* call me that *fucking* name ever again."

CHAPTER 34

Shadows curled around her hand, and Saskia watched them snake across her skin in strands of black and purple. Opening her palm, whisps of smoke like magic appeared. Within the black depths was the faintest shimmer of gold before the dark purple mixed into it.

They were arguing. Well, she wasn't, but everyone else was. They were back in the same conference room they had arrived in, the wall of windows filled with morning light that bathed the room. Saskia was leaned back in her chair, mostly ignoring the voices around her as she focused on the shadows and magic dancing between her fingers.

When she had woken up… when *she* had woken up, it felt like breathing after being near death. She had been trapped within her own mind, chained by foreign magic, but even so, she had fought for nearly fourteen years. Her body and mind protesting the humanity forced on her.

Talan had made to call her Sarah; the thought of the name made her lip curl in disgust, but she had shut him down. A needle drop would have echoed in the silence that followed.

Brean swept in to help her stand and suggested they move to a more discreet location. Saskia had barely heard her, pushing off the witch's help and staring after the head of auburn hair that had disappeared behind the now-closed ballroom doors.

"Brother," she had whispered.

"*Brother?*"

She ignored Talan's incredulous stare and made to go after Reign when Brean stepped in front of her. "Come, let's speak now, and you can find him after."

Saskia had almost shoved the witch off of her, but a dark warning glance over the petite woman from the king had her complying.

Now, she flicked her gaze up at the three who argued about current and future events, and she wished her shadows would fill the room so she could disappear. The king was seated in the chair at the end of the table. Brean leaned against the windows, her arms folded across her black blouse, and Talan was across from her, now fully dressed. She could feel his gaze flicker to her every so often.

"You can't make her stay here," Brean said, exasperated. "She's not a prisoner, Savven."

Savven waved a dismissive hand. "Letting her walk right into Avian's territory would either be an execution for her or for us. The coin hasn't landed yet on who has the favourable odds."

"That isn't your choice to make," growled Talan.

The king shot Talan an annoyed look. "She's too powerful to do as she pleases. It could jeopardise everything."

"Oh, I'm sorry, I forgot your *precious* kingdom is a top priority," Talan sneered.

Blue eyes flashed in a warning. "You don't understand, Shifter."

The room shuddered with the king's power, and Saskia tilted her head, eyeing him.

"What," she said softly, "Does he not understand?"

The conference room went quiet, all eyes snapping to her.

When the king didn't answer, she straightened, her gaze calculating, the shadows curling up her arm. "Go on, Your Majesty. *Enlighten us.*"

Savven sighed, and after a moment, he leaned forward, fingers interlocked on the long desk, the rolled sleeves of his black button-down stretching around his forearms as he looked directly at Saskia. "I failed your parents. Your mother, his father."

Brean shifted by the windows as if she knew what the king spoke of, but Saskia paid her no mind.

"Avian is the product of what happened to his father, Ezra, after his father saved my cousin. Levina, your mother, *his* mother, is the result of what happened when she tried to save our kingdom. Our people. Our home. I thought Ezra lost, and Levina dead trying to go after him. I was wrong on both counts."

Her heart dropped a fraction at the mention of her mother. The image of her decapitated body seared into her memory.

"Avian's father was a close friend who took a killing blow to my cousin. Because of his immortal heritage, he survived, but it changed him. The shadows took over, and he did… unspeakable things, but he was only a puppet. The true villain was a shade called Nazar, who was using Ezra to build up an army of the undead before he tried to kill him and take over. Your mother was Ezra's prisoner after she made a bargain with him to try and save our people, and Avian was the outcome of that."

Saskia folded her arms over her chest. "How do you know this?"

"Because I lived through it… and your mother sought me out sometime after the fall with Avian. He was only four, but the signs were there. He wasn't like us, like the Fae. He was different. Just as you are."

"What signs?" Saskia asked.

"The blood. He craved blood all the time. Your mother kept him fed on animal blood, but I found him just before he attacked one of my people. I told your mother, and Brean tried to put a containment spell on his urges, but it was too much. It didn't last, and your mother took Avian into the mountains, away from humans and Fae alike, where I suspect she met your father."

"What the fuck."

Saskia glanced at Talan.

Talan narrowed amber eyes on the king, his biceps flexing as he crossed his arms over his white henley. The sunlight lit up behind him, giving his chocolate curls a golden glow, his olive skin vibrant. He looked too handsome for his own good despite the circumstances.

Her mate.

Her jaw twitched with the thought. It was insanity. But it all made sense. From the very beginning, it had been there, slowly fighting the magic hold on her, bringing them closer and closer. She knew it the moment she saw him when she awoke. His scent alone, like a campfire in the summer, warm, inviting and peaceful, made her want to curl around him and never leave his side. Still, every trained instinct in her stood firm in keeping him at bay until they could talk privately.

"You're holding her prisoner because you feel *guilty?*" Talan questioned darkly.

Savven looked at Talan, frowning. "I'm not holding her prisoner; I'm keeping her safe while also keeping my people safe until we can figure out a better way of handling this. If Avian gets his claws into Saskia, there's no telling what will happen. He's powerful, more powerful than I've ever seen but—" he turned to Saskia "—but there is power in you too, Saskia. You and Avian are the first of your kind. Until we can figure out how to avoid an all-out war, I cannot allow you to leave."

"Savven..."

Brean approached the male quietly, his back to her as he stood before the long stretch of windows overlooking his city. His black hair was skewed, shoulders tensed, she wanted to ease the stress building in his muscles.

"Savven," she whispered, laying her hand on his shoulder and coming around to look up at him.

Blue eyes flicked briefly down at her, and she tilted her head, giving him a small, knowing smile. "You can't keep her here forever."

"If it keeps her alive, then I'll do what I must," he replied, his mouth set in a stubborn line.

Smiling, she shook her head, brushing away a curl that fell. "What will I do with you?"

"Let me love you."

Brean scowled at him when he spoke in the Fae tongue. "Savven."

He raised his brows. "Little witch?"

"You know that's not fair," she said, pursing her lips.

That earned her a small smile.

"Many things in this life are not fair," he mused, giving her his full attention.

Brean should have backed up a step when he turned, their bodies brushing against one another, but she couldn't make herself move. His heat made her heart stutter, and her skin flushed, a shiver running down her spine.

Savven leaned down until he was close enough for her to kiss with ease if she so chose, but she didn't. Instead, she knitted her fingers together behind her back, restraining herself.

"One day," he murmured softly, "I will tell you in every language so you will always know how I feel."

His voice was like a caress along her skin, and she watched his eyes drop to her mouth, lingering. Brean licked her lips quickly, and his gaze snapped back to hers, heat filling those depthless blues.

"If I had known who she was sooner, I would have done something about it then. But now, my hands are tied, and this is the only thing I can do."

"But to make her a prisoner?" Brean argued, trying not to think of how near he was and how much she wanted to press closer.

"She's free to wander wherever she wants, so long as it's not out of Álfheimr Towers—just until I figure out a solution. Avian poses a risk to everything we've built. To our people's safety, their homes, *our* home. I can't just let that all go. I can't lose another one."

Brean's heart lurched at his words, her breath catching, and she looked up at him through her lashes. "*Our* people?"

Savven's jaw flexed, and he inched closer. Raising a hand, he cupped her cheek, his thumb stroking the skin there. "They are your people as much as they are mine. This is your home, my home, *our home.* I will not allow it to fall."

She leaned into his touch and sighed. He was doing what he had to for their sake. He was doing what he thought was right, but Brean knew better... she knew Death was waiting in the shadows for them all.

CHAPTER 35

Saskia hesitated; her fist raised to knock on the dark wood door in front of her, but something inside of her coward at what lay beyond it.

Flexing her hand to disperse the energy tingling at her fingertips, she dropped it to her side, finger tapping her thigh instead as she faced off with the door.

"Saskia?"

She sighed. "Yes?"

Talan eased up behind her. "What's going on?" His tone was hesitant as if he was approaching a rabid animal.

She didn't blame him. She felt feral. Her mind was a slew of memories and images of her past, present, and thoughts of her future. Saskia was ready to free fall off the side of Álfheimr Towers if only to put her mind to rest. The overwhelming scent of Talan behind her was not helping.

She was spiralling into a sea of emotions, falling too fast to grasp onto one to make heads or tails of what was happening.

Dropping her head, she sighed deeply. "Talan," she whispered.

He stepped closer to her.

"I need… a moment." She turned to face him. His brows were furrowed with concern, confusion in his eyes mixed with a longing from the sudden life-altering bond thrust upon them when she had awoken.

Closing her eyes, she took a deep breath before opening them and stepping closer to him. Palm pressed against his chest, feeling his heartbeat behind his ribs; she let the steady *thump-thump* centre her.

He wrapped a warm, callused hand over hers, his amber eyes turning molten, nostrils flaring as he scented her. He could smell her now, and she frowned, anger spiking through her again in a short burst before she pushed it down. She would be angry later. Instead, she stared up at the male before her, who looked at her so softly and adoringly that it added to the spiralling mass of emotions she didn't know what to do with.

Talan, while she could see it pained him to do so, leaned forward, kissed her cheek tenderly and stepped back. Saskia shivered when his heat disappeared. She nearly pulled him back but stopped herself, stepping back instead, furthering the distance.

"Wait for me?" she asked quietly.

"It would seem I've waited my entire life for you," he mused wryly. "What's a little longer?"

Something burned her eyes, and Saskia blinked. Realising his words struck her where it counted, and tears formed. Pursing her lips, she sniffed and cleared her eyes. She couldn't afford to be sentimental right now.

"I promise, Puppy, you get me next," she said with a crooked smile.

He stared at her so intensely that heat started to coil in her core. He smirked, and she scowled, smacking him with a huff.

Talan glanced at the door behind her, smirk dropping, before he walked around her to his room. "If he tries anything, I will kill him," he promised darkly. "Brother or not, Princess."

Saskia watched him slip into his room, and the door clicked shut. She was alone.

Silence enveloped the hall, and she turned to the door again, her heart rate speeding. The nerves she had felt came back tenfold, and her finger began tapping on her thigh again.

She paused, her finger stilling.

A memory flooded her mind of her running through the clotheslines behind their home as a child, no more than five years old. Her mother hanging washed items to dry in the sunshine…

"Saskia," her mother said exasperated, "watch where you're running. Don't pull the clothes off."

Saskia wrinkled her nose, hands grasping the sheet tangled around her face she had run into and pulled it free. "Sorry, mamma."

Her mother chuckled, shaking her head, and Saskia watched her stare at the large basket of wet clothes. Blonde brows furrowing, her mother's hair glowing golden in the light, Saskia watched her finger tap the side of her jean-clad thigh.

Holding a little finger up, head cocked to the side, Saskia brought her finger down and copied her mother's movements, tapping it on the side of her leg. After a moment, she looked up at her mother and asked, "Why don't you use magic to dry them?"

Her laughter made Saskia smile, and she turned and scooped her up into her arms. "I find magic makes me lazy, and when I'm lazy, my mind tends to overthink things, little one. So, I do things like humans to keep myself occupied."

"Can I help?" Saskia asked, bending forward until she was nearly hanging upside down in her mother's arms, grabbing for a damp sheet.

Her mother's laughter filled the air. "Of course, little one."

The memory faded, and Saskia raised a brow at the finger frozen mid-tap beside her leg. Her mother had always been with her. It was in her small nuances of everyday living, and that thought alone brought more tears to her eyes, and she quickly blinked them away.

Steeling away her emotions, lips pursed in determination, Saskia raised a fist to the door and knocked.

The tension was thick and awkward as Reign and Saskia stared at one another.

She was leaning on the vanity of his wardrobe, arms crossed and staring at him expressionless. He was on the opposite side of the room, standing by the wall of windows, his face just as unreadable.

A wave of emotions spiralled through Reign like a torrent of air, heart hammering, blood rushing through his ears; but he barely moved, eyes fixated on the female before him.

Fourteen years… he had been searching and *waiting* for fourteen years.

"Saskia."

Her name was barely a breath on his lips, but she heard him. She shifted against his vanity before going preternaturally still.

She was as he remembered. Long black hair, mossy green eyes, tan skin, but her eyes… her eyes were hard, untrusting. Still, there was *something* beyond that, something he was feeling similarly. He could feel the anxious tension in his muscles, and he knew in the tight lines of her shoulders and the hard press of her mouth that she was feeling it, too.

His sister had been the hunter this whole time, is still a hunter. Like every other hunter before… she had become one of them, and… "Saskia," he said again, clearer this time.

She tilted her head a fraction, eyes narrowing on him.

Jaw flexing, he straightened, pushing up the sleeves of his black thermal. "I…" He what? What would or could he say to fix this? Where would he start? His *sister* was *alive*. It was the only thing his mind could fixate on, and he didn't know how to approach it, especially when she looked at him like a stranger.

"Saskia, I—"

"—Tell me what happened that night," she interrupted.

His brows furrowed.

"Tell me what I'm missing." Her voice was beginning to shake. "Make me understand why my brother is working with the *monster* who helped slaughter our parents."

Reign could see the fury rolling off her, the hurt mixed into it, and his chest cracked when he saw it directed at him. The betrayal was evident in her eyes.

"The night I lost you," he began, "The night our parents were murdered was the worst moment of my life." He combed a hand through his hair, growling low in frustration. "You don't understand—"

"—You betrayed them," she said darkly, shadows flickering at her fingertips.

"You don't understand," he tried again.

Saskia scoffed. "I think I do."

"I did it for you!" Reign snarled.

Silence.

Her mouth wobbled, but he watched her bite back the tears, clenching her jaw.

He stepped towards her slowly, his chest cracking the closer he got to her. "I did it all for you, Saskia." His whisper was broken, throat constricting with every emotion racing through him. "I *failed* you as your brother. They took you, and I wasn't fast enough. I watched them drive off with my little sister, our parent's mangled bodies in the foyer of our home, and I was left alone with the aftermath." The truth out loud felt like a dagger to his chest, pain ripping through him with every spoken truth. He hadn't allowed himself to speak of what happened for fourteen years, and now... now it was all coming out like a broken dam.

"I overheard Avian and your abductor arguing when you were locked in the car. Avian had made a deal with him that he could have our parents so long as Avian got you. But the male went back on their deal, slaughtered our parents, and then took you." His voice was shaking, and he curled his fingers into fists before shoving them into the front pockets of his black jeans, the sunlight streaming between them like a barrier. "Avian was just coming into his power then. Whoever your abductor is was stronger than him, and when they drove off with you, I... I... I ran as fast as I could, Saskia. But you were gone, and all I had left was the memory of what used to be our family."

She hadn't moved since he started talking, her face unreadable, so he swallowed the knot in his throat and said, "I made a promise to myself to find you. I didn't know how I would find you, or where, or if you would be dead or alive. But I would find you. I would bring you home."

"Why Avian?"

Her question was soft and reserved; he almost didn't hear it.

"Because I knew he would find you. He was my lifeline to you." Tears burned his eyes at the unspeakable things he had seen and done in the last fourteen years, but he wouldn't regret them. No. Not when before him stood the very reason for his heinous acts.

"He's a monster," she intoned bitterly.

"If me becoming a monster as well to save my sister makes me the bad guy, then damn me to eternal fire, Saskia. But I wouldn't change my decision for anything in this world. Because I am standing before you, looking at my sister who is alive, breathing, healthy... but *alive*." He shook his head in disbelief, licking his lips. "I thought when I finally found you that you would be *dead*. Dead, Saskia!" His voice was raising with every word, and Reign could feel himself beginning to shake from the nerves and relief he felt coursing through his body. "Do you understand what it's like seeing your little sister taken after your parents are slaughtered and then making the conscious decision to befriend the enemy just so I could spend over a decade of my eternal life searching for you? Praying that every hunter who came to us, who struck a deal with Avian, who I brought to this Gods forsaken city, would have some sort of tie or knowledge of you. But they all died the same way, and none knew of you. You had *vanished* from this world, and now you stand before me. You don't understand."

Reign was shaking, and his eyes burned, but he didn't move. Slowly, so slowly, Saskia unwound her arms, walking silently towards him. Her face was impassive, the sun streaking across her cheekbones as she stopped before him.

Saskia looked up at him, her green eyes searching. "You're right, I don't understand. I spent fourteen years being beaten, trained, and honed to kill those like us." Tears brimmed her eyes, making the mossy green turn emerald. Reign could see the internal battle within as she fought back her emotions. But she wasn't winning, and a tear streaked down her cheek. "You did what you had to to find me. You became a monster because of a monster." She made to touch him, but her hand dropped back to her side. "And so did I."

Reign reached for his sister instead and found her hand shaking at her side.

Another tear fell down her cheek, her mouth pressing into a stubborn line. Breathing heavily through her nose, he watched her try and fail to tame her tears, but they continued a silent trek down her face.

"I guess we've both been in hell… brother."

His world teetered when she called him brother, and he fell to his knees before her. "I'm so sorry," he whispered through his tears. He didn't care. He let them fall, every emotion vanishing except one: relief. It crashed through him with tidal wave force, drowning out the mindless, bloody torment he had endured for so long and cleansing the carnage from his soul. "I'm so sorry, sister."

Saskia kneeled before him silently, staring at him nearly eye-level, her eyes glassy and wide, reminding him so much of the little girl he had known. Without a word, she pulled him into her arms for the first time in fourteen years, and Reign cried openly as he held onto his little sister. Sunlight streamed around them as it bathed their dark world with light.

CHAPTER 36

Numb, tired, green eyes stared back at her as Saskia braced her hands on the black marble counter of the modern bathroom. A towel was wrapped around her still-damp body, steam curling in the air from her shower. The inlaid lights of the mirror covering the wall were too bright, too white. It exposed every imperfection and flaw across her body… but there wasn't any. Just scars, but all human traces were wiped from her.

A stranger stared back.

Straightening, Saskia dropped the towel around her feet, delicate pointed ears poked through long black hair, wet and curling around her arms as she traced a finger over one of the scars. Her only reminder of what once was.

Naked and exposed to the too-bright lights, Saskia studied her face and her body and searched for traces of *her*. But which version of her was she looking for?

Black and purple shadows glimmered across her damp tan skin. She tilted her head, regarding them. They feathered from her hand to her collarbones, her breasts, wrapping around her torso before it curled back to the hand she offered and sank into her skin.

A scar from the lick of a whip slashed the small part of her waist on her left side, and she traced it, remembering who gave it to her.

"You are a soldier. A killer. A thing of nightmares. If I say march, you march; if I say kill, you kill!*"*

Florin's voice echoed in her memories, and she frowned. She had failed in one of their training simulations because she wouldn't kill the fox she had been hunting and was punished for it.

She killed every animal after that.

Another scar, a burn mark on her hip from Naschta.

Another on her bicep from a hunt.

Another and another and another... she turned her wrists over, seeing the faint silver lines from the garrotte wire still there.

These scars she knew, and they knew her. But when she looked up slowly at the beautiful, weary reflection staring back at her, all she saw was a stranger staring back, and a silent tear trailed down her cheek.

Nostrils flaring, her gut clenching with anger and guilt and... grief, she sucked in a ragged breath turning on the stainless faucet. The sound of water filled the room, drowning out the ringing in her ears. She rolled her head back, trying to loosen the tension, but it didn't work, and a soft sob slipped past her lips instead.

When she looked back at herself, all she saw was a child. Once smiling, full of laughter, love, and family, but now she was broken. Little pieces of a once beautiful life destroyed.

A shiver wracked her body, her nipples peaking at the ice filling her blood and goosebumps rose along her arms. Turning the faucet to hot, she waited until steam rose, and she shoved her frozen fingers under the stream.

The discomfort of the heat centred her. She sucked in a tight breath, watching her fingers go from pale to bright red until pain stabbed through her chest, and a guttural sob ripped out of her as she watched the water turn to blood.

Bright red covered her skin, and she lifted shaking hands in the air, watching the crimson liquid turn black and drip down her wrists.

Saskia screamed, short and sharp. It was her parent's blood on her hands, and she stumbled away from the counter, back crashing against the frosted glass shower wall. She fell to her knees, staring at her hands, shaking uncontrollably.

There was so much blood.

"Saskia!?"

A bang on the bathroom door, followed by persistent pounding, echoed in the space, but she couldn't hear it.

"Saskia!"

Her name was a distant echo, and she blinked slowly, feeling her world spin out of control. A control she had so delicately put together to survive the world she lived in, but it was spinning and spinning and spinning....

Hands grabbed her by the shoulders, bright golden eyes infiltrating her vision.

"Saskia!"

She trembled, looking down at her crimson-stained skin, and lifted her trembling hands. "Look," she sobbed, her throat clenching around the word. "Look at their blood on my hands. M-my—my fault. It's all my fault!"

A large, callused hand wrapped around her bloodied ones while another hand tipped her chin up.

Gentle gold eyes stared down at her as Talan forced her to look away from her parents' blood. "No, Saskia. It's not your fault."

She made to show him her hands, but he held firm. "Just look," she cried, her eyes burning with the tears dripping from her jaw.

"I am," he said quietly.

But he wasn't looking at her hands.

"Look," she said feebly; her energy was waning, the world slowly steadying the longer he stayed with her, her hands beginning to shake as the cold returned.

"I am," he repeated. He held onto her chin, forcing her gaze on him. "I am looking, Saskia. I see you, I promise. I see you."

"Their blood—"

"—is not on your hands." Talan reached for her discarded towel, took her hands, and turned them up so she could see the blood collecting on her palms.

Saskia bit back her whimper and watched, instead, as he wiped the blood from her hands.

He wiped the towel across her palms and the backs of her hands until the red staining her skin was gone. Clean, tan hands stared back at her.

"I thought the blood of my brothers and parents would stain my skin forever. I carried that weight with me, and a part of me still does," he murmured, setting the towel aside. "It's a heavy burden to bear, and if I didn't have anyone, it might have become too heavy. But I had my sister when I lost my parents, and when I lost my brothers... I had you."

Saskia blinked, staring at him through waterlogged lashes.

"Whether we were mated or just fated to meet, Saskia, you made the burden of my brother's deaths so much easier to bear until I realised I had let go of it entirely. Not because I had forgotten them, but because I realised their fates were not mine to control... just like your parents."

She shook her head in protest, but he took hold of her chin between his thumb and forefinger.

"Their blood is not on your hands. I don't know exactly what happened, and maybe we will talk about it one day. However, I know this: you were a child, Saskia," he stated firmly, his tone still gentle, but a line of steel went through it that made her listen. "What could you have done differently that would have altered the course the Gods' chose for them?"

It was a rhetorical question she tried and failed to answer regardless.

He offered the towel to her.

She looked at it, staring at it silently before she took it and opened it up, expecting the stain of blood.

"You're not alone, not anymore. Lean on me... I'm right here. I'm not going anywhere."

It was clean. The towel was clean. The faucet was still running with scalding hot water, the cold hard press of marble was biting into her knees painfully, and that's when she saw the bathroom door. Half was attached to the doorframe, and the other half was splintered apart like he had torn it off.

He noticed her stare and smiled sheepishly, rubbing the back of his neck. "Do you think they uphold the *break it you buy it* rule?"

Saskia laughed, startling herself and her frazzled nerves, but the sound felt good, and she did it again, looking at him. Despite Talan's firm ridge of masculinity, a sense of distress underlined it. She took in his dishevelled hair and the slight crinkle of worry around his beautiful eyes.

"You look like a mess," she commented with a huff.

He smirked. "Speak for yourself."

She smiled, sighed, and the laughter slowly died. "I'm sorry," she whispered, defeated.

Talan's hands went under her arms, and he pulled her into his lap, repositioning them against the shower as he wrapped his arms around her and held her close. His warmth seeped into her frozen bones, and Saskia felt the ice slowly begin to melt.

"Don't be," he said quietly against her hair.

And for the first time in her life, she wasn't.

She couldn't sleep, even with Talan's soft even snoring in her ear. Laying on her back, his thick arm draped over her stomach protectively. He had carried her to her bed and made to tuck her in and leave when she had stopped him.

"Don't," she had whispered. "Don't go."

He hadn't moved, so Saskia opened her legs and pulled him between them, dragging his mouth to hers. She needed to feel something, anything, and he made her feel safe, so she nearly found herself begging him to stay when he broke their kiss despite her whimper of protest. But Talan had gently pressed her onto her back in the middle of her bed, kneeled before her, hands wrapped around her lean, tawny legs, and looked up at her like a male worshipping a goddess.

"This is not about me or us, Princess," he had growled against her thigh, placing a soft kiss on her inner leg. "Maybe tomorrow or the day after, but right now, I'm going to devour you."

And he had.

His mouth sucking, teasing, licking until she couldn't breathe except to gasp his name before she crashed over the edge with her orgasm, thighs locked around his face, one hand fisted in his hair, the other in her black sheets.

Afterwards, he cleaned her up with a warm rag, picked her up and tucked her into bed. He didn't have a chance to ask if he could stay before she pulled back the other side of the comforter, looking at him expectedly. He turned off the lights and silently crawled into bed beside her, pulling her into his chest and wrapping his arms around her… where they were now.

But Saskia hadn't slept, not yet. Instead, she lay comfortable in the oversized king bed, thoughts racing over the future and the past before they clashed in her brain, and she frowned. Holding her left hand above her face, her new vision heightened in the darkness. She watched the black bargain digging into her flesh.

The thorns were trailing down her forearm now, stabbing into her skin, but she didn't feel the pain. She ignored the prick of sensation and eyed the miniature roses instead. They were dying. Saskia watched a petal fall and disappear off her skin.

Time was running out.

Talan made a soft sound, muttering something in his sleep, and rolled over. Saskia glanced at him, slowly dropping her hand. Staring at his ruffled chocolate curls and broad muscled back, she sat up slowly, ghosted a kiss over his shoulder and slipped out of bed.

Shadows filtered into the room, and she brought them closer to her, wrapping around the sounds she made to muffle them as she quickly dressed. She made a mental note to thank the assistant, if she ever made it back, for bringing her new clothes as she slipped into dark skinny jeans, a simple fitted black long-sleeve, and her boots. Finding her belt and checking the push blade in the buckle, she pulled it on before reaching for the black shoulder holster.

The gun was heavy in her hands, and she stared at it for a long moment. Shadows curled around the barrel before she slipped it into the holster, the press snug against her ribs, comforting.

Talan tossed, and Saskia took a final parting look at him before slipping out of the room.

Álfheimr Towers was a tomb of silence, dark and brooding as the night crept in around her. White marble halls allowed for a quick escape through the main halls before she spotted her target and made a direct path for the duelling wood doors of the ballroom.

Her neck tingled, and Saskia paused, going preternaturally still. Her hearing was enhanced now, and her ears twitched at the slight change in the air.

"Come out, Your Majesty," she drolled quietly, raising her brow to the shadows on her left.

"Call me Savven, please," he replied simply, stepping out of the darkness on bare feet, dressed in a plain white t-shirt and black joggers. Despite his face still partially hidden in shadows, there was enough dim light to see as keen blue eyes fixed on her.

She tilted her head at him regarding the king. "Lurking in the shadows to catch me?"

"No," he said simply. "I figured if I had told you not to go, and tried to confine you, you would do the opposite."

Her brow arched. "Oh?"

Savven shrugged a shoulder. "Like mother like daughter."

She frowned but didn't say anything.

"Well? Are you going to go?" he asked expectedly.

Not daring to take her eyes off him, she crossed her arms over her chest. "Are you going to stop me?"

"No."

His simple answer made her glare suspiciously at him.

Savven chuckled under his breath and combed a hand through his hair. He looked like he had rolled out of bed to find her. Her nostrils flared, scenting something floral on him, something human as Talan had once described but not dying. Vanilla and spice were mixed into the scent, and Saskia had a brief thought that he had just been with a particular red-headed woman.

"If I could do more, I would have already, but I can't. I have a city to govern, people to protect." He glanced at the doors leading to the ballroom. "I can't start a war right now, not another one. My people have already paid the price for one war, to subject them to another…." Savven looked at her thoughtfully. "I've seen a lot of death in my lifetime, more than I care to see. So have they."

"I thought you were against me going after him?" she asked.

The king shrugged. "For all I know, you're going for a midnight walk, so who am I to stop you? It's a beautiful spring night."

"A walk…" she echoed slowly.

"A walk," he said more firmly.

Realisation dawned on her, and she pursed her lips. "Don't want to soil your hands?"

His smile turned bitter. "My soul is plenty soiled, and there will never be a day I don't feel the weight of each death. But I'm tired, and this is not my battle to fight."

Saskia could see the weariness in his eyes, and she almost— almost—felt pity for the king. "Well, Your Majesty, I have a walk to finish."

Savven tilted his head in regard, eyes flickering to the ballroom doors. "There is an easier way down. Your first jump is always a bit of a rough landing. I don't suggest it be from thirty stories up."

Chuckling, she shot him a quick wink, ambling towards the doors. "Where's the fun in that?"

The door was heavy as Saskia pulled it open. It swung silently on well-oiled hinges. When he didn't respond, she paused, looked back at him and found him watching her quiet and reverent.

They stared at each other for a pause before the king said in a soft, commanding voice, "May the Gods watch after you, Saskia of the Fae."

Saskia watched him disappear into the dark hall, frowning at the title he used. Not because it felt wrong, but because it felt like she belonged.

Huffing, Saskia turned on her boot heels, slipped through the double doors and walked across the ballroom, the space echoing the quiet taps of her shoes before she used her shadows to throw open the French doors to the balcony.

Icy spring air blasted her face, but she ignored the shiver that wanted to crawl down her spine, her black hair loose around her as it danced in the wind. The one thing she hadn't been able to find was a hair tie, and she frowned in annoyance when a curl brushed her cheek.

Shadows curled around her fingers, and Saskia braced on the black wrought iron bannister before she jumped up onto it.

Her toes balanced on the narrow ledge, the city spread before like a sea of twinkling lights and nondescript pillars and hills. Saskia felt her heart lurch with a very human reaction of fear, nearly making her jump back to safety. Her newly immortal heart skidded across her ribs, and she swallowed the knot that formed in her throat.

When she looked down, all she saw was darkness and impending death, and she took in a shaking breath, nails biting into her palms as she curled her fingers into fists.

"No," she whispered into the abyss. "It's all in your head, Saskia." Whether it was her words or her name on her tongue that reminded her what she was, her heart rate slowly stilled its erratic thump.

Saskia closed her eyes, leaning into the wind that curled around her, perfectly balanced on her toes, and breathed.

In… out… in…

She wasn't human.

Not anymore.

Not ever.

… Out.

Shadows coiled around her tighter and tighter until they filled the air, and she inhaled the cold wind beating her face, centring her mind and stretching her arms wide.

Alec's terrified face filled her memory, and Saskia's eyes flew open. The world tumbled into darkness as she leapt into the waiting shadows that consumed her.

CHAPTER 37

"Get up!" Talan roared through the door to Reign's room.

His fist banged on the wood, threatening to shatter this one, too. He was only in dark grey sweatpants, his chest and feet bare, his body still warm from bed. He had woken to an empty bed and room, and the bond between him and Sar—Saskia was oddly… silent.

Since the magic was lifted over her and the bond snapped into place, it shimmered with an energy between them that only got stronger when they were together. He could feel her emotions down it; it was like a comforting tug from the other end, but now… he couldn't feel her at all.

The bond was cold, pulled tight like it stretched across an ocean. So, when he had woken to an empty bed and silent bond, he grabbed the balled-up sweats on Saskia's bedroom floor, pulled them on and stalked out of her room directly to Reign's.

Talan could smell Saskia around the male's door faintly; their scents were nearly identical, but Reign's was more male, like deep wooded mountains and cold like stone, and it only fuelled his torrent of emotions. Brother or not, he couldn't care less right now, raising his fist to bang on the door again.

Dark brown eyes glared coldly at Talan as the door swung open suddenly.

"I will kill y—"

"She's gone."

The two males stared at each other.

"What," Reign asked slowly.

Talan stepped up to him, nostrils flaring with the first emotion he could identify: fear. Bitter and tangy in his nose. "She's. Gone."

The Fae male in front of him went preternaturally still, staring at Talan with wide, shocked eyes, and for the first time since he met the male, Talan saw that same fear reflected in him.

CHAPTER 38

SIX DAYS LEFT...

"Right where I left you," Saskia muttered, picking up the discarded blade on the ground that had fallen during her first climb up the glassy mountainside. She ran her finger over it, watching blood well up, and just as quickly the skin mended, she raised a brow at her finger. She didn't know if she would ever get used to that.

The blade was still surprisingly sharp, and she weighed it in her palm, looking up.

If the sky could be seen, it would have been bright blue with the last dregs of sunrise, but now, as she looked up, all she saw was dark, angry grey clouds and a low ceiling of fog that curled around the middle basin of the mountain.

The path ahead and behind her was still a desolate graveyard. The body of the Gogmagog was pecked through and torn into by various animals. Half of its ribcage was exposed and rotting, the stench almost unbearable as it hung in the air with an oily sheen that made her nose wrinkle in disgust.

Beyond the decaying body, Saskia knew the Carpathian Forest lay in waiting, and within those trees, across the mountain range, was a small dying village and a manor that held a dark secret.

Saskia's eyes narrowed, almost as if she could see the manor and Florin through the stone gorge.

Lips curling in a sneer, she checked the rage blooming in her stomach and tightened her grip on the blade.

First things first.

She turned her attention back to the mountain.

There had been no *rough landing* as the king had warned because she hadn't fallen the whole thirty stories—maybe only three, before she was whisked between shadows. She had thought of Alec, and her power flooded from her and opened a void in the darkness that had taken her to the Carpathian Forest just before the obsidian mountain.

It had surprised her initially, not expecting to be tossed into a portal rather than meeting hard earth when she jumped. But a small, quiet part of her whispered of the deep well of magic burrowed in her bones, and her surprise wore off quickly.

Magic coiled purple and black around her hand to the blade's tip, and she tilted her head, watching them slither across the metal. Silently, she called them back to her, a soft, barely there tug within on the magic she had been taken from, and the shadows retreated into her.

It was as easy as breathing, she relished how it flowed and ebbed through her limbs with so much power. Her power and Fae heritage were slowly filling in the pieces that had once been gaping wounds. Saskia rolled her shoulders back with determination.

Shoving the blade into her right boot, she grabbed a razor-sharp ledge and began her climb up.

Her muscles sighed with the use and the ease of bearing her

own weight, feeling lighter and more agile than she had in her life. There was something to be said about Fae agility that she could get used to. She barely had a moment to think before seeing the lip of the entrance.

Pausing, she eyed a small ledge to her right before she leveraged her foot into the glassy side and pushed herself off. She was airborne for all of two seconds. Then she was slamming into jagged rock, fingers digging into the small lip, core tightening when her body swung, feet anchoring onto a jutting ridge.

The entrance was just ahead, and she didn't think, didn't let herself look down even though she knew the dreary fog had encapsulated her view of the ground. She was among the clouds now, so she climbed hand over foot, up and up and up the last fifteen feet.

Pulling herself up into the cave mouth, her breathing even and controlled compared to her first climb, she glanced into the darkness, seeing the narrow doorway hidden in the shadows. But those shadows obeyed her now, parting with a subtle twitch of her finger to see a dim flicker of firelight from within the stairwell.

With a short glance over her shoulder to the world beyond the mountain where the fog and the tips of trees and stone ridges were visible, she knew there was a gilded tower made of gold and marble where everyone would know she was gone by now. But she didn't care. She had never labelled herself a team player, and just like the Fae king had said, this wasn't their fight, and she always finished a hunt.

Saskia turned away from the world at her back and smiled faintly, cold and murderous. Cracking her neck, she stalked into the waiting darkness.

"Ding-dong, bitch. Daddy's home."

The overhead motion-sensor lights didn't flick on this time as Saskia walked beneath them, making quick work of the mountain passage. The layout of the mountain was imprinted into her memory.

She was cloaked in shadows, her power seeping from her skin like wisps of smoke until she blended in with her surroundings. If anyone were to glance in her direction, if they stared *really* hard, they might see the faint shimmer of gold and dark purple threading into the pitch black that was the other half of her power.

The hall curved, thick wooden doors with their small cutouts encased with iron bars lining one side of the hallway just as she remembered it. Her nostrils flared, smelling the scent of piss, and... she paused, eyes landing on one door in particular.

The door looked like all the others, but when she faced off with it, she could feel the sheen of magic over it. Her shadows disappeared when her hand got close to it, fingers exposed in the dark hallway that suddenly flooded with light from overhead.

Saskia growled in annoyance, staring pensively up at the ceiling when she retracted her hand, shadows curling around her exposed skin. The light flickered off a second later.

A low growl filtered into the silence, and her eyes flickered to the door just beyond the iron bars. Golden eyes glowed from within, and soon, a body followed. Saskia's heart stopped.

"Alec?" she breathed.

Molten eyes widened in the slightest, but the tiny wolf pup kept its teeth bared, fluffy cream-coloured ears flattened against its skull, tail between its legs.

He was... cute. Saskia stared and stared, and... she didn't know what to think as Alec looked blindly into the darkness of his cell. Was it Alec?

"Alec?" she whispered, louder this time.

The pup ceased its growling, head tilted in the way dogs do and softly whined. His ears perked up, and she watched him back up a step.

Damn the fucking lights.

Saskia willed the shadows away, snatching the leash back on her well of power, and the lights flared on, nearly blinding.

"Alec," she said firmly, showing her face in the door.

He barked once and proceeded to bare his teeth again in a warning growl.

The sound was small and unthreatening, but Saskia flinched nonetheless. Alec didn't recognise her.

"It's me," she said softly.

But was it her? Saskia leaned her forehead against the bars, sighing. "It's me, Alec. It's… it's Sarah." That name tasted vile on her tongue, and she had to refrain from wincing with disgust. Her hatred for that single name made her fingers curl tighter around the bars. "I know I look different, but you have to trust me, Alec. It's me. It's Sarah."

Golden eyes widened, taking up nearly half of his face, and he bounded for the door, rearing up to place his paws on the door. He whined loud and long, tail wagging.

"You're a…" A *shifter*. But she couldn't make herself finish that sentence, because that would mean Florin did what he did to not just her but Alec too. But *why*. Why Alec?

Wrapping her hands around the bars, she pressed her face to the iron, feeling the magic sting her palms, but she ignored their bite and looked down at Alec.

"I'm going to get you out. Can you shift back, Alec?" She looked down the hall, the light remaining on her, and she shifted her feet the longer she stayed in one spot. She needed to move, but she wouldn't leave Alec behind.

Alec pushed off the door, stepping back. He looked down at the ground, whining, and turned in a circle, ears pressed back, but after a moment, he looked up at Saskia and shook his head.

She huffed out a defeated breath.

Fuck.

Saskia yanked at the door handle. It didn't move, not even a little. Wrapping both hands around the iron bars, she leveraged a foot on the obsidian wall and used every ounce of her newfound Fae strength to pull.

It still didn't move. The door was practically cemented into the stone.

She pulled again and again and again, a rough sound of frustration grating against her throat when it didn't so much as shift a fraction, the magic biting into her palms more and more.

"Fuck!" she snapped, leaning on the door, hands dropping from the bars, closing her eyes as she tried to think of a way to open it.

The magic around the door lessened when she stopped trying, and she knew there was no getting it open. Not right now. It was locked tight, and she didn't have the key… but she knew who did.

Alec whined.

Saskia opened her eyes and looked down at his golden stare as he reared up on his paws again. "Alec," she said slowly.

He tilted his head, showing he heard her.

"I need you to be brave for a little bit longer. Can you do that?"

He only blinked.

"I can't get the door open," she continued, "but I'm going to. Do you understand?"

This time, he gave a little yip, more of a snap of his teeth.

"I need to leave you here for now, but I *will* return for you. I will come and get you. Do you understand?"

Fuck, fuck, *fuck.*

She did not like this one bit.

Alec pressed off the door and sat back on his haunches, the faint bit of light showcasing his small cream and brown fur body, tail wagging negligibly across the stone floor.

Okay, she could do this.

"I need you to figure out how to shift back, Alec. Can you do that?" Another soft yip. "Good," she said with a firm press of her mouth. Letting out a harsh breath through her nose, she gave him a short nod and stepped away from the door. "I will come back for you."

His soft yip was followed by a low whine, and her heart clenched painfully in her chest, but she forced herself to walk away.

She didn't call on her shadows, the lights flaring to life with every step she took, the dark hall a looming presence at her back, her chest squeezing painfully the more distance she put between herself and Alec.

Saskia frowned, taking the familiar stairwell down into a spiral corridor. Why did Florin conceal Alec… why did he *take* Alec. Did he kill his parents, too? Why did he kill her parents? Her jaw flexed with so many unanswered questions, but she sniffed back her disdain. If she had any say in it, the answers were coming sooner

rather than later.
     Someone was going to start talking.

❧ 363 ❧

"She went for a *walk*," Talan stated incredulously.

This conference room was starting to grate on him as he braced both his hands on the long table, leaning forward to stare at the king seated in his high-back chair at the end. Every time they were in this room, some sort of bad news or revelation happened, and he was really fucking tired of it.

The king looked up with a casually arched black brow, a tablet in his hand with a 3D hologram of an artefact hovering above it. "That's what I said."

Talan growled low, a promise of pain, the wolf within wanting to surface.

"You just let her walk out of the tower? I thought you didn't want her to leave."

Talan looked back at the male behind him who spoke. Reign was leaning against the white marble wall, arms crossed over his black long sleeve, tailored black pants making him look like a dark cloud that promised a storm, if the murderous look in his brown eyes was any indication.

The longer he stared at the male, the more he saw the slight familiar resemblance between him and his mate. He had a lot of questions, and *none* of them were getting answered.

His head swivelled back to the king and the witch who stood on his right, another tablet in her hands with a mountain landscape floating above it.

"I did say she wasn't a prisoner," the king commented coolly, flicking a finger at the mountainscape that turned to give a different vantage point. "Send the excavation team out to see if they can locate an entrance or tunnel system into the mountain."

Brean nodded, tapping on the tablet, the sunlight creating a halo around her cream colour silk blouse and cream cigarette pants. Her fiery curls were half pulled from her face and streaming down her back. "The team has been notified. ETA to the site is two hours."

"So that's it? You just let her walk out without trying to stop her?"

The king set the tablet aside, fixed the rolled cuff of his evergreen button-down, and leaned back in his chair, sparing Reign a contemplative look. "You say I didn't try to stop her, but was it my job to stop her in the first place?"

"Oh, I'm sorry, Savven, I forgot you're a king, so you don't fight your own battles," Reign sneered.

Talan raised a brow at his blatant disrespect. He could scent the rage seeping from the male and knew he was out for blood.

A shadow passed over Savven's face, but it was there and gone in the blink of an eye, his calm demeanour a mask for the power Talan knew was bubbling beneath the king's perfect exterior.

"Says the right hand of the most prevalent murderer of this new world." Savven grabbed the tablet, tapping on it as he continued. "Do you think Avian can't fight his own battles as well? Or just me?"

"It's different," Reign seethed, pushing off the wall.

Talan moved out of the way as the male nearly threw a chair against the wall with how forcibly he moved it to brace on the table, glaring at the king.

"Reign, you need to calm down," Talan muttered. This wasn't helping.

Reign whipped around, snarling at him, brown eyes nearly black. "*Shut. Up.* You know *nothing*, dog! She is your *mate*, and you're standing here like she isn't in grave danger!"

His words felt like a physical blow, and Talan had to refrain from flinching. She is his mate, he's right, but that didn't make her his to control. She was still the woman—the female—he had first met in the forest a week ago. "You don't know her," he said carefully. And to be fair, neither did Talan, not entirely—mated or not. But he knew she worked alone and would do anything for the little boy trapped within the mountain.

Reign snorted in disgust. "You're undeserving of her."

Talan growled low and primal.

"How is it different?" Savven drolled, interrupting them while still looking at something on the tablet.

"What?" snapped Reign.

Savven sighed like this conversation was a chore. "You said it's different. Me and Avian. I don't corrupt my people to make them follow me, but Avian does. I personally don't see the comparison."

Reign slammed a fist down, rattling the long table. "I didn't have a choice!"

"You did."

"I did it for my *sister*!"

Savven looked up at that. "You and Levina do not share blood, correct?"

Reign paused, and Savven continued.

"You all share very similar familiar traits, even after all this time. It's quite surprising. Your *sister*, as well. Stubbornness. Wouldn't you agree, Brean?"

Brean coughed into her hand, amber eyes going wide, and Talan could see her hiding the faint smile behind her hand.

"Notably," she replied dryly, arching a brow at the tablet he showed her.

Talan sighed through his nose. This was not how this meeting was supposed to go. Fuck. This was going nowhere, and he was itching to leave so he could find the earliest flight back to that Godsforsaken mountain, or at least the nearest airport to it in Brasov.

Brean painted on a professional smile, hugging the tablet to her chest. "His Majesty has kindly requested his helicopter to stand by for you."

Brows raised at them; Talan frowned. Had he spoken out loud?

Savven leaned back in his chair, arms on the rests, a bored look on his face, looking every bit of a Fae king. "Do try not to damage it. I *will* make you pay for the cost of repairs purely out of spite."

Reign snorted. "That's the best you can do?"

"Reign," Talan hissed, "Let's go. Now." He put a hand on the male's shoulder, but Reign jerked, shaking it off.

"Don't touch me, Dog," Reign warned.

Talan saw red, grabbed him by the arm, and yanked him to face him. "Lets. Go. *Now,*" he growled, the beast within rising to the surface.

Reign opened his mouth to snap a reply but closed it, glaring at the king and Brean. He yanked his arm free of Talan, who had an iron grip around his bicep and stalked out of the room.

Silence stretched between the three of them, and Talan rubbed the back of his neck with a low breath, his black t-shirt tightening around his bicep as the muscle flexed. "I'm sorry." He looked at the two behind him. "Thank you, Your Majesty and… Brean."

Brean gave him a small, crooked smile. Savven just tilted his head in reply.

Talan stalked after Reign, wanting a word with the male before they stepped foot onto the chopper.

"What the fuck was that?" Talan snarled, catching up to the male who power-walked to the elevator. A male assistant standing by greeted them with a smile that quickly fell off his dark bronze face as they approached.

"His Majesty—"

"Reign, answer me!" Talan ignored the assistant as he tried to speak, and the male's hazel eyes widened when he and Reign faced off.

Quickly pressing the button going up, Talan saw the male from the corner of his eye take a couple healthy steps away from them. Probably a good idea considering the rage he felt coming from Reign.

Reign's laugh was full of acid. "You have no idea what Avian is capable of."

"You don't know Sar—Saskia," he countered.

That earned him a snort. "I know her better than you do."

The doors opened, and the three stepped in, the assistant between them wide-eyed.

"No, you don't," Talan said softly. "You knew her as a child." He looked at Reign over the shorter assistant's brown hair. "In case you haven't noticed, she's all grown up now."

Reign's lips curled in a snarl. "Do not talk to me like you know my sister better than I do."

Talan shrugged a shoulder, facing the gold reflection of the polished elevator door. "Neither of us knows her, but I know the kind of female she is right now." The doors opened, and he stepped back out.

Icy spring wind cut across his face, the bright blue cloudless sky above them a false promise of warmth. He ignored the cold, his blood heating the longer the male behind simmered. The scent of his anger was poison in Talan's nose, bitter and rancid, and his hands balled into fists at his side.

The male assistant let out a squeak of surprise. Talan looked behind him to see Reign push him out of the way, his emotions a warning across his face, there was no doubt that his judgement was clouded.

Reign and Talan saw the black helicopter sitting on the heliport near the ledge of the tower, eyes fixed on the spinning electric blue blades. Reign made to walk towards it, and Talan stopped him.

A rock sunk in Talan's gut when he halted the male, but it sunk further when Reign snapped dark eyes at him.

"What?"

"Let me go first," Talan said. "I'm superstitious." It was a lie.

Reign snorted, rolled his eyes, and waved a hand towards the chopper. "After you, Puppy."

Fuck, his mind whispered repeatedly. The tang of Reign's anger put him on edge. He couldn't let him around Saskia, not right now. It could put her in danger, brother or not. He knew clouded judgment made for bad outcomes; he had seen it time and time again, maybe not in the same context of life and death, but the premiss still stood.

He was almost to the chopper, the blades above creating a vortex of wind, his dark brown hair whipping across his forehead. The wolf in him pressed against his bones, his fingers slowly curled into fists as power flooded into his limbs. His blood raged in his ears, and his heart pounded like a drum against his ribs, and just as he made to step onto the chopper, he swung.

His fist connected with Reign's face, the sound of the bones in his hands cracking against his skull. If he had been more aware of his hand, he would feel the pain radiating up his arm, but he didn't. His blood rushed through his ears with adrenaline.

Reign didn't have a moment to register what happened. He collapsed on the roof, Talan above him, and he gritted his jaw, trying to push down the power raging inside him as the beast demanded he shift.

Slowly, he raised his gaze to the wide-eyed assistant, who startled when he saw Talan looking at him and took a step back. Again, probably for the best, based on how he was feeling.

Toeing Reign's hand with his black boot to ensure he was still alive, the male moaned, his head moving slightly, his auburn hair dishevelled.

"I do know her better," Talan said softly. "Because if she were here now, she would have punched you herself." He looked again at the assistant whose hazel eyes were darting between him and Reign. "Sorry."

And he turned on his heels and climbed into the helicopter, watching Reign slowly regain consciousness.

Raising a brow, he shook his head and looked down at his hand when they were airborne. His knuckles were bright red and split but slowly healing when a bone popped into place.

Fuck he had a hard head.

Savven sighed, annoyed. "Alright, thank you, Tarkin. See that he's taken to a healer." The call ended, and he put his mobile on the table, rubbing his hand over his eyes.

Brean perched on the ledge beside his chair, and he leaned back, shaking his head, hand going to her knee as he turned to watch the sky, fingers tracing small circles on her pant leg.

"What happened, Savven?" Brean inquired softly.

He looked up at her pretty face and just shook his head irritably. "I hope for all the Gods sakes that Tatius has a *very* good reason for all of this."

CHAPTER 40

They were all dead.

All of them.

They had been drained. Their bodies emaciated, every bone protruding from their grey flesh with sickening detail. Some had their eyes closed, others were wide open, cloudy gazes staring into the void.

Saskia stared at the old man on the floor, her brows furrowed, and she swallowed back her guilt. She hadn't made it back in time. The row of cages alongside the Goliath cave had become an open tomb.

She closed her eyes, taking in a long, steady breath.

You can't save everyone, her mind whispered to her.

Her eyes opened, and she frowned.

When she turned her back on the cages, the sterile tables glared back at her. Tables that had once been occupied by a sea of comatose Fae bodies hooked up to bags of blood were now empty.

Where did they go?

To her right, the tables extended into the jaws of the cave where lights didn't extend or simply weren't on. She watched the shadows shift and slither over a table. They were different from her own, and she narrowed her eyes at them, watching them retract from the too-bright white LEDs.

These shadows were true darkness, and she couldn't suppress the shiver of fear that went down her spine when she saw a clawed hand reach from the darkness and stretch towards her.

That was where she had to go.

"Fuck," she whispered, her voice still echoing around her.

Finger tapping against her thigh, knowing she got the trait from her mother, was a comfort as she notched her chin higher and walked into the darkness.

It was cold, like ice, and her skin *burned* as pain lanced across her arm. Saskia stepped out of the shadows as quickly as she could into a seemingly empty throne room, watching a black tar hand reach for her, and she stumbled away from it with disgust. A quick glance at her left arm had her noting a jagged laceration across the bargain branded into her skin.

The vines, roses, and long needle-like thorns constricted around her forearm, nearly to her wrist, and the blood that trailed down her skin was absorbed into the bargain. The laceration mended quickly, and to her surprise, the tattoo on her skin, the hourglass counting down to her death... vanished.

Saskia held up her arm, examining the bare, fully healed, tan skin.

The bargain had been fulfilled.

A slow clap filled the throne room, the hair on her neck rising. Without moving, she slowly scanned the room. The silver throne was unoccupied, the towering obsidian pillars nearly cloaked in shadows, and a corona of fire orbs hung above the middle of the hall, barely lighting the dark space.

"You know, I did suspect. But one must never get their hopes up. Isn't that right… *sister?*"

Avian's voice carried through the hall, and she whipped around, facing the wall of darkness she had just come from. His voice was everywhere all at once, and she stepped back beneath the orbs of light. There was darkness around her, slowly encroaching on the dimly lit space.

Her breathing came in short, sharp procession, and she forced it to slow, to steady. Listening for any movement. But there was none. The silence was deafening. It rang in her ears along with her heartbeat.

"He was hoping I would kill you," Avian's voice said again. "He wrote to me, stating he would like to meet. To amend what he did, to make an alliance, but instead, he sent *you.*"

Shadows curled around her hands, but unlike the cold, endless darkness within the hall, hers brought her the comfort she needed at that moment.

"Did you know?" Avian's voice scoffed. "He thought I would tie up his loose ends since you were concealed so well. Or perhaps he really thought you would kill me, and then he would never have to worry. He could have you take control of my newborns, and the world would be his for the taking."

She opened her mouth, eyes flicking from one shadow to another, turning slowly to keep her eye on the hall. "What loose ends?"

"Don't lie to me, Sister," Avian chuckled darkly. "I see you now. I smell you now. I know you know what happened that night."

"I don't," she snapped quickly. It was true. She knew most of what happened, but she didn't know why it happened.

Avian laughed, the sound raking down her skin. "The truth smells so sweet, did you know that? Our emotions have a scent to them."

Her hand itched to reach for the dagger in her boot or the gun pressed to her ribs, but she refrained. She couldn't afford to lose either, not yet.

Despite wanting to murder Florin for what he's done, his lesson still rang in her head that she has remembered time and time again:

"Never make the first move."

"So, tell me, sister. Did your master ever tell you why he wanted our mother dead?"

Images of her parent's bodies and decapitated heads filled Saskia's memory, and she swallowed down her bile.

"Enlighten me," she seethed through clenched teeth.

"*Revenge.*"

The word was whispered against her ear as if he had pressed his cold lips there, and she spun, swinging a fist through nothing.

Avian's laugh reverberated through the hall.

"I wanted you, and he wanted our parents. It was a win-win if you ask me." He paused and asked, "He goes by Florin now?"

Her eyes narrowed. "I have places to be, so if you could get to the point." The shadows pressed closer, and she staggered her stance, eyeing them. She had power, the duel-coloured shadows curling around her hands, but if she were honest with herself, she didn't know how to use it, not to its full extent.

"He stole you from me." Avian's voice became bitter and cold. "He broke our agreement. I was to have you! But he took you from me! You were the key to my uprising!" His words filled the expanding darkness, piercing her ears.

He paused for a heartbeat, and his voice became manic and higher pitched. Saskia braced herself.

"But now—now I see I didn't need you, Sister! I have built up my army. I have created the ultimate undead soldiers, and now they stand by for my command. Half-breeds who would have been nothing in this life can now be part of the change! Join me! Join me, Sister!"

Saskia's blood froze, her heart hammering.

Hell fucking no.

"Join me, and we will end the line of half-breeds and humans together. The Fae will rise again, and together, we will reign over them all!"

The shadows were nearly to her feet, and now she could see the hungry demonic smiles from within. The sliver of yellow firelight above her wavered under the cool breath of darkness pressing around them, threatening to extinguish, and she gritted her teeth.

Smiling bitterly, Saskia laughed under her breath and dug her feet into the stone, bracing for what was about to come. "Go to hell."

Avian chuckled. "Pity."

And then the light went out.

⚜ 377 ⚜

CHAPTER 41

"You are both darkness and light, my Saskia."
Her mother's words whispered through her mind as she opened her eyes, blinking rapidly. A sharp gasp filled the silence, too loud in her ears, when all she saw was darkness. She was swallowed into its depths, the throne room gone, the firelight smothered, and the air as still as the dead.

Heart hammering in her chest, feeling like she was being watched, she slowly turned, trying to find a way out.

A soft purple glow faintly began to shine, and she looked down. Her power was alive, thrumming through her body until it seeped from her bones and wrapped around her. She couldn't see the black within the abyss. But the purple... her father's side, the side that tamed the darkness she knew curled within, waiting, glowed brighter and brighter until it was practically neon.

"What an interesting trick, Sister."

Avian's voice came from everywhere. It moved through the darkness, and Saskia whipped around, searching the shadows.

The neon glow of purple followed her, and she slowly extended her hand. Tendrils of purple coiled into the air, cutting a trail through the endless black. It did nothing to light up the darkness, but it wouldn't be smothered, unlike the fire. It did not waver or give under the consuming weight of the abyss. It was searching for a way out, shifting and curving randomly, and Saskia wondered if the pillars were there.

"You can try and try and try, but you will never find an escape."

Avian's voice pressed against her ear, and her blood froze. She whirled. No one was there, at least not that she could see, as she raised a hand to the darkness before her.

"Try again," he taunted.

The sound was sharp behind her, the neon light flying in that direction. Eyes wide, she saw nothing. Fear crawled down her skin, and she could smell the sour tang of it on herself.

It was cold, the temperature dropping rapidly. Saskia's breath clouded in the light of her hand, and a soft ticking, like claws on stone, scratched to her right.

She turned.

There was nothing. But she couldn't see past the glow of her power that reached out to explore the space.

"*Boo.*"

His voice whispered against the shell of her ear, and Saskia bit back her sharp intake of breath, whipping to her left.

"Is this how you fight?! By hiding in the shadows and trying to scare me?" she snapped, heart thudding behind her ribs.

That awful scratching sound came from behind her this time, more claws. She knew it was the heinous creatures she saw within the darkness. The same demons she suspected lurked within Avian.

"No," Avian remarked simply. "This is how I play with my *food.*"

And then pain erupted across her back.

It felt like jagged knives tore across her shoulder blades, slicing to the bone, and she couldn't restrain the guttural scream that left her lips.

Hands locked onto her wrists like shackles, their touch branding her skin, and spread her arms wide. The flesh of her wrists *burned,* and she refrained from crying out from the pain, even when she turned watery eyes to her right hand. A face made from nightmares was lit up by the bright purple glow of her shadows, and she jerked back.

It was disgusting.

A gaunt face made of seeping tar, hollow eyes, and a smile full of razor teeth stared back at her. She had seen a lot of creatures over the years, some demonic, others not so much, but never had she seen something straight from the pits of the underworld.

The demon's hand was latched onto her, and she watched as its razor-like nails dug into her further. Its touch leaving behind bands of burned flesh. Her eyes snapped to her fingers, watching them tremble.

She was shaking.

She was afraid.

She had *never* been afraid like this before.

This was a living nightmare, the demons pressing closer, and she knew they could taste her fear.

"I expected more from you, Sister. How disappointing," Avian sighed, and she could feel his breath skim her cheek, the scent of blood strong.

Pursing her lips, she breathed unsteadily through her nose and jerked her head away at his touch when he skimmed an unseen finger down her cheek.

"Tut-tut, that's not very nice," Avian chided with a click of his tongue.

She glared and spit blindly into the space in front of her. "Fuck you."

"Ohh, there's that spirit. I'll admit I was afraid you had gone soft after you regained your memories."

Saskia didn't say anything. She couldn't. Had she gone soft?

"Oh well, enough of that." Avian's fingers wrapped around her jaw, his sharp nails prying her mouth open when she fought him. "Open wide, Sister."

She fought him and the demons holding her with everything she could. Her arms threatened to pull straight from their sockets, her skin melting around her wrists as the grips on her wrists tightened. Saskia collapsed to her knees, pain jarring her bones, her jaw still hinged open by Avian, and she could feel hot tears cutting a path down her cheeks.

She was terrified, and she *hated* that she was. Her whole body shook, pain consuming every nerve ending, muscle, and ligament right down to her voice and, last, her mind. She couldn't see Avian, and the glow of her power was beginning to wane from her, the demon's faces from the corner of her eyes starting to morph into shadows.

The glowing power was useless, and a strangled sob escaped when she thought of Alec in that cell all alone, waiting for her. He was waiting for her, but she was here, she wasn't coming. She had promised him she would come.

"This could have been a whole lot easier for you if you hadn't fought me," Avian said in a contemplative tone, suddenly all business. "But I think I prefer it this way. I do like it when they struggle. Goodbye, Sister."

And then a burning trail of liquid went down her throat, and she gagged, choking and sputtering. Fire filled her frozen limbs, scorching her from the inside out, invisible claws burrowing into her bones and muscles. Avian and the demons released her, and she collapsed onto the stone floor.

The purple glow flickered, becoming hazy and distorted. Saskia's body twitched involuntarily, and she dragged a leaden hand across the stone, her mouth open as she tried to suck in small gasps of air.

She watched with fading vision as the purple light went out, and she went with it.

CHAPTER 42

Avian stared down at his sister with a cool disposition after his shadows dispersed. "Pity," he murmured, toeing her body.

She didn't stir.

Kneeling, he brushed a curling lock of her long black hair from her face, exposing her rose-bud mouth, high cheekbones, and long black lashes. "You look so much like our mother, I wish you hadn't forced my hand, Sister."

Her wounds had already healed on her back, though her bright red blood was splattered on the black stone in wet droplets around her.

"We could have ruled this world *together* had you just complied. I could have shown you how to use that power within you to its full potential." Avian frowned, standing. "But that's all you'll ever be—potential."

Saskia's eyes opened, and Avian smiled at her milky white stare as she stood.

"Now, you'll just be a puppet," he said softly. "While full Fae, you are still a halfling of dark and light. I suspected you might not become a perfect soldier but rather a perfect toy, and I'm glad to see I was right." Avian leaned in close, examining her face, searching her eyes for signs of life. "I always wondered if you could see what was going on while trapped within or if you simply go into a comatose state. I guess I'll never know." He snapped his fingers, the sound echoing in the throne room.

The door beside his throne opened, and a skeletal human woman appeared nearby.

He didn't bother looking at her, studying his sister's tan face, a cold smile curling the corners of his mouth. "Bring me the child."

CHAPTER 43

She was staring at herself—her younger self.

Saskia blinked slowly, and so did the child. She moved her hand to her face, fingers brushing her cheek, and so did child her.

Eyes darting past her younger self, she noted the dark purple space, a black tar-like substance slowly creeping over the walls, and before her was a screen—no… that wasn't a screen. Avian was staring at her, and she… wasn't killing him. Her eyes snapped to her younger self, who was just watching her.

Sitting up, she brushed her black hair over her shoulder and stood, walking over to the large screen. Raising a hand, she pressed against it, her fingers spreading wide when met with a barrier.

"Bring me the child."

His voice was distorted like she was listening through a wall, and she bashed her fist into the invisible barrier.

"No!" she screamed.

"He can't hear you," said a soft little girl's voice.

Her voice.

Saskia whirled to her younger self, who had stood, wearing a simple black dress, her hair loose down her back, and was now observing Avian as he walked away.

"Who are you?" Saskia bit out, watching the child suspiciously.

Little Saskia tilted her head and extended a hand. "A memory."

She flicked a brief glance at the offered hand. "I don't have time for that. I need to get out of this first." She whirled and tried to smash her fist through the barrier. "Wake up!" But she wasn't asleep; this much she was learning, and her command was ignored. She was just a prisoner of her own mind, locked in her body without control of it.

"I know." Younger her took a single step towards her, gathering her attention. "Take my hand."

Identical green eyes stared at each other.

Saskia pursed her lips, sucking in a deep, resigned breath through her nose. With one more look to the throne room, she narrowed her gaze on her younger self and took her hand.

It happened in a blink.

There and gone.

She was transported from the entrapment of her mind to... a forest.

It was peak summertime; towering evergreens surrounded her, a warm wind grazed her cheek, and beams of sunlight filtered in through the long branches overhead.

Child's laughter filled the air, and Saskia turned to see a version of herself running towards her. Curly black hair, a banner behind her, cheeks full and rosy, skin freckled and sun-kissed. She couldn't have been more than six, dressed in a dark blue sundress with pink flowers on the straps that slipped off her shoulders.

Saskia chuckled, watching herself fix the straps with an annoyed huff.

This all felt so familiar, and she turned with a furrowed brow, watching, waiting. Someone was coming. She knew it. Shadows condensed and curled within the forest but avoided the sunlight beams like they were poison.

She knew this memory, faint as it might be…

Avian stepped from the thickening darkness, and Saskia paused, her head tilting curiously.

"Hello," she said softly.

"Hello," he replied.

Saskia glanced around the forest, wondering if she should run back, the house just in sight beyond the trees. She shouldn't have snuck away; mama was going to be upset with her. Her eyes snapped to the male when he stepped closer, and she frowned.

"Why are you alone?"

He cocked his head, arching a brow. "But I'm not alone; you're here."

He was right, but Saskia frowned further.

"I know your parents, Saskia. They tell me about you."

"They do?" He knew her name and her mama and papa. "Do you want to come to our house?"

"No," he said solemnly, "I'm afraid I can't today. But I did want to give you something, Saskia."

"Me?" She didn't know this male, not that she could recall, but he knew her mama and papa, so he must be okay. Looking him up and down with large green eyes, she watched him hesitantly. "What is it?"

He knelt and crooked a finger at her to come closer.

She took a single step, earning her a short, dry laugh from the male.

Shadows lifted from the earth around him, curling like smoke, and he looked at her while he circled his hands around the darkness and formed it into a miniature dark horse.

It had glowing silver eyes and reared up, galloping around her.

Saskia shrieked with laughter, clapping her hands in excitement. As it ran and bounded through the air, darkness streamed around her until it built and built. Her laughter died, and her smile slipped from her face.

Her heart shuddered with fear as the darkness consumed her, the sunlight disappearing. Saskia screamed, something pulsating beneath her skin until a glowing purple light exploded from her hands, and the darkness absorbed it like the light.

It was quiet for only a second before thin, splintered cracks of purple glowed within the void, and the darkness seemed to scream in agony.

Saskia reached for the shadows with her hand. The darkness exploded around her at her touch, and she blinked rapidly.

The forest was filled with black glimmering particles, gold flecks shimmering with light between them, suspended in the air. Saskia stared, wide-eyed in awe, the male before her forgotten as she stretched a hand to the shimmering flecks.

At her touch, every single one flew to her, sinking into her flesh, and she gasped at the overwhelming sensation of energy coursing through her tiny body. When she looked down at her hand, she yelped.

Purple shadows curled around her bare arms, but now black was coiled with it, gold sparkling through the darkness before they sunk into her skin, and she absorbed the dark with the light.

Her eyes turned watery as fear and anger made her small mouth purse. She turned her narrowed eyes to the male now standing and looking at her the same way she looked at something when she really wanted it.

"That wasn't nice!" And then she was running, sprinting as fast as her little legs could carry her back home. "Mama!"

Saskia stood in the forest, watching her younger self run away. She remembered now. Her mother had been looking for her, and she had gotten scolded and her bottom swatted for running off without telling anyone. Then her father had come home and asked if she wanted to go for ice cream and the bad male was forgotten and she hadn't told them what he or she had done.

Her head whipped to her left, watching Avian with fury in her gaze. He was smirking, the dark part holding her hostage within her mind, allowing her to see his memory as well.

"Soon, little sister. Soon," he whispered darkly.

"Like hell," she snarled and lunged for him.

But he was just a memory, and the world melted away into darkness, and she squinted her eyes at the lack of light, letting her eyes adjust.

She was back, trapped within her mind.

Something stung her fingers, and she jerked back. But she didn't move. She was stuck. That black tar seeping along the walls of her mind coated the entire floor, coating everything. It anchored her feet, slowly crawling up her jean-clad legs, her skin burning beneath the fabric.

Gritting her teeth, she looked at the throne room, and her stomach curdled. Large, tear-filled golden eyes looked up at her as Alec, naked as a babe, screamed at her.

"SARAH!"

Saskia flinched both at the name and the terror in his small face. He had managed to shift back, but now she was holding him by the neck, and her eyes widened at what she realised was happening.

"No!" she screamed, fighting at the darkness holding her.

It was at her waist now, half of her body on fire, the other half contorting in her restraints.

Avian's cold blue eyes infiltrated her field of vision, standing behind Alec.

"Let him go, you bastard!" she screamed again. The tar holding her hands prisoner was to her shoulders now, crawling along her clavicle. A tendril of it reached for her jaw like a snake, and she jerked her face away.

"Now, Sister, whether you can hear me or not, there is something you must know," Avian started calmly as if discussing the weather. *"Your master sent you to me with the task of killing me... but did you know you were meant to die all along? You're not the only one I made a bargain with recently. Your life for his part of my army. Now, of course, I couldn't give him half, but a fraction, yes. Soon, my pets will storm the world with his help, and the Fae will rise."*

Alec whimpered, half screaming, half sobbing her name again, clawing at her hand around his neck. *"Sar-Sarah..."*

Avian sighed, shooting Alec an annoyed look. *"This one is a loose end your master wanted discarded now that this fabricated life of yours is over. I thought it would be fitting if you did the honours."*

His smile was cold as ice, his eyes becoming shards of glass as they cut a vicious look to Alec, who growled.

"Leave my sister alone! Leave us alone!" he screamed, voice breaking and thrashing in her hold as he tried to claw the air where Avian had been. He barely moved, her grip firm. She knew because she could see her fingers digging into his flesh.

Saskia's body followed Avian; Alec forced to move with her.

"No," Saskia whispered, feeling the sticky tar liquid crawling up the side of her face. "No, let him go," she commanded herself. "Let him go, let him go, *LET HIM GO!*"

But her body didn't listen to her.

One of her eyes went black, her free one fixated on Avian's back and then on Alec's watery gaze.

He had stopped trembling, though his mouth wobbled, and he whispered in a soft, barely there voice. *"It's okay, Sarah."*

She sobbed, hot tears scorching a path from her free eyes, the tar seeping over her mouth, trying to muffle the sound.

"I love you," Alec whispered, barely audible through the barrier.

The scream that tore from Saskia filled the darkness of her mind.

"Kill the boy."

And then she began to squeeze, and Alec's eyes bulged.

"NO!" Her heart was racing, her breathing being suffocated as her vision went black, and she screamed again into the void until she was consumed by Avian's darkness.

It was small at first, a minuscule hairline crack, and then another appeared, and then another until hundreds of tiny bright purple cracks splintered across the pitch, coating her mind, and the darkness imploded.

CHAPTER 44

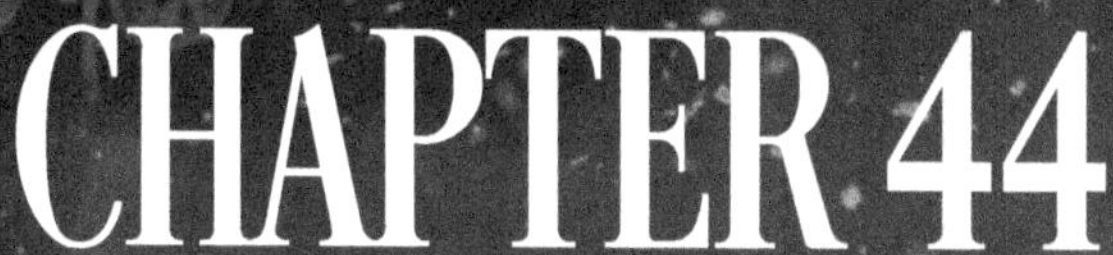

Alec stared up at her, tears streaming down his face silently as she quickly released his neck, and he took in a sucking breath. She held up a finger to her mouth, and he quickly quieted.

Saskia looked at Avian through lowered brows, feeling an electric current to her power pulsating beneath her skin. She had absorbed his darkness and *cleansed* it. It was still there, moving within her, but it was hers now, and Saskia tilted her head, eyeing Avian's exposed back.

Slowly and silently, she kneeled and slipped her short blade free of her boot. Weighing it in her hand as she palmed it, she looked at Alec briefly.

"Close your eyes," she mouthed to him.

Nodding slowly, he closed his eyes.

Standing, Saskia faced off with Avian's exposed back, weapon at her side, and tugged on the cord of power within her as she morphed into shadows.

Avian chuckled softly, walking up the steps of the dais. "Who knew this would all be so easy. My father was too weak; his compassion overruled his sense, but now the world will be mine! Where shadows lay, the world will fall!"

He whipped around and froze when the shadows concealing Saskia slipped behind the silver throne.

"Where did she go?!" he bellowed, voice echoing back at him.

Alec flinched, but he didn't open his eyes.

Good boy, she thought.

Avian made to step down, but with a single thought from her, shadows lashed out and wrapped around his body, snapping him back against the throne so violently it shuddered from impact.

Purple and black slithered around Avian like constrictors, restraining him. His head dropped back, and he laughed, the sound full of acid. "Ah, Sister. Learning to play in the dark, are we?"

Loosening the leash on the shadows, she walked around the throne, her boots silent on the stone and the blade still in her hand.

"I told you we would be great together," Avian continued, a calculating, manic gleam lighting his eyes. "Look at the power within you. Look at what you can do. Just think of what we could do together!"

She leaned in close, dragging the point of her blade across his cheek. A dribble of black blood trailed down his narrow jaw.

Avian's eyes flashed, and he jerked against his restraints, pieces of his long black hair falling across his eyes. "I am darkness incarnate! You do not scare me!" The veins in his neck bulged as he screamed in her face, trying to call on his power. But hers was stronger.

Saskia laughed softly and leaned in close, pressing her lips to his ear. "And I am the shadows within, *Brother*."

A sickening crunch filled the hall, the tip of her blade nicking her bottom lip. She kissed his temple gently and leaned back, stepping away to view her handy work.

Avian twitched uncontrollably; her short blade skewed between his ears. Slack-jawed, his eyes slowly tried to move towards her before they froze and dropped to the ground as his body slumped, lifeless. Her restraints vanished around him.

What she saw next made her lip curl back in disgust. That same black tar he had forced down her throat and consumed her within her mind clawed its way out of his open mouth.

"Ugh," she said with revulsion and flicked out a finger.

A tendril of purple slipped out and wrapped around the pitch of darkness. It wiggled violently in the hold of her power, squeezing it tighter and tighter until it froze and, a second later, combusted.

It was quicker this time. The dark part of her power absorbed the cleansed shadows until nothing was left.

It would never hurt anyone again.

Saskia walked down the dais and scooped Alec into her arms. He quickly wrapped his arms around her neck and legs around her waist. "Keep your eyes closed," she whispered into his tangled curly hair. He obeyed by tucking his head into the crook of her neck and holding on tight.

"I got you," she said gently, holding him close.

Her shadows curled in front of her. Thinking of the forest beside the gorge, she stepped through them with Alec.

Saskia kneeled on the forest floor, Alec still in her arms and wrapped around her. "Alec," she said softly, soothing a hand over his head. "We're safe now."

He jerked back and shoved out of her arms, stumbling over a lone branch, his face bright red and splotchy, lashes thick with his tears.

"Did you see anything?" Saskia asked gently, wanting to reach for him but waiting.

He shook his head, fists balled at his sides. He turned his face away from her, bare chest heaving. She could feel his anger bubbling.

"Good," she murmured. "Can you look at me?"

The air was stale beside the gorge, but a sense of impending freedom filled her, and she swallowed the lump forming in her throat. She wasn't free yet. There was still one more person she had to pay a visit to.

"Alec," she said, finally reaching for him.

He sobbed, hitting his fist into her shoulder. He punched her the way she taught him, and it landed a solid blow, though it didn't hurt. He shoved her this time, again and again and again as he cried.

"I thought you were dead!" he yelled in a broken voice, sounding so small and scared. "He said you were dead!"

Saskia took every hit, sitting back on her haunches until his shoves became less and less, and he threw his arms around her neck and collapsed against her.

She instantly wrapped her arms around him and scooped him close, feeling his weight like an anchor to reality. She had gotten him out, and they were out. *They were out.* "No one will ever hurt you again, not me, not *anyone*," she cooed, holding him close.

"I thought you were gone," he whimpered in a wobbling voice.

"I know," she soothed. Her gaze narrowed on the forest beyond them, and she knew there was one more place she had to go. "Alec…"

He pulled back, whipping the back of his hand over his cheeks, blinking back his tears. "Yeah?"

Sighing, she levelled him a look that said she needed him to pay attention. He sat upright, and she knew he was listening. "There's something I need to do. One last thing."

His large eyes blinked back at her before his small mouth twisted into a scowl, and his eyes burned molten. "Are you going to go take care of Florin?"

'Take care of' was a nice way to put it, she thought idly.

"Yes," she said. There was no reason to sugarcoat it.

"Naschta was snooping around your room again before Florin took me," Alec commented, his brows folding in the middle. "You should take care of her, too."

Saskia chuckled, standing with him still in her arms. "Is that so?"

Alec hummed, nodding vigorously, wrapping his arms around her neck again.

Her shadows gathered, and she stepped through them as he told her about telling Naschta off for trying to get in her room before Florin restrained him, and he ended up in a cell in the mountain.

She had to breathe through the anger boiling her blood by the time they walked into a white marble office, and a pretty red-haired witch startled behind a glass desk, emerald sparks igniting at her fingertips.

Alec peeked over at Brean, offering her a small smile. Brean smiled at him and arched a brow at Saskia with narrowed eyes.

Saskia shifted him on her hip and cocked her head. "I need a favour."

CHAPTER 45

"Look after him."

Those were the words she said to the witch before setting Alec down and explaining that she might not be back for a little bit but that she would come back *again*.

Brean had stood there, arms crossed over her cream blouse, staring down at Alec with a soft glint in her eyes. With a snap of her fingers, emerald sparks danced in the air and produced a sweater that plopped into her waiting hand.

Saskia watched the witch kneel and crook her finger at Alec, who walked shyly towards her, wide-eyed.

"You're growing into a young lad," Brean had said softly in her lilting accent. *"We can't have you go running around naked as a wee bairn."*

The sweater hung to his shins, but Alec wiggled his hands free of the long sleeves and nodded in understanding.

"They rip off when I... when I..." Alec's voice had trailed off as he looked down at his hands, fiddling with the sweater.

Saskia knelt beside the witch in front of Alec. *"Don't worry,"* she had said, brushing a curl from his face. *"I have a friend who is just like you."*

Alec's eyes had widened, and he smiled brightly at her. *"I remember him! You kind of smell like him now."*

Brean had snorted, eyes glimmering with amusement, and ruffled Alec's hair, scooping him into her arms and standing. *"Let's not tease her for now. We can do that when she comes back."*

Saskia shook her head at the memory. Alec was safe. That was all that mattered.

Grey clouds rumbled overhead, the smell of rain hanging in the air, and she breathed deeply, turning her face to the sky and inhaling the cool breeze as it brushed through her long curly hair. She was perched on the side of the mountain beside her village, the ancient town nestled between the mountain gorge below her. And for a moment, as she gazed up at the sky, she thought of Fiason, wondering if she would see the Vilon flying above her, scouting for food or Deathwalkers.

Her hunt in Rome felt like a lifetime ago, but perhaps it was. The concept of time was no longer prevalent to her as she turned away from the sky, her mind narrowing on her next hunt.

She could see the manor from her perch in the tree she chose, crouched on a midlevel branch in one of the thousands of evergreens around her. Smoke wafted from one of the four chimneys, and she slit her eyes in thought, tilting her head.

That was the kitchen chimney, which meant Haveaurd was cooking. No one used the kitchen except him and Saskia. Usually, he was boiling something foul-smelling over the hearth that would cause her to leave and return when he was gone. She paused on that thought. It had smelled faintly like copper one day before Haveaurd had added spices to it, and the smell had made her gag.

Her fingers curled into fists, anger burning a hole in her gut.

It had been blood.

Bracing on the branch, she stood, and with one last glance to the village, she pushed off. Her body arched above the treetops below, and she snapped her arms in front of her as she dove headfirst into the forest.

She tucked her body into a ball, grunting roughly when the ground impacted her shoulder as she rolled out of the fall and onto her feet, sprinting down the mountain.

How's that for a landing, Your Majesty? She thought smugly.

The forest whipped by her in a palette of green and brown, the soft, damp soil below cushioning her fleeting feet. She was fast. Really fast, and Saskia found herself grinning, just for a moment, as her body *soared* down the mountain.

Her joy was short-lived when she skidded to a sudden halt just before the treeline ended. She was breathing hard, but not from her run or the adrenaline she could feel coursing through her body. She was just beyond the manor and its cold stone fortress, and memories of her past spilt into her mind, shocking her core when they were of her first arrival to the manor and the hell she endured for *years.*

This had been her prison disguised as a salvation.

Bile rose in her throat, and she swallowed it down, hand to the back of her throat.

Breathing through the spiralling emotions, her neck tingled, and she paused, blinked, and slipped her gun free. Spinning quickly, gun raised to the thick brush to her right, she chambered a round and waited.

Molten gold eyes peaked from the brambles, and something familiar, something bonded, tugged within her.

Sarah rolled her eyes, huffing, and lowered her gun, holstering it. "What the fuck, Talan?"

A soft whine confirmed her suspicions, and two fluffy silver ears with red tips popped free of the bushes before his massive silver and red body followed.

Talan spit out something from his maw and shifted.

Saskia eyed the semi-wet jeans in the dirt before her gaze slowly trailed up the very naked male body in front of her. His thick muscles flexed under her stare, and she slowed her gaze when she got to his broad chest and wide shoulders.

His jaw flexed when she finally dragged her eyes to his, and she glared at his cocky smile.

"Shut up," she growled.

She blamed their mating bond.

His smile slowly fell, and he grabbed his jeans, pulling them on. He didn't have a shirt or shoes, but even half naked, he looked wholly at home within the forest and comfortable in his own skin.

"Saskia," he started.

She held up a terse hand, silencing him. "What are you doing here?"

He rubbed a hand across the back of his neck. "I thought you might need some company."

"How the hell did you even get here so quickly?"

"I found a helicopter, took it for a joy ride, made a detour to Tamblin when I finally felt you down the bond, and from there, I ran." He was ticking down his fingers as if counting from a list of everything he had done. "I'm faster on all fours, and you're not an easy female to keep up with."

She shook her head with a scoff, her insides twisting into knots. She was a mix of anger, longing, lust, and happiness. But the longer he stood there shirtless, the more angry she got. The mating bond was messing with her head, she pursed her lips, fighting it.

She should *not* be happy he's here.

Glaring, she crossed her arms. "Despite your pet name for me, I'm not some princess that needs saving."

"No, you're not," he agreed. "But you're a female worth protecting, and I always protect what's mine."

"I am not yours," she snarled, but even she could hear the lack of venom behind her words.

She was so tired of fighting.

Saskia glanced away from his intent stare, chewing on her words.

She heard Talan sigh, and then his finger was tucked under her chin, turning her face to him. His eyes were no longer molten and full of power, but rather, they were warm, and she shifted under its scrutiny, his body heat emanating from him in waves. His scent was overwhelming, nearly making her dizzy.

"You became mine the moment you held a danger to my throat and threatened to remove my favourite appendage."

His voice was a low rumble, warm and solid, and Saskia searched his eyes for the lie. All she found was raw honesty and the taste of the truth, sweet and evident, on her tongue.

Talan stroked his thumb across her cheek, stepping closer until their bodies brushed with every breath. "It doesn't matter if you have brown eyes or green. If you have brown hair or black. It doesn't matter if you're human or Fae. Because whether you are Sarah or Saskia, that doesn't change who you are." He leaned in, his breath fanning across her lips. "And I will follow you to the ends of this world."

And then he was kissing her. The hand holding her chin slipped to the back of her head, tangling in her hair as the other banded around her waist and pulled her flush against his bare chest.

Despite her better judgement, Saskia melted at his touch and relaxed into the kiss, parting her lips to his. He groaned low and claiming as his tongue swept into her mouth and he deepened the kiss.

His hand wandered over her long sleeve, fingers creeping under the hem and skimming the underside of her bra.

Saskia chuckled and pulled back, arching her brow. He gave her a sheepish smile and kissed the tip of her nose.

Stepping back, she smoothed a hand over her hair with a low breath, wishing she had found a hair tie, and looked at the manor from beyond the treeline.

"You're going to get yourself killed," she remarked.

Talan stepped up beside her, his muscled torso flexing when he stretched his arms above his head, regarding the manor. He shot her a wicked smirk, and Saskia couldn't help but grin as he said, "You wound me, Princess. I might not be able to kill anyone on two feet, but I can rip out a throat on four."

CHAPTER 46

Wood splinted in the air, the double doors slamming open as Saskia blasted her power through them.

She cocked her head, stepping into the foyer. Something silver caught her eye, and she dodged to her left. Her hand lashed out, catching the dagger by its hilt as it flew by her head. Eyeing it, she weighed it in her hand before flipping it and hurling it back.

"Come out, Naschta. I have someone who wants to play," she called in a sing-song.

A hand caught the blade, and russet curls and cold green eyes filled her vision as Naschta rounded the corner of her hiding spot, barefoot and dressed in black leggings and a white t-shirt.

Saskia smirked at the female before her, smelling the rot rolling off her.

It had all been a lie formulated by Florin. The memories, who she was, and her identity. It was all lies, and now, as she stared Naschta down, the memories came back of that night.

She had been there when her parents were murdered. She was Florin's accomplice. She hadn't grown up with Naschta like she had thought. It was all an illusion curated carefully by magic.

Naschta's eyes roved over Saskia, cocking her hip and bringing a hand up to study her nails, bored. "So, I take it, you know?"

"Tell me two things—how and why?" Saskia asked, shadows curling around her hands and up her arms.

"Cute trick," Naschta smirked, eyeing the shadows before she lifted a small silver pendant around her neck. It was a simple round medallion, the same one Alec had worn, nothing special etched on it. But now Saskia could feel magic emanating from it, even from the doorway.

Naschta's face shimmered, and then she looked like a little girl, a teenager, and now an adult. Finally, her face changed. Her ears elongated, the tips poking through her unruly hair, and her cheekbones heightened, eyebrows arching as her eyes turned black.

"I didn't have the power to produce such a long-term glamour, but Florin cared for me like he always does. He had this medallion made for me so you would stop asking questions after we had your memories sealed."

She spoke about Florin like he was her lover, and Saskia wanted to gag.

"But you ask why?" Like pools of endless abyss, her black eyes blinked at Saskia like she was stupid. "Why wouldn't we? Humans treated me like trash beneath their feet." She spat on the ground, rage morphing her, what would be beautiful, face. "Florin found me in the slums and took me under his wing. He trained me and said he planned to bring Fae to power again. I believed him."

Naschta snorted, her black eyes turning green again. "Look how much good that did. He used you for his own amusement after slaughtering your parents until he knew he had the upper hand and sent you and that *dog* to your deaths. You were simply there to entertain us, and the boy was simply there to make the lie look real until he got rid of you both. The busy old hags in the village were growing suspicious, so Florin found him during a slaughter. It was very convenient." She paused, smiling bitterly at Saskia. "Do you know how easy it was to kill your parents? Their heads ripped off their bodies like they were nothing, their defences down and unsuspecting. Hearing your mother's scream was the cherry on top."

Power swirled in her gut, pulsating against her bones, but she restrained herself, keeping her face void of emotion.

"With Avian's newborn army, the Fae will rise to power, and we will cleanse the human scum from our world!"

Saskia arched a brow. "Are you finished?"

Naschta hissed, her canines lengthening a fraction.

Saskia watched them lengthen, still interested when they had evolved to that but snapped her gaze back to the female in front of her. "That *dog's* name is Alec, and you'll be happy to know he's *alive* and *safe* with the King of the Fae."

"He is not my king!"

She snorted. "Tell that to his face. I'm sure he'll find it amusing." Saskia's lips lifted into a cutting smile. "And Avian is dead, and so are his newborns." A partial lie.

Green eyes turned black again, and Naschta took a threatening step towards her. "He is not!"

Saskia chuckled, "Cross my heart."

Naschta crouched low, her dagger in hand, hissing, "I'm going to tear you apart."

She shrugged, stepping out of the way of the door. "Tell that to him."

The female paused, confusion flashing briefly on her face. "Wha—"

Her words became a scream as a silver and red-tipped wolf lunged through the air like a bullet. Paws the size of her face and claws extended, his muzzle wrinkled back into a snarl, long teeth snapping for Naschta's face.

She turned and fled.

Fucking coward.

Talan landed once, the dark green carpet runner under his paws sliding, and his body slammed into the empty suits of armour, clattering to the ground loudly. Shaking his head, he leapt again, his jaws wrapping around her hair and snatching her back.

Naschta screeched in pain, long nails slashing at Talan's face, but he held her firm, dragging her across the floor.

He let her go suddenly, and she scrambled away, throwing a sloppy punch when he advanced. He was the size of a miniature horse, standing level with Naschta, and she didn't stand a chance.

Saskia almost—*almost*—felt bad for her when she watched her make a run for it again.

Talan threw her a look as if to say *really?* He caught the female by the ankle, and bones crunched on stone as Naschta's head slammed on the ground, and he dragged her back to the middle of the foyer.

With a jerk of his head, Naschta was thrown onto her back, hands coming up to shove him off, tears streaming down her twisted face. Her eyes were black and rage-filled; a bloody scream filled the stone walls when his claws sliced through her stomach, gutting her.

A door slammed open from within the manor, and Saskia briefly glanced down the hall towards the kitchen. Perfect timing.

Naschta's hands were black with her blood, trying to put her organs back into her body. Livid eyes turned to Saskia, catching her in the corner watching. "You fucking bitch!" she seethed through the black oozing from the corners of her mouth.

"Oh," Saskia said causally, touching her chest, affronted. "I'm the bitch?" She snorted dryly. "Turnabout is fair play, *Sister.*"

Naschta's black eyes bulged in their sockets, and Talan's maw opened wide before he sank his teeth into her chest. Her screams would be permanently etched into the stone walls before they died abruptly, and Talan *ripped.* Her sternum pulled free of her body, leaving her chest cavity exposed.

He dropped her ribs and flesh on the carpet, staining it black, and buried his teeth into her chest, tearing her heart from her body and eating it.

If Naschta wasn't dead before, she was now.

Talan trotted over to Saskia, tongue lolling out of his mouth happily, black blood coating the silver fur around his face.

Saskia chuckled, scratching the space behind his ear. "Good boy."

He barked once, and she rolled her eyes, pausing on the mountain of a male storming down the hall, his eyes wholly black and pinned on Saskia. "Looks like we have company."

Talan swivelled his head to Haveaurd with a huff.

"Think you can handle him?" Saskia questioned.

He growled, offended.

Haveaurd froze down the hall, eyes fixed on Naschta's torn body.

Saskia's lips pressed into a line, eyeing the male. "Good, because I have someone I need to pay a visit to."

Talan nudged her hand with his nose. *Go*, he seemed to say silently before he was bounding towards Haveaurd, teeth bared and a savage snarl ripping through the air.

CHAPTER 47

Haveaurd's screams were still echoing within the manor, for a brief moment Saskia wondered exactly *what* Talan was doing to him. But she knew she would find out soon enough.

Her eyes fixated on the dark wood door to Florin's office, the tarnished silver handle taunting her as she stood outside of it.

She could just apparat into his office. She could walk through the shadows and slit his throat. But that would be too easy, and she deserved to look him in the eye when she killed him.

Saskia reached for the knob, and the door swung open silently. She stood at the entry, and from within, Florin looked up from his desk.

"Hello, Saskia," he said cordially, closing the ledger he was logging in. "I was wondering when it would be my turn."

Her eyes roved over Florin, taking in the small, minute physical changes she noticed.

Lies, lies, *lies.*

His ears were arched to delicate points. His cropped hair was more of a dirty blonde now, a cold, toying smirk shadowing his lips. He was still tall and well-built, but there was something agile about him; he seemed leaner. The demon she had suspected lay dormant within had revealed itself at last as Florin cocked his head, studying her approach into his study with pitch black eyes.

"I assume you have questions," he said, unbothered, leaning back into his black leather chair.

Saskia walked over to the arsenal lining one side of his study. "No, not plural," she remarked, taking a pretty military green P365 with copper accents down from its mount. She stared down the barrel, admiring the laser pointer. "Just one. One question." She put the gun back and turned to look at him.

Florin wasn't sitting at his desk anymore. He had gotten up and leaned against its ledge, legs crossed at the ankles, arms folded across his muscular chest. Dressed in all black, he looked menacing. And if Saskia didn't know him, hadn't been trained by him, and known what he did to her and her family... she might have been scared. Instead, she just felt a calm numbness sweep through her.

He waved a hand for her to continue.

Saskia didn't speak for a long moment, primarily out of spite because fuck him. When she saw annoyance flash across his face, the muscle under his left eye twitching, she waited for a hair longer before she finally asked, "Who are you?"

His teeth were too perfect, too white, when he flashed her a sharp smile. "My true name is Laudin of the High Fae of Álfheimr. In the old world, I rose to power as Ezra's right hand—Avian's father," he clarified. "His mother—*your* mother, was also there as Ezra's prisoner."

Laudin frowned, glancing at the row of history books. "What those books don't tell you is that we were close, *so close* to taking back the natural world of Fae and bringing a more structured power to the throne." He looked at Saskia over his shoulder. "I wanted your mother at my side to do that. I wanted to save her from Ezra's bargain. She was pregnant, after all. If she had taken my deal, I would have killed Ezra for her and saved her from him."

From one monster to another, she thought.

He spoke as if he were a savour in all of this—as if he were the good guy, and she had it all wrong. But she remembered the feel of her parent's blood on her skin, the feeling fresh in her mind like it had happened yesterday and not fourteen years ago.

Saskia circled the study slowly, dragging her fingers along the desk, leaving fingerprints on the metal she knew he would hate. She looked down at the ledge casually. *Expenses* was scrawled in gold script on the brown leather, a silver letter opener beside it.

She looked up through lowered brows, continuing her slow procession. "You know what I think?" He arched a brow. "I think you're full of shit."

Laudin's face morphed, his nose wrinkling and brows folding in the middle as he snarled, "I tried to help her, and what did Levina do? She spat in my face and insulted me! Your whore of a mother deserved everything that came to her and more. I only wish I had kept my promise and cut her babe from her womb."

Saskia refrained from flinching, instead holding onto the power pressed along her skin. Not yet.

"But this is better, isn't it?" he sniffed with a hungry look. "I got to kill her and her bastard husband, train her off-breed daughter how to kill her own kind, and then pit her children against one another whilst gaining a newborn army in the process to take back control of our world!" He barked a laugh, shaking his head in awe. "I amaze even myself."

"Well then, let's settle it." She nodded to the two crossed katanas on top of his bookshelves. Black and gold cord-wrapped handles were accented by a decorative thin black marble guard. They were purely for show, but Laudin's eyes flicked up to the blades regardless.

His smile was contemplative.

She waved a hand down her body. "Loose ends, right?"

"Magic?"

"No," she replied with a shake of her head, despite the overwhelming feeling of her power arcing through her body in waves that made her clench her hands behind her back. "Weapons only. To the death."

Saskia held out a hand, waiting.

Laudin studied it before he huffed out a laugh like he was amusing a child. "Weapons only. To the death," he mimicked.

Magic sparked between their hands as the deal was struck. There was no tattoo as a reminder; simply, the heavy weight of magic settled over them, watching and waiting.

This was going to be quick.

A katana flew towards her, and she caught it. As soon as her blade was free of its scabbard, Laudin was moving.

Fuck, he was quick.

His desk clattered against the wall as Laudin effortlessly pushed it out of the way. He was strong, stronger than Saskia, but he trained her.

He always taught her to wait for the first move, but she didn't, not this time.

Her blade cut through the air with lethal precision as he turned back to her, but Laudin was quick with his draw. Sparks danced between them, lighting up the abyss in his black eyes.

Saskia faltered under his weight, pressing against him. He growled through gritted teeth and threw her back. She stumbled and caught her footing, her back hitting the bookshelf.

Righting herself, she spun, bringing her blade across her body, meeting Laudin blow for blow. His study wasn't small, but it wasn't meant for combat, and Saskia found herself flung across the space, the back of Laudin's hand connecting solidly with her cheek.

She rolled out of the fall, dropped her katana, and spun on her knees, sending the silver letter opener she had snagged off his desk flying.

Laudin roared when the tip sunk into his kneecap.

On command, she disappeared into the shadows, her power flowing like an endless living well.

Laudin whipped around, stumbling on his bad knee.

She appeared behind him. Shadows shot across his chest, and with a single thought, his body was spinning through the air. He crashed into the bookshelves, the letter opener lodging itself further into his bone when he landed on it.

He screamed.

Saskia smirked.

"You *cheated*!" he spat, his lip bleeding black. Laudin braced on his hand, trying to shove to his feet.

"Did I?" No, she hadn't, and that thought made her smile, truly smile at the male she had answered to for too long.

Black and purple shadows wrapped around his neck, his veins bulging black under their constriction. Saskia could feel the hungry hum of her power, and she used it to fling his body to the wall where his desk was toppled beside.

With inhuman speed, she picked up the discarded katana, arched her arm back and threw it towards the wall as his body slammed into the stone.

Laudin's eyes bugged when the blade crossed his neck, nicking the sink, a dribble of blood dripping down the collum of his throat. Her power held him pinned until she picked up his discarded blade by the bookshelf and threw that one, too.

Head pinned between both blades, she released her shadows. Laudin's body dropped onto the sharp edges. Luckily for him, they hadn't been sharpened in a long time, so the edges didn't decapitate him completely, much to her relief.

Saskia looked around the destroyed study. "Sorry about the mess."

"You cheated!" he repeated with a snarl, though his voice broke away when his neck strained against the blades.

"We agreed to weapons only," Saskia confirmed. "Did we not?"

He spat black blood at her, the residue staining his perfect teeth. "Yes!"

"But you forget," she said casually, walking towards him until only a foot of space separated them. "I *am* a weapon. One you forged yourself, Florin. Or have you forgotten the reminders you left me with?"

Magic pressed in on her, commanding her, waiting for her to fulfil the bargain struck.

Laudin reached for her, and shadows lashed out, stretching his arms wide and anchoring him to the wall like one of his prized toys behind her.

"Tut-tut," she chastised.

"It's *Laudin*," he seethed through clenched teeth. The blades were sinking deeper and deeper.

Saskia shrugged, unholstering her gun. "It's all a lie, anyway, right? What's to say that's even your name?"

When he didn't reply, she looked up from her gun. His eyes were locked on the weapon in her hand, and she smirked.

"You want to know the best part about all of this?" she asked, facing the male pinned to the wall, wrinkling her nose at the stench of rot. He looked pathetic. The monster she had known, the torment she had endured, was all gone.

His eyes darted up to her, no longer black but dark brown.

There was fear there, deep, deep down, but it was there.

"You're going to die a nobody. Laudin is already dead. He died in the old world. And Florin, well, no one will remember him. A little human nobody." With one hand, she raised the gun between his furrowed brows, finger on the trigger. "My mother thought you were full of shit, and so does her daughter."

Laudin's eyes turned black as pitch, and he flashed his teeth, spitting a clot of black blood at her, not caring about the blades cutting into his throat. "You're going to shoot me like a pathetic human?!"

Saskia narrowed her eyes and gave him a cutting smile. "Welcome to the twenty-second century, asshole."

And she pulled the trigger.

CHAPTER 48

The sound of the gun was deafening in the study, the 10mm cobalt ignition round leaving the chamber in a glowing neon blue spiral. The same rounds the little voice in the back of her mind had told her to bring instead of her regular ammunition, the same ones she bought from an illegal arms dealer on a hunt in France years ago for 'just in case', was now lodged into the middle of Laudin's skull.

His head slammed back into the stone, the rock cracking behind him. The butt of the round blinked blue once, twice, and Saskia smiled at Laudin, his eyes going wide. His cry was cut short on the third blink of light, the round combusting in his skull.

Saskia closed her eyes as brain matter sprayed the room like fertiliser. Hot blood coated her skin. Grimacing, she used the bottom of her shirt to wipe it off her face. His body dropped free of the blades, and she looked down at the headless corpse with revulsion.

Checking her weapon, she popped the safety on and slipped it back into its holster.

A slow clap filled the study, and Saskia's head darted up, one hand wreathed in shadows, the other going back to her gun simultaneously. A pair of dark eyes watched her, these ones naturally black and depthless, as a young woman, probably no more than seventeen, in a simple black floor-length gown sat in the forgotten leather desk chair that had somehow ended up beside the mounted armoury her long fingers drumming on the narrow armrests.

Glossy black hair hung chin length and pin straight, her face indifferent, a thin-lipped smile barely visible. "Tatius," she said before Saskia could finish opening her mouth to question her.

Tatius leaned to the side, looking around Saskia's body. Saskia followed her line of sight.

"Your handy work?"

Saskia cocked her head regarding the young female. "Who are you?"

How the hell did she get in here?

Tatius rolled her eyes. "Forgive me, I forget you new ones don't know your Gods."

Gods. Plural.

Her brows shot to her hairline.

"I am Tatius, the God of Death—that was such a good shot," she said, her attention returning to Laudin's body.

"You're a God?" Saskia said slowly.

Did the Gods still exist from the old world?

Seeing the one before her was confirmation enough that they do.

"It's quite well done. I couldn't have asked for better if I had done it myself. Your new advancements in weaponry are exciting. You almost don't need magic anymore—almost," she mused thoughtfully.

Saskia's dull laugh got the young God's attention, who scowled at her.

"What is so funny?"

"Nothing, you're just… so young."

Storm clouds passed over Tatius's face. "You will watch your tongue."

Saskia relaxed somewhat and dropped the hand still hovering by her holster, and let her shadows disperse. "Look at the last guy who told me what to do."

Those black eyes chilled, and Tatius's face relaxed into amusement, reclining into the chair. "I like you."

"I can't say it's mutual."

A soft scoff and the God steepled her fingers over her stomach. "Do you know why I'm here?"

"Enlighten me," drawled Saskia, exasperated.

Tatius sighed like the weight of all her Godliness was on her delicate shoulders. Saskia wanted to roll her eyes, but she refrained.

"I was minding my business, as us Gods do, when I came across a lucrative opportunity. You see, as the God of Death, I only eat when there are souls to be had. But because of the immortal lifespan of the Fae, we so *conveniently* gave them, and the veil splitting the worlds, well, you can see why I did what I did."

Tatius looked at Saskia as if what she said had made any sense.

"I'm sorry," she said slowly. "Can you rephrase that?"

She looked like she would rather do anything else but that, though she said all the same, "A soul does not taste appealing when it is corrupted," she said slowly as if it were obvious and she was talking to a child.

Saskia gave her a deadpanned look at her tone. "I understand you just fine," she snapped. "I'm not deaf or stupid."

"Could have fooled me," mumbled the God.

Huffing, Saskia shook her head and walked towards the door. "I'm leaving."

"Wait," commanded Tatius.

Saskia paused at the door, glaring at the female in the chair. "What?"

"I'm here to say… thank… you."

The words sounded so foreign coming from the female that

Saskia almost laughed. She dropped her hand from the doorknob, crossed her arms, and waited by the door, listening.

"Balwin and Nazar were making ugly work of the world. They struck a deal, and I saw the death of my creation coming into fruition. Towards the end there, I was *very* hungry. God of Death and all with no souls to feast on except the occasional, bound to the world of magic with the divide. You can imagine."

She could not imagine. Saskia crossed her arms, tilting her head. "Is that so?"

"I saw a means to… both ends. The end of their tyranny and my hunger."

"You were hangry," she clarified.

"No!" snapped Tatius. "I was, what do you say here, killing two birds with a stone."

Saskia shook her head. "Did you know?"

Tatius nodded, rocking back in the chair. It squeaked once. She frowned and stopped. "Yes, and with Avian born of darkness, it would have spread rampant like a disease through this new world. That one," she pointed to Laudin's body, "was not helping any. So, when I saw your birth, your life, I knew you would be the answer. The balance between light and dark this world craves." Tatius leaned forward, an ancient look passing over her face. "Because one cannot exist without the other."

Her blood ran cold at the realisation. "You're why my parents are dead?"

"No," Tatius answered simply, correcting, "Laudin is the reason your parents are dead. The darkness corrupts everything, Saskia. Not even the Gods can control it all. I saw what would happen to your parents, but I am Death, so who am I to stop it?"

"You made everything happen. Everything the history books of Fae write about regarding the fall and everything before it. It was all you." Red filled Saskia's vision, and she took a threatening step towards the God.

Tatius pinched the bridge of her nose, holding up a finger. "I did not make *everything* happen. Some things are simply made by design, destined to happen regardless of what I want. I just simply… pulled a couple strings of fate and manipulated a couple individuals—that I'm not proud of," she added quickly.

Saskia suspected that was a blatant lie.

"But that's neither here nor there. Balwin's bargain with Nazar set off a chain of events. I simply took the opportunity to right it while also gaining something from it in return."

Her jaw worked as she chewed on her questions. She didn't know what to ask first, and Tatius ignored her regardless, speaking.

"Laudin was going to kill your mother no matter what I did. That was predestined. Even fate is out of a God's hands. Your father, too, unfortunately. But I can alter the course fate takes. So, I made sure that instead of Laudin killing you the night he brought you back to the manor, Brean intercepted him."

Saskia paused her thoughts, her full attention on the God.

"Brean is very convincing. She sold herself well; I applaud her."

"What are you talking about?" Saskia whispered. "That's not what she told me happened."

Tatius smirked. "She came here. You were never brought to the Fae. Brean located you by a tracking spell. I gave her a swath of your mother's torn gown I stole from her cell many years ago; you are half of her, after all." She almost looked saddened, recalling the past, and offered Saskia a small smile. "Brean told Laudin about all the children she had masked over the years—not a lie—some Fae wanting to blend in with this new society. After a few drinks, a little hypnosis potion in his beer, and her flirting with him, she managed to convince him that if he really wanted to get revenge on Levina, he would raise you as a human, train you to kill your own, and then have your own brother kill you off. He rises in power and gets what he wants."

Brean had… saved her. The witch's quiet, expressive face filled her mind, and the emotions in her gaze when she saw Saskia for the first time in the conference room. "No one knows what she did," she said slowly.

"No."

"Why?" Saskia asked, frowning.

"Because had she failed, you would have died, and the world too. She was the only hope left to tie up… the loose ends, as you called yourself earlier—yes, I was watching. Avian and Laudin were my loose ends."

Tatius stood, half a head shorter than Saskia, and brushed a hand over the fitted bodice of her dress, its modest neckline revealing just enough of her delicate pale décolletage. She dusted her skirts off before she righted herself, offering Saskia a tight smile. "Don't think too poorly of me, Saskia. I was very hungry for the last, ah, six hundred years, give or take a millennia. Or do, I don't care either way. It's all done with—finally."

Saskia shook her head, running a disbelieving hand through her hair. "So, that's it? You use me and countless others as *pawns*—"

"—Don't spend the rest of your very long, very immortal life being bitter at what I had to do," she interrupted with a long sigh. "Go, enjoy it with your mate. Don't say I didn't give you anything." Tatius clapped her hands, smiling to herself. "Well, I'll be off. Souls to feed on, people to torment—humans truly are so delectably tasty, and they're always dying. It's so convenient, really."

She didn't know what to say, her mouth opening and closing with confusion. What the fuck was happening right now?

Tatius wiggled her fingers at her in goodbye. "Just take this as a *growing* opportunity, I know I did."

With a final smirk, she vanished.

CHAPTER 49

Brean brushed an unruly curl from the little boy's brow, smiling softly down at him as he slept on a velvet green chaise, a cream knit blanket over him.

She had brought him to her room where she had him bathe and, with the help of her magic, had fitted some clothes to his small body. He was wearing her personal cream knit sweater, now shrunk to size to fit him, and when Alec was in the shower, she had walked to Savven's room, stolen a pair of his grey joggers, and shrunk them down as well.

Something warm and nurturing filled her chest when she laid eyes on the boy, naked and covered in grime. When Saskia had to leave, he had almost started crying, and she could tell from the dirty streaks cutting down his cheeks that it wouldn't have been the first time that day.

But Brean had soothed him with reassurance that she would be back, and when the hunter was gone and no tears were shed, she had told Alec that after he was cleaned, she would show him Álfheimr Towers. And she did, until he started yawning, and she picked him up and walked him to the dark library.

Long windows were equally spaced apart in the room, with thick cream drapes; black marble floors reflected the world from the windows with a dark green rug thrown down in the middle. Black, deep-set bookshelves were filled with an array of novels on three of the four walls, on the empty one, a velvet green chaise was pressed against it, holding Alec as he slept.

She had sat at a desk with him in her lap and opened the tablet that now lay silent on the black wood. Alec had curled against her as she started reading a children's story she had found in the archives. It was an ancient story about Fae magic and one girl chosen to protect them all. Images had projected from the tablet as she read, showing him the story as it unfolded. He was startled at first, wide-eyed and curious. Alec had poked at the image, giggled when his finger went through it, and proceeded to ask her a multitude of questions before he settled, and she continued.

He had fallen asleep shortly after, and she had just held him, stroking a finger over his brow until she finally stood and settled him on the chaise.

She hadn't held a baby, or a child—ever, yet there was something familiar about the action. Like she was made to do just that. It was the most natural, instinctual thing she had done, and she smiled sadly, knowing she might not get that opportunity now.

"Why do you look like you're about to cry?" intoned a bored female voice.

Brean whirled, putting herself between the boy and whoever was there, her magic flaring at her fingertips. She faltered when she saw Tatius. She was older, no longer a child, but it was the God of Death. There was no denying that.

Her cold black eyes roved over Brean, and Tatius lifted her brows in response, waiting for a reply.

"I—" her words died on her tongue. Notching her chin, she

stared the God down and tried again. "Have you come for me then?"

Right to the point. Brean didn't think she had it in herself to prolong this. She had been denying herself in this new life for the sake of others because she knew, one day, it would all end. Because her life was a clock slowly counting down to this moment.

"Hm," Tatius hummed with a purse of her thin lips. "So, you're ready then?"

She nodded once, a quick jerk of her chin. "Yes."

"Well, get on with it."

Brean stared at the God, and Tatius stared back at her, waiting.

An awkward silence filled the library.

"I—but—"

"Oh," Tatius sighed, "You want me to do that thing, right."

Brean was so confused. She squinted her eyes, looking at the God. "Are you well?"

She had never seen Death so at… odds before.

"Yes, actually," Tatius said amicably. Her black eyes flickered to the door to Brean's left, and she rolled them slightly with an exasperated sigh. "Your knight in shining armour is on his way. It would seem his wards around this… palace—or whatever it is, alerted him to my arrival. They're quite strong, did you know?"

Brean nodded mutely, flabbergasted.

"Do you want to wait? Say goodbye and," Tatius waved a nonchalant hand towards the door, "whatever else you do in these moments?"

"No." Brean looked down at Alec, her gaze softening, and then turned it to the door, picturing Savven's face. Her heart cracked at the thought of saying goodbye, and she knew if she saw him, she wouldn't know how to say the words. "No," she said again, looking back at Tatius.

Tatius nodded thoughtfully, staring at Brean briefly before she clapped her hands, startling Brean. "Well, that's it then. I'll be off. Say hello to his majesty for me."

Brean stepped towards Death, her face twisting with puzzlement. "Wait, what? I thought…?"

"I know what you thought," Tatius said. "And normally I would. I am a greedy God, after all. *Buuut* I'm feeling generous today."

She paused, tapping a finger on her chin. "Maybe she was right. Maybe I was hangry." Tatius said this primarily to herself before she cocked her head. "Does hangry mean what I think it means? No, wait, never mind. I don't care enough."

Brean's heart was beating like a hummingbird's wings in her chest, hope slowly blossoming, her hands shaking by her side. "Tatius, you're not..."

The God of Death smiled, almost kindly, at Brean. "Don't thank me yet. Immortality can become *very* dull."

Her knees were going to give out, her legs shaking as a weight that had been living on her shoulders for over a hundred years finally lifted.

Tatius arched a brow at the door again and said in a wondering tone. "You know, had you been born Fae, you and your king would be mates. Funny how you found each other despite the odds." She looked at Brean, and despite her youthful face, an ancient sort of power filled her eyes as she said in a low, echoing tone, "Consider your deal with me void, Brean Mackenzie."

Brean's knees gave out as the door to the library flew open, Tatius vanishing, and she landed on the plush rug, Savven's hands catching her by the shoulders.

"Brean!" Savven said urgently.

"Wh-whats going on?" Alec asked, startled awake from Savven's entrance.

Her shoulders were shaking. Her whole body was shaking. She couldn't stop. Tatius was gone.

Savven kneeled before her, cupping her face in his hands and gently turning her to face him.

Her silent laughter slipped out, filling the library, tears streaming down her face uncontrollably. "Savven," she gasped. "Savven I..."

He searched her face, his dark blue eyes so beautiful she could get lost in them.

"What," he breathed, fear filling his handsome face.

She reached up and grabbed the hands holding her, smiling. "I'm *free.*"

"What," he whispered.

"I'm free!" Brean laughed. "Tatius released me from our

bargain!" Pure, unending joy filled her, and she threw her arms around Savven, nearly knocking them both over.

His arms banded around her tightly, anchoring her to this new reality, excitement lighting his gaze.

Home.

She was home for good.

Savven freed a hand from around her and cupped her cheek, asking in a shaking voice, "Are you sure?"

"Yes," she breathed, and then she was kissing him.

His mouth met hers in a kiss that tilted her world.

Savven's hand tangled into her hair, pressing her body to his as he claimed what was his, what had always been his, what she had wanted to give him but couldn't. Brean submitted to his embrace, laughing and crying through their kiss as joy overflowed from her.

She had a family—a home, and she had never had to say goodbye again.

Savven pulled back, leaning his forehead against hers, and then she saw his tears. She smiled, full and toothy, as she brought a hand up and wiped them away.

"You'll have all of me now?" he asked roughly, hope in his tone.

He was shaking, and Brean wrapped her arms around him, nodding. "Yes," she laughed. "Yes!"

And then he was kissing her again, slow and sweet. Every ounce of love he had for her in the press of his lips, and Brean smiled.

Alec was watching them with a look of disgust from the chaise. "Ew."

And then they were all laughing.

CHAPTER 50

Haveaurd was in pieces. Literal pieces as Saskia arched a brow, stepping over a beefy finger, her lip curling at the smell.

The foyer was painted black. She was impressed, but she would never tell Talan that, or maybe she would. She hadn't decided yet.

Talan was sitting on the manor's steps outside, dressed in his jeans, shirtless and barefoot.

"You know, I could steal some of Florin's old clothes for you.

He looked up at her approach, watching her sit beside him. "You look like shit."

She snorted. "Speak for yourself."

They were both covered in black blood, hair caked in clotted pieces. Her shirt was torn along the ribs, probably when she slammed against the bookshelf, and her jeans smelled horrible.

Talan groaned and popped his back, stretching, before smelling the blood on his forearm. He gagged. "I need a shower first before I think about clothes."

"There's a shower in my room."

He looked at her deadpan. "I don't know how I feel about showering here."

Saskia shrugged, staring at the forest. "You having a problem with where you shower is highly amusing. I know I'm going to shower."

"Can I join you?" he asked with a wicked grin.

She snorted. "Maybe."

Comfortable silence filled the space between them when neither of them spoke. A soft, undemanding silence as the world around them settled, and the blood on their clothes and skin dried down.

"So, what now, Princess?"

His pet name for her was almost comforting after the havoc surrounding them. Saskia pulled a folded slip of paper from her pocket and opened it up, staring at the eleven-digit phone number scrawled in pen. Brean had slipped it to her before she left so she could call Alec when it was all over.

She made a mental note to grab her burner phone from her old room.

"Well, first a shower, and then... there's an army of newborns, I'm assuming, running around without a master."

Talan winced at that thought. "Gre-*eat*."

A soft breeze brushed over them, and Saskia breathed deeply. The smell of earth rose around them, fresh and invigorating the way it did before a storm. Saskia looked towards the mountains, the grey clouds turning black and whispering through the tree tops, and she knew when the storm passed, the ground was wet, and the forest was thrumming with life—that's where they'd be.

"Oh, I know that look," Talan muttered.

Saskia's smile was wicked, green eyes practically glowing with predatory promise as she stood and offered a hand to him. "Let's go hunting."

EPILOGUE

SOMEWHERE IN THE UNIVERSE...

Tatius, barefoot, stepped from star to star until she reached the cluster of planets suspended in deep space, her black hair floating lazily around her face. Thin lips twisting into a ghostly smile, she leapt from the stars onto Pluto.

From Pluto to Neptune and Uranus until, she grabbed the hem of her long black dress and jumped from the smaller blue planet to the rocky rings of Saturn.

She was humming under her breath, amusement coursing through her. With a single thought, golden light paved a path across the expansive rings and their mountain-sized rocks. But compared to Tatius, those mountains were only boulders, and she walked right across, hopping onto Saturn's body.

She could see the small blue and green planet from her position, and Tatius grinned wickedly, leaping across the expanse between Saturn and Jupiter.

Picking up her skirts, she laid down on her stomach across the largest planet, kicking her feet behind her. She was positively giddy.

It had all worked out. If she were being honest, there was a point where she wasn't sure if it would. But, of course, it did. She's a God, so of course it would. She always gets her way. And now, there was a buffet of souls at her disposal, and it would never run dry.

Tatius crooked a finger, and Earth floated to her outstretched palm. With the planet floating before her, she rolled onto her back, hooking a leg over her bent knee, her foot tapped idly at the Milky Way.

"Well, you were fun to play with while it lasted," she commented wistfully to the small planet. She twirled a finger over it, watching storm clouds form and brew over an unsuspecting country.

With a dismissive sigh, Tatius flicked the planet away and sat up, a tendril of her short hair brushing her cheek.

"Hmm," she hummed, drumming her fingers on Jupiter.

She could sense her boredom already returning, trickling in like an annoying pest, and she huffed. Looking towards the cosmos expanding across a vast universe of stars, planets, and moons, she spotted something that made her lips curl up slyly. Eyes narrowed on a nebula, where nestled between its vibrant purple and orange was an unsuspecting planet she had long since forgotten about through the aeons.

Tatius cocked her head like a cat eyeing its prey, and she giggled, her boredom fading.

"It would be rude not to say hello, wouldn't it?"

THE END.

ACKNOWLEDGEMENTS

Holy shit.

It's finished.

As the reader, don't take this the wrong way, but thank God!

This series happened by accident, and don't get me wrong, I absolutely loved the journey along the way. But as this story comes to an end, I can safely say I'm excited to see what the writing future holds for me.

But—with that said, I have to take the time to thank the ones who helped make it possible.

First of all, God. Without Him, none of this would be possible.

To my editor, Brandy — I know life is crazy with home, kids, and crazy southern storms, but thank you for being a constant with me from the start of all this. I'm so proud of how far you've come.

To my alpha reader, Jazmyn — I love you. Thank you for easing my concerns.

To my narrator, Ashlyn — for being a one-of-a-kind magician and bringing a voice to my characters.

To my Barnes & Noble friends in Fort Lauderdale — thank you for being a constant support.

To my fiancé — for being the amazing man he is, and for the love and grace he's shown me.

To my family — for always cheering me on.

And finally, to you, the reader. You have been with me from the beginning of Anabelle's story to the end of the worlds as we know it. Thank you for traversing with me through this world — with wars, villains, meddling gods, magic, romance, and so much more. Thank you for experiencing it all with me.

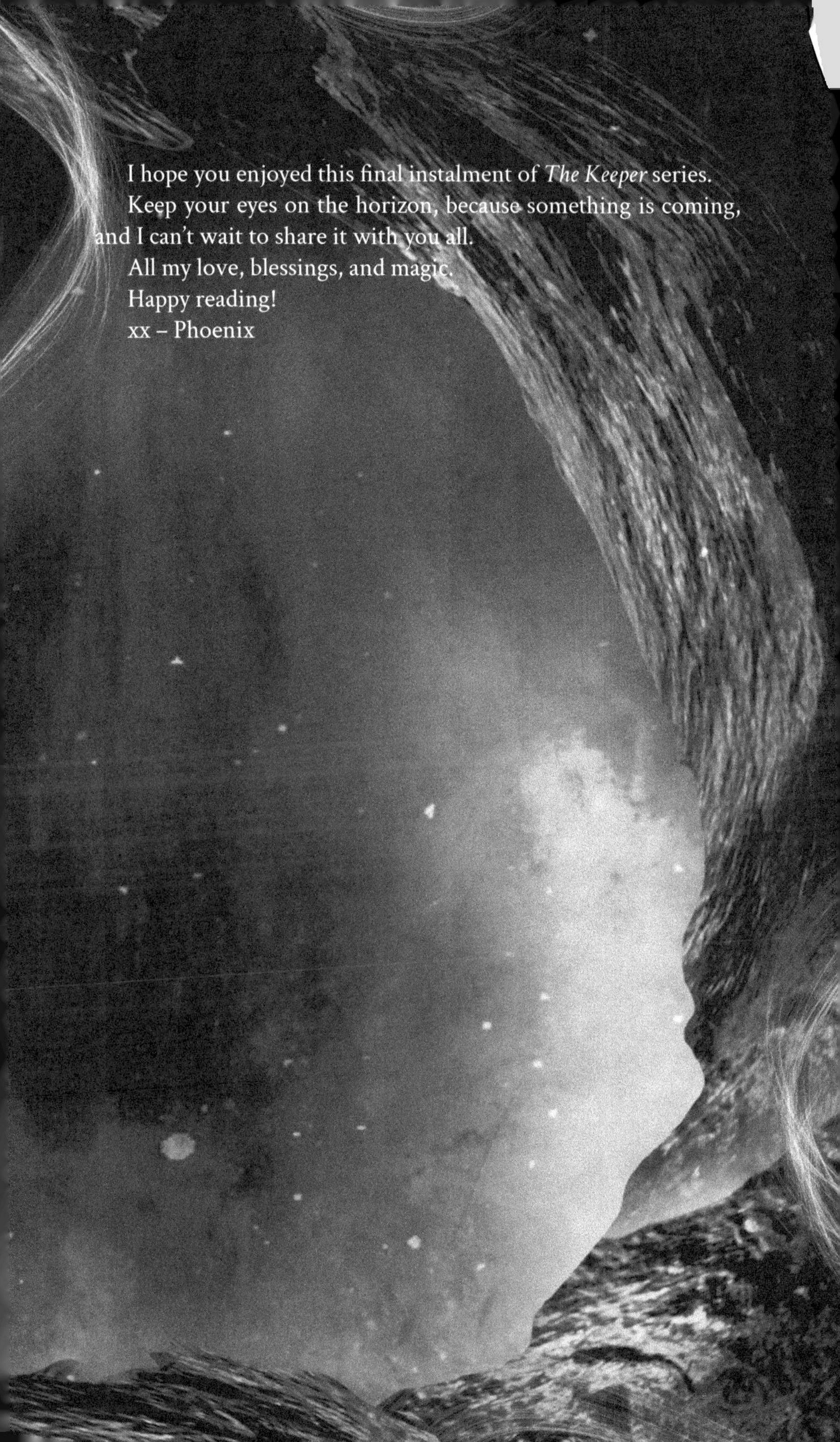

I hope you enjoyed this final instalment of *The Keeper* series.
Keep your eyes on the horizon, because something is coming,
and I can't wait to share it with you all.
All my love, blessings, and magic.
Happy reading!
xx – Phoenix